The Short Works of George Meredith

George Meredith, OM, was born in Portsmouth, England on February 12th, 1828, a son and grandson of naval outfitters. His mother died when he was only five.

As a fourteen year old teenager he was sent to a Moravian School in Neuwied, Germany, staying there for two years.

After reading law he was articled as a solicitor, but quickly abandoned that career path for journalism and poetry. He collaborated with Edward Gryffydh Peacock, son of Thomas Love Peacock in publishing a privately circulated literary magazine, the Monthly Observer.

At age twenty-one he married Mary Ellen Nicolls, Edward Peacock's beautiful widowed sister, and mother of a child, on August 8th, 1849. Mary Ellen was twenty-eight. The marriage produced one child; Arthur (1853–1890).

Meredith collected his early writings, all previously published in periodicals, in an 1851 volume, Poems.

In 1856 he posed as the model for The Death of Chatterton, a well-known picture by the English Pre-Raphaelite painter Henry Wallis, which romantised the teenage Chatterton's demise.

Although Meredith received some publicity for this his wife received rather more attention from Wallis because of it. Mary Ellen ran off with Wallis in 1858, shortly before giving birth to a child that all assumed to be Wallis. Tragically she died three years later.

From that dreadful experience emerged a collection of sonnets entitled Modern Love in 1862 together with much of his first major novel; The Ordeal of Richard Feverel.

Meredith married Marie Vulliamy on September 20th, 1864 and they settled in Surrey. Together they had two children; William (born in 1865) and Mariette (born in 1874).

He continued writing novels and poetry, often inspired by nature. He had a keen understanding of comedy and his Essay on Comedy (1877) remains a reference work in the history of comic theory.

In The Egoist, published in 1879, he applies some of his theories of comedy in one of his most thoughtful and enduring novels.

During most of his career, he had difficulty crossing over from critical acclamation to popular success. It was only in 1885 that his first genuine commercial success appeared; Diana of the Crossways.

An artist's life throughout the ages, when not subsidised by a patron, is often difficult. Meredith found it no different. With an unreliable income stream he sought to bolster that with a job as a publisher's reader.

The company that gave him this lifeline was Chapman & Hall (an eminent publishing house who could include Charles Dickens, William Makepeace Thackeray, Elizabeth Barrett Browning and Anthony

Trollope on their roster). His advice to the company was very well received and made him influential in the world of letters.

To this influence he was able to add a circle of friends that included William and Dante Gabriel Rossetti, Algernon Charles Swinburne, Cotter Morison, Leslie Stephen, Robert Louis Stevenson, George Gissing and J. M. Barrie.

In 1868 Meredith was introduced to Thomas Hardy. Hardy had submitted his first novel, The Poor Man and the Lady. Meredith felt the book was too bitter a satire on the rich and told Hardy to put it aside as it was likely it would be savaged by reviewers and destroy his nascent career. Meredith had received the same reaction with The Ordeal of Richard Feverel. Although it had brought him success it was judged so shocking that Mudie's circulating library cancelled an order of 300 copies.

But these years, creatively, were very prolific and successful for Meredith. Novels and poems flowed from his pen including everything from The Adventures of Harry Richmond to Diana of the Crossways and many poetry volumes include The Lark Ascending (which later inspired the Vaughan Williams music)

In 1886, tragedy struck the Meredith household when his second wife, Marie Vulliamy, died of cancer.

Whilst his personal life was producing horrendous scars he was receiving many accolades. Oscar Wilde was a fan. In The Decay of Lying, (originally published in the January 1889 issue of The Nineteenth Century) he says of Meredith "Ah, Meredith! Who can define him? His style is chaos illumined by flashes of lightning".

In 1891 Meredith was even the subject of homage when Sir Arthur Conan Doyle in his Sherlock Holmes short story The Boscombe Valley Mystery, (published in the popular Strand magazine) when Sherlock Holmes turns to Watson during case discussions and says "And now let us talk about George Meredith, if you please, and we shall leave all minor matters until tomorrow."

Before his death, Meredith was honoured from many quarters: he succeeded Lord Tennyson as president of the Society of Authors; in 1905 he was appointed to the Order of Merit by King Edward VII.

George Meredith, aged 81, died at his home in Box Hill, Surrey on May 18th, 1909. He is buried in the cemetery at Dorking, Surrey.

Index of Contents

FARINA
THE WHITE ROSE CLUB
THE TAPESTRY
WORD
THE WAGER
THE SILVER ARROW
THE LILIES OF THE VALLEY
THE MISSIVES
THE MONK
THE RIDE AND THE RACE

THE COMBAT ON DRACHENFELS
THE GOSHAWK LEADS
WERNER'S ECK
THE WATER-LADY
THE RESCUE
THE PASSAGE OF THE RHINE
THE BACK-BLOWS OF SATHANAS
THE ENTRY INTO COLOGNE
CONCLUSION
THE CASE OF GENERAL OPLE AND LADY CAMPER
CHAPTER I
CHAPTER VIII
THE TALE OF CHLOE AN EPISODE IN THE HISTORY OF BEAU BEAMISH
CHAPTER I
CHAPTER II
CHAPTER III
CHAPTER IV
CHAPTER V
CHAPTER VI
CHAPTER VII
CHAPTER VIII
CHAPTER IX
CHAPTER X
THE HOUSE ON THE BEACH - A REALISTIC TALE
CHAPTER I
CHAPTER II
CHAPTER III
CHAPTER IV
CHAPTER V
CHAPTER VI
CHAPTER VII
CHAPTER VIII
CHAPTER IX
CHAPTER X
CHAPTER XI
CHAPTER XII
THE GENTLEMAN OF FIFTY AND THE DAMSEL OF NINETEEN (An early uncompleted fragment.)
CHAPTER I - HE
CHAPTER II - SHE
CHAPTER III - HE
CHAPTER IV - SHE
CHAPTER V - HE
CHAPTER VI - SHE
THE SENTIMENTALISTS - AN UNFINISHED COMEDY
DRAMATIS PERSONAE
SCENE I
SCENE II

SCENE III
SCENE IV
SCENE V
SCENE VI
SCENE VII
SCENE VIII
GEORGE MEREDITH – A CONCISE BIBLIOGRAPHY

FARINA

THE WHITE ROSE CLUB

In those lusty ages when the Kaisers lifted high the golden goblet of Aachen, and drank, elbow upward, the green-eyed wine of old romance, there lived, a bow-shot from the bones of the Eleven Thousand Virgins and the Three Holy Kings, a prosperous Rhinelander, by name Gottlieb Groschen, or, as it was sometimes ennobled, Gottlieb von Groschen; than whom no wealthier merchant bartered for the glory of his ancient mother-city, nor more honoured burgess swallowed impartially red juice and white under the shadow of his own fig-tree.

Vine-hills, among the hottest sun-bibbers of the Rheingau, glistened in the roll of Gottlieb's possessions; corn-acres below Cologne; basalt-quarries about Linz; mineral-springs in Nassau, a legacy of the Romans to the genius and enterprise of the first of German traders. He could have bought up every hawking crag, owner and all, from Hatto's Tower to Rheineck. Lore-ley, combing her yellow locks against the night-cloud, beheld old Gottlieb's rafts endlessly stealing on the moonlight through the iron pass she peoples above St. Goar. A wailful host were the wives of his raftsmen widowed there by her watery music!

This worthy citizen of Cologne held vasty manuscript letters of the Kaiser addressed to him:

'Dear Well-born son and Subject of mine, Gottlieb!' and he was easy with the proudest princes of the Holy German Realm. For Gottlieb was a money-lender and an honest man in one body. He laid out for the plenteous harvests of usury, not pressing the seasons with too much rigour. 'I sow my seed in winter,' said he, 'and hope to reap good profit in autumn; but if the crop be scanty, better let it lie and fatten the soil.'

'Old earth's the wisest creditor,' he would add; 'she never squeezes the sun, but just takes what he can give her year by year, and so makes sure of good annual interest.'

Therefore when people asked Gottlieb how he had risen to such a pinnacle of fortune, the old merchant screwed his eye into its wisest corner, and answered slyly, 'Because I've always been a student of the heavenly bodies'; a communication which failed not to make the orbs and systems objects of ardent popular worship in Cologne, where the science was long since considered alchymic, and still may be.

Seldom could the Kaiser go to war on Welschland without first taking earnest counsel of his Well-born son and Subject Gottlieb, and lightening his chests. Indeed the imperial pastime must have ceased, and the Kaiser had languished but for him. Cologne counted its illustrious citizen something more than man. The burghers doffed when he passed; and scampish leather-draggled urchins gazed after him with praeternatural respect on their hanging chins, as if a gold-mine of great girth had walked through the awe-struck game.

But, for the young men of Cologne he had a higher claim to reverence as father of the fair Margarita, the White Rose of Germany; a noble maiden, peerless, and a jewel for princes.

The devotion of these youths should give them a name in chivalry. In her honour, daily and nightly, they earned among themselves black bruises and paraded discoloured countenances, with the humble hope to find it pleasing in her sight. The tender fanatics went in bands up and down Rhineland, challenging wayfarers and the peasantry with staff and beaker to acknowledge the supremacy of their mistress. Whoso of them journeyed into foreign parts, wrote home boasting how many times his head had been broken on behalf of the fair Margarita; and if this happened very often, a spirit of envy was created, which compelled him, when he returned, to verify his prowess on no less than a score of his rivals. Not to possess a beauty-scar, as the wounds received in these endless combats were called, became the sign of inferiority, so that much voluntary maiming was conjectured to be going on; and to obviate this piece of treachery, minutes of fights were taken and attested, setting forth that a certain glorious cut or crack was honourably won in fair field; on what occasion; and from whom; every member of the White Rose Club keeping his particular scroll, and, on days of festival and holiday, wearing it haughtily in his helm. Strangers entering Cologne were astonished at the hideous appearance of the striplings, and thought they never had observed so ugly a race; but they were forced to admit the fine influence of beauty on commerce, seeing that the consumption of beer increased almost hourly. All Bavaria could not equal Cologne for quantity made away with.

The chief members of the White Rose Club were Berthold Schmidt, the rich goldsmith's son; Dietrich Schill, son of the imperial saddler; Heinrich Abt, Franz Endermann, and Ernst Geller, sons of chief burghers, each of whom carried a yard-long scroll in his cap, and was too disfigured in person for men to require an inspection of the document. They were dangerous youths to meet, for the oaths, ceremonies, and recantations they demanded from every wayfarer, under the rank of baron, were what few might satisfactorily perform, if lovers of woman other than the fair Margarita, or loyal husbands; and what none save trained heads and stomachs could withstand, however naturally manful. The captain of the Club was he who could drink most beer without intermediate sighing, and whose face reckoned the proudest number of slices and mixture of colours. The captaincy was most in dispute between Dietrich Schill and Berthold Schmidt, who, in the heat and constancy of contention, were gradually losing likeness to man. 'Good coin,' they gloried to reflect, 'needs no stamp.'

One youth in Cologne held out against the standing tyranny, and chose to do beauty homage in his own fashion, and at his leisure. It was Farina, and oaths were registered against him over empty beer-barrels. An axiom of the White Rose Club laid it down that everybody must be enamoured of Margarita, and the conscience of the Club made them trebly suspicious of those who were not members. They had the consolation of knowing that Farina was poor, but then he was affirmed a student of Black Arts, and from such a one the worst might reasonably be feared. He might bewitch Margarita!

Dietrich Schill was deputed by the Club to sound the White Rose herself on the subject of Farina, and one afternoon in the vintage season, when she sat under the hot vine-poles among maiden friends, eating ripe grapes, up sauntered Dietrich, smirking, cap in hand, with his scroll trailed behind him.

'Wilt thou?' said Margarita, offering him a bunch.

'Unhappy villain that I am!' replied Dietrich, gesticulating fox-like refusal; 'if I but accept a favour, I break faith with the Club.'

'Break it to pleasure me,' said Margarita, smiling wickedly.

Dietrich gasped. He stood on tiptoe to see if any of the Club were by, and half-stretched out his hand. A mocking laugh caused him to draw it back as if stung. The grapes fell. Farina was at Margarita's feet offering them in return.

'Wilt thou?' said Margarita, with softer stress, and slight excess of bloom in her cheeks.

Farina put the purple cluster to his breast, and clutched them hard on his heart, still kneeling.

Margarita's brow and bosom seemed to be reflections of the streaming crimson there. She shook her face to the sky, and affected laughter at the symbol. Her companions clapped hands. Farina's eyes yearned to her once, and then he rose and joined in the pleasantry.

Fury helped Dietrich to forget his awkwardness. He touched Farina on the shoulder with two fingers, and muttered huskily: 'The Club never allow that.'

Farina bowed, as to thank him deeply for the rules of the Club. 'I am not a member, you know,' said he, and strolled to a seat close by Margarita.

Dietrich glared after him. As head of a Club he understood the use of symbols. He had lost a splendid opportunity, and Farina had seized it. Farina had robbed him.

'May I speak with Mistress Margarita?' inquired the White Rose chief, in a ragged voice.

'Surely, Dietrich! do speak,' said Margarita.

'Alone?' he continued.

'Is that allowed by the Club?' said one of the young girls, with a saucy glance.

Dietrich deigned no reply, but awaited Margarita's decision. She hesitated a second; then stood up her full height before him; faced him steadily, and beckoned him some steps up the vine-path. Dietrich bowed, and passing Farina, informed him that the Club would wring satisfaction out of him for the insult.

Farina laughed, but answered, 'Look, you of the Club! beer-swilling has improved your manners as much as fighting has beautified your faces. Go on; drink and fight! but remember that the Kaiser's coming, and fellows with him who will not be bullied.'

'What mean you?' cried Dietrich, lurching round on his enemy.

'Not so loud, friend,' returned Farina. 'Or do you wish to frighten the maidens? I mean this, that the Club had better give as little offence as possible, and keep their eyes as wide as they can, if they want to be of service to Mistress Margarita.'

Dietrich turned off with a grunt.

'Now!' said Margarita.

She was tapping her foot. Dietrich grew unfaithful to the Club, and looked at her longer than his mission warranted. She was bright as the sunset gardens of the Golden Apples. The braids of her yellow hair were bound in wreaths, and on one side of her head a saffron crocus was stuck with the bell downward. Sweetness, song, and wit hung like dews of morning on her grape-stained lips. She wore a scarlet corset with bands of black velvet across her shoulders. The girlish gown was thin blue stuff, and fell short over her firm-set feet, neatly cased in white leather with buckles. There was witness in her limbs and the way she carried her neck of an amiable, but capable, dragon, ready, when aroused, to bristle up and guard the Golden Apples against all save the rightful claimant. Yet her nether lip and little white chin-ball had a dreamy droop; her frank blue eyes went straight into the speaker: the dragon slept. It was a dangerous charm. 'For,' says the minnesinger, 'what ornament more enchants us on a young beauty than the soft slumber of a strength never yet called forth, and that herself knows not of! It sings double things to the heart of knighthood; lures, and warns us; woos, and threatens. 'Tis as nature, shining peace, yet the mother of storm.'

'There is no man,' rapturously exclaims Heinrich von der Jungferweide, 'can resist the desire to win a sweet treasure before which lies a dragon sleeping. The very danger prattles promise.'

But the dragon must really sleep, as with Margarita.

'A sham dragon, shamming sleep, has destroyed more virgins than all the heathen emperors,' says old Hans Aepfelmann of Duesseldorf.

Margarita's foot was tapping quicker.

'Speak, Dietrich!' she said.

Dietrich declared to the Club that at this point he muttered, 'We love you.' Margarita was glad to believe he had not spoken of himself. He then informed her of the fears entertained by the Club, sworn to watch over and protect her, regarding Farina's arts.

'And what fear you?' said Margarita.

'We fear, sweet mistress, he may be in league with Sathanas,' replied Dietrich.

'Truly, then,' said Margarita, 'of all the youths in Cologne he is the least like his confederate.'

Dietrich gulped and winked, like a patient recovering wry-faced from an abhorred potion.

'We have warned you, Fraulein Groschen!' he exclaimed. 'It now becomes our duty to see that you are not snared.'

Margarita reddened, and returned: 'You are kind. But I am a Christian maiden and not a Pagan soldan, and I do not require a body of tawny guards at my heels.'

Thereat she flung back to her companions, and began staining her pretty mouth with grapes anew.

THE TAPESTRY WORD

Fair maids will have their hero in history. Siegfried was Margarita's chosen. She sang of Siegfried all over the house. 'O the old days of Germany, when such a hero walked!' she sang.

'And who wins Margarita,' mused Farina, 'happier than Siegfried, has in his arms Brunhild and Chrimhild together!'

Crowning the young girl's breast was a cameo, and the skill of some cunning artist out of Welschland had wrought on it the story of the Drachenfels. Her bosom heaved the battle up and down.

This cameo was a north star to German manhood, but caused many chaste expressions of abhorrence from Aunt Lisbeth, Gottlieb's unmarried sister, who seemed instinctively to take part with the Dragon. She was a frail-fashioned little lady, with a face betokening the perpetual smack of lemon, and who reigned in her brother's household when the good wife was gone. Margarita's robustness was beginning to alarm and shock Aunt Lisbeth's sealed stock of virtue.

'She must be watched, such a madl as that,' said Aunt Lisbeth. 'Ursula! what limbs she has!'

Margarita was watched; but the spy being neither foe nor friend, nothing was discovered against her. This did not satisfy Aunt Lisbeth, whose own suspicion was her best witness. She allowed that Margarita dissembled well.

'But,' said she to her niece, 'though it is good in a girl not to flaunt these naughtinesses in effrontery, I care for you too much not to say—Be what you seem, my little one!'

'And that am I!' exclaimed Margarita, starting up and towering.

'Right good, my niece,' Lisbeth squealed; 'but now Frau Groschen lies in God's acre, you owe your duty to me, mind! Did you confess last week?'

'From beginning to end,' replied Margarita.

Aunt Lisbeth fixed pious reproach on Margarita's cameo.

'And still you wear that thing?'

'Why not?' said Margarita.

'Girl! who would bid you set it in such a place save Satan? Oh, thou poor lost child! that the eyes of the idle youths may be drawn there! and thou become his snare to others, Margarita! What was that Welsh wandering juggler but the foul fiend himself, mayhap, thou maiden of sin! They say he has been seen in Cologne lately. He was swarthy as Satan and limped of one leg. Good Master in heaven, protect us! it was Satan himself I could swear!'

Aunt Lisbeth crossed brow and breast.

Margarita had commenced fingering the cameo, as if to tear it away; but Aunt Lisbeth's finish made her laugh outright.

'Where I see no harm, aunty, I shall think the good God is,' she answered; 'and where I see there's harm, I shall think Satan lurks.'

A simper of sour despair passed over Aunt Lisbeth. She sighed, and was silent, being one of those very weak reeds who are easily vanquished and never overcome.

'Let us go on with the Tapestry, child,' said she.

Now, Margarita was ambitious of completing a certain Tapestry for presentation to Kaiser Heinrich on his entry into Cologne after his last campaign on the turbaned Danube. The subject was again her beloved Siegfried slaying the Dragon on Drachenfels. Whenever Aunt Lisbeth indulged in any bitter virginity, and was overmatched by Margarita's frank maidenhood, she hung out this tapestry as a flag of truce. They were working it in bits, not having contrivances to do it in a piece. Margarita took Siegfried and Aunt Lisbeth the Dragon. They shared the crag between them. A roguish gleam of the Rhine toward Nonnenwerth could be already made out, Roland's Corner hanging like a sentinel across the chanting island, as one top-heavy with long watch.

Aunt Lisbeth was a great proficient in the art, and had taught Margarita. The little lady learnt it, with many other gruesome matters, in the Palatine of Bohemia's family. She usually talked of the spectres of Hollenbogenblitz Castle in the passing of the threads. Those were dismal spectres in Bohemia, smelling of murder and the charnel-breath of midnight. They uttered noises that wintered the blood, and revealed sights that stiffened hair three feet long; ay, and kept it stiff!

Margarita placed herself on a settle by the low-arched window, and Aunt Lisbeth sat facing her. An evening sun blazoned the buttresses of the Cathedral, and shadowed the workframes of the peaceful couple to a temperate light. Margarita unrolled a sampler sheathed with twists of divers coloured threads, and was soon busy silver-threading Siegfried's helm and horns.

'I told you of the steward, poor Kraut, did I not, child?' inquired Aunt Lisbeth, quietly clearing her throat.

'Many times!' said Margarita, and went on humming over her knee

'Her love was a Baron,
A Baron so bold;
She loved him for love,
He loved her for gold.'

'He must see for himself, and be satisfied,' continued Aunt Lisbeth; 'and Holy Thomas to warn him for an example! Poor Kraut!'

'Poor Kraut!' echoed Margarita.

'The King loved wine, and the Knight loved wine,
And they loved the summer weather:
They might have loved each other well,
But for one they loved together.'

'You may say, poor Kraut, child!' said Aunt Lisbeth. 'Well! his face was before that as red as this dragon's jaw, and ever after he went about as white as a pullet's egg. That was something wonderful!' 'That was it!' chimed Margarita.

'O the King he loved his lawful wife,
The Knight a lawless lady:
And ten on one-made ringing strife,
Beneath the forest shady.'

'Fifty to one, child!' said Aunt Lisbeth: 'You forget the story. They made Kraut sit with them at the jabbering feast, the only mortal there. The walls were full of eye-sockets without eyes, but phosphorus instead, burning blue and damp.'

'Not to-night, aunty dear! It frightens me so,' pleaded Margarita, for she saw the dolor coming.

'Night! when it's broad mid-day, thou timid one! Good heaven take pity on such as thou! The dish was seven feet in length by four broad. Kraut measured it with his eye, and never forgot it. Not he! When the dish-cover was lifted, there he saw himself lying, boiled!

'"I did not feel uncomfortable then," Kraut told us. "It seemed natural."

'His face, as it lay there, he says, was quite calm, only a little wrinkled, and piggish-looking-like. There was the mole on his chin, and the pucker under his left eyelid. Well! the Baron carved. All the guests were greedy for a piece of him. Some cried out for breast; some for toes. It was shuddering cold to sit and hear that! The Baroness said, "Cheek!"'

'Ah!' shrieked Margarita, 'that can I not bear! I will not hear it, aunt; I will not!'

'Cheek!' Aunt Lisbeth reiterated, nodding to the floor.

Margarita put her fingers to her ears.

'Still, Kraut says, even then he felt nothing odd. Of course he was horrified to be sitting with spectres as you and I should be; but the first tremble of it was over. He had plunged into the bath of horrors, and there he was. I 've heard that you must pronounce the names of the Virgin and Trinity, sprinkling water round you all the while for three minutes; and if you do this without interruption, everything shall disappear. So they say. "Oh! dear heaven of mercy!" says Kraut, "what I felt when the Baron laid his long hunting-knife across my left cheek!"'

Here Aunt Lisbeth lifted her eyes to dote upon Margarita's fright. She was very displeased to find her niece, with elbows on the window-sill and hands round her head, quietly gazing into the street.

She said severely, 'Where did you learn that song you were last singing, Margarita? Speak, thou girl!'

Margarita laughed.

'The thrush, and the lark, and the blackbird,
They taught me how to sing:
And O that the hawk would lend his eye,
And the eagle lend his wing.'

'I will not hear these shameless songs,' exclaimed Aunt Lisbeth.

'For I would view the lands they view,
And be where they have been:
It is not enough to be singing
For ever in dells unseen!'

A voice was heard applauding her. 'Good! right good! Carol again, Gretelchen! my birdie!'

Margarita turned, and beheld her father in the doorway. She tripped toward him, and heartily gave him their kiss of meeting. Gottlieb glanced at the helm of Siegfried.

'Guessed the work was going well; you sing so lightsomely to-day, Grete! Very pretty! And that's Drachenfels? Bones of the Virgins! what a bold fellow was Siegfried, and a lucky, to have the neatest lass in Deutschland in love with him. Well, we must marry her to Siegfried after all, I believe! Aha? or somebody as good as Siegfried. So chirrup on, my darling!'

'Aunt Lisbeth does not approve of my songs,' replied Margarita, untwisting some silver threads.

'Do thy father's command, girl!' said Aunt Lisbeth.

'And doing his command,
Should I do a thing of ill,
I'd rather die to his lovely face,
Than wanton at his will.'

'There—there,' said Aunt Lisbeth, straining out her fingers; 'you see, Gottlieb, what over-indulgence brings her to. Not another girl in blessed Rhineland, and Bohemia to boot, dared say such words!— than—I can't repeat them!—don't ask me!—She's becoming a Frankish girl!'

'What ballad's that?' said Gottlieb, smiling.

'The Ballad of Holy Ottilia; and her lover was sold to darkness. And she loved him—loved him—'

'As you love Siegfried, you little one?'

'More, my father; for she saw Winkried, and I never saw Siegfried. Ah! if I had seen Siegfried! Never mind. She loved him; but she loved Virtue more. And Virtue is the child of God, and the good God forgave her for loving Winkried, the Devil's son, because she loved Virtue more, and He rescued her as she was being dragged down—down—down, and was half fainting with the smell of brimstone— rescued her and had her carried into His Glory, head and feet, on the wings of angels, before all men, as a hope to little maidens.

'And when I thought that I was lost
I found that I was saved,
And I was borne through blessed clouds,
Where the banners of bliss were waved.'

'And so you think you, too, may fall in, love with Devils' sons, girl?' was Aunt Lisbeth's comment.

'Do look at Lisbeth's Dragon, little Heart! it's so like!' said Margarita to her father.

Old Gottlieb twitted his hose, and chuckled.

'She's my girl! that may be seen,' said he, patting her, and wheezed up from his chair to waddle across to the Dragon. But Aunt Lisbeth tartly turned the Dragon to the wall.

'It is not yet finished, Gottlieb, and must not be looked at,' she interposed. 'I will call for wood, and see to a fire: these evenings of Spring wax cold': and away whimpered Aunt Lisbeth.

Margarita sang:

'I with my playmates,
In riot and disorder,
Were gathering herb and blossom
Along the forest border.'

'Thy mother's song, child of my heart!' said Gottlieb; 'but vex not good Lisbeth: she loves thee!'

'And do you think she loves me?
And will you say 'tis true?
O, and will she have me,
When I come up to woo?'

'Thou leaping doe! thou chattering pie!' said Gottlieb.

'She shall have ribbons and trinkets,
And shine like a morn of May,
When we are off to the little hill-church,
Our flowery bridal way.'

'That she shall; and something more!' cried Gottlieb. 'But, hark thee, Gretelchen; the Kaiser will be here in three days. Thou dear one! had I not stored and hoarded all for thee, I should now have my feet on a hearthstone where even he might warm his boot. So get thy best dresses and jewels in order, and look thyself; proud as any in the land. A simple burgher's daughter now, Grete; but so shalt thou not end, my butterfly, or there's neither worth nor wit in Gottlieb Groschen!'

'Three days!' Margarita exclaimed; 'and the helm not finished, and the tapestry-pieces not sewed and joined, and the water not shaded off.—Oh! I must work night and day.'

'Child! I'll have no working at night! Your rosy cheeks will soon be sucked out by oil-light, and you look no better than poor tallow Court beauties—to say nothing of the danger. This old house saw Charles the Great embracing the chief magistrate of his liege city yonder. Some swear he slept in it. He did not sneeze at smaller chambers than our Kaisers abide. No gold ceilings with cornice carvings, but plain wooden beams.'

'Know that the men of great renown,
Were men of simple needs:
Bare to the Lord they laid them down,
And slept on mighty deeds.'

'God wot, there's no emptying thy store of ballads, Grete: so much shall be said of thee. Yes; times are changeing: We're growing degenerate. Look at the men of Linz now to what they were! Would they have let the lads of Andernach float down cabbage-stalks to them without a shy back? And why? All because they funk that brigand-beast Werner, who gets redemption from Laach, hard by his hold, whenever he commits a crime worth paying for. As for me, my timber and stuffs must come down stream, and are too good for the nixen under Rhine, or think you I would acknowledge him with a toll, the hell-dog? Thunder and lightning! if old scores could be rubbed out on his hide!'

Gottlieb whirled a thong-lashing arm in air, and groaned of law and justice. What were they coming to!

Margarita softened the theme with a verse:

'And tho' to sting his enemy,
Is sweetness to the angry bee,
The angry bee must busy be,
Ere sweet of sweetness hiveth he.

The arch thrill of his daughter's voice tickled Gottlieb. 'That's it, birdie! You and the proverb are right. I don't know which is best,

'Better hive
And keep alive
Than vengeance wake
With that you take.'

A clatter in the cathedral square brought Gottlieb on his legs to the window. It was a company of horsemen sparkling in harness. One trumpeter rode at the side of the troop, and in front a standard-bearer, matted down the chest with ochre beard, displayed aloft to the good citizens of Cologne, three brown hawks, with birds in their beaks, on an azure stardotted field.

'Holy Cross!' exclaimed Gottlieb, low in his throat; 'the arms of Werner! Where got he money to mount his men? Why, this is daring all Cologne in our very teeth! 'Fend that he visit me now! Ruin smokes in that ruffian's track. I 've felt hot and cold by turns all day.'

The horsemen came jingling carelessly along the street in scattered twos and threes, laughing together, and singling out the maidens at the gable-shadowed windows with hawking eyes. The good citizens of Cologne did not look on them favourably. Some showed their backs and gruffly banged their doors: others scowled and pocketed their fists: not a few slunk into the side alleys like well-licked curs, and scurried off with forebent knees. They were in truth ferocious-looking fellows these trusty servants of the robber Baron Werner, of Werner's Eck, behind Andernach. Leather, steel, and dust, clad them from head to foot; big and black as bears; wolf-eyed, fox-nosed. They glistened bravely in the falling beams of the sun, and Margarita thrust her fair braided yellow head a little forward over her father's shoulder to catch the whole length of the grim cavalcade. One of the troop was not long in discerning the young beauty. He pointed her boldly out to a comrade, who approved his appetite, and referred her to a third. The rest followed lead, and Margarita was as one spell-struck when she became aware that all those hungry eyes were preying on hers. Old Gottlieb was too full of his own fears to think for her, and when he drew in his head rather suddenly, it was with a dismal foreboding that Werner's destination in Cologne was direct to the house of Gottlieb Groschen, for purposes only too well to be divined.

'Devil's breeches!' muttered Gottlieb; 'look again, Grete, and see if that hell-troop stop the way outside.'

Margarita's cheeks were overflowing with the offended rose.

'I will not look at them again, father.'

Gottlieb stared, and then patted her.

'I would I were a man, father!'

Gottlieb smiled, and stroked his beard.

'Oh! how I burn!'

And the girl shivered visibly.

'Grete! mind to be as much of a woman as you can, and soon such raff as this you may sweep away, like cobwebs, and no harm done.'

He was startled by a violent thumping at the streetdoor, and as brazen a blast as if the dead were being summoned. Aunt Lisbeth entered, and flitted duskily round the room, crying:

'We are lost: they are upon us! better death with a bodkin! Never shall it be said of me; never! the monsters!'

Then admonishing them to lock, bar, bolt, and block up every room in the house, Aunt Lisbeth perched herself on the edge of a chair, and reversed the habits of the screech-owl, by being silent when stationary.

'There's nothing to fear for you, Lisbeth,' said Gottlieb, with discourteous emphasis.

'Gottlieb! do you remember what happened at the siege of Mainz? and poor Marthe Herbstblum, who had hoped to die as she was; and Dame Altknopfchen, and Frau Kaltblut, and the old baker, Hans Topf's sister, all of them as holy as abbesses, and that did not save them! and nothing will from such godless devourers.'

Gottlieb was gone, having often before heard mention of the calamity experienced by these fated women.

'Comfort thee, good heart, on my breast,' said Margarita, taking Lisbeth to that sweet nest of peace and fortitude.

'Margarita! 'tis your doing! have I not said—lure them not, for they swarm too early upon us! And here they are! and, perhaps, in five minutes all will be over!

Herr Je!—What, you are laughing! Heavens of goodness, the girl is delighted!'

Here a mocking ha-ha! accompanied by a thundering snack at the door, shook the whole house, and again the trumpet burst the ears with fury.

This summons, which seemed to Aunt Lisbeth final, wrought a strange composure in her countenance. She was very pale, but spread her dress decently, as if fear had departed, and clasped her hands on her knees.

'The will of the Lord above must be done,' said she; 'it is impious to complain when we are given into the hand of the Philistines. Others have been martyred, and were yet acceptable.'

To this heroic speech she added, with cold energy: 'Let them come!'

'Aunt,' cried Margarita, 'I hear my father's voice with those men. Aunty! I will not let him be alone. I must go down to him. You will be safe here. I shall come to you if there's cause for alarm.'

And in spite of Aunt Lisbeth's astonished shriek of remonstrance, she hurried off to rejoin Gottlieb.

THE WAGER

Ere Margarita had reached the landing of the stairs, she repented her haste and shrank back. Wrapt in a thunder of oaths, she distinguished: ''Tis the little maiden we want; let's salute her and begone! or cap your skull with something thicker than you've on it now, if you want a whole one, happy father!'

'Gottlieb von Groschen I am,' answered her father, 'and the Kaiser—'

''S as fond of a pretty girl as we are! Down with her, and no more drivelling! It's only for a moment, old Measure and Scales!'

'I tell you, rascals, I know your master, and if you're not punished for this, may I die a beggar!' exclaimed Gottlieb, jumping with rage.

'May you die as rich as an abbot! And so you will, if you don't bring her down, for I've sworn to see her; there 's the end of it, man!'

'I'll see, too, if the laws allow this villany!' cried Gottlieb. 'Insulting a peaceful citizen! in his own house! a friend of your emperor! Gottlieb von Groschen!'

'Groschen? We're cousins, then! You wouldn't shut out your nearest kin? Devil's lightning! Don't you know me? Pfennig? Von Pfennig! This here's Heller: that's Zwanziger: all of us Vons, every soul! You're not decided? This'll sharpen you, my jolly King Paunch!'

And Margarita heard the ruffian step as if to get swing for a blow. She hurried into the passage, and slipping in front of her father, said to his assailant:

'You have asked for me! I am here!'

Her face was colourless, and her voice seemed to issue from between a tightened cord. She stood with her left foot a little in advance, and her whole body heaving and quivering: her arms folded and pressed hard below her bosom: her eyes dilated to a strong blue: her mouth ashy white. A strange lustre, as of suppressed internal fire, flickered over her.

'My name 's Schwartz Thier, and so 's my nature!' said the fellow with a grin; 'but may I never smack lips with a pretty girl again, if I harm such a young beauty as this! Friendly dealing's my plan o' life.'

'Clear out of my house, then, fellow, and here's money for you,' said Gottlieb, displaying a wrathfully-trembling handful of coin.

'Pish! money! forty times that wouldn't cover my bet! And if it did? Shouldn't I be disgraced? jeered at for a sheep-heart? No, I'm no ninny, and not to be diddled. I'll talk to the young lady! Silence, out there! all's going proper': this to his comrades through the door. 'So, my beautiful maiden! thus it stands: We saw you at the window, looking like a fresh rose with a gold crown on. Here are we poor fellows come to welcome the Kaiser. I began to glorify you. "Schwartz Thier!" says Henker Rothhals to me, "I'll wager you odds you don't have a kiss of that fine girl within twenty minutes, counting from the hand-smack!" Done! was my word, and we clapped our fists together. Now, you see, that's straightforward! All I want is, not to lose my money and be made a fool of—leaving alone that sugary mouth which makes mine water'; and he drew the back of his hand along his stubbled jaws: 'So, come! don't hesitate! no harm to you, my beauty, but a compliment, and Schwartz Thier's your friend and anything else you like for ever after. Come, time's up, pretty well.'

Margarita leaned to her father a moment as if mortal sickness had seized her. Then cramping her hands and feet, she said in his ear, 'Leave me to my own care; go, get the men to protect thee'; and ordered Schwartz Thier to open the door wide.

Seeing Gottlieb would not leave her, she joined her hands, and begged him. 'The good God will protect me! I will overmatch these men. Look, my father! they dare not strike me in the street: you they would fell without pity. Go! what they dare in a house, they dare not in the street.'

Schwartz Thier had opened the door. At sight of Margarita, the troop gave a shout.

'Now! on the doorstep, full in view, my beauteous one! that they may see what a lucky devil I am—and have no doubts about the handing over.'

Margarita looked behind. Gottlieb was still there, every member of him quaking like a bog under a heavy heel. She ran to him. 'My father! I have a device wilt thou spoil it, and give me to this beast? You can do nothing, nothing! protect yourself and save me!'

'Cologne! broad day!' muttered Gottlieb, as if the enormity had prostrated his belief in facts; and moved slowly back.

Margarita strode to the door-step. Schwartz Thier was awaiting her, his arm circled out, and his leering face ducked to a level with his victim's. This rough show of gallantry proved costly to him. As he was gently closing his iron hold about her, enjoying before hand with grim mouthridges the flatteries of triumph, Margarita shot past him through the door, and was already twenty paces beyond the troop before either of them thought of pursuing her. At the first sound of a hoof, Henker Rothhals seized the rider's bridle-rein, and roared: 'Fair play for a fair bet! leave all to the Thier!' The Thier, when he had recovered from his amazement, sought for old Gottlieb to give him a back-hit, as Margarita foresaw that he would. Not finding him at hand, out lumbered the fellow as swiftly as his harness would allow, and caught a glimpse of Margarita rapidly fleeting up the cathedral square.

'Only five minutes, Schwartz Thier!' some of the troop sung out.

'The devil can do his business in one,' was the retort, and Schwartz Thier swung himself on his broad-backed charger, and gored the fine beast till she rattled out a blast of sparkles from the flint.

In a minute he drew up in front of Margarita.

'So! you prefer settling this business in the square.

Good! my choice sweetheart!' and he sprang to her side.

The act of flight had touched the young girl's heart with the spirit of flight. She crouched like a winded hare under the nose of the hound, and covered her face with her two hands. Margarita was no wisp in weight, but Schwartz Thier had her aloft in his arm as easily as if he had tossed up a kerchief.

'Look all, and witness!' he shouted, lifting the other arm.

Henker Rothhals and the rest of the troop looked, as they came trotting to the scene, with the coolness of umpires: but they witnessed something other than what Schwartz Thier proposed. This was the sight of a formidable staff, whirling an unfriendly halo over the head of the Thier, and descending on it with such honest intent to confound and overthrow him, that the Thier succumbed to its force without argument, and the square echoed blow and fall simultaneously. At the same time the wielder of this sound piece of logic seized Margarita, and raised a shout in the square for all true men to stand by him in rescuing a maiden from the clutch of brigands and ravishers. A crowd was collecting, but seemed to consider the circle now formed by the horsemen as in a manner charmed, for only one, a fair slender youth, came forward and ranged himself beside the stranger.

'Take thou the maiden: I'll keep to the staff,' said this latter, stumbling over his speech as if he was in a foreign land among old roots and wolfpits which had already shaken out a few of his teeth, and made him cautious about the remainder.

'Can it be Margarita!' exclaimed the youth, bending to her, and calling to her: 'Margarita! Fraulein Groschen!'

She opened her eyes, shuddered, and said: 'I was not afraid! Am I safe?'

'Safe while I have life, and this good friend.'

'Where is my father?'

'I have not seen him.'

'And you—who are you? Do I owe this to you?'

'Oh! no! no! Me you owe nothing.'

Margarita gazed hurriedly round, and at her feet there lay the Thier with his steel-cap shining in dints, and three rivulets of blood coursing down his mottled forehead. She looked again at the youth, and a blush of recognition gave life to her cheeks.

'I did not know you. Pardon me. Farina! what thanks can reward such courage! Tell me! shall we go?'

'The youth eyed her an instant, but recovering himself, took a rapid survey, and called to the stranger to follow and help give the young maiden safe conduct home.

'Just then Henker Rothhals bellowed, 'Time's up!' He was answered by a chorus of agreement from the troop. They had hitherto patiently acted their parts as spectators, immovable on their horses. The assault on the Thier was all in the play, and a visible interference of fortune in favour of Henker Rothhals. Now general commotion shuttled them, and the stranger's keen hazel eyes read their intentions rightly when he lifted his redoubtable staff in preparation for another mighty swoop, this time defensive. Rothhals, and half a dozen others, with a war-cry of curses, spurred their steeds at once to ride him down. They had not reckoned the length and good-will of their antagonist's weapon. Scarce were they in motion, when round it whizzed, grazing the nostrils of their horses with a precision that argued practice in the feat, and unhorsing two, Rothhals among the number. He dropped heavily on his head, and showed signs of being as incapable of combat as the Thier. A cheer burst from the crowd, but fell short.

The foremost of their number was struck flat to the earth by a fellow of the troop.

Calling on St. George, his patron saint, the stranger began systematically to make a clear ring in his path forward. Several of the horsemen essayed a cut at his arm with their long double-handed swords, but the horses could not be brought a second time to the edge of the magic circle; and the blood of these warriors being thoroughly up, they now came at him on foot. In their rage they would have made short work with the three, in spite of the magistracy of Cologne, had they not been arrested by cries of 'Werner! Werner!'

At the South-west end of the square, looking Rhinewards, rode the marauder Baron, in full armour, helm and hauberk, with a single retainer in his rear. He had apparently caught sight of the brawl, and, either because he distinguished his own men, or was seeking his natural element, hastened up for his share in it, which was usually that of the king of beasts. His first call was for Schwartz Thier. The men made way, and he beheld his man in no condition to make military responses. He shouted for Henker Rothhals, and again the men opened their ranks mutely, exhibiting the two stretched out in diverse directions, with their feet slanting to a common point. The Baron glared; then caught off his mailed glove, and thrust it between his teeth. A rasping gurgle of oaths was all they heard, and presently surged up,

'Who was it?'

Margarita's eyes were shut. She opened them fascinated with horror. There was an unearthly awful and comic mixture of sounds in Werner's querulous fury, that was like the noise of a complaining bear, rolling up from hollow-chested menace to yawning lament. Never in her life had Margarita such a shock of fear. The half gasp of a laugh broke on her trembling lips. She stared at Werner, and was falling; but Farina's arm clung instantly round her waist. The stranger caught up her laugh, loud and hearty.

'As for who did it, Sir Baron,' he cried, is a cheery tone, 'I am the man! As you may like to know why—and that's due to you and me both of us—all I can say is, the Black Muzzle yonder lying got his settler for merry-making with this peaceful maiden here, without her consent—an offence in my green island they reckon a crack o' the sconce light basting for, I warrant all company present,' and he nodded sharply about. 'As for the other there, who looks as if a rope had been round his neck once and shirked its duty, he counts his wages for helping the devil in his business, as will any other lad here who likes to come on and try.'

Werner himself, probably, would have given him the work he wanted; but his eye had sidled a moment over Margarita, and the hardly-suppressed applause of the crowd at the stranger's speech failed to bring his ire into action this solitary time.

'Who is the maiden?' he asked aloud.

'Fraulein von Groschen,' replied Farina.

'Von Groschen! Von Groschen! the daughter of Gottlieb Groschen?—Rascals!' roared the Baron, turning on his men, and out poured a mud-spring of filthy oaths and threats, which caused Henker Rothhals, who had opened his eyes, to close them again, as if he had already gone to the place of heat.

'Only lend me thy staff, friend,' cried Werner.

'Not I! thwack 'em with your own wood,' replied the stranger, and fell back a leg.

Werner knotted his stringy brows, and seemed torn to pieces with the different pulling tides of his wrath. He grasped the mane of his horse and flung abroad handfuls, till the splendid animal reared in agony.

'You shall none of you live over this night, villains! I 'll hang you, every hag's son! My last orders were,— Keep quiet in the city, ye devil's brood. Take that! and that!' laying at them with his bare sword. 'Off with you, and carry these two pigs out of sight quickly, or I'll have their heads, and make sure o' them.'

The latter injunction sprang from policy, for at the head of the chief street there was a glitter of the city guard, marching with shouldered spears.

'Maiden,' said Werner, with a bull's bow, 'let me conduct thee to thy father.'

Margarita did not reply; but gave her hand to Farina, and took a step closer to the stranger.

Werner's brows grew black.

'Enough to have saved you, fair maid,' he muttered hoarsely. 'Gratitude never was a woman's gift. Say to your father that I shall make excuses to him for the conduct of my men.'

Whereupon, casting a look of leisurely scorn toward the guard coming up in the last beams of day, the Baron shrugged his huge shoulders to an altitude expressing the various contemptuous shades of feudal coxcombry, stuck one leather-ruffled arm in his side, and jolted off at an easy pace.

'Amen!' ejaculated the stranger, leaning on his staff. 'There are Barons in my old land; but never a brute beast in harness.'

Margarita stood before him, and took his two hands.

'You will come with me to my father! He will thank you. I cannot. You will come?'

Tears and a sob of relief started from her.

The city guard, on seeing Werner's redoubtable back turned, had adopted double time, and now came panting up, while the stranger bent smiling under a fresh overflow of innocent caresses. Margarita was caught to her father's breast.

'You shall have vengeance for this, sweet chuck,' cried old Gottlieb in the intervals of his hugs.

'Fear not, my father; they are punished': and Margarita related the story of the stranger's prowess, elevating him into a second Siegfried. The guard huzzaed him, but did not pursue the Baron.

Old Gottlieb, without hesitation, saluted the astonished champion with a kiss on either cheek.

'My best friend! You have saved my daughter from indignity! Come with us home, if you can believe that a home where the wolves come daring us, dragging our dear ones from our very doorsteps. Come, that we may thank you under a roof at least. My little daughter! Is she not a brave lass?'

'She's nothing less than the white rose of Germany,' said the stranger, with a good bend of the shoulders to Margarita.

'So she's called,' exclaimed Gottlieb; 'she 's worthy to be a man!'

'Men would be the losers, then, more than they could afford,' replied the stranger, with a ringing laugh.

'Come, good friend,' said Gottlieb; 'you must need refreshment. Prove you are a true hero by your appetite. As Charles the Great said to Archbishop Turpin, "I conquered the world because Nature gave me a gizzard; for everywhere the badge of subjection is a poor stomach." Come, all! A day well ended, notwithstanding!'

THE SILVER ARROW

At the threshold of Gottlieb's house a number of the chief burgesses of Cologne had corporated spontaneously to condole with him. As he came near, they raised a hubbub of gratulation. Strong were the expressions of abhorrence and disgust of Werner's troop in which these excellent citizens clothed their outraged feelings; for the insult to Gottlieb was the insult of all. The Rhinestream taxes were provoking enough to endure; but that the licence of these free-booting bands should extend to the homes of free and peaceful men, loyal subjects of the Emperor, was a sign that the evil had reached from pricks to pokes, as the saying went, and must now be met as became burgesses of ancient Cologne, and by joint action destroyed.

'In! in, all of you!' said Gottlieb, broadening his smile to suit the many. 'We 'll talk about that in-doors. Meantime, I've got a hero to introduce to you: flesh and blood! no old woman's coin and young girl's dream-o'day: the honest thing, and a rarity, my masters. All that over some good Rhine-juice from above Bacharach. In, and welcome, friends!'

Gottlieb drew the stranger along with him under the carved old oak-wood portals, and the rest paired, and reverentially entered in his wake. Margarita, to make up for this want of courtesy, formed herself the last of the procession. She may have had another motive, for she took occasion there to whisper something to Farina, bringing sun and cloud over his countenance in rapid flushes. He seemed to remonstrate in dumb show; but she, with an attitude of silence, signified her wish to seal the conversation, and he drooped again. On the door step she paused a moment, and hung her head pensively, as if moved by a reminiscence. The youth had hurried away some strides. Margarita looked after him. His arms were straightened to his flanks, his hands clenched, and straining out from the wrist. He had the aspect of one tugging against the restraint of a chain that suddenly let out link by link to his whole force.

'Farina!' she called; and wound him back with a run. 'Farina! You do not think me ungrateful? I could not tell my father in the crowd what you did for me. He shall know. He will thank you. He does not understand you now, Farina. He will. Look not so sorrowful. So much I would say to you.'

So much was rushing on her mind, that her maidenly heart became unruly, and warned her to beware.

The youth stood as if listening to a nightingale of the old woods, after the first sweet stress of her voice was in his ear. When she ceased, he gazed into her eyes. They were no longer deep and calm like forest lakes; the tender-glowing blue quivered, as with a spark of the young girl's soul, in the beams of the moon then rising.

'Oh, Margarita!' said the youth, in tones that sank to sighs: 'what am I to win your thanks, though it were my life for such a boon!'

He took her hand, and she did not withdraw it. Twice his lips dwelt upon those pure fingers.

'Margarita: you forgive me: I have been so long without hope. I have kissed your hand, dearest of God's angels!'

She gently restrained the full white hand in his pressure.

'Margarita! I have thought never before death to have had this sacred bliss. I am guerdoned in advance for every grief coming before death.'

She dropped on him one look of a confiding softness that was to the youth like the opened gate of the innocent garden of her heart.

'You pardon me, Margarita? I may call you my beloved? strive, wait, pray, hope, for you, my star of life?'

Her face was so sweet a charity!

'Dear love! one word!—or say nothing, but remain, and move not. So beautiful you are! Oh, might I kneel to you here; dote on you; worship this white hand for ever.'

The colour had passed out of her cheeks like a blissful western red leaving rich paleness in the sky; and with her clear brows levelled at him, her bosom lifting more and more rapidly, she struggled against the charm that was on her, and at last released her hand.

'I must go. I cannot stay. Pardon you? Who might not be proud of your love!—Farewell!'

She turned to move away, but lingered a step from him, hastily touching her bosom and either hand, as if to feel for a brooch or a ring. Then she blushed, drew the silver arrow from the gathered gold-shot braids above her neck, held it out to him, and was gone.

Farina clutched the treasure, and reeled into the street. Half a dozen neighbours were grouped by the door.

'What 's the matter in Master Groschen's house now?' one asked, as he plunged into the midst of them.

'Matter?' quoth the joy-drunken youth, catching at the word, and mused off into raptures; 'There never was such happiness! 'Tis paradise within, exile without. But what exile! A star ever in the heavens to lighten the road and cheer the path of the banished one'; and he loosened his vest and hugged the cold shaft on his breast.

'What are you talking and capering at, fellow?' exclaimed another: 'Can't you answer about those shrieks, like a Christian, you that have just come out of the house? Why, there's shrieking now! It 's a woman. Thousand thunders! it sounds like the Frau Lisbeth's voice. What can be happening to her?'

'Perhaps she's on fire,' was coolly suggested between two or three.

'Pity to see the old house burnt,' remarked one.

'House! The woman, man! the woman!'

'Ah!' replied the other, an ancient inhabitant of Cologne, shaking his head, 'the house is oldest!'

Farina, now recovering his senses, heard shrieks that he recognized as possible in the case of Aunt Lisbeth dreading the wickedness of an opposing sex, and alarmed by the inrush of old Gottlieb's numerous guests. To confirm him, she soon appeared, and hung herself halfway out of one of the upper windows, calling desperately to St. Ursula for aid. He thanked the old lady in his heart for giving him a pretext to enter Paradise again; but before even love could speed him, Frau Lisbeth was seized and dragged remorselessly out of sight, and he and the rosy room darkened together.

Farina twice strode off to the Rhine-stream; as many times he returned. It was hard to be away from her. It was harder to be near and not close. His heart flamed into jealousy of the stranger. Everything threatened to overturn his slight but lofty structure of bliss so suddenly shot into the heavens. He had but to remember that his hand was on the silver arrow, and a radiance broke upon his countenance, and a calm fell upon his breast. 'It was a plight of her troth to me,' mused the youth. 'She loves me! She would not trust her frank heart to speak. Oh, generous young girl! what am I to dare hope for such a prize? for I never can be worthy. And she is one who, giving her heart, gives it all. Do I not know her? How lovely she looked thanking the stranger! The blue of her eyes, the warm-lighted blue, seemed to grow full on the closing lids, like heaven's gratitude. Her beauty is wonderful. What wonder, then, if he loves her? I should think him a squire in his degree. There are squires of high birth and low.'

So mused Farina with his arms folded and his legs crossed in the shadow of Margarita's chamber. Gradually he fell into a kind of hazy doze. The houses became branded with silver arrows. All up the Cathedral stone was a glitter, and dance, and quiver of them. In the sky mazed confusion of arrowy flights and falls. Farina beheld himself in the service of the Emperor watching these signs, and expecting on the morrow to win glory and a name for Margarita. Glory and the name now won, old Gottlieb was just on the point of paternally blessing them, when a rude pat aroused him from the delicious moon-dream.

'Hero by day! house-guard by night! That tells a tale,' said a cheerful voice.

The moon was shining down the Cathedral square and street, and Farina saw the stranger standing solid and ruddy before him. He was at first prompted to resent such familiar handling, but the stranger's face was of that bland honest nature which, like the sun, wins everywhere back a reflection of its own kindliness.

'You are right,' replied Farina; 'so it is!'

'Pretty wines inside there, and a rare young maiden. She has a throat like a nightingale, and more ballads at command than a piper's wallet. Now, if I hadn't a wife at home.'

'You're married?' cried Farina, seizing the stranger's hand.

'Surely; and my lass can say something for herself on the score of brave looks, as well as the best of your German maids here, trust me.'

Farina repressed an inclination to perform a few of those antics which violent joy excites, and after rushing away and back, determined to give his secret to the stranger.

'Look,' said he in a whisper, that opens the private doors of a confidence.

But the stranger repeated the same word still more earnestly, and brought Farina's eyes on a couple of dark figures moving under the Cathedral.

'Some lamb's at stake when the wolves are prowling,' he added: ''Tis now two hours to the midnight. I doubt if our day's work be over till we hear the chime, friend.'

'What interest do you take in the people of this house that you watch over them thus?' asked Farina.

The stranger muffled a laugh in his beard.

'An odd question, good sooth. Why, in the first place, we like well whatso we have done good work for. That goes for something. In the second, I've broken bread in this house. Put down that in the reckoning. In the third; well! in the third, add up all together, and the sum total's at your service, young sir.'

Farina marked him closely. There was not a spot on his face for guile to lurk in, or suspicion to fasten on. He caught the stranger's hand.

'You called me friend just now. Make me your friend. Look, I was going to say: I love this maiden! I would die for her. I have loved her long. This night she has given me a witness that my love is not vain. I am poor. She is rich. I am poor, I said, and feel richer than the Kaiser with this she has given me! Look, it is what our German girls slide in their back-hair, this silver arrow!'

'A very pretty piece of heathenish wear!' exclaimed the stranger.

'Then, I was going to say—tell me, friend, of a way to win honour and wealth quickly; I care not at how rare a risk. Only to wealth, or high baronry, will her father give her!'

The stranger buzzed on his moustache in a pause of cool pity, such as elders assume when young men talk of conquering the world for their mistresses: and in truth it is a calm of mind well won!

'Things look so brisk at home here in the matter of the maiden, that I should say, wait a while and watch your chance. But you're a boy of pluck: I serve in the Kaiser's army, under my lord: the Kaiser will be here in three days. If you 're of that mind then, I doubt little you may get posted well: but, look again! there's a ripe brew yonder. Marry, you may win your spurs this night even; who knows?—'S life! there's a tall fellow joining those two lurkers.'

'Can you see into the murk shadow, Sir Squire?'

'Ay! thanks to your Styrian dungeons, where I passed a year's apprenticeship:

"I learnt to watch the rats and mice
At play, with never a candle-end.
They play'd so well; they sang so nice;
They dubb'd me comrade; called me friend!"

So says the ballad of our red-beard king's captivity. All evil has a good:

"When our toes and chins are up,
Poison plants make sweetest cup"

as the old wives mumble to us when we're sick. Heigho! would I were in the little island well home again, though that were just their song of welcome to me, as I am a Christian.'

'Tell me your name, friend,' said Farina.

'Guy's my name, young man: Goshawk's my title. Guy the Goshawk! so they called me in my merry land. The cap sticks when it no longer fits. Then I drove the arrow, and was down on my enemy ere he could ruffle a feather. Now, what would be my nickname?

"A change so sad, and a change so bad,
Might set both Christian and heathen a sighing:
Change is a curse, for it's all for the worse:
Age creeps up, and youth is flying!"

and so on, with the old song. But here am I, and yonder's a game that wants harrying; so we'll just begin to nose about them a bit.'

He crossed to the other side of the street, and Farina followed out of the moonlight. The two figures and the taller one were evidently observing them; for they also changed their position and passed behind an angle of the Cathedral.

'Tell me how the streets cross all round the Cathedral you know the city,' said the stranger, holding out his hand.

Farina traced with his finger a rough map of the streets on the stranger's hand.

'Good! that's how my lord always marks the battlefield, and makes me show him the enemy's posts. Forward, this way!'

He turned from the Cathedral, and both slid along close under the eaves and front hangings of the houses. Neither spoke. Farina felt that he was in the hands of a skilful captain, and only regretted the want of a weapon to make harvest of the intended surprise; for he judged clearly that those were fellows of Werner's band on the look-out. They wound down numberless intersections of narrow streets with irregular-built houses standing or leaning wry-faced in row, here a quaint-beamed cottage, there almost a mansion with gilt arms, brackets, and devices. Oil-lamps unlit hung at intervals by the corners, near a pale Christ on crucifix. Across the passages they hung alight. The passages and alleys were too dusky and close for the moon in her brightest ardour to penetrate; down the streets a slender lane of white beams could steal: 'In all conscience,' as the good citizens of Cologne declared, 'enough for those heathen hounds and sons of the sinful who are abroad when God's own blessed lamp is out.' So, when there was a moon, the expense of oil was saved to the Cologne treasury, thereby satisfying the virtuous.

After incessant doubling here and there, listening to footfalls, and themselves eluding a chase which their suspicious movements aroused, they came upon the Rhine. A full flood of moonlight burnished the knightly river in glittering scales, and plates, and rings, as headlong it rolled seaward on from under crag and banner of old chivalry and rapine. Both greeted the scene with a burst of pleasure. The grey mist of flats on the south side glimmered delightful to their sight, coming from that drowsy crowd and press of habitations; but the solemn glory of the river, delaying not, heedless, impassioned-pouring on in some sublime conference between it and heaven to the great marriage of waters, deeply shook Farina's enamoured heart. The youth could not restrain his tears, as if a magic wand had touched him. He trembled with love; and that delicate bliss which maiden hope first showers upon us like a silver rain when she has taken the shape of some young beauty and plighted us her fair fleeting hand, tenderly embraced him.

As they were emerging into the spaces of the moon, a cheer from the stranger arrested Farina.

'Seest thou? on the wharf there! that is the very one, the tallest of the three. Lakin! but we shall have him.'

Wrapt in a long cloak, with low pointed cap and feather, stood the person indicated. He appeared to be meditating on the flow of the water, unaware of hostile presences, or quite regardless of them. There was a majesty in his height and air, which made the advance of the two upon him more wary and respectful than their first impulse had counselled. They could not read his features, which were mantled behind voluminous folds: all save a pair of very strange eyes, that, even as they gazed directly downward, seemed charged with restless fiery liquid.

The two were close behind him: Guy the Goshawk prepared for one of those fatal pounces on the foe that had won him his title. He consulted Farina mutely, who Nodded readiness; but the instant after, a cry of anguish escaped from the youth:

'Lost! gone! lost! Where is it? where! the arrow! The Silver Arrow! My Margarita!'

Ere the echoes of his voice had ceased lamenting into the distance, they found themselves alone on the wharf.

THE LILIES OF THE VALLEY

'He opened like a bat!' said the stranger.

'His shadow was red!' said Farina.

'He was off like an arrow!' said the stranger.

'Oh! pledge of my young love, how could I lose thee!' exclaimed the youth, and his eyes were misted with tears.

Guy the Goshawk shook his brown locks gravely.

'Bring me a man, and I 'll stand up against him, whoever he be, like a man; but this fellow has an ill scent and foreign ways about him, that he has! His eye boils all down my backbone and tingles at my finger-tips. Jesu, save us!'

'Save us!' repeated Farina, with the echo of a deadened soul.

They made the sign of the Cross, and purified the place with holy ejaculations.

'I 've seen him at last; grant it be for the last time! That's my prayer, in the name of the Virgin and Trinity,' said Guy. 'And now let's retrace our steps: perchance we shall hunt up that bauble of yours, but I'm not fit for mortal work this night longer.'

Burdened by their black encounter, the two passed again behind the Cathedral. Farina's hungry glances devoured each footmark of their track. Where the moon held no lantern for him, he went on his knees, and groped for his lost treasure with a miser's eager patience of agony, drawing his hand slowly over the stony kerb and between the interstices of the thick-sown flints, like an acute-feeling worm. Despair grew heavy in his breast. At every turning he invoked some good new saint to aid him, and ran over all the propitiations his fancy could suggest and his religious lore inspire. By-and-by they reached the head of the street where Margarita dwelt. The moon was dipping down, and paler, as if touched with a warning of dawn. Chill sighs from the open land passed through the spaces of the city. On certain coloured gables and wood-crossed fronts, the white light lingered; but mostly the houses were veiled in dusk, and Gottlieb's house was confused in the twilight with those of his neighbours, notwithstanding its greater stateliness and the old grandeur of its timbered bulk. They determined to take up their position there again, and paced on, Farina with his head below his shoulders, and Guy nostril in air, as if uneasy in his sense of smell.

On the window-ledge of a fair-fitted domicile stood a flower-pot, a rude earthen construction in the form of a river-barge, wherein grew some valley lilies that drooped their white bells over the sides.

The Goshawk eyed them wistfully.

'I must smell those blessed flowers if I wish to be saved!' and he stamped resolve with his staff.

Moved by this exclamation, Farina gazed up at them.

'How like a company of maidens they look floating in the vessel of life!' he said.

Guy curiously inspected Farina and the flower-pot, shrugged, and with his comrade's aid, mounted to a level with it, seized the prize and redescended.

'There,' he cried, between long luxurious sniffs, 'that chases him out of the nostril sooner than aught else, the breath of a fresh lass-like flower! I was tormented till now by the reek of the damned rising from under me. This is heaven's own incense, I think!'

And Guy inhaled the flowers and spake prettily to them.

'They have a melancholy sweetness, friend,' said Farina. 'I think of whispering Fays, and Elf, and Erl, when their odour steals through me. Do not you?'

'Nay, nor hope to till my wits are clean gone,' was the Goshawk's reply. 'To my mind, 'tis an honest flower, and could I do good service by the young maiden who there set it, I should be rendering back good service done; for if that flower has not battled the devil in my nose this night, and beaten him, my head's a medlar!'

'I scarce know whether as a devout Christian I should listen to that, friend,' Farina mildly remonstrated. 'Lilies are indeed emblems of the saints; but then they are not poor flowers of earth, being transfigured, lustrous unfadingly. Oh, Cross and Passion! with what silver serenity thy glory enwraps me, gazing on these fair bells! I look on the white sea of the saints. I am enamoured of fleshly anguish and martyrdom. All beauty is that worn by wan-smiling faces wherein Hope sits as a crown on Sorrow, and the pale ebb of mortal life is the twilight of joy everlasting. Colourless peace! Oh, my beloved! So walkest thou for my soul on the white sea ever at night, clad in the straight fall of thy spotless virgin linen; bearing in thy hand the lily, and leaning thy cheek to it, where the human rose is softened to a milky bloom of red, the espousals of heaven with earth; over thee, moving with thee, a wreath of sapphire stars, and the solitude of purity around!'

'Ah!' sighed the Goshawk, dandling his flower-pot; 'the moon gives strokes as well's the sun. I' faith, moon-struck and maid-struck in one! He'll be asking for his head soon. This dash of the monk and the minstrel is a sure sign. That 's their way of loving in this land: they all go mad, straight off. I never heard such talk.'

Guy accompanied these remarks with a pitiful glance at his companion.

'Come, Sir Lover! lend me a help to give back what we've borrowed to its rightful owner. 'S blood! but I feel an appetite. This night-air takes me in the wind like a battering ram. I thought I had laid in a stout four-and-twenty hours' stock of Westphalian Wurst at Master Groschen's supper-table. Good stuff, washed down with superior Rhine wine; say your Liebfrauenmilch for my taste; though, when I first tried it, I grimaced like a Merry-Andrew, and remembered roast beef and Glo'ster ale in my prayers.'

The Goshawk was in the act of replacing the pot of lilies, when a blow from a short truncheon, skilfully flung, struck him on the neck and brought him to the ground. With him fell the lilies. He glared to the right and left, and grasped the broken flower-pot for a return missile; but no enemy was in view to test his accuracy of aim.

The deep-arched doorways showed their empty recesses the windows slept.

'Has that youth played me false?' thought the discomfited squire, as he leaned quietly on his arm. Farina was nowhere near.

Guy was quickly reassured.

'By my fay, now! that's a fine thing! and a fine fellow! and a fleet foot! That lad 'll rise! He'll be a squire some day. Look at him. Bowels of a'Becket! 'tis a sight! I'd rather see that, now, than old Groschen 's supper-table groaning with Wurst again, and running a river of Rudesheimer! Tussle on! I'll lend a hand if there's occasion; but you shall have the honour, boy, an you can win it.'

This crying on of the hound was called forth by a chase up the street, in which the Goshawk beheld Farina pursue and capture a stalwart runaway, who refused with all his might to be brought back, striving every two and three of his tiptoe steps to turn against the impulse Farina had got on his neck and nether garments.

'Who 'd have thought the lad was so wiry and mettlesome, with his soft face, blue eyes, and lank locks? but a green mead has more in it than many a black mountain. Hail, and well done! if I could dub you knight, I would: trust me!' and he shook Farina by the hand.

Farina modestly stood aside, and allowed the Goshawk to confront his prisoner.

'So, Sir Shy-i'the-dark! gallant Stick-i'the-back! Squire Truncheon, and Knight of the noble order of Quicksilver Legs! just take your stand at the distance you were off me when you discharged this instrument at my head. By 'r lady! I smart a scratch to pay you in coin, and it's lucky for you the coin is small, or you might reckon on it the same, trust me. Now, back!'

The Goshawk lunged out with the truncheon, but the prisoner displayed no hesitation in complying, and fell back about a space of fifteen yards.

'I suppose he guesses I've never done the stupid trick before,' mused Guy, 'or he would not be so sharp.' Observing that Farina had also fallen back in a line as guard, Guy motioned him to edge off to the right more, bawling, 'Never mind why!'

'Now,' thought Guy, 'if I were sure of notching him, I'd do the speech part first; but as I'm not—throwing truncheons being no honourable profession anywhere—I'll reserve that. The rascal don't quail. We'll see how long he stands firm.'

The Goshawk cleared his wrist, fixed his eye, and swung the truncheon meditatively to and fro by one end. He then launched off the shoulder a mighty down-fling, calmly, watching it strike the prisoner to earth, like an ox under the hammer.

'A hit!' said he, and smoothed his wrist.

Farina knelt by the body, and lifted the head on his breast. 'Berthold! Berthold!' he cried; 'no further harm shall hap to you, man! Speak!'

'You ken the scapegrace?' said Guy, sauntering up.

''Tis Berthold Schmidt, son of old Schmidt, the great goldsmith of Cologne.'

'St. Dunstan was not at his elbow this time!'

'A rival of mine,' whispered Farina.

'Oho!' and the Goshawk wound a low hiss at his tongue's tip. 'Well! as I should have spoken if his ears had been open: Justice struck the blow; and a gentle one. This comes of taking a flying shot, and not standing up fair. And that seems all that can be said. Where lives he?'

Farina pointed to the house of the Lilies.

'Beshrew me! the dog has some right on his side. Whew! yonder he lives? He took us for some night-prowlers. Why not come up fairly, and ask my business?

Smelling a flower is not worth a broken neck, nor defending your premises quite deserving a hole in the pate. Now, my lad, you see what comes of dealing with cut and run blows; and let this be a warning to you.'

They took the body by head and feet, and laid him at the door of his father's house. Here the colour came to his cheek, and they wiped off the streaks of blood that stained him. Guy proved he could be tender with a fallen foe, and Farina with an ill-fated rival. It was who could suggest the soundest remedies, or easiest postures. One lent a kerchief and nursed him; another ran to the city fountain and fetched him water. Meantime the moon had dropped, and morning, grey and beamless, looked on the house-peaks and along the streets with steadier eye. They now both discerned a body of men, far down, fronting Gottlieb's house, and drawn up in some degree of order. All their charity forsook them at once.

'Possess thyself of the truncheon,' said Guy: 'You see it can damage. More work before breakfast, and a fine account I must give of myself to my hostess of the Three Holy Kings!'

Farina recovered the destructive little instrument.

'I am ready,' said he. 'But hark! there's little work for us there, I fancy. Those be lads of Cologne, no grunters of the wild. 'Tis the White Rose Club. Always too late for service.'

Voices singing a hunting glee, popular in that age, swelled up the clear morning air; and gradually the words became distinct.

The Kaiser went a-hunting,
A-hunting, tra-ra:
With his bugle-horn at springing morn,
The Kaiser trampled bud and thorn:
Tra-ra!

And the dew shakes green as the horsemen rear,
And a thousand feathers they flutter with fear;
And a pang drives quick to the heart of the deer;
For the Kaiser's out a-hunting,
Tra-ra!
Ta, ta, ta, ta,
Tra-ra, tra-ra,

Ta-ta, tra-ra, tra-ra!

the owner of the truncheon awoke to these reviving tones, and uttered a faint responsive 'Tra-ra!'

'Hark again!' said Farina, in reply to the commendation of the Goshawk, whose face was dimpled over with the harmony.

The wild boar lay a-grunting,
A-grunting, tra-ra!
And, boom! comes the Kaiser to hunt up me?
Or, queak! the small birdie that hops on the tree?
Tra-ra!
O birdie, and boar, and deer, lie tame!
For a maiden in bloom, or a full-blown dame,
Are the daintiest prey, and the windingest game,
When Kaisers go a-hunting,
Tra-ra!
Ha, ha, ha, ha,
Tra-ra, tra-ra,
Ha-ha, tra-ra, tra-ra!

The voices held long on the last note, and let it die in a forest cadence.

"Fore Gad! well done. Hurrah! Tra-ra, ha-ha, tra-ra! That's a trick we're not half alive to at home,' said Guy. 'I feel friendly with these German lads.'

The Goshawk's disposition toward German lads was that moment harshly tested by a smart rap on the shoulder from an end of German oak, and a proclamation that he was prisoner of the hand that gave the greeting, in the name of the White Rose Club. Following that, his staff was wrested from him by a dozen stout young fellows, who gave him no time to get his famous distance for defence against numbers; and he and Farina were marched forthwith to the chorusing body in front of Gottlieb Groschen's house.

THE MISSIVES

Of all the inmates, Gottlieb had slept most with the day on his eyelids, for Werner hung like a nightmare over him. Margarita lay and dreamed in rose-colour, and if she thrilled on her pillowed silken couch like a tense-strung harp, and fretted drowsily in little leaps and starts, it was that a bird lay in her bosom, panting and singing through the night, and that he was not to be stilled, but would musically utter the sweetest secret thoughts of a love-bewitched maiden. Farina's devotion she knew his tenderness she divined: his courage she had that day witnessed. The young girl no sooner felt that she could love worthily, than she loved with her whole strength. Muffed and remote came the hunting-song under her pillow, and awoke dreamy delicate curves in her fair face, as it thinned but did not banish her dream. Aunt Lisbeth also heard the song, and burst out of her bed to see that the door and window were secured against the wanton Kaiser. Despite her trials, she had taken her spell of sleep; but being possessed of some mystic maiden belief that in cases of apprehended peril from man, bed was a rock of refuge and fortified defence, she crept back there, and allowed the sun to rise without her. Gottlieb's voice could not awaken her to the household duties she loved to perform with such a doleful visage. She heard him open his window, and parley in angry tones with the musicians below.

'Decoys!' muttered Aunt Lisbeth; 'be thou alive to them, Gottlieb!'

He went downstairs and opened the street door, whereupon the scolding and railing commenced anew.

'Thou hast given them vantage, Gottlieb, brother mine,' she complained; 'and the good heavens only can say what may result from such indiscreetness.'

A silence, combustible with shuffling of feet in the passage and on the stairs, dinned horrors into Aunt Lisbeth's head.

'It was just that sound in the left wing of Hollenbogenblitz,' she said: 'only then it was night and not morning. Ursula preserve me!'

'Why, Lisbeth! Lisbeth!' cried Gottlieb from below. 'Come down! 'tis full five o' the morning. Here's company; and what are we to do without the woman?'

'Ah, Gottlieb! that is like men! They do not consider how different it is for us!' which mysterious sentence being uttered to herself alone, enjoyed a meaning it would elsewhere have been denied.

Aunt Lisbeth dressed, and met Margarita descending. They exchanged the good-morning of young maiden and old.

'Go thou first,' said Aunt Lisbeth.

Margarita gaily tripped ahead.

'Girl!' cried Aunt Lisbeth, 'what's that thing in thy back hair?'

'I have borrowed Lieschen's arrow, aunt. Mine has had an accident.'

'Lieschen's arrow! An accident! Now I will see to that after breakfast, Margarita.'

'Tra-ra, ta-ta, tra-ra, tra-ra,' sang Margarita.

'The wild boar lay a-grunting,
A-grunting, tra-ra.'

'A maiden's true and proper ornament! Look at mine, child! I have worn it fifty years. May I deserve to wear it till I am called! O Margarita! trifle not with that symbol.'

'"O birdie, and boar, and deer, lie tame!"

I am so happy, aunty.'

'Nice times to be happy in, Margarita.'

"Be happy in Spring, sweet maidens all,
For Autumn's chill will early fall."

So sings the Minnesinger, aunty; and

"'A maiden in the wintry leaf
Will spread her own disease of grief."

I love the Minnesingers! Dear, sweet-mannered men they are! Such lovers! And men of deeds as well as song: sword on one side and harp on the other. They fight till set of sun, and then slacken their armour to waft a ballad to their beloved by moonlight, covered with stains of battle as they are, and weary!'

'What a girl! Minnesingers! Yes; I know stories of those Minnesingers. They came to the castle—Margarita, a bead of thy cross is broken. I will attend to it. Wear the pearl one till I mend this. May'st thou never fall in the way of Minnesingers. They are not like Werner's troop. They do not batter at doors: they slide into the house like snakes.'

'Lisbeth! Lisbeth!' they heard Gottlieb calling impatiently.

'We come, Gottlieb!' and in a low murmur Margarita heard her say: 'May this day pass without trouble and shame to the pious and the chaste.'

Margarita knew the voice of the stranger before she had opened the door, and on presenting herself, the hero gave her a guardian-like salute.

'One may see,' he said, 'that it requires better men than those of Werner to drive away the rose from that cheek.'

Gottlieb pressed the rosy cheek to his shoulder and patted her.

'What do you think, Grete? You have now forty of the best lads in Cologne enrolled to protect you, and keep guard over the house night and day. There! What more could a Pfalzgrafin ask, now? And voluntary service; all to be paid with a smile, which I daresay my lady won't refuse them. Lisbeth, you know our friend. Fear him not, good Lisbeth, and give us breakfast. Well, sweet chuck, you're to have royal honours paid you. I warrant they've begun good work already in locking up that idle moony vagabond, Farina—'

'Him? What for, my father? How dared they! What has he done?'

'O, start not, my fairy maid! A small matter of breakage, pet! He tried to enter Cunigonde Schmidt's chamber, and knocked down her pot of lilies: for which Berthold Schmidt knocked him down, and our friend here, out of good fellowship, knocked down Berthold. However, the chief offender is marched off to prison by your trusty guard, and there let him cool himself. Berthold shall tell you the tale himself: he'll be here to breakfast, and receive your orders, mistress commander-in-chief.'

The Goshawk had his eye on Margarita. Her teeth were tight down on her nether lip, and her whole figure had a strange look of awkwardness, she was so divided with anger.

'As witness of the affair, I think I shall make a clearer statement, fair maiden,' he interposed. 'In the first place, I am the offender. We passed under the window of the Fraulein Schmidt, and 'twas I mounted to greet the lilies. One shoot of them is in my helm, and here let me present them to a worthier holder.'

He offered the flowers with a smile, and Margarita took them, radiant with gratitude.

'Our friend Berthold,' he continued, 'thought proper to aim a blow at me behind my back, and then ran for his comrades. He was caught, and by my gallant young hero, Farina; concerning whose character I regret that your respected father and I differ: for, on the faith of a soldier and true man, he's the finest among the fine fellows I've yet met in Germany, trust me. So, to cut the story short, execution was done upon Berthold by my hand, for an act of treachery. He appears to be a sort of captain of one of the troops, and not affectionately disposed to Farina; for the version of the affair you have heard from your father is a little invention of Master Berthold's own. To do him justice, he seemed equally willing to get me under the cold stone; but a word from your good father changed the current; and as I thought I could serve our friend better free than behind bars, I accepted liberty. Pshaw! I should have accepted it any way, to tell the truth, for your German dungeons are mortal shivering ratty places. So rank me no hero, fair Mistress Margarita, though the temptation to seem one in such sweet eyes was beginning to lead me astray. And now, as to our business in the streets at this hour, believe the best of us.'

'I will! I do!' said Margarita.

'Lisbeth! Lisbeth!' called Gottlieb. 'Breakfast, little sister! our champion is starving. He asks for wurst, milk-loaves, wine, and all thy rarest conserves. Haste, then, for the honour of Cologne is at stake.'

Aunt Lisbeth jingled her keys in and out, and soon that harmony drew a number of domestics with platters of swine flesh, rolls of white wheaten bread, the perpetual worst, milk, wine, barley-bread, and household stores of dainties in profusion, all sparkling on silver, relieved by spotless white cloth. Gottlieb beheld such a sunny twinkle across the Goshawk's face at this hospitable array, that he gave the word of onset without waiting for Berthold, and his guest immediately fell to, and did not relax in his exertions for a full half-hour by the Cathedral clock, eschewing the beer with a wry look made up of scorn and ruefulness, and drinking a well-brimmed health in Rhine wine all round. Margarita was pensive: Aunt Lisbeth on her guard. Gottlieb remembered Charles the Great's counsel to Archbishop Turpin, and did his best to remain on earth one of its lords dominant.

'Poor Berthold!' said he. ''Tis a good lad, and deserves his seat at my table oftener. I suppose the flower-pot business has detained him. We'll drink to him: eh, Grete?'

'Drink to him, dear father!—but here he is to thank you in person.'

Margarita felt a twinge of pity as Berthold entered. The livid stains of his bruise deepened about his eyes, and gave them a wicked light whenever they were fixed intently; but they looked earnest; and spoke of a combat in which he could say that he proved no coward and was used with some cruelty. She turned on the Goshawk a mute reproach; yet smiled and loved him well when she beheld him stretch a hand of welcome and proffer a brotherly glass to Berthold. The rich goldsmith's son was occupied in studying the horoscope of his fortunes in Margarita's eyes; but when Margarita directed his attention to Guy, he turned to him with a glance of astonishment that yielded to cordial greeting.

'Well done, Berthold, my brave boy! All are friends who sit at table,' said Gottlieb. 'In any case, at my table:

"'Tis a worthy foe
Forgives the blow
Was dealt him full and fairly,"

says the song; and the proverb takes it up with, "A generous enemy is a friend on the wrong side"; and no one's to blame for that, save old Dame Fortune. So now a bumper to this jovial make-up between you. Lisbeth! you must drink it.'

The little woman bowed melancholy obedience.

'Why did you fling and run?' whispered Guy to Berthold.

'Because you were two against one.'

'Two against one, man! Why, have you no such thing as fair play in this land of yours? Did you think I should have taken advantage of that?'

'How could I tell who you were, or what you would do?' muttered Berthold, somewhat sullenly.

'Truly no, friend! So you ran to make yourself twenty to two? But don't be down on the subject. I was going to say, that though I treated you in a manner upright, 'twas perhaps a trifle severe, considering your youth: but an example's everything; and I must let you know in confidence, that no rascal truncheon had I flung in my life before; so, you see, I gave you all the chances.'

Berthold moved his lips in reply; but thinking of the figure of defeat he was exhibiting before Margarita, caused him to estimate unfavourably what chances had stood in his favour.

The health was drunk. Aunt Lisbeth touched the smoky yellow glass with a mincing lip, and beckoned Margarita to withdraw.

'The tapestry, child!' she said. 'Dangerous things are uttered after the third glass, I know, Margarita.'

'Do you call my champion handsome, aunt?'

'I was going to speak to you about him, Margarita. If I remember, he has rough, good looks, as far as they go. Yes: but thou, maiden, art thou thinking of him? I have thrice watched him wink; and that, as we know, is a habit of them that have sold themselves. And what is frail womankind to expect from such a brawny animal?'

'And oh! to lace his armour up,
And speed him to the field;
To pledge him in a kissing-cup,
The knight that will not yield!

I am sure he is tender, aunt. Notice how gentle he looks now and then.'

'Thou girl! Yes, I believe she is madly in love with him. Tender, and gentle! So is the bear when you're outside his den; but enter it, maiden, and try! Thou good Ursula, preserve me from such a fate.'

'Fear not, dear aunt! Have not a fear of it! Besides, it is not always the men that are bad. You must not forget Dalilah, and Lot's wife, and Pfalzgrafin Jutta, and the Baroness who asked for a piece of poor Kraut. But, let us work, let us work!'

Margarita sat down before Siegfried, and contemplated the hero. For the first time, she marked a resemblance in his features to Farina: the same long yellow hair scattered over his shoulders as that flowing from under Siegfried's helm; the blue eyes, square brows, and regular outlines. 'This is a marvel,' thought Margarita. 'And Farina! it was to watch over me that he roamed the street last night, my best one! Is he not beautiful?' and she looked closer at Siegfried.

Aunt Lisbeth had begun upon the dragon with her usual method, and was soon wandering through skeleton halls of the old palatial castle in Bohemia. The woolly tongue of the monster suggested fresh horrors to her, and if Margarita had listened, she might have had fair excuses to forget her lover's condition; but her voice only did service like a piece of clock-work, and her mind was in the prison with Farina. She was long debating how to win his release; and meditated so deeply, and exclaimed in so many bursts of impatience, that Aunt Lisbeth found her heart melting to the maiden. 'Now,' said she, 'that is a well-known story about the Electress Dowager of Bavaria, when she came on a visit to the castle; and, my dear child, be it a warning. Terrible, too!' and the little woman shivered pleasantly. 'She had—I may tell you this, Margarita—yes, she had been false to her wedded husband.—You understand, maiden; or, no! you do not understand: I understand it only partly, mind. False, I say—'

'False—not true: go on, dear aunty,' said Margarita, catching the word.

'I believe she knows as much as I do!' ejaculated Aunt Lisbeth; 'such are girls nowadays. When I was young-oh! for a maiden to know anything then—oh! it was general reprobation. No one thought of confessing it. We blushed and held down our eyes at the very idea. Well, the Electress! she was—you must guess. So she called for her caudle at eleven o'clock at night. What do you think that was? Well, there was spirit in it: not to say nutmeg, and lemon, and peach kernels. She wanted me to sit with her, but I begged my mistress to keep me from the naughty woman: and no friend of Hilda of Bayern was Bertha of Bohmen, you may be sure. Oh! the things she talked while she was drinking her caudle.

Isentrude sat with her, and said it was fearful!—beyond blasphemy! and that she looked like a Bible witch, sitting up drinking and swearing and glaring in her nightclothes and nightcap. She was on a journey into Hungary, and claimed the hospitality of the castle on her way there. Both were widows. Well, it was a quarter to twelve. The Electress dropped back on her pillow, as she always did when she had finished the candle. Isentrude covered her over, heaped up logs on the fire, wrapped her dressing-gown about her, and prepared to sleep. It was Winter, and the wind howled at the doors, and rattled the windows, and shook the arras—Lord help us! Outside was all snow, and nothing but forest; as you saw when you came to me there, Gretelchen. Twelve struck. Isentrude was dozing; but she says that after the last stroke she woke with cold. A foggy chill hung in the room. She looked at the Electress, who had not moved. The fire burned feebly, and seemed weighed upon: Herr Je!—she thought she heard a noise. No. Quite quiet! As heaven preserve her, says slip, the smell in that room grew like an open grave, clammily putrid. Holy Virgin! This time she was certain she heard a noise; but it seemed on both sides of her. There was the great door leading to the first landing and state-room; and opposite exactly there was the panel of the secret passage. The noises seemed to advance as if step by step, and grew louder in each ear as she stood horrified on the marble of the hearth. She looked at the Electress again, and her eyes were wide open; but for all Isentrude's calling, she would not wake. Only think! Now the noise increased, and was a regular tramp-grate, tramp-screw sound-coming nearer and nearer: Saints of mercy! The apartment was choking with vapours. Isentrude made a dart, and robed herself behind a curtain of the bed just as the two doors opened. She could see through a slit in the woven work, and winked her eyes which she had shut close on hearing the scream of the door-hinges—winked her eyes to catch a sight for moment—we are such sinful, curious creatures!—What she saw then, she says she shall never forget; nor I! As she was a living woman, there she saw the two dead princes, the Prince Palatine of Bohemia and the Elector of Bavaria, standing front to front at the foot of the bed, all in white armour, with drawn swords, and attendants holding pine-torches. Neither of them spoke. Their vizors were down; but she knew them by their arms and bearing: both tall, stately presences, good knights in their day, and had fought against the Infidel! So one of them pointed to the bed, and then a torch was lowered, and the fight commenced. Isentrude saw the sparks fly, and the steel struck till it was shattered; but they fought on, not caring for wounds, and snorting with fury as they grew hotter. They fought a whole hour. The poor girl was so eaten up with looking on, that she let go the curtain and stood quite exposed among them. So, to steady herself, she rested her hand on the foot of the bed; and—think what she felt—a hand as cold as ice locked hers, and get from it she could not! That instant one of the princes fell. It was Bohmen. Bayern sheathed his sword, and waved his hand, and the attendants took up the slaughtered ghost, feet and shoulders, and bore him to the door of the secret passage, while Bayern strode after—'

'Shameful!' exclaimed Margarita. 'I will speak to Berthold as he descends. I hear him coming. He shall do what I wish.'

'Call it dreadful, Grete! Dreadful it was. If Berthold would like to sit and hear—Ah! she is gone. A good girl! and of a levity only on the surface.'

Aunt Lisbeth heard Margarita's voice rapidly addressing Berthold. His reply was low and brief. 'Refuses to listen to anything of the sort,' Aunt Lisbeth interpreted it. Then he seemed to be pleading, and Margarita uttering short answers. 'I trust 'tis nothing a maiden should not hear,' the little lady exclaimed with a sigh.

The door opened, and Lieschen stood at the entrance.

'For Fraulein Margarita,' she said, holding a letter halfway out.

'Give it,' Aunt Lisbeth commanded.

The woman hesitated—''Tis for the Fraulein.'

'Give it, I tell thee!' and Aunt Lisbeth eagerly seized the missive, and subjected it to the ordeal of touch. It was heavy, and contained something hard. Long pensive pressures revealed its shape on the paper. It was an arrow. 'Go!' said she to the woman, and, once alone, began, bee-like, to buzz all over it, and finally entered. It contained Margarita's Silver Arrow. 'The art of that girl!' And the writing said:

'SWEETEST MAIDEN!

'By this arrow of our betrothal, I conjure thee to meet me in all haste without the western gate, where, burning to reveal to thee most urgent tidings that may not be confided to paper, now waits, petitioning the saints, thy

'FARINA.'

Aunt Lisbeth placed letter and arrow in a drawer; locked it; and 'always thought so.' She ascended the stairs to consult with Gottlieb. Roars of laughter greeted her just as she lifted the latch, and she retreated abashed.

There was no time to lose. Farina must be caught in the act of waiting for Margarita, and by Gottlieb, or herself. Gottlieb was revelling. 'May this be a warning to thee, Gottlieb,' murmured Lisbeth, as she hooded her little body in Margarita's fur-cloak, and determined that she would be the one to confound Farina.

Five minutes later Margarita returned. Aunt Lisbeth was gone. The dragon still lacked a tip to his forked tongue, and a stream of fiery threads dangled from the jaws of the monster. Another letter was brought into the room by Lieschen.

'For Aunt Lisbeth,' said Margarita, reading the address. 'Who can it be from?'

'She does not stand pressing about your letters,' said the woman; and informed Margarita of the foregoing missive.

'You say she drew an arrow from it?' said Margarita, with burning face. 'Who brought this? tell me!' and just waiting to hear it was Farina's mother, she tore the letter open, and read:

'DEAREST LISBETH!

'Thy old friend writes to thee; she that has scarce left eyes to see the words she writes. Thou knowest we are a fallen house, through the displeasure of the Emperor on my dead husband. My son, Farina, is my only stay, and well returns to me the blessings I bestow upon him. Some call him idle: some think him too wise. I swear to thee, Lisbeth, he is only good. His hours are devoted to the extraction of essences—to no black magic. Now he is in trouble-in prison. The shadow that destroyed his dead father threatens him. Now, by our old friendship, beloved Lisbeth! intercede with Gottlieb, that he may plead for my son before the Emperor when he comes—'

Margarita read no more. She went to the window, and saw her guard marshalled outside. She threw a kerchief over her head, and left the house by the garden gate.

THE MONK

By this time the sun stood high over Cologne. The market-places were crowded with buyers and sellers, mixed with a loitering swarm of soldiery, for whose thirsty natures winestalls had been tumbled up. Barons and knights of the empire, bravely mounted and thickly followed, poured hourly into Cologne from South Germany and North. Here, staring Suabians, and round-featured warriors of the East

Kingdom, swaggered up and down, patting what horses came across them, for lack of occupation for their hands. Yonder, huge Pomeranians, with bosks of beard stiffened out square from the chin, hurtled mountainous among the peaceable inhabitants. Troopers dismounted went straddling, in tight hose and loose, prepared to drink good-will to whomsoever would furnish the best quality liquor for that solemn pledge, and equally ready to pick a quarrel with them that would not. It was a scene of flaring feathers, wide-flapped bonnets, flaunting hose, blue and battered steel plates, slashed woollen haunch-bags, leather-leggings, ensigns, and imperious boots and shoulders. Margarita was too hurried in her mind to be conscious of an imprudence; but her limbs trembled, and she instinctively quickened her steps. When she stood under the sign of the Three Holy Kings, where dwelt Farina's mother, she put up a fervent prayer of thanks, and breathed freely.

'I had expected a message from Lisbeth,' said Frau Farina; 'but thou, good heart! thou wilt help us?'

'All that may be done by me I will do,' replied Margarita; 'but his mother yearns to see him, and I have come to bear her company.'

The old lady clasped her hands and wept.

'Has he found so good a friend, my poor boy! And trust me, dear maiden, he is not unworthy, for better son never lived, and good son, good all! Surely we will go to him, but not as thou art. I will dress thee. Such throngs are in the streets: I heard them clattering in early this morning. Rest, dear heart, till I return.'

Margarita had time to inspect the single sitting-room in which her lover lived. It was planted with bottles, and vases, and pipes, and cylinders, piling on floor, chair, and table. She could not suppress a slight surprise of fear, for this display showed a dealing with hidden things, and a summoning of scattered spirits. It was this that made his brow so pale, and the round of his eye darker than youth should let it be! She dismissed the feeling, and assumed her own bright face as Dame Farina reappeared, bearing on her arm a convent garb, and other apparel. Margarita suffered herself to be invested in the white and black robes of the denial of life.

'There!' said the Frau Farina, 'and to seal assurance, I have engaged a guard to accompany us. He was sorely bruised in a street combat yesterday, and was billeted below, where I nursed and tended him, and he is grateful, as man should be-though I did little, doing my utmost—and with him near us we have nought to fear.'

'Good,' said Margarita, and they kissed and departed. The guard was awaiting them outside.

'Come, my little lady, and with thee the holy sister! 'Tis no step from here, and I gage to bring ye safe, as sure as my name's Schwartz Thier!—Hey? The good sister's dropping. Look, now! I'll carry her.'

Margarita recovered her self-command before he could make good this offer.

'Only let us hasten there,' she gasped.

The Thier strode on, and gave them safe-conduct to the prison where Farina was confined, being near one of the outer forts of the city.

'Thank and dismiss him,' whispered Margarita.

'Nay! he will wait-wilt thou not, friend! We shall not be long, though it is my son I visit here,' said Frau Farina.

'Till to-morrow morning, my little lady! The lion thanked him that plucked the thorn from his foot, and the Thier may be black, but he's not ungrateful, nor a worse beast than the lion.'

They entered the walls and left him.

For the first five minutes Schwartz Thier found employment for his faculties by staring at the shaky, small-paned windows of the neighbourhood. He persevered in this, after all novelty had been exhausted, from an intuitive dread of weariness. There was nothing to see. An old woman once bobbed out of an attic, and doused the flints with water. Harassed by increasing dread of the foul nightmare of nothing-to-do, the Thier endeavoured to establish amorous intelligence with her. She responded with an indignant projection of the underjaw, evanishing rapidly. There was no resource left him but to curse her with extreme heartiness. The Thier stamped his right leg, and then his left, and remembered the old woman as a grievance five minutes longer. When she was clean forgotten, he yawned. Another spouse of the moment was wanted, to be wooed, objurgated, and regretted. The prison-gate was in a secluded street. Few passengers went by, and those who did edged away from the ponderous, wanton-eyed figure of lazy mischief lounging there, as neatly as they well could. The Thier hailed two or three. One took to his legs, another bowed, smirked, gave him a kindly good-day, and affected to hear no more, having urgent business in prospect. The Thier was a faithful dog, but the temptation to betray his trust and pursue them was mighty. He began to experience an equal disposition to cry and roar. He hummed a ballad—

'I swore of her I'd have my will,
And with him I'd have my way:
I learn'd my cross-bow over the hill:
Now what does my lady say?

Give me the good old cross-bow, after all, and none of these lumbering puff-and-bangs that knock you down oftener than your man!

'A cross stands in the forest still,
And a cross in the churchyard grey:
My curse on him who had his will,
And on him who had his way!

Good beginning, bad ending! 'Tisn't so always. "Many a cross has the cross-bow built," they say. I wish I had mine, now, to peg off that old woman, or somebody. I'd swear she's peeping at me over the gable, or behind some cranny. They're curious, the old women, curse 'em! And the young, for that matter. Devil a young one here.

'When I'm in for the sack of a town,
What, think ye, I poke after, up and down?
Silver and gold I pocket in plenty,
But the sweet tit-bit is my lass under twenty.

I should like to be in for the sack of this Cologne. I'd nose out that pretty girl I was cheated of yesterday. Take the gold and silver, and give me the maiden! Her neck's silver, and her hair gold. Ah! and her cheeks roses, and her mouth-say no more! I'm half thinking Werner, the hungry animal, has cast wolf's eyes on her. They say he spoke of her last night. Don't let him thwart me. Thunderblast him! I owe him a grudge. He's beginning to forget my plan o' life.'

A flight of pigeons across the blue top of the street abstracted the Thier from these reflections. He gaped after them in despair, and fell to stretching and shaking himself, rattling his lungs with loud reports. As he threw his eyes round again, they encountered those of a monk opposite fastened on him in penetrating silence. The Thier hated monks as a wild beast shuns fire; but now even a monk was welcome.

'Halloo!' he sung out.

The monk crossed over to him.

'Friend!' said he, 'weariness is teaching thee wantonness. Wilt thou take service for a night's work, where the danger is little, the reward lasting?'

'As for that,' replied the Thier, 'danger comes to me like greenwood to the deer, and good pay never yet was given in promises. But I'm bound for the next hour to womankind within there. They're my masters; as they've been of tough fellows before me.'

'I will seek them, and win their consent,' said the monk, and so left him.

'Quick dealing!' thought the Thier, and grew brisker. 'The Baron won't want me to-night: and what if he does? Let him hang himself—though, if he should, 'twill be a pity I'm not by to help him.'

He paced under the wall to its farthest course. Turning back, he perceived the monk at the gateway.

'A sharp hand!' thought the Thier.

'Intrude no question on me,' the monk began; 'but hold thy peace and follow: the women release thee, and gladly.'

'That's not my plan o' life, now! Money down, and then command me': and Schwartz Thier stood with one foot forward, and hand stretched out.

A curl of scorn darkened the cold features of the monk.

He slid one hand into a side of his frock above the girdle, and tossed a bag of coin.

'Take it, if 'tis in thee to forfeit the greater blessing,' he cried contemptuously.

The Thier peeped into the bag, and appeared satisfied.

'I follow,' said he; 'lead on, good father, and I'll be in the track of holiness for the first time since my mother was quit of me.'

The monk hurried up the street and into the marketplace, oblivious of the postures and reverences of the people, who stopped to stare at him and his gaunt attendant. As they crossed the square, Schwartz Thier spied Henker Rothhals starting from a wine-stall on horseback, and could not forbear hailing him. Before the monk had time to utter a reproach, they were deep together in a double-shot of query and reply.

'Whirr!' cried the Thier, breaking on some communication. 'Got her, have they? and swung her across stream? I'm one with ye for my share, or call me sheep!'

He waved his hand to the monk, and taking hold of the horse's rein, ran off beside his mounted confederate, heavily shod as he was.

The monk frowned after him, and swelled with a hard sigh.

'Gone!' he exclaimed, 'and the accursed gold with him! Well did a voice warn me that such service was never to be bought!'

He did not pause to bewail or repent, but returned toward the prison with rapid footsteps, muttering: 'I with the prison-pass for two; why was I beguiled by that bandit? Saw I not the very youth given into my hands there, he that was with the damsel and the aged woman?'

THE RIDE AND THE RACE

Late in the noon a horseman, in the livery of the Kaiser's body-guard, rode dry and dusty into Cologne, with tidings that the Kaiser was at Hammerstein Castle, and commanding all convocated knights, barons, counts, and princes, to assemble and prepare for his coming, on a certain bare space of ground within two leagues of Cologne, thence to swell the train of his triumphal entry into the ancient city of his empire.

Guy the Goshawk, broad-set on a Flemish mare, and a pack-horse beside him, shortly afterward left the hotel of the Three Holy Kings, and trotted up to Gottlieb's door.

'Tent-pitching is now my trade,' said he, as Gottlieb came down to him. 'My lord is with the Kaiser. I must say farewell for the nonce. Is the young lady visible?'

'Nor young, nor old, good friend,' replied Gottlieb, with a countenance somewhat ruffled. 'I dined alone for lack of your company. Secret missives came, I hear, to each of them, and both are gadding. Now what think you of this, after the scene of yesterday?—Lisbeth too!'

'Preaches from the old text, Master Groschen; "Never reckon on womankind for a wise act." But farewell! and tell Mistress Margarita that I take it ill of her not giving me her maiden hand to salute before parting. My gravest respects to Frau Lisbeth. I shall soon be sitting with you over that prime vintage of yours, or fortune's dead against me.'

So, with a wring of the hand, Guy put the spur to his round-flanked beast, and was quickly out of Cologne on the rough roadway.

He was neither the first nor the last of the men-at-arms hastening to obey the Kaiser's mandate. A string of horse and foot in serpentine knots stretched along the flat land, flashing colours livelier than the spring-meadows bordering their line of passage. Guy, with a nod for all, and a greeting for the best-disposed, pushed on toward the van, till the gathering block compelled him to adopt the snail's pace of the advance party, and gave him work enough to keep his two horses from being jammed with the mass. Now and then he cast a weather-eye on the heavens, and was soon confirmed in an opinion he had repeatedly ejaculated, that 'the first night's camping would be a drencher.' In the West a black bank of cloud was blotting out the sun before his time. Northeast shone bare fields of blue lightly touched with loosefloating strips and flakes of crimson vapour. The furrows were growing purple-dark, and gradually a low moaning obscurity enwrapped the whole line, and mufed the noise of hoof, oath, and waggon-wheel in one sullen murmur.

Guy felt very much like a chopped worm, as he wriggled his way onward in the dusk, impelled from the rear, and reduced to grope after the main body. Frequent and deep counsel he took with a trusty flask suspended at his belt. It was no pleasant reflection that the rain would be down before he could build up anything like shelter for horse and man. Still sadder the necessity of selecting his post on strange ground, and in darkness. He kept an anxious look-out for the moon, and was presently rejoiced to behold a broad fire that twinkled branchy beams through an east-hill orchard.

'My lord calls her Goddess,' said Guy, wistfully. 'The title's outlandish, and more the style of these foreigners but she may have it to-night, an she 'll just keep the storm from shrouding her bright eye a matter of two hours.'

She rose with a boding lustre. Drifts of thin pale upper-cloud leaned down ladders, pure as virgin silver, for her to climb to her highest seat on the unrebellious half-circle of heaven.

'My mind's made up!' quoth Guy to the listening part of himself. 'Out of this I'll get.'

By the clearer ray he had discerned a narrow track running a white parallel with the general route. At the expense of dislocating a mile of the cavalcade, he struck into it. A dyke had to be taken, some heavy fallows crossed, and the way was straight before him. He began to sneer at the slow jog-trot and absence of enterprise which made the fellows he had left shine so poorly in comparison with the Goshawk, but a sight of two cavaliers in advance checked his vanity, and now to overtake them he tasked his fat Flemish mare with unwonted pricks of the heel, that made her fling out and show more mettle than speed.

The objects of this fiery chase did not at first awake to a sense of being pursued. Both rode with mantled visages, and appeared profoundly inattentive to the world outside their meditations. But the Goshawk was not to be denied, and by dint of alternately roaring at them and upbraiding his two stumping beasts, he at last roused the younger of the cavaliers, who called to his companion loudly: without effect it seemed, for he had to repeat the warning. Guy was close up with them, when the youth exclaimed:

'Father! holy father! 'Tis Sathanas in person!'

The other rose and pointed trembling to a dark point in the distance as he vociferated:

'Not here! not here; but yonder!'

Guy recognized the voice of the first speaker, and cried:

'Stay! halt a second! Have you forgotten the Goshawk?'

'Never!' came the reply, 'and forget not Farina!'

Spur and fleeter steeds carried them out of hearing ere Guy could throw in another syllable. Farina gazed back on him remorsefully, but the Monk now rated his assistant with indignation.

'Thou weak one! nothing less than fool! to betray thy name on such an adventure as this to soul save the saints!'

Farina tossed back his locks, and held his forehead to the moon. All the Monk's ghostly wrath was foiled by the one little last sweet word of his beloved, which made music in his ears whenever annoyance sounded.

'And herein,' say the old writers, 'are lovers, who love truly, truly recompensed for their toils and pains; in that love, for which they suffer, is ever present to ward away suffering not sprung of love: but the disloyal, who serve not love faithfully, are a race given over to whatso this base world can wreak upon them, without consolation or comfort of their mistress, Love; whom sacrificing not all to, they know not to delight in.'

The soul of a lover lives through every member of him in the joy of a moonlight ride. Sorrow and grief are slow distempers that crouch from the breeze, and nourish their natures far from swift-moving things. A true lover is not one of those melancholy flies that shoot and maze over muddy stagnant pools. He must be up in the great air. He must strike all the strings of life. Swiftness is his rapture. In his wide arms he embraces the whole form of beauty. Eagle-like are his instincts; dove-like his desires. Then the fair moon is the very presence of his betrothed in heaven. So for hours rode Farina in a silver-fleeting glory; while the Monk as a shadow, galloped stern and silent beside him. So, crowning them in the sky, one half was all love and light; one, blackness and fell purpose.

THE COMBAT ON DRACHENFELS

Not to earth was vouchsafed the honour of commencing the great battle of that night. By an expiring blue-shot beam of moonlight, Farina beheld a vast realm of gloom filling the hollow of the West, and the moon was soon extinguished behind sluggish scraps of iron scud detached from the swinging bulk of ruin, as heavily it ground on the atmosphere in the first thunder-launch of motion.

The heart of the youth was strong, but he could not view without quicker fawning throbs this manifestation of immeasurable power, which seemed as if with a stroke it was capable of destroying creation and the works of man. The bare aspect of the tempest lent terrors to the adventure he was engaged in, and of which he knew not the aim, nor might forecast the issue. Now there was nothing to illumine their path but such forked flashes as lightning threw them at intervals, touching here a hill with clustered cottages, striking into day there a May-blossom, a patch of weed, a single tree by the wayside. Suddenly a more vivid and continuous quiver of violet fire met its reflection on the landscape, and Farina saw the Rhine-stream beneath him.

'On such a night,' thought he, 'Siegfried fought and slew the dragon!'

A blast of light, as from the jaws of the defeated dragon in his throes, made known to him the country he traversed. Crimsoned above the water glimmered the monster-haunted rock itself, and mid-channel beyond, flat and black to the stream, stretched the Nuns' Isle in cloistral peace.

'Halt!' cried the Monk, and signalled with a peculiar whistle, to which he seemed breathlessly awaiting an answer. They were immediately surrounded by longrobed veiled figures.

'Not too late?' the Monk hoarsely asked of them.

'Yet an hour!' was the reply, in soft clear tones of a woman's voice.

'Great strength and valour more than human be mine,' exclaimed the Monk, dismounting.

He passed apart from them; and they drew in a circle, while he prayed, kneeling.

Presently he returned, and led Farina to a bank, drawing from some hiding-place a book and a bell, which he gave into the hands of the youth.

'For thy soul, no word!' said the Monk, speaking down his throat as he took in breath. 'Nay! not in answer to me! Be faithful, and more than earthly fortune is thine; for I say unto thee, I shall not fail, having grace to sustain this combat.'

Thereupon he commenced the ascent of Drachenfels.

Farina followed. He had no hint of the Monk's mission, nor of the part himself was to play in it. Such a load of silence gathered on his questioning spirit, that the outcry of the rageing elements alone prevented him from arresting the Monk and demanding the end of his service there. That outcry was enough to freeze speech on the very lips of a mortal. For scarce had they got footing on the winding path of the crags, when the whole vengeance of the storm was hurled against the mountain. Huge boulders were loosened and came bowling from above: trees torn by their roots from the fissures whizzed on the eddies of the wind: torrents of rain foamed down the iron flanks of rock, and flew off in hoar feathers against the short pauses of darkness: the mountain heaved, and quaked, and yawned a succession of hideous chasms.

'There's a devil in this,' thought Farina. He looked back and marked the river imaging lurid abysses of cloud above the mountain-summit—yea! and on the summit a flaming shape was mirrored.

Two nervous hands stayed the cry on his mouth.

'Have I not warned thee?' said the husky voice of the Monk. 'I may well watch, and think for thee as for a dog. Be thou as faithful!'

He handed a flask to the youth, and bade him drink. Farina drank and felt richly invigorated. The Monk then took bell and book.

'But half an hour,' he muttered, 'for this combat that is to ring through centuries.'

Crossing himself, he strode wildly upward. Farina saw him beckon back once, and the next instant he was lost round an incline of the highest peak.

The wind that had just screamed a thousand death-screams, was now awfully dumb, albeit Farina could feel it lifting hood and hair. In the unnatural stillness his ear received tones of a hymn chanted below; now sinking, now swelling; as though the voices faltered between prayer and inspiration. Farina caught on a projection of crag, and fixed his eyes on what was passing on the height.

There was the Monk in his brown hood and wrapper, confronting—if he might trust his balls of sight—the red-hot figure of the Prince of Darkness.

As yet no mortal tussle had taken place between them. They were arguing: angrily, it was true: yet with the first mutual deference of practised logicians. Latin and German was alternately employed by both. It thrilled Farina's fervid love of fatherland to hear the German Satan spoke: but his Latin was good, and his command over that tongue remarkable; for, getting the worst of the argument, as usual, he revenged himself by parodying one of the Church canticles with a point that discomposed his adversary, and caused him to retreat a step, claiming support against such shrewd assault.

'The use of an unexpected weapon in warfare is in itself half a victory. Induce your antagonist to employ it as a match for you, and reckon on completely routing him...' says the old military chronicle.

'Come!' said the Demon with easy raillery. 'You know your game—I mine! I really want the good people to be happy; dancing, kissing, propagating, what you will. We quite agree. You can have no objection to me, but a foolish old prejudice—not personal, but class; an antipathy of the cowl, for which I pardon you! What I should find in you to complain of—I have only to mention it, I am sure—is, that perhaps you do speak a little too much through your nose.'

The Monk did not fall into the jocular trap by retorting in the same strain.

'Laugh with the Devil, and you won't laugh longest,' says the proverb.

Keeping to his own arms, the holy man frowned.

'Avaunt, Fiend!' he cried. 'To thy kingdom below! Thou halt raged over earth a month, causing blights, hurricanes, and epidemics of the deadly sins. Parley no more! Begone!'

The Demon smiled: the corners of his mouth ran up to his ears, and his eyes slid down almost into one.

'Still through the nose!' said he reproachfully.

'I give thee Five Minutes!' cried the Monk.

'I had hoped for a longer colloquy,' sighed the Demon, jogging his left leg and trifling with his tail.

'One Minute!' exclaimed the Monk.

'Truly so!' said the Demon. 'I know old Time and his habits better than you really can. We meet every Saturday night, and communicate our best jokes. I keep a book of them Down There!'

And as if he had reason to remember the pavement of his Halls, he stood tiptoe and whipped up his legs.

'Two Minutes!'

The Demon waved perfect acquiescence, and continued:

'We understand each other, he and I. All Old Ones do. As long as he lasts, I shall. The thing that surprises me is, that you and I cannot agree, similar as we are in temperament, and playing for the long odds, both of us. My failure is, perhaps, too great a passion for sport, aha! Well, 'tis a pity you won't try and live on the benevolent principle. I am indeed kind to them who commiserate my condition. I give them all they want, aha! Hem! Try and not believe in me now, aha! Ho!... Can't you? What are eyes? Persuade yourself you're dreaming. You can do anything with a mind like yours, Father Gregory! And consider the luxury of getting me out of the way so easily, as many do. It is my finest suggestion, aha! Generally I myself nudge their ribs with the capital idea—You're above bribes? I was going to observe—'

'Three!'

'Observe, that if you care for worldly honours, I can smother you with that kind of thing. Several of your first-rate people made a bargain with me when they were in the fog, and owe me a trifle. Patronage they call it. I hook the high and the low. Too-little and too-much serve me better than Beelzebub. A weak stomach is certainly more carnally virtuous than a full one. Consequently my kingdom is becoming too respectable. They've all got titles, and object to being asked to poke the fire without—Honourable-and-with-Exceeding-Brightness-Beaming Baroness This! Admirably-Benignant-Down-looking Highness That! Interrupts business, especially when you have to ask them to fry themselves, according to the rules... Would you like Mainz and the Rheingau?... You don't care for Beauty—Puella, Puellae? I have plenty of them, too, below. The Historical Beauties warmed up at a moment's notice. Modern ones made famous between morning and night—Fame is the sauce of Beauty. Or, no—eh?'

'Four!'

'Not quite so fast, if you please. You want me gone. Now, where's your charity? Do you ask me to be always raking up those poor devils underneath? While I'm here, they've a respite. They cannot think you kind, Father Gregory! As for the harm, you see, I'm not the more agreeable by being face to face with you—though some fair dames do take to my person monstrously. The secret is, the quantity of small talk I can command: that makes them forget my smell, which is, I confess, abominable, displeasing to myself, and my worst curse. Your sort, Father Gregory, are somewhat unpleasant in that particular—if I may judge by their Legate here. Well, try small talk. They would fall desperately in love with polecats and skunks if endowed with small talk. Why, they have become enamoured of monks before now! If skunks, why not monks? And again—'

'Five!'

Having solemnly bellowed this tremendous number, the holy man lifted his arms to begin the combat.

Farina felt his nerves prick with admiration of the ghostly warrior daring the Second Power of Creation on that lonely mountain-top. He expected, and shuddered at thought of the most awful fight ever yet chronicled of those that have taken place between heroes and the hounds of evil: but his astonishment was great to hear the Demon, while Bell was in air and Book aloft, retreat, shouting, 'Hold!'

'I surrender,' said he sullenly. 'What terms?'

'Instantaneous riddance of thee from face of earth.'

'Good!—Now,' said the Demon, 'did you suppose I was to be trapped into a fight? No doubt you wish to become a saint, and have everybody talking of my last defeat.... Pictures, poems, processions, with the Devil downmost! No. You're more than a match for me.'

'Silence, Darkness!' thundered the Monk, 'and think not to vanquish thy victor by flatteries. Begone!'

And again he towered in his wrath.

The Demon drew his tail between his legs, and threw the forked, fleshy, quivering end over his shoulder. He then nodded cheerfully, pointed his feet, and finicked a few steps away, saying: 'I hope we shall meet again.'

Upon that he shot out his wings, that were like the fins of the wyver-fish, sharpened in venomous points.

'Commands for your people below?' he inquired, leering with chin awry. 'Desperate ruffians some of those cowls. You are right not to acknowledge them.'

Farina beheld the holy man in no mood to let the Enemy tamper with him longer.

The Demon was influenced by a like reflection; for, saying, 'Cologne is the city your Holiness inhabits, I think?' he shot up rocket-like over Rhineland, striking the entire length of the stream, and its rough-bearded castle-crests, slate-ledges, bramble-clefts, vine-slopes, and haunted valleys, with one brimstone flash. Frankfort and the far Main saw him and reddened. Ancient Trier and Mosel; Heidelberg and Neckar; Limberg and Lahn, ran guilty of him. And the swift artery of these shining veins, Rhine, from his snow cradle to his salt decease, glimmered Stygian horrors as the Infernal Comet, sprung over Bonn, sparkled a fiery minute along the face of the stream, and vanished, leaving a seam of ragged flame trailed on the midnight heavens.

Farina breathed hard through his teeth.

'The last of him was awful,' said he, coming forward to where the Monk knelt and grasped his breviary, 'but he was vanquished easily.'

'Easily?' exclaimed the holy man, gasping satisfaction: 'thou weakling! is it for thee to measure difficulties, or estimate powers? Easily? thou worldling! and so are great deeds judged when the danger's past! And what am I but the humble instrument that brought about this wondrous conquest! the poor tool of this astounding triumph! Shall the sword say, This is the battle I won! Yonder the enemy I overthrow! Bow to me, ye lords of earth, and worshippers of mighty acts? Not so! Nay, but the sword is honoured in the hero's grasp, and if it break not, it is accounted trusty. This, then, this little I may claim, that I was trusty! Trusty in a heroic encounter! Trusty in a battle with earth's terror! Oh! but this must not be said. This is to think too much! This is to be more than aught yet achieved by man!'

The holy warrior crossed his arms, and gently bowed his head.

'Take me to the Sisters,' he said. 'The spirit has gone out of me! I am faint, and as a child!'

Farina asked, and had, his blessing.

'And with it my thanks!' said the Monk. 'Thou hast witnessed how he can be overcome! Thou hast looked upon a scene that will be the glory of Christendom! Thou hast beheld the discomfiture of Darkness before the voice of Light! Yet think not much of me: account me little in this matter! I am but an instrument! but an instrument!—and again, but an instrument!'

Farina drew the arms of the holy combatant across his shoulders and descended Drachenfels.

The tempest was as a forgotten anguish. Bright with maiden splendour shone the moon; and the old rocks, cherished in her beams, put up their horns to blue heaven once more. All the leafage of the land shook as to shake off a wicked dream, and shuddered from time to time, whispering of old fears quieted, and present peace. The heart of the river fondled with the image of the moon in its depths.

'This is much to have won for earth,' murmured the Monk. 'And what is life, or who would not risk all, to snatch such loveliness from the talons of the Fiend, the Arch-foe? Yet, not I! not I! say not, 'twas I did this!'

Soft praises of melody ascended to them on the moist fragrance of air. It was the hymn of the Sisters.

'How sweet!' murmured the Monk. 'Put it from me! away with it!'

Rising on Farina's back, and stirruping his feet on the thighs of the youth, he cried aloud: 'I charge ye, whoso ye be, sing not this deed before the emperor! By the breath of your nostrils; pause! ere ye whisper aught of the combat of Saint Gregory with Satan, and his victory, and the marvel of it, while he liveth; for he would die the humble monk he is.'

He resumed his seat, and Farina brought him into the circle of the Sisters. Those pure women took him, and smoothed him, lamenting, and filling the night with triumphing tones.

Farina stood apart.

'The breeze tells of dawn,' said the Monk; 'we must be in Cologne before broad day.'

They mounted horse, and the Sisters grouped and reverenced under the blessings of the Monk.

'No word of it!' said the Monk warningly. 'We are silent, Father!' they answered. 'Cologne-ward!' was then his cry, and away he and Farina, flew.

THE GOSHAWK LEADS

Morning was among the grey eastern clouds as they rode upon the camp hastily formed to meet the Kaiser. All there was in a wallow of confusion. Fierce struggles for precedence still went on in the neighbourhood of the imperial tent ground, where, under the standard of Germany, lounged some veterans of the Kaiser's guard, calmly watching the scramble. Up to the edge of the cultivated land nothing was to be seen but brawling clumps of warriors asserting the superior claims of their respective lords. Variously and hotly disputed were these claims, as many red coxcombs testified. Across that point where the green field flourished, not a foot was set, for the Kaiser's care of the farmer, and affection for good harvests, made itself respected even in the heat of those jealous rivalries. It was said of him, that he would have camped in a bog, or taken quarters in a cathedral, rather than trample down a green blade of wheat, or turn over one vine-pole in the empire. Hence the presence of Kaiser Heinrich was never hailed as Egypt's plague by the peasantry, but welcome as the May month wherever he went.

Father Gregory and Farina found themselves in the centre of a group ere they drew rein, and a cry rose, 'The good father shall decide, and all's fair,' followed by, 'Agreed! Hail and tempest! he's dropped down o' purpose.'

'Father,' said one, 'here it is! I say I saw the Devil himself fly off Drachenfels, and flop into Cologne. Fritz here, and Frankenbauch, saw him too. They'll swear to him: so 'll I. Hell's thunder! will we. Yonder fellows will have it 'twas a flash o' lightning, as if I didn't see him, horns, tail, and claws, and a mighty sight 'twas, as I'm a sinner.'

A clash of voices, for the Devil and against him, burst on this accurate description of the Evil spirit. The Monk sank his neck into his chest.

'Gladly would I hold silence on this, my sons,' said he, in a supplicating voice.

'Speak, Father,' cried the first spokesman, gathering courage from the looks of the Monk.

Father Gregory appeared to commune with himself deeply. At last, lifting his head, and murmuring, 'It must be,' he said aloud:

''Twas verily Satan, O my sons! Him this night in mortal combat I encountered and overcame on the summit of Drachenfels, before the eyes of this youth; and from Satan I this night deliver ye! an instrument herein as in all other.'

Shouts, and a far-spreading buzz resounded in the camp. Hundreds had now seen Satan flying off the Drachenstein. Father Gregory could no longer hope to escape from the importunate crowds that beset him for particulars. The much-contested point now was, as to the exact position of Satan's tail during his airy circuit, before descending into Cologne. It lashed like a lion's. 'Twas cocked, for certain! He sneaked it between his legs like a lurcher! He made it stumpy as a brown bear's! He carried it upright as a pike!

'O my sons! have I sown dissension? Have I not given ye peace?' exclaimed the Monk.

But they continued to discuss it with increasing frenzy.

Farina cast a glance over the tumult, and beheld his friend Guy beckoning earnestly. He had no difficulty in getting away to him, as the fetters of all eyes were on the Monk alone.

The Goshawk was stamping with excitement.

'Not a moment to be lost, my lad,' said Guy, catching his arm. 'Here, I've had half-a-dozen fights already for this bit of ground. Do you know that fellow squatting there?'

Farina beheld the Thier at the entrance of a tumbledown tent. He was ruefully rubbing a broken head.

'Now,' continued Guy, 'to mount him is the thing; and then after the wolves of Werner as fast as horse-flesh can carry us. No questions! Bound, are you? And what am I? But this is life and death, lad! Hark!'

The Goshawk whispered something that sucked the blood out of Farina's cheek.

'Look you—what's your lockjaw name? Keep good faith with me, and you shall have your revenge, and the shiners I promise, besides my lord's interest for a better master: but, sharp! we won't mount till we're out of sight o' the hell-scum you horde with.'

The Thier stood up and staggered after them through the camp. There was no difficulty in mounting him horses were loose, and scampering about the country, not yet delivered from their terrors of the last night's tempest.

'Here be we, three good men!' exclaimed Guy, when they were started, and Farina had hurriedly given him the heads of his adventure with the Monk. 'Three good men! One has helped to kick the devil: one has served an apprenticeship to his limb: and one is ready to meet him foot to foot any day, which last should be myself. Not a man more do we want, though it were to fish up that treasure you talk of being under the Rhine there, and guarded by I don't know how many tricksy little villains. Horses can be ferried across at Linz, you say?'

'Ay, thereabout,' grunted the Thier.

'We're on the right road, then!' said Guy. 'Thanks to you both, I've had no sleep for two nights—not a wink, and must snatch it going—not the first time.'

The Goshawk bent his body, and spoke no more. Farina could not get a word further from him. By the mastery he still had over his rein, the Goshawk alone proved that he was of the world of the living. Schwartz Thier, rendered either sullen or stunned by the latest cracked crown he had received, held his jaws close as if they had been nailed.

At Linz the horses were well breathed. The Goshawk, who had been snoring an instant before, examined them keenly, and shook his calculating head.

'Punch that beast of yours in the ribs,' said he to Farina. 'Ah! not a yard of wind in him. And there's the coming back, when we shall have more to carry. Well: this is my lord's money; but i' faith, it's going in a good cause, and Master Groschen will make it all right, no doubt; not a doubt of it.'

The Goshawk had seen some excellent beasts in the stables of the Kaiser's Krone; but the landlord would make no exchange without an advance of silver. This done, the arrangement was prompt.

'Schwartz Thier!—I've got your name now,' said Guy, as they were ferrying across, 'you're stiff certain they left Cologne with the maiden yesternoon, now?'

'Ah, did they! and she's at the Eck safe enow by this time.'

'And away from the Eck this night she shall come, trust me!'

'Or there will I die with her!' cried Farina.

'Fifteen men at most, he has, you said,' continued Guy.

'Two not sound, five true as steel, and the rest shillyshally. 'Slife, one lock loose serves us; but two saves us: five we're a match for, throwing in bluff Baron; the remainder go with victory.'

'Can we trust this fellow?' whispered Farina.

'Trust him!' roared Guy. 'Why, I've thumped him, lad; pegged and pardoned him. Trust him? trust me! If Werner catches a sight of that snout of his within half-a-mile of his hold, he'll roast him alive.'

He lowered his voice: 'Trust him? We can do nothing without him. I knocked the devil out of him early this morning. No chance for his Highness anywhere now. This Eck of Werner's would stand a siege from the Kaiser in person, I hear. We must into it like weasels; and out as we can.'

Dismissing the ferry-barge with stern injunctions to be in waiting from noon to noon, the three leapt on their fresh nags.

'Stop at the first village,' said Guy; 'we must lay in provision. As Master Groschen says, "Nothing's to be done, Turpin, without provender."'

'Goshawk!' cried Farina; 'you have time; tell me how this business was done.'

The only reply was a soft but decided snore, that spoke, like a voluptuous trumpet, of dreamland and its visions.

At Sinzig, the Thier laid his hand on Guy's bridle, with the words, 'Feed here,' a brief, but effective, form of signal, which aroused the Goshawk completely. The sign of the Trauben received them. Here, wurst reeking with garlic, eggs, black bread, and sour wine, was all they could procure. Farina refused to eat, and maintained his resolution, in spite of Guy's sarcastic chiding.

'Rub down the beasts, then, and water them,' said the latter. 'Made a vow, I suppose,' muttered Guy.

'That's the way of those fellows. No upright manly take-the-thing-as-it-comes; but fly-sky-high whenever there's a dash on their heaven. What has his belly done to offend him? It will be crying out just when we want all quiet. I wouldn't pay Werner such a compliment as go without a breakfast for him. Not I! Would you, Schwartz Thier?'

'Henker! not I!' growled the Thier. 'He'll lose one sooner.'

'First snatch his prey, or he'll be making, God save us! a meal for a Kaiser, the brute.'

Guy called in the landlady, clapped down the score, and abused the wine.

'Sir,' said the landlady, 'ours is but a poor inn, and we do our best.'

'So you do,' replied the Goshawk, softened; 'and I say that a civil tongue and rosy smiles sweeten even sour wine.'

The landlady, a summer widow, blushed, and as he was stepping from the room, called him aside.

'I thought you were one of that dreadful Werner's band, and I hate him.'

Guy undeceived her.

'He took my sister,' she went on, 'and his cruelty killed her. He persecuted me even in the lifetime of my good man. Last night he came here in the middle of the storm with a young creature bright as an angel, and sorrowful—'

'He's gone, you're sure?' broke in Guy.

'Gone! Oh, yes! Soon as the storm abated he dragged her on. Oh! the way that young thing looked at me, and I able to do nothing for her.'

'Now, the Lord bless you for a rosy Christian!' cried Guy, and, in his admiration, he flung his arm round her and sealed a ringing kiss on each cheek.

'No good man defrauded by that! and let me see the fellow that thinks evil of it. If I ever told a woman a secret, I'd tell you one now, trust me. But I never do, so farewell! Not another?'

Hasty times keep the feelings in a ferment, and the landlady was extremely angry with Guy and heartily forgave him, all within a minute.

'No more,' said she, laughing: 'but wait; I have something for you.'

The Goshawk lingered on a fretting heel. She was quickly under his elbow again with two flasks leaning from her bosom to her arms.

'There! I seldom meet a man like you; and, when I do, I like to be remembered. This is a true good wine, real Liebfrauenmilch, which I only give to choice customers.'

'Welcome it is!' sang Guy to her arch looks; 'but I must pay for it.'

'Not a pfennig!' said the landlady.

'Not one?'

'Not one!' she repeated, with a stamp of the foot.

'In other coin, then,' quoth Guy; and folding her waist, which did not this time back away, the favoured Goshawk registered rosy payment on a very fresh red mouth, receiving in return such lively discount, that he felt himself bound in conscience to make up the full sum a second time.

'What a man!' sighed the landlady, as she watched the Goshawk lead off along the banks; 'courtly as a knight, open as a squire, and gentle as a page!'

WERNER'S ECK

A league behind Andernach, and more in the wintry circle of the sun than Laach, its convenient monastic neighbour, stood the castle of Werner, the Robber Baron. Far into the South, hazy with afternoon light, a yellow succession of sandhills stretched away, spouting fire against the blue sky of an elder world, but now dead and barren of herbage. Around is a dusty plain, where the green blades of spring no sooner peep than they become grimed with sand and take an aged look, in accordance with the ungenerous harvests they promise. The aridity of the prospect is relieved on one side by the lofty woods of Laach, through which the sun setting burns golden-red, and on the other by the silver sparkle of a narrow winding stream, bordered with poplars, and seen but a glistening mile of its length by all the thirsty hills. The Eck, or Corner, itself, is thick-set with wood, but of a stunted growth, and lying like a dark patch on the landscape. It served, however, entirely to conceal the castle, and mask every movement of the wary and terrible master. A trained eye advancing on the copse would hardly mark the glimmer of the turrets over the topmost leaves, but to every loophole of the walls lies bare the circuit of the land. Werner could rule with a glance the Rhine's course down from the broad rock over Coblentz to the white tower of Andernach. He claimed that march as his right; but the Mosel was no hard ride's distance, and he gratified his thirst for rapine chiefly on that river, delighting in it, consequently, as much as his robber nature boiled over the bound of his feudal privileges.

Often had the Baron held his own against sieges and restrictions, bans and impositions of all kinds. He boasted that there was never a knight within twenty miles of him that he had not beaten, nor monk of the same limit not in his pay. This braggadocio received some warrant from his yearly increase of licence; and his craft and his castle combined, made him a notable pest of the region, a scandal to the abbey whose countenance he had, and a frightful infliction on the poorer farmers and peasantry.

The sun was beginning to slope over Laach, and threw the shadows of the abbey towers half-way across the blue lake-waters, as two men in the garb of husbandmen emerged from the wood. Their feet plunged heavily and their heads hung down, as they strode beside a wain mounted with straw, whistling an air of stupid unconcern; but a close listener might have heard that the lumbering vehicle carried a human voice giving them directions as to the road they were to take, and what sort of behaviour to observe under certain events. The land was solitary. A boor passing asked whether toll or tribute they were conveying to Werner. Tribute, they were advised to reply, which caused him to shrug and curse as he jogged on. Hearing him, the voice in the wain chuckled grimly. Their next speech was with a trooper, who overtook them, and wanted to know what they had in the wain for Werner. Tribute, they replied, and won the title of 'brave pigs' for their trouble.

'But what's the dish made of?' said the trooper, stirring the straw with his sword-point.

'Tribute,' came the answer.

'Ha! You've not been to Werner's school,' and the trooper swung a sword-stroke at the taller of the two, sending a tremendous shudder throughout his frame; but he held his head to the ground, and only seemed to betray animal consciousness in leaning his ear closer to the wain.

'Blood and storm! Will ye speak?' cried the trooper.

'Never talk much; but an ye say nothing to the Baron,'—thrusting his hand into the straw—'here's what's better than speaking.'

'Well said!—Eh? Liebfrauenmilch? Ho, ho! a rare bleed!'

Striking the neck of the flask on a wheel, the trooper applied it to his mouth, and ceased not deeply ingurgitating till his face was broad to the sky and the bottle reversed. He then dashed it down, sighed, and shook himself.

'Rare news! the Kaiser's come: he'll be in Cologne by night; but first he must see the Baron, and I'm post with the order. That's to show you how high he stands in the Kaiser's grace. Don't be thinking of upsetting Werner yet, any of you; mind, now!'

'That's Blass-Gesell,' said the voice in the wain, as the trooper trotted on: adding, ''gainst us.'

'Makes six,' responded the driver.

Within sight of the Eck, they descried another trooper coming toward them. This time the driver was first to speak.

'Tribute! Provender! Bread and wine for the high Baron Werner from his vassals over Tonnistein.'

'And I'm out of it! fasting like a winter wolf,' howled the fellow.

He was in the act of addressing himself to an inspection of the wain's contents, when a second flask lifted in air, gave a sop to his curiosity. This flask suffered the fate of the former.

'A Swabian blockhead, aren't you?'

'Ay, that country,' said the driver. 'May be, Henker Rothhals happens to be with the Baron?'

'To hell with him! I wish he had my job, and I his, of watching the yellow-bird in her new cage, till she's taken out to-night, and then a jolly bumper to the Baron all round.'

The driver wished him a fortunate journey, strongly recommending him to skirt the abbey westward, and go by the Ahr valley, as there was something stirring that way, and mumbling, 'Makes five again,' as he put the wheels in motion.

'Goshawk!' said his visible companion; 'what do you say now?'

'I say, bless that widow!'

'Oh! bring me face to face with this accursed Werner quickly, my God!' gasped the youth.

'Tusk! 'tis not Werner we want—there's the Thier speaking. No, no, Schwartz Thier! I trust you, no doubt; but the badger smells at a hole, before he goes inside it. We're strangers, and are allowed to miss our way.'

Leaving the wain in Farina's charge, he pushed through a dense growth of shrub and underwood, and came crouching on a precipitous edge of shrouded crag, which commanded a view of the stronghold, extending round it, as if scooped clean by some natural action, about a stone'sthrow distant, and nearly level with the look-out tower. Sheer from a deep circular basin clothed with wood, and bottomed with grass and bubbling water, rose a naked moss-stained rock, on whose peak the castle firmly perched, like a spying hawk. The only means of access was by a narrow natural bridge of rock flung from this insulated pinnacle across to the mainland. One man, well disposed, might have held it against forty.

'Our way's the best,' thought Guy, as he meditated every mode of gaining admission. 'A hundred men an hour might be lost cutting steps up that steep slate; and once at the top we should only have to be shoved down again.'

While thus engaged, he heard a summons sounded from the castle, and scrambled back to Farina.

'The Thier leads now,' said he, 'and who leads is captain. It seems easier to get out of that than in. There's a square tower, and a round. I guess the maiden to be in the round. Now, lad, no crying out— You don't come in with us; but back you go for the horses, and have them ready and fresh in yon watered meadow under the castle. The path down winds easy.'

'Man!' cried Farina, 'what do you take me for?—go you for the horses.'

'Not for a fool,' Guy rejoined, tightening his lip; 'but now is your time to prove yourself one.'

'With you, or without you, I enter that castle!'

'Oh! if you want to be served up hot for the Baron's supper-mess, by all means.'

'Thunder!' growled Schwartz Thier, 'aren't ye moving?'

The Goshawk beckoned Farina aside.

'Act as I tell you, or I'm for Cologne.'

'Traitor!' muttered the youth.

'Swearing this, that if we fail, the Baron shall need a leech sooner than a bride.'

'That stroke must be mine!'

The Goshawk griped the muscle of Farina's arm till the youth was compelled to slacken it with pain.

'Could you drive a knife through a six-inch wood-wall? I doubt this wild boar wants a harder hit than many a best man could give. 'Sblood! obey, sirrah. How shall we keep yon fellow true, if he sees we're at points?'

'I yield,' exclaimed Farina with a fall of the chest; 'but hear I nothing of you by midnight—Oh! then think not I shall leave another minute to chance. Farewell! haste! Heaven prosper you! You will see her, and die under her eyes. That may be denied to me. What have I done to be refused that last boon?'

'Gone without breakfast and dinner,' said Guy in abhorrent tones.

A whistle from the wain, following a noise of the castlegates being flung open, called the Goshawk away, and he slouched his shoulders and strode to do his part, without another word. Farina gazed after him, and dropped into the covert.

THE WATER-LADY

'Bird of lovers! Voice of the passion of love! Sweet, deep, disaster-toning nightingale!' sings the old minnesinger; 'who that has not loved, hearing thee is touched with the wand of love's mysteries, and yearneth to he knoweth not whom, humbled by overfulness of heart; but who, listening, already loveth, heareth the language he would speak, yet faileth in; feeleth the great tongueless sea of his infinite desires stirred beyond his narrow bosom; is as one stript of wings whom the angels beckon to their silver homes: and he leaneth forward to ascend to them, and is mocked by his effort: then is he of the fallen, and of the fallen would he remain, but that tears lighten him, and through the tears stream jewelled shafts dropt down to him from the sky, precious ladders inlaid with amethyst, sapphire, blended jasper, beryl, rose-ruby, ether of heaven flushed with softened bloom of the insufferable Presences: and lo, the ladders dance, and quiver, and waylay his eyelids, and a second time he is mocked, aspiring: and after the third swoon standeth Hope before him with folded arms, and eyes dry of the delusions of tears, saying, Thou hast seen! thou hast felt! thy strength hath reached in thee so far! now shall I never die in thee!'

'For surely,' says the minstrel, 'Hope is not born of earth, or it were perishable. Rather know her the offspring of that embrace strong love straineth the heavens with. This owe we to thy music, bridal nightingale! And the difference of this celestial spirit from the smirking phantasy of whom all stand soon or late forsaken, is the difference between painted day with its poor ambitious snares, and night lifting its myriad tapers round the throne of the eternal, the prophet stars of everlasting time! And the one dieth, and the other liveth; and the one is unregretted, and the other walketh in thought-spun raiment of divine melancholy; her ears crowded with the pale surges that wrap this shifting shore; in her eyes a shape of beauty floating dimly, that she will not attain this side the water, but broodeth on evermore.

'Therefore, hold on thy cherished four long notes, which are as the very edge where exultation and anguish melt, meet, and are sharpened to one ecstasy, death-dividing bird! Fill the woods with passionate chuckle and sob, sweet chaplain of the marriage service of a soul with heaven! Pour out thy holy wine of song upon the soft-footed darkness, till, like a priest of the inmost temple, 'tis drunken with fair intelligences!'

Thus the old minstrels and minnesingers.

Strong and full sang the nightingales that night Farina held watch by the guilty castle that entombed his living beloved. The castle looked itself a denser shade among the moonthrown shadows of rock and tree. The meadow spread like a green courtyard at the castle's foot. It was of lush deep emerald grass, softly mixed with grey in the moon's light, and showing like jasper. Where the shadows fell thickest, there was yet a mist of colour. All about ran a brook, and babbled to itself. The spring crocus lifted its head in moist midgrasses of the meadow, rejoiced with freshness. The rugged heights seemed to clasp this one innocent spot as their only garden-treasure; and a bank of hazels hid it from the castle with a lover's arm.

'The moon will tell me,' mused Farina; 'the moon will signal me the hour! When the moon hangs over the round tower, I shall know 'tis time to strike.'

The song of the nightingales was a full unceasing throb.

It went like the outcry of one heart from branch to branch. The four long notes, and the short fifth which leads off to that hurried gush of music, gurgling rich with passion, came thick and constant from under the tremulous leaves.

At first Farina had been deaf to them. His heart was in the dungeon with Margarita, or with the Goshawk in his dangers, forming a thousand desperate plans, among the red-hot ploughshares of desperate action. Finally, without a sense of being wooed, it was won. The tenderness of his love then mastered him.

'God will not suffer that fair head to come to harm!' he thought, and with the thought a load fell off his breast.

He paced the meadows, and patted the three pasturing steeds. Involuntarily his sight grew on the moon. She went so slowly. She seemed not to move at all. A little wing of vapour flew toward her; it whitened, passed, and the moon was slower than before. Oh! were the heavens delaying their march to look on this iniquity? Again and again he cried, 'Patience, it is not time!' He flung himself on the grass. The next moment he climbed the heights, and was peering at the mass of gloom that fronted the sky. It reared such a mailed head of menace, that his heart was seized with a quivering, as though it had been struck. Behind lay scattered some small faint-winkling stars on sapphire fields, and a stain of yellow light was in a breach of one wall.

He descended. What was the Goshawk doing? Was he betrayed? It was surely now time? No; the moon had not yet smitten the face of the castle. He made his way through the hazel-bank among flitting nightmoths, and glanced up to measure the moon's distance. As he did so, a first touch of silver fell on the hoary flint.

'Oh, young bird of heaven in that Devil's clutch!'

Sounds like the baying of boar-hounds alarmed him. They whined into silence.

He fell back. The meadow breathed peace, and more and more the nightingales volumed their notes. As in a charmed circle of palpitating song, he succumbed to languor. The brook rolled beside him fresh as an infant, toying with the moonlight. He leaned over it, and thrice waywardly dipped his hand in the clear translucence.

Was it his own face imaged there?

Farina bent close above an eddy of the water. It whirled with a strange tumult, breaking into lines and lights a face not his own, nor the moon's; nor was it a reflection. The agitation increased. Now a wreath of bubbles crowned the pool, and a pure water-lily, but larger, ascended wavering.

He started aside; and under him a bright head, garlanded with gemmed roses, appeared. No fairer figure of woman had Farina seen. Her visage had the lustrous white of moonlight, and all her shape undulated in a dress of flashing silver-white, wonderful to see. The Lady of the Water smiled on him, and ran over with ripples and dimples of limpid beauty. Then, as he retreated on the meadow grass, she swam toward him, and taking his hand, pressed it to her. After her touch the youth no longer feared. She curved her finger, and beckoned him on. All that she did was done flowingly. The youth was a shadow in her silver track as she passed like a harmless wave over the closed crocuses; but the crocuses shivered and swelled their throats of streaked purple and argent as at delicious rare sips of a wine. Breath of violet, and ladysmock, and valley-lily, mingled and fluttered about her. Farina was as a man working the day's intent in a dream. He could see the heart in her translucent, hanging like a cold dingy ruby. By the purity of his nature he felt that such a presence must have come but to help. It might be Margarita's guardian fairy!

They passed the hazel-bank, and rounded the castlecrag, washed by the brook and, beneath the advancing moon, standing in a ring of brawling silver. The youth with his fervid eyes marked the old weather-stains and scars of long defiance coming into colour. That mystery of wickedness which the towers had worn in the dusk, was dissolved, and he endured no more the almost abashed sensation of competing littleness that made him think there was nought to do, save die, combating single-handed such massive power. The moon shone calmly superior, like the prowess of maiden knights; and now the harsh frown of the walls struck resolution to his spirit, and nerved him with hate and the contempt true courage feels when matched against fraud and villany.

On a fallen block of slate, cushioned with rich brown moss and rusted weather-stains, the Water-Lady sat, and pointed to Farina the path of the moon toward the round tower. She did not speak, and if his lips parted, put her cold finger across them. Then she began to hum a soft sweet monotony of song, vague and careless, very witching to hear. Farina caught no words, nor whether the song was of days in dust or in flower, but his mind bloomed with legends and sad splendours of story, while she sang on the slate-block under sprinkled shadows by the water.

He had listened long in trance, when the Water-Lady hushed, and stretched forth a slender forefinger to the moon. It stood like a dot over the round tower. Farina rose in haste. She did not leave him to ask her aid, but took his hand and led him up the steep ascent. Halfway to the castle, she rested. There, concealed by bramble-tufts, she disclosed the low portal of a secret passage, and pushed it open without effort. She paused at the entrance, and he could see her trembling, seeming to wax taller, till she was like a fountain glittering in the cold light. Then she dropped, as drops a dying bet, and cowered into the passage.

Darkness, thick with earth-dews, oppressed his senses. He felt the clammy walls scraping close on him. Not the dimmest lamp, or guiding sound, was near; but the lady went on as one who knew her way. Passing a low-vaulted dungeon-room, they wound up stairs hewn in the rock, and came to a door, obedient to her touch, which displayed a chamber faintly misted by a solitary bar of moonlight. Farina perceived they were above the foundation of the castle. The walls gleamed pale with knightly harness, habergeons gaping for heads, breastplates of blue steel, halbert, and hand-axe, greaves, glaives, boar-spears, and polished spur-fixed heel-pieces. He seized a falchion hanging apart, but the lady stayed his arm, and led to another flight of stone ending in a kind of corridor. Noises of laughter and high feasting beset him at this point. The Lady of the Water sidled her head, as to note a familiar voice; and then drew him to a looped aperture.

Farina beheld a scene that first dazzled, but, as it grew into shape, sank him with dismay. Below, and level with the chamber he had left, a rude banqueting-hall glowed, under the light of a dozen flambeaux, with smoking boar's flesh, deer's flesh, stone-flagons, and horn-beakers. At the head of this board sat Werner, scarlet with furious feasting, and on his right hand, Margarita, bloodless as a beautiful martyr bound to the fire. Retainers of Werner occupied the length of the hall, chorusing the Baron's speeches, and drinking their own healths when there was no call for another. Farina saw his beloved alone. She was dressed as when he parted with her last. The dear cameo lay on her bosom, but not heaving proudly as of old. Her shoulders were drooped forward, and contracted her bosom in its heaving. She would have had a humbled look, but for the marble sternness of her eyes. They were fixed as eyes that see the way of death through all earthly objects.

'Now, dogs!' cried the Baron, 'the health of the night! and swell your lungs, for I'll have no cat's cry when Werner's bride is the toast. Monk or no monk's leave, she's mine. Ay, my pretty one! it shall be made right in the morning, if I lead all the Laach rats here by the nose. Thunder! no disrespect to Werner's bride from Pope or abbot. Now, sing out!—or wait! these fellows shall drink it first.'

He stretched and threw a beaker of wine right and left behind him, and Farina's despair stiffened his limbs as he recognized the Goshawk and Schwartz Thier strapped to the floor. Their beards were already moist with previous libations similarly bestowed, and they received this in sullen stillness; but Farina thought he observed a rapid glance of encouragement dart from beneath the Goshawk's bent brows, as Margarita momentarily turned her head half-way on him.

'Lick your chaps, ye beasts, and don't say Werner stints vermin good cheer his nuptial-night. Now,' continued the Baron, growing huskier as he talked louder: 'Short and ringing, my devil's pups:—Werner and his Bride! and may she soon give you a young baron to keep you in better order than I can, as, if she does her duty, she will.'

The Baron stood up, and lifted his huge arm to lead the toast.

'Werner and his Bride!'

Not a voice followed him. There was a sudden intimation of the call being echoed; but it snapped, and ended in shuffling tones, as if the hall-door had closed on the response.

'What 's this?' roared the Baron, in that caged wild beast voice Margarita remembered she had heard in the Cathedral Square.

No one replied.

'Speak! or I'll rot you a fathom in the rock, curs!'

'Herr Baron!' said Henker Rothhals impressively; 'the matter is, that there's something unholy among us.'

The Baron's goblet flew at his head before the words were uttered.

'I'll make an unholy thing of him that says it,' and Werner lowered at them one by one.

'Then I say it, Herr Baron!' pursued Henker Rothhals, wiping his frontispiece: 'The Devil has turned against you at last. Look up there—Ah, it's gone now; but where's the man sitting this side saw it not?'

The Baron made one spring, and stood on the board.

'Now! will any rascal here please to say so?'

Something in the cruel hang of his threatening hatchet jaw silenced many in the act of confirming the assertion.

'Stand out, Henker Rotthals!'

Rotthals slid a hunting-knife up his wrist, and stepped back from the board.

'Beast!' roared the Baron, 'I said I wouldn't shed blood to-night. I spared a traitor, and an enemy—'

'Look again!' said Rothhals; 'will any fellow say he saw nothing there.'

While all heads, including Werner's, were directed to the aperture which surveyed them, Rothhals tossed his knife to the Goshawk unperceived.

This time answers came to his challenge, but not in confirmation. The Baron spoke with a gasping gentleness.

'So you trifle with me? I'm dangerous for that game. Mind you of Blass-Gesell? I made a better beast of him by sending him three-quarters of the road to hell for trial.' Bellowing, 'Take that!' he discharged a broad blade, hitherto concealed in his right hand, straight at Rothhals. It fixed in his cheek and jaw, wringing an awful breath of pain from him as he fell against the wall.

'There's a lesson for you not to cross me, children!' said Werner, striding his stumpy legs up and down the crashing board, and puffing his monstrous girth of chest and midriff. 'Let him stop there awhile, to show what comes of thwarting Werner!—Fire-devils! before the baroness, too!—Something unholy is there? Something unholy in his jaw, I think!—Leave it sticking! He's against meat last, is he? I'll teach you who he's for!—Who speaks?'

All hung silent. These men were animals dominated by a mightier brute.

He clasped his throat, and shook the board with a jump, as he squeaked, rather than called, a second time 'Who spoke?'

He had not again to ask. In this pause, as the Baron glared for his victim, a song, so softly sung that it sounded remote, but of which every syllable was clearly rounded, swelled into his ears, and froze him in his angry posture.

'The blood of the barons shall turn to ice,
And their castle fall to wreck,
When a true lover dips in the water thrice,
That runs round Werner's Eck.

'Round Werner's Eck the water runs;
The hazels shiver and shake:
The walls that have blotted such happy suns,
Are seized with the ruin-quake.

'And quake with the ruin, and quake with rue,
Thou last of Werner's race!
The hearts of the barons were cold that knew
The Water-Dame's embrace.

'For a sin was done, and a shame was wrought,
That water went to hide:
And those who thought to make it nought,
They did but spread it wide.

'Hold ready, hold ready to pay the price,
And keep thy bridal cheer:
A hand has dipped in the water thrice,
And the Water-Dame is here.'

THE RESCUE

The Goshawk was on his feet. 'Now, lass,' said he to Margarita, 'now is the time!' He took her hand, and led her to the door. Schwartz Thier closed up behind her. Not a man in the hall interposed. Werner's head moved round after them, like a dog on the watch; but he was dumb. The door opened, and Farina entered. He bore a sheaf of weapons under his arm. The familiar sight relieved Werner's senses from the charm. He shouted to bar the prisoners' passage. His men were ranged like statues in the hall. There was a start among them, as if that terrible noise communicated an instinct of obedience, but no more. They glanced at each other, and remained quiet.

The Goshawk had his eye on Werner. 'Stand back, lass!' he said to Margarita. She took a sword from Farina, and answered, with white lips and flashing eyes, 'I can fight, Goshawk!'

'And shall, if need be; but leave it to me now, returned Guy.

His eye never left the Baron. Suddenly a shriek of steel rang. All fell aside, and the combatants stood opposed on clear ground. Farina, took Margarita's left hand, and placed her against the wall between the Thier and himself. Werner's men were well content to let their master fight it out. The words spoken by Henker Rothhals, that the Devil had forsaken him, seemed in their minds confirmed by the weird song which every one present could swear he heard with his ears. 'Let him take his chance, and try his own luck,' they said, and shrugged. The battle was between Guy, as Margarita's champion, and Werner.

In Schwartz Thier's judgement, the two were well matched, and he estimated their diverse qualities from sharp experience. 'For short work the Baron, and my new mate for tough standing to 't!' Farina's summary in favour of the Goshawk was, 'A stouter heart, harder sinews, and a good cause. The combat was generally regarded with a professional eye, and few prayers. Margarita solely there asked aid from above, and knelt to the Virgin; but her, too, the clash of arms and dire earnest of mortal fight aroused to eager eyes. She had not dallied with heroes in her dreams. She was as ready to second Siegfried on the crimson field as tend him in the silken chamber.

It was well that a woman's heart was there to mark the grace and glory of manhood in upright foot-to-foot encounter. For the others, it was a mere calculation of lucky hits. Even Farina, in his anxiety for her, saw but the brightening and darkening of the prospect of escape in every attitude and hard-ringing blow. Margarita was possessed with a painful exaltation. In her eyes the bestial Baron now took a nobler form and countenance; but the Goshawk assumed the sovereign aspect of old heroes, who, whether persecuted or favoured of heaven, still maintained their stand, remembering of what stuff they were, and who made them.

'Never,' say the old writers, with a fervour honourable to their knowledge of the elements that compose our being, 'never may this bright privilege of fair fight depart from us, nor advantage of it fail to be taken! Man against man, or beast, singly keeping his ground, is as fine rapture to the breast as Beauty in her softest hour affordeth. For if woman taketh loveliness to her when she languisheth, so surely doth man in these fierce moods, when steel and iron sparkle opposed, and their breath is fire, and their lips white with the lock of resolution; all their faculties knotted to a point, and their energies alive as the daylight to prove themselves superior, according to the laws and under the blessing of chivalry.'

'For all,' they go on to improve the comparison, 'may admire and delight in fair blossoming dales under the blue dome of peace; but 'tis the rare lofty heart alone comprehendeth, and is heightened by, terrific splendours of tempest, when cloud meets cloud in skies black as the sepulchre, and Glory sits like a flame on the helm of Ruin'

For a while the combatants aired their dexterity, contenting themselves with cunning cuts and flicks of the sword-edge, in which Werner first drew blood by a keen sweep along the forehead of the Goshawk. Guy had allowed him to keep his position on the board, and still fought at his face and neck. He now jerked back his body from the hip, and swung a round stroke at Werner's knee, sending him in retreat with a snort of pain. Before the Baron could make good his ground, Guy was level with him on the board.

Werner turned an upbraiding howl at his men. They were not disposed to second him yet. They one and all approved his personal battle with Fate, and never more admired him and felt his power; but the affair was exciting, and they were not the pillars to prop a falling house.

Werner clenched his two hands to his ponderous glaive, and fell upon Guy with heavier fury. He was becoming not unworth the little womanly appreciation Margarita was brought to bestow on him. The voice of the Water-Lady whispered at her heart that the Baron warred on his destiny, and that ennobles all living souls.

Bare-headed the combatants engaged, and the headpiece was the chief point of attack. No swerving from blows was possible for either: ward, or take; a false step would have ensured defeat. This also induced caution. Many a double stamp of the foot was heard, as each had to retire in turn.

'Not at his head so much, he'll bear battering there all night long,' said Henker Rothhals in a breathing interval. Knocks had been pretty equally exchanged, but the Baron's head certainly looked the least vulnerable, whereas Guy exhibited several dints that streamed freely. Yet he looked, eye and bearing, as fresh as when they began, and the calm, regular heave of his chest contrasted with Werner's quick gasps. His smile, too, renewed each time the Baron paused for breath, gave Margarita heart. It was not a taunting smile, but one of entire confidence, and told all the more on his adversary. As Werner led off again, and the choice was always left him, every expression of the Goshawk's face passed to full light in his broad eyes.

The Baron's play was a reckless fury. There was nothing to study in it. Guy became the chief object of speculation. He was evidently trying to wind his man.

He struck wildly, some thought. Others judged that he was a random hitter, and had no mortal point in aim. Schwartz Thier's opinion was frequently vented. 'Too round a stroke—down on him! Chop-not slice!'

Guy persevered in his own fashion. According to Schwartz Thier, he brought down by his wilfulness the blow that took him on the left shoulder, and nigh broke him. It was a weighty blow, followed by a thump of sound. The sword-edge swerved on his shoulder-blade, or he must have been disabled. But Werner's crow was short, and he had no time to push success. One of the Goshawk's swooping under-hits half severed his right wrist, and the blood spirted across the board. He gasped and seemed to succumb, but held to it still, though with slackened force. Guy now attacked. Holding to his round strokes, he accustomed Werner to guard the body, and stood to it so briskly right and left, that Werner grew bewildered, lost his caution, and gave ground. Suddenly the Goshawk's glaive flashed in air, and chopped sheer down on Werner's head. So shrewd a blow it was against a half-formed defence, that the Baron dropped without a word right on the edge of the board, and there hung, feebly grasping with his fingers.

'Who bars the way now?' sang out Guy.

No one accepted the challenge. Success clothed him with terrors, and gave him giant size.

'Then fare you well, my merry men all,' said Guy. 'Bear me no ill-will for this. A little doctoring will right the bold Baron.'

He strode jauntily to the verge of the board, and held his finger for Margarita to follow. She stepped forward. The men put their beards together, muttering. She could not advance. Farina doubled his elbow, and presented sword-point. Three of the ruffians now disputed the way with bare steel. Margarita looked at the Goshawk. He was smiling calmly curious as he leaned over his sword, and gave her an encouraging nod. She made another step in defiance. One fellow stretched his hand to arrest her. All her maidenly pride stood up at once. 'What a glorious girl!' murmured the Goshawk, as he saw her face suddenly flash, and she retreated a pace and swung a sharp cut across the knuckles of her assailant, daring him, or one of them, with hard, bright eyes, beautifully vindictive, to lay hand on a pure maiden.

'You have it, Barenleib!' cried the others, and then to Margarita: 'Look, young mistress! we are poor fellows, and ask a trifle of ransom, and then part friends.'

'Not an ace!' the Goshawk pronounced from his post.

'Two to one, remember.'

'The odds are ours,' replied the Goshawk confidently.

They ranged themselves in front of the hall-door. Instead of accepting this challenge, Guy stepped to Werner, and laid his moaning foe length-wise in an easier posture. He then lifted Margarita on the board, and summoned them with cry of 'Free passage!' They answered by a sullen shrug and taunt.

'Schwartz Thier! Rothhals! Farina! buckle up, and make ready then,' sang Guy.

He measured the length, of his sword, and raised it. The Goshawk had not underrated his enemies. He was tempted to despise them when he marked their gradually lengthening chaps and eyeballs.

Not one of them moved. All gazed at him as if their marrows were freezing with horror.

'What's this?' cried Guy.

They knew as little as he, but a force was behind them irresistible against their efforts. The groaning oak slipped open, pushing them forward, and an apparition glided past, soft as the pallid silver of the moon. She slid to the Baron, and put her arms about him, and sang to him. Had the Water-Lady laid an iron hand on all those ruffians, she could not have held them faster bound than did the fear of her presence. The Goshawk drew his fair charge through them, followed by Farina, the Thier, and Rothhals. A last glimpse of the hall showed them still as old cathedral sculpture staring at white light on a fluted pillar of the wall.

Low among the swarthy sandhills behind the Abbey of Laach dropped the round red moon. Soft lengths of misty yellow stole through the glens of Rhineland. The nightingales still sang. Closer and closer the moon came into the hushed valleys.

There is a dell behind Hammerstein Castle, a ring of basking sward, girdled by a silver slate-brook, and guarded by four high-peaked hills that slope down four long wooded corners to the grassy base. Here, it is said, the elves and earthmen play, dancing in circles with laughing feet that fatten the mushroom. They would have been fulfilling the tradition now, but that the place was occupied by a sturdy group of mortals, armed with staves. The intruders were sleepy, and lay about on the inclines. Now and then two got up, and there rang hard echoes of oak. Again all were calm as cud-chewing cattle, and the white water ran pleased with quiet.

It may be that the elves brewed mischief among them; for the oaken blows were becoming more frequent. One complained of a kick: another demanded satisfaction for a pinch. 'Go to,' drawled the accused drowsily in both cases, 'too much beer last night!' Within three minutes, the company counted a pair of broken heads. The East was winning on the West in heaven, and the dusk was thinning. They began to mark, each, whom he had cudgelled. A noise of something swiftly in motion made them alert. A roebuck rushed down one of the hills, and scampered across the sward. The fine beast went stretching so rapidly away as to be hardly distinct.

'Sathanas once more!' they murmured, and drew together.

The name passed through them like a watchword.

'Not he this time,' cried the two new-comers, emerging from the foliage. 'He's safe under Cologne—the worse for all good men who live there! But come! follow to the Rhine! there 's work for us on the yonder side, and sharp work.'

'Why,' answered several, 'we 've our challenge with the lads of Leutesdorf and Wied to-day.'

'D' ye see this?' said the foremost of the others, pointing to a carved ivory white rose in his cap.

'Brothers!' he swelled his voice, 'follow with a will, for the White Rose is in danger!'

Immediately they ranked, and followed zealously through the buds of young bushes, and over heaps of damp dead leaves, a half-hour's scramble, when they defiled under Hammerstein, and stood before the Rhine. Their leader led up the river, and after a hasty walk, stopped, loosened his hood, and stripped.

'Now,' said he, strapping the bundle to his back, 'let me know the hound that refuses to follow his leader when the White Rose is in danger.'

'Long live Dietrich!' they shouted. He dropped from the bank, and waded in. He was soon supported by the remainder of the striplings, and all struck out boldly into mid-stream.

Never heard history of a nobler Passage of the Rhine than this made between Andernach and Hammerstein by members of the White Rose Club, bundle on back, to relieve the White Rose of Germany from thrall and shame!

They were taken far down by the rapid current, and arrived panting to land. The dressing done, they marched up the pass of Tonnistein, and took a deep draught at the spring of pleasant waters there open to wayfarers. Arrived at the skirts of Laach, they beheld two farmer peasants lashed back to back against a hazel. They released them, but could gain no word of information, as the fellows, after a yawn and a wink, started off, all heels, to make sure of liberty. On the shores of the lake the brotherhood descried a body of youths, whom they hailed, and were welcomed to companionship.

'Where's Berthold?' asked Dietrich.

He was not present.

'The more glory for us, then,' Dietrich said.

It was here seriously put to the captain, whether they should not halt at the abbey, and reflect, seeing that great work was in prospect.

'Truly,' quoth Dietrich, 'dying on an empty stomach is heathenish, and cold blood makes a green wound gape. Kaiser Conrad should be hospitable, and the monks honour numbers. Here be we, thirty and nine; let us go!'

The West was dark blue with fallen light. The lakewaters were growing grey with twilight. The abbey stood muffled in shadows. Already the youths had commenced battering at the convent doors, when they were summoned by the voice of the Goshawk on horseback. To their confusion they beheld the White Rose herself on his right hand. Chapfallen Dietrich bowed to his sweet mistress.

'We were coming to the rescue,' he stammered.

A laugh broke from the Goshawk. 'You thought the lady was locked up in the ghostly larder; eh!'

Dietrich seized his sword, and tightened his belt.

'The Club allows no jesting with the White Rose, Sir Stranger.'

Margarita made peace. 'I thank you all, good friends. But quarrel not, I pray you, with them that save me at the risk of their lives.'

'Our service is equal,' said the Goshawk, flourishing, 'Only we happen to be beforehand with the Club, for which Farina and myself heartily beg pardon of the entire brotherhood.'

'Farina!' exclaimed Dietrich. 'Then we make a prisoner instead of uncaging a captive.'

'What 's this?' said Guy.

'So much,' responded Dietrich. 'Yonder's a runaway from two masters: the law of Cologne, and the conqueror of Satan; and all good citizens are empowered to bring him back, dead or alive.'

'Dietrich! Dietrich! dare you talk thus of the man who saved me?' cried Margarita.

Dietrich sullenly persisted.

'Then, look!' said the White Rose, reddening under the pale dawn; 'he shall not, he shall not go with you.'

One of the Club was here on the point of speaking to the White Rose,—a breach of the captain's privilege. Dietrich felled him unresisting to earth, and resumed:

'It must be done, Beauty of Cologne! the monk, Father Gregory, is now enduring shame and scorn for lack of this truant witness.'

'Enough! I go!' said Farina.

'You leave me?' Margarita looked tender reproach. Weariness and fierce excitement had given a liquid flame to her eyes and an endearing darkness round their circles that matched strangely with her plump youth. Her features had a soft white flush. She was less radiant, but never looked so bewitching. An aspect of sweet human languor caught at the heart of love, and raised tumults.

'It is a duty,' said Farina.

'Then go,' she beckoned, and held her hand for him to kiss. He raised it to his lips. This was seen of all the Club.

As they were departing with Farina, and Guy prepared to demand admittance into the convent, Dietrich chanced to ask how fared Dame Lisbeth. Schwartz Thier was by, and answered, with a laugh, that he had quite forgotten the little lady.

'We took her in mistake for you, mistress! She was a one to scream! The moment she was kissed—mum as a cloister. We kissed her, all of us, for the fun of it. No harm—no harm! We should have dropped her when we found we had the old bird 'stead of the young one, but reckoned ransom, ye see. She's at the Eck, rattling, I's wager, like last year's nut in the shell!'

'Lisbeth! Lisbeth! poor Lisbeth; we will return to her. Instantly,' cried Margarita.

'Not you,' said Guy.

'Yes! I!'

'No!' said Guy.

'Gallant Goshawk! best of birds, let me go!'

'Without me or Farina, never! I see I shall have no chance with my lord now. Come, then, come, fair Irresistible! come, lads. Farina can journey back alone. You shall have the renown of rescuing Dame Lisbeth.'

'Farina! forget not to comfort my father,' said Margarita.

Between Margarita's society and Farina's, there was little dispute in the captain's mind which choice to make. Farina was allowed to travel single to Cologne; and Dietrich, petted by Margarita, and gently jeered by Guy, headed the Club from Laach waters to the castle of the Robber Baron.

THE BACK-BLOWS OF SATHANAS

Monk Gregory was pacing the high road between the Imperial camp and suffering Cologne. The sun had risen through interminable distances of cloud that held him remote in a succession of receding mounds and thinner veils, realm beyond realm, till he showed fireless, like a phantom king in a phantom land. The lark was in the breast of morning. The field-mouse ran along the furrows. Dews hung red and grey on the weedy banks and wayside trees. At times the nostril of the good father was lifted, and he beat his breast, relapsing into sorrowful contemplation. Passed-any citizen of Cologne, the ghostly head sunk into its cowl. 'There's a black raven!' said many. Monk Gregory heard them, and murmured, 'Thou hast me, Evil one! thou hast me!'

It was noon when Farina came clattering down from the camp.

'Father,' said he, 'I have sought thee.'

'My son!' exclaimed Monk Gregory with silencing hand, 'thou didst not well to leave me contending against the tongues of doubt. Answer me not. The maiden! and what weighed she in such a scale?—No more! I am punished. Well speaks the ancient proverb:

"Beware the back-blows of Sathanas!"

I, that thought to have vanquished him! Vanity has wrecked me, in this world and the next. I am the victim of self-incense. I hear the demons shouting their chorus—"Here comes Monk Gregory, who called himself Conqueror of Darkness!" In the camp I am discredited and a scoff; in the city I am spat upon, abhorred. Satan, my son, fights not with his fore-claws. 'Tis with his tail he fights, O Farina!—Listen, my son! he entered to his kingdom below Cologne, even under the stones of the Cathedral Square, and the stench of him abominably remaineth, challenging the nostrils of holy and unholy alike. The Kaiser cannot approach for him; the citizens are outraged. Oh! had I held my peace in humbleness, I had truly conquered him. But he gave me easy victory, to inflate me. I shall not last. Now this only is left, my son; that thou bear living testimony to the truth of my statement, as I bear it to the folly!'

Farina promised, in the face of all, he would proclaim and witness to his victory on Drachenfels.

'That I may not be ranked an impostor!' continued the Monk. 'And how great must be the virtue of them that encounter that dark spirit! Valour availeth nought. But if virtue be not in' ye, soon will ye be puffed to bursting with that devil's poison, self-incense. Surely, my son, thou art faithful; and for this service I can reward thee. Follow me yet again.'

On the road they met Gottlieb Groschen, hastening to the camp. Dismay rumpled the old merchant's honest jowl. Farina drew rein before him.

'Your daughter is safe, worthy Master Groschen,' said he.

'Safe?' cried Gottlieb; 'where is she, my Grete?'

Farina briefly explained. Gottlieb spread out his arms, and was going to thank the youth. He saw Father Gregory, and his whole frame narrowed with disgust.

'Are you in company with that pestilent animal, that curse of Cologne!'

'The good Monk—,' said Farina.

'You are leagued with him, then, sirrah! Expect no thanks from me. Cologne, I say, is cursed! Meddling wretches! could ye not leave Satan alone? He hurt us not. We were free of him. Cologne, I say, is cursed! The enemy of mankind is brought by you to be the deadly foe of Cologne.'

So saying, Gottlieb departed.

'Seest thou, my son,' quoth the Monk, 'they reason not!'

Farina was dejected. Willingly would he, for his part, have left the soul of Evil a loose rover for the sake of some brighter horizon to his hope.

No twinge of remorse accompanied Gottlieb. The Kaiser had allotted him an encampment and a guard of honour for his household while the foulness raged, and there Gottlieb welcomed back Margarita and Aunt Lisbeth on the noon after his meeting with Farina. The White Rose had rested at Laach, and was blooming again. She and the Goshawk came trotting in advance of the Club through the woods of Laach, startling the deer with laughter, and sending the hare with her ears laid back all across country. In vain Dietrich menaced Guy with the terrors of the Club: Aunt Lisbeth begged of Margarita not to leave her with the footmen in vain. The joyous couple galloped over the country, and sprang the ditches, and leapt the dykes, up and down the banks, glad as morning hawks, entering Andernach at a round pace; where they rested at a hostel as capable of producing good Rhine and Mosel wine then as now. Here they had mid-day's meal laid out in the garden for the angry Club, and somewhat appeased them on their arrival with bumpers of the best Scharzhofberger. After a refreshing halt, three boats were hired. On their passage to the river, they encountered a procession of monks headed by the Archbishop of Andernach, bearing a small figure of Christ carved in blackthorn and varnished: said to work miracles, and a present to the good town from two Hungarian pilgrims.

'Are ye for Cologne?' the monks inquired of them.

'Direct down stream!' they answered.

'Send, then, hither to us Gregory, the conqueror of Darkness, that he may know there is gratitude on earth and gratulation for great deeds,' said the monks.

So with genuflexions the travellers proceeded, and entered the boats by the Archbishop's White Tower. Hammerstein Castle and Rheineck they floated under; Salzig and the Ahr confluence; Rolandseck and Nonnenwerth; Drachenfels and Bonn; hills green with young vines; dells waving fresh foliage. Margarita sang as they floated. Ancient ballads she sang that made the Goshawk sigh for home, and affected the Club with delirious love for the grand old water that was speeding them onward. Aunt Lisbeth was not to be moved. She alone held down her head. She looked not Gottlieb in the face as he embraced her. Nor to any questioning would she vouchsafe reply. From that time forth, she was charity to woman; and the exuberant cheerfulness and familiarity of the men toward her soon grew kindly and respectful. The dragon in Aunt Lisbeth was destroyed. She objected no more to Margarita's cameo.

The Goshawk quickly made peace with his lord, and enjoyed the commendation of the Kaiser. Dietrich Schill thought of challenging him; but the Club had graver business: and this was to pass sentence on Berthold Schmidt for the crime of betraying the White Rose into the hands of Werner. They had found Berthold at the Eck, and there consented to let him remain until ransom was paid for his traitorous body. Berthold in his mad passion was tricked by Werner, and on his release, by payment of the ransom, submitted to the judgement of the Club, which condemned him to fight them all in turn, and then endure banishment from Rhineland; the Goshawk, for his sister's sake, interceding before a harsher tribunal.

THE ENTRY INTO COLOGNE

Seven days Kaiser Heinrich remained camped outside Cologne. Six times in six successive days the Kaiser attempted to enter the city, and was foiled.

'Beard of Barbarossa!' said the Kaiser, 'this is the first stronghold that ever resisted me.'

The warrior bishops, electors, pfalzgrafs, and knights of the Empire, all swore it was no shame not to be a match for the Demon.

'If,' said the reflective Kaiser, 'we are to suffer below what poor Cologne is doomed to undergo now, let us, by all that is savoury, reform and do penance.'

The wind just then setting on them dead from Cologne made the courtiers serious. Many thought of their souls for the first time.

This is recorded to the honour of Monk Gregory.

On the seventh morning, the Kaiser announced his determination to make a last trial.

It was dawn, and a youth stood before the Kaiser's tent, praying an audience.

Conducted into the presence of the Kaiser, the youth, they say, succeeded in arousing him from his depression, for, brave as he was, Kaiser Heinrich dreaded the issue. Forthwith order was given for the cavalcade to set out according to the rescript, Kaiser Heinrich retaining the youth at his right hand. But the youth had found occasion to visit Gottlieb and Margarita, each of whom he furnished with a flash, [flask?] curiously shaped, and charged with a distillation.

As the head of the procession reached the gates of Cologne, symptoms of wavering were manifest.

Kaiser Heinrich commanded an advance, at all cost.

Pfalzgraf Nase, as the old chronicles call him in their humour, but assuredly a great noble, led the van, and pushed across the draw-bridge.

Hesitation and signs of horror were manifest in the assemblage round the Kaiser's person. The Kaiser and the youth at his right hand were cheery. Not a whit drooped they! Several of the heroic knights begged the Kaiser's permission to fall back.

'Follow Pfalzgraf Nase!' the Kaiser is reported to have said.

Great was the wonderment of the people of Cologne to behold Kaiser Heinrich riding in perfect stateliness up the main street toward the Cathedral, while right and left of him bishops and electors were dropping incapable.

The Kaiser advanced till by his side the youth rode sole.

'Thy name?' said the Kaiser.

He answered: 'A poor youth, unconquerable Kaiser! Farina I am called.'

'Thy recompense?' said the Kaiser.

He answered: 'The hand of a maiden of Cologne, most gracious Kaiser and master!'

'She is thine!' said the Kaiser.

Kaiser Heinrich looked behind him, and among a host grasping the pommels of their saddles, and reeling vanquished, were but two erect, a maiden and an old man.

'That is she, unconquerable Kaiser!' Farina continued, bowing low.

'It shall be arranged on the spot,' said the Kaiser.

A word from Kaiser Heinrich sealed Gottlieb's compliance.

Said he: 'Gracious Kaiser and master! though such a youth could of himself never have aspired to the possession of a Groschen, yet when the Kaiser pleads for him, objection is as the rock of Moses, and streams consent. Truly he has done Cologne good service, and if Margarita, my daughter, can be persuaded—'

The Kaiser addressed her with his blazing brows.

Margarita blushed a ready autumn of rosy-ripe acquiescence.

'A marriage registered yonder!' said the Kaiser, pointing upward.

'I am thine, murmured Margarita, as Farina drew near her.

'Seal it! seal it!' quoth the Kaiser, in hearty good humour; 'take no consent from man or maid without a seal.'

Farina tossed the contents of a flask in air, and saluted his beloved on the lips.

This scene took place near the charred round of earth where the Foulest descended to his kingdom below.

Men now pervaded Cologne with flasks, purifying the atmosphere. It became possible to breathe freely.

'We Germans,' said Kaiser Heinrich, when he was again surrounded by his courtiers, 'may go wrong if we always follow Pfalzgraf Nase; but this time we have been well led.' Whereat there was obsequious laughter.

The Pfalzgraf pleaded a susceptible nostril.

'Thou art, I fear, but a timid mortal,' said the Kaiser.

'Never have I been found so on the German Field, Imperial Majesty!' returned the Pfalzgraf. 'I take glory to myself that this Nether reek overcomes me.'

'Even that we must combat, you see!' exclaimed Kaiser Heinrich; 'but come all to a marriage this night, and take brides as soon as you will, all of you. Increase, and give us loyal subjects in plenty. I count prosperity by the number of marriages in my empire!'

The White Rose Club were invited by Gottlieb to the wedding, and took it in vast wrath until they saw the Kaiser, and such excellent stout German fare present, when immediately a battle raged as to who should do the event most honour, and was in dispute till dawn: Dietrich Schill being the man, he having consumed wurst the length of his arm, and wine sufficient to have floated a St. Goar salmon; which was long proudly chronicled in his family, and is now unearthed from among the ancient honourable records of Cologne.

The Goshawk was Farina's bridesman, and a very spiriting bridesman was he! Aunt Lisbeth sat in a corner, faintly smiling.

'Child!' said the little lady to Margarita when they kissed at parting, 'your courage amazes me. Do you think? Do you know? Poor, sweet bird, delivered over hand and foot!'

'I love him! I love him, aunty! that's all I know,' said Margarita: 'love, love, love him!'

'Heaven help you!' ejaculated Aunt Lisbeth.

'Pray with me,' said Margarita.

The two knelt at the foot of the bride-bed, and prayed very different prayers, but to the same end. That done, Aunt Lisbeth helped undress the White Rose, and trembled, and told a sad nuptial anecdote of the Castle, and put her little shrivelled hand on Margarita's heart, and shrieked.

'Child! it gallops!' she cried.

''Tis happiness,' said Margarita, standing in her hair.

'May it last only!' exclaimed Aunt Lisbeth.

'It will, aunty! I am humble: I am true'; and the fair girl gathered the frill of her nightgown.

'Look not in the glass,' said Lisbeth; 'not to-night! Look, if you can, to-morrow.'

She smoothed the White Rose in her bed, tucked her up, and kissed her, leaving her as a bud that waits for sunshine.

CONCLUSION

The shadow of Monk Gregory was seen no more in Cologne. He entered the Calendar, and ranks next St. Anthony. For three successive centuries the towns of Rhineland boasted his visits in the flesh, and the conqueror of Darkness caused dire Rhenish feuds.

The Tailed Infernal repeated his famous Back-blow on Farina. The youth awoke one morning and beheld warehouses the exact pattern of his own, displaying flasks shaped even as his own, and a Farina to right and left of him. In a week, they were doubled. A month quadrupled them. They increased.

'Fame and Fortune,' mused Farina, 'come from man and the world: Love is from heaven. We may be worthy, and lose the first. We lose not love unless unworthy. Would ye know the true Farina? Look for him who walks under the seal of bliss; whose darling is for ever his young sweet bride, leading him from snares, priming his soul with celestial freshness. There is no hypocrisy can ape that aspect. Least of all, the creatures of the Damned! By this I may be known.'

Seven years after, when the Goshawk came into Cologne to see old friends, and drink some of Gottlieb's oldest Rudesheimer, he was waylaid by false Farinas; and only discovered the true one at last, by chance, in the music-gardens near the Rhine, where Farina sat, having on one hand Margarita, and at his feet three boys and one girl, over whom both bent lovingly, like the parent vine fondling its grape bunches in summer light.

THE CASE OF GENERAL OPLE AND LADY CAMPER

CHAPTER I

An excursion beyond the immediate suburbs of London, projected long before his pony-carriage was hired to conduct him, in fact ever since his retirement from active service, led General Ople across a famous common, with which he fell in love at once, to a lofty highway along the borders of a park, for which he promptly exchanged his heart, and so gradually within a stone's-throw or so of the river-side, where he determined not solely to bestow his affections but to settle for life. It may be seen that he was of an adventurous temperament, though he had thought fit to loosen his sword-belt. The pony-carriage, however, had been hired for the very special purpose of helping him to pass in review the lines of what he called country houses, cottages, or even sites for building, not too remote from sweet London: and as when Coelebs goes forth intending to pursue and obtain, there is no doubt of his bringing home a wife, the circumstance that there stood a house to let, in an airy situation, at a certain distance in hail of the metropolis he worshipped, was enough to kindle the General's enthusiasm. He would have taken the first he saw, had it not been for his daughter, who accompanied him, and at the age of eighteen was about to undertake the management of his house. Fortune, under Elizabeth Ople's guiding restraint, directed him to an epitome of the comforts. The place he fell upon is only to be described in the tongue of auctioneers, and for the first week after taking it he modestly followed them by terming it bijou. In time, when his own imagination, instigated by a state of something more than mere contentment, had been at work on it, he chose the happy phrase, 'a gentlemanly residence.' For it was, he declared, a small estate. There was a lodge to it, resembling two sentry-boxes forced into union, where in one half an old couple sat bent, in the other half lay compressed; there was a backdrive to discoverable stables; there was a bit of grass that would have appeared a meadow if magnified; and there was a wall round the kitchen-garden and a strip of wood round the flower-garden. The prying of the outside world was impossible. Comfort, fortification; and gentlemanliness made the place, as the General said, an ideal English home.

The compass of the estate was half an acre, and perhaps a perch or two, just the size for the hugging love General Ople was happiest in giving. He wisely decided to retain the old couple at the lodge, whose members were used to restriction, and also not to purchase a cow, that would have wanted pasture. With the old man, while the old woman attended to the bell at the handsome front entrance with its gilt-spiked gates, he undertook to do the gardening; a business he delighted in, so long as he could perform it in a gentlemanly manner, that is to say, so long as he was not overlooked. He was perfectly concealed from the road. Only one house, and curiously indeed, only one window of the house, and further to show the protection extended to Douro Lodge, that window an attic, overlooked him. And the house was empty.

The house (for who can hope, and who should desire a commodious house, with conservatories, aviaries, pond and boat-shed, and other joys of wealth, to remain unoccupied) was taken two seasons later by a lady, of whom Fame, rolling like a dust-cloud from the place she had left, reported that she was eccentric. The word is uninstructive: it does not frighten. In a lady of a certain age, it is rather a characteristic of aristocracy in retirement. And at least it implies wealth.

General Ople was very anxious to see her. He had the sentiment of humble respectfulness toward aristocracy, and there was that in riches which aroused his admiration. London, for instance, he was not afraid to say he thought the wonder of the world. He remarked, in addition, that the sacking of London would suffice to make every common soldier of the foreign army of occupation an independent gentleman for the term of his natural days. But this is a nightmare! said he, startling himself with an abhorrent dream of envy of those enriched invading officers: for Booty is the one lovely thing which the military mind can contemplate in the abstract. His habit was to go off in an explosion of heavy sighs when he had delivered himself so far, like a man at war with himself.

The lady arrived in time: she received the cards of the neighbourhood, and signalized her eccentricity by paying no attention to them, excepting the card of a Mrs. Baerens, who had audience of her at once. By express arrangement, the card of General Wilson Ople, as her nearest neighbour, followed the card of the rector, the social head of the district; and the rector was granted an interview, but Lady Camper was not at home to General Ople. She is of superior station to me, and may not wish to associate with me, the General modestly said. Nevertheless he was wounded: for in spite of himself, and without the slightest wish to obtrude his own person, as he explained the meaning that he had in him, his rank in the British army forced him to be the representative of it, in the absence of any one of a superior rank. So that he was professionally hurt, and his heart being in his profession, it may be honestly stated that he was wounded in his feelings, though he said no, and insisted on the distinction. Once a day his walk for constitutional exercise compelled him to pass before Lady Camper's windows, which were not bashfully withdrawn, as he said humorously of Douro Lodge, in the seclusion of half-pay, but bowed out imperiously, militarily, like a generalissimo on horseback, and had full command of the road and levels up to the swelling park-foliage. He went by at a smart stride, with a delicate depression of his upright bearing, as though hastening to greet a friend in view, whose hand was getting ready for the shake. This much would have been observed by a housemaid; and considering his fine figure and the peculiar shining silveriness of his hair, the acceleration of his gait was noticeable. When he drove by, the pony's right ear was flicked, to the extreme indignation of a mettlesome little animal. It ensued in consequence that the General was borne flying under the eyes of Lady Camper, and such pace displeasing him, he reduced it invariably at a step or two beyond the corner of her grounds.

But neither he nor his daughter Elizabeth attached importance to so trivial a circumstance. The General punctiliously avoided glancing at the windows during the passage past them, whether in his wild career or on foot. Elizabeth took a side-shot, as one looks at a wayside tree. Their speech concerning Lady Camper was an exchange of commonplaces over her loneliness: and this condition of hers was the more perplexing to General Ople on his hearing from his daughter that the lady was very fine-looking, and not so very old, as he had fancied eccentric ladies must be. The rector's account of her, too, excited the mind. She had informed him bluntly, that she now and then went to church to save appearances, but was not a church-goer, finding it impossible to support the length of the service; might, however, be reckoned in subscriptions for all the charities, and left her pew open to poor people, and none but the poor. She had travelled over Europe, and knew the East. Sketches in watercolours of the scenes she had visited adorned her walls, and a pair of pistols, that she had found useful, she affirmed, lay on the writing-desk in her drawing-room. General Ople gathered from the rector that she had a great contempt for men: yet it was curiously varied with lamentations over the weakness of women. 'Really she cannot possibly be an example of that,' said the General, thinking of the pistols.

Now, we learn from those who have studied women on the chess-board, and know what ebony or ivory will do along particular lines, or hopping, that men much talked about will take possession of their thoughts; and certainly the fact may be accepted for one of their moves. But the whole fabric of our knowledge of them, which we are taught to build on this originally acute perception, is shattered when we hear, that it is exactly the same, in the same degree, in proportion to the amount of work they have to do, exactly the same with men and their thoughts in the case of women much talked about. So it was with General Ople, and nothing is left for me to say except, that there is broader ground than the chessboard. I am earnest in protesting the similarity of the singular couples on common earth, because otherwise the General is in peril of the accusation that he is a feminine character; and not simply was he a gallant officer, and a veteran in gunpowder strife, he was also (and it is an extraordinary thing that a genuine humility did not prevent it, and did survive it) a lord and conqueror of the sex. He had done his pretty bit of mischief, all in the way of honour, of course, but hearts had knocked. And now, with his bright white hair, his close-brushed white whiskers on a face burnt brown, his clear-cut features, and a winning droop of his eyelids, there was powder in him still, if not shot.

There was a lamentable susceptibility to ladies' charms. On the other hand, for the protection of the sex, a remainder of shyness kept him from active enterprise and in the state of suffering, so long as indications of encouragement were wanting. He had killed the soft ones, who came to him, attracted by the softness in him, to be killed: but clever women alarmed and paralyzed him. Their aptness to question and require immediate sparkling answers; their demand for fresh wit, of a kind that is not furnished by publications which strike it into heads with a hammer, and supply it wholesale; their various reading; their power of ridicule too; made them awful in his contemplation.

Supposing (for the inflammable officer was now thinking, and deeply thinking, of a clever woman), supposing that Lady Camper's pistols were needed in her defence one night: at the first report proclaiming her extremity, valour might gain an introduction to her upon easy terms, and would not be expected to be witty. She would, perhaps, after the excitement, admit his masculine superiority, in the beautiful old fashion, by fainting in his arms. Such was the reverie he passingly indulged, and only so could he venture to hope for an acquaintance with the formidable lady who was his next neighbour. But the proud society of the burglarious denied him opportunity.

Meanwhile, he learnt that Lady Camper had a nephew, and the young gentleman was in a cavalry regiment. General Ople met him outside his gates, received and returned a polite salute, liked his appearance and manners and talked of him to Elizabeth, asking her if by chance she had seen him. She replied that she believed she had, and praised his horsemanship. The General discovered that he was an excellent sculler. His daughter was rowing him up the river when the young gentleman shot by, with a splendid stroke, in an outrigger, backed, and floating alongside presumed to enter into conversation, during which he managed to express regrets at his aunt's turn for solitariness. As they belonged to sister branches of the same Service, the General and Mr. Reginald Roller had a theme in common, and a passion. Elizabeth told her father that nothing afforded her so much pleasure as to hear him talk with Mr. Roller on military matters. General Ople assured her that it pleased him likewise. He began to spy about for Mr. Roller, and it sometimes occurred that they conversed across the wall; it could hardly be avoided. A hint or two, an undefinable flying allusion, gave the General to understand that Lady Camper had not been happy in her marriage. He was pained to think of her misfortune; but as she was not over forty, the disaster was, perhaps, not irremediable; that is to say, if she could be taught to extend her forgiveness to men, and abandon her solitude. 'If,' he said to his daughter, 'Lady Camper should by any chance be induced to contract a second alliance, she would, one might expect, be humanized, and we should have highly agreeable neighbours.' Elizabeth artlessly hoped for such an event to take place.

She rarely differed with her father, up to whom, taking example from the world around him, she looked as the pattern of a man of wise conduct.

And he was one; and though modest, he was in good humour with himself, approved himself, and could say, that without boasting of success, he was a satisfied man, until he met his touchstone in Lady Camper.

CHAPTER II

This is the pathetic matter of my story, and it requires pointing out, because he never could explain what it was that seemed to him so cruel in it, for he was no brilliant son of fortune, he was no great pretender, none of those who are logically displaced from the heights they have been raised to, manifestly created to show the moral in Providence. He was modest, retiring, humbly contented; a gentlemanly residence appeased his ambition. Popular, he could own that he was, but not meteorically; rather by reason of his willingness to receive light than his desire to shed it. Why, then, was the terrible test brought to bear upon him, of all men? He was one of us; no worse, and not strikingly or perilously better; and he could not but feel, in the bitterness of his reflections upon an inexplicable destiny, that the punishment befalling him, unmerited as it was, looked like absence of Design in the scheme of things, Above. It looked as if the blow had been dealt him by reckless chance. And to believe that, was for the mind of General Ople the having to return to his alphabet and recommence the ascent of the laborious mountain of understanding.

To proceed, the General's introduction to Lady Camper was owing to a message she sent him by her gardener, with a request that he would cut down a branch of a wychelm, obscuring her view across his grounds toward the river. The General consulted with his daughter, and came to the conclusion, that as he could hardly despatch a written reply to a verbal message, yet greatly wished to subscribe to the wishes of Lady Camper, the best thing for him to do was to apply for an interview. He sent word that he would wait on Lady Camper immediately, and betook himself forthwith to his toilette. She was the niece of an earl.

Elizabeth commended his appearance, 'passed him,' as he would have said; and well she might, for his hat, surtout, trousers and boots, were worthy of an introduction to Royalty. A touch of scarlet silk round the neck gave him bloom, and better than that, the blooming consciousness of it.

'You are not to be nervous, papa,' Elizabeth said.

'Not at all,' replied the General. 'I say, not at all, my dear,' he repeated, and so betrayed that he had fallen into the nervous mood. 'I was saying, I have known worse mornings than this.' He turned to her and smiled brightly, nodded, and set his face to meet the future.

He was absent an hour and a half.

He came back with his radiance a little subdued, by no means eclipsed; as, when experience has afforded us matter for thought, we cease to shine dazzlingly, yet are not clouded; the rays have merely grown serener. The sum of his impressions was conveyed in the reflective utterance—'It only shows, my dear, how different the reality is from our anticipation of it!'

Lady Camper had been charming; full of condescension, neighbourly, friendly, willing to be satisfied with the sacrifice of the smallest branch of the wych-elm, and only requiring that much for complimentary reasons.

Elizabeth wished to hear what they were, and she thought the request rather singular; but the General begged her to bear in mind, that they were dealing with a very extraordinary woman; 'highly accomplished, really exceedingly handsome,' he said to himself, aloud.

The reasons were, her liking for air and view, and desire to see into her neighbour's grounds without having to mount to the attic.

Elizabeth gave a slight exclamation, and blushed.

'So, my dear, we are objects of interest to her ladyship,' said the General.

He assured her that Lady Camper's manners were delightful. Strange to tell, she knew a great deal of his antecedent history, things he had not supposed were known; 'little matters,' he remarked, by which his daughter faintly conceived a reference to the conquests of his dashing days. Lady Camper had deigned to impart some of her own, incidentally; that she was of Welsh blood, and born among the mountains. 'She has a romantic look,' was the General's comment; and that her husband had been an insatiable traveller before he became an invalid, and had never cared for Art. 'Quite an extraordinary circumstance, with such a wife!' the General said.

He fell upon the wych-elm with his own hands, under cover of the leafage, and the next day he paid his respects to Lady Camper, to inquire if her ladyship saw any further obstruction to the view.

'None,' she replied. 'And now we shall see what the two birds will do.'

Apparently, then, she entertained an animosity to a pair of birds in the tree.

'Yes, yes; I say they chirp early in the morning,' said General Ople.

'At all hours.'

'The song of birds...?' he pleaded softly for nature.

'If the nest is provided for them; but I don't like vagabond chirping.'

The General perfectly acquiesced. This, in an engagement with a clever woman, is what you should do, or else you are likely to find yourself planted unawares in a high wind, your hat blown off, and your coat-tails anywhere; in other words, you will stand ridiculous in your bewilderment; and General Ople ever footed with the utmost caution to avoid that quagmire of the ridiculous. The extremer quags he had hitherto escaped; the smaller, into which he fell in his agile evasions of the big, he had hitherto been blest in finding none to notice.

He requested her ladyship's permission to present his daughter. Lady Camper sent in her card.

Elizabeth Ople beheld a tall, handsomely-mannered lady, with good features and penetrating dark eyes, an easy carriage of her person and an agreeable voice, but (the vision of her age flashed out under the compelling eyes of youth) fifty if a day. The rich colouring confessed to it. But she was very pleasing, and Elizabeth's perception dwelt on it only because her father's manly chivalry had defended the lady against one year more than forty.

The richness of the colouring, Elizabeth feared, was artificial, and it caused her ingenuous young blood a shudder. For we are so devoted to nature when the dame is flattering us with her gifts, that we loathe the substitute omitting to think how much less it is an imposition than a form of practical adoration of the genuine.

Our young detective, however, concealed her emotion of childish horror.

Lady Camper remarked of her, 'She seems honest, and that is the most we can hope of girls.'

'She is a jewel for an honest man,' the General sighed, 'some day!'

'Let us hope it will be a distant day.'

'Yet,' said the General, 'girls expect to marry.'

Lady Camper fixed her black eyes on him, but did not speak.

He told Elizabeth that her ladyship's eyes were exceedingly searching: 'Only,' said he, 'as I have nothing to hide, I am able to submit to inspection'; and he laughed slightly up to an arresting cough, and made the mantelpiece ornaments pass muster.

General Ople was the hero to champion a lady whose airs of haughtiness caused her to be somewhat backbitten. He assured everybody, that Lady Camper was much misunderstood; she was a most remarkable woman; she was a most affable and highly intelligent lady. Building up her attributes on a splendid climax, he declared she was pious, charitable, witty, and really an extraordinary artist. He laid particular stress on her artistic qualities, describing her power with the brush, her water-colour sketches, and also some immensely clever caricatures. As he talked of no one else, his friends heard enough of Lady Camper, who was anything but a favourite. The Pollingtons, the Wilders, the Wardens, the Baerens, the Goslings, and others of his acquaintance, talked of Lady Camper and General Ople rather maliciously. They were all City people, and they admired the General, but mourned that he should so abjectly have fallen at the feet of a lady as red with rouge as a railway bill. His not seeing it showed the state he was in. The sister of Mrs. Pollington, an amiable widow, relict of a large City warehouse, named Barcop, was chilled by a falling off in his attentions. His apology for not appearing at garden parties was, that he was engaged to wait on Lady Camper.

And at one time, her not condescending to exchange visits with the obsequious General was a topic fertile in irony. But she did condescend. Lady Camper came to his gate unexpectedly, rang the bell, and was let in like an ordinary visitor. It happened that the General was gardening—not the pretty occupation of pruning—he was digging—and of necessity his coat was off, and he was hot, dusty, unpresentable. From adoring earth as the mother of roses, you may pass into a lady's presence without purification; you cannot (or so the General thought) when you are caught in the act of adoring the mother of cabbages. And though he himself loved the cabbage equally with the rose, in his heart respected the vegetable yet more than he esteemed the flower, for he gloried in his kitchen garden, this was not a secret for the world to know, and he almost heeled over on his beam ends when word was brought of the extreme honour Lady Camper had done him. He worked his arms hurriedly into his fatigue jacket, trusting to get away to the house and spend a couple of minutes on his adornment; and with any other visitor it might have been accomplished, but Lady Camper disliked sitting alone in a room. She was on the square of lawn as the General stole along the walk. Had she kept her back to him, he might have rounded her like the shadow of a dial, undetected. She was frightfully acute of hearing. She turned while he was in the agony of hesitation, in a queer attitude, one leg on the march, projected by a frenzied tip-toe of the hinder leg, the very fatallest moment she could possibly have selected for unveiling him.

Of course there was no choice but to surrender on the spot.

He began to squander his dizzy wits in profuse apologies. Lady Camper simply spoke of the nice little nest of a garden, smelt the flowers, accepted a Niel rose and a Rohan, a Cline, a Falcot, and La France.

'A beautiful rose indeed,' she said of the latter, 'only it smells of macassar oil.'

'Really, it never struck me, I say it never struck me before,' rejoined the General, smelling it as at a pinch of snuff. 'I was saying, I always ....' And he tacitly, with the absurdest of smiles, begged permission to leave unterminated a sentence not in itself particularly difficult

'I have a nose,' observed Lady Camper.

Like the nobly-bred person she was, according to General Ople's version of the interview on his estate, when he stood before her in his gardening costume, she put him at his ease, or she exerted herself to do so; and if he underwent considerable anguish, it was the fault of his excessive scrupulousness regarding dress, propriety, appearance.

He conducted her at her request to the kitchen garden and the handful of paddock, the stables and coach-house, then back to the lawn.

'It is the home for a young couple,' she said.

'I am no longer young,' the General bowed, with the sigh peculiar to this confession. 'I say, I am no longer young, but I call the place a gentlemanly residence. I was saying, I...'

'Yes, yes!' Lady Camper tossed her head, half closing her eyes, with a contraction of the brows, as if in pain.

He perceived a similar expression whenever he spoke of his residence.

Perhaps it recalled happier days to enter such a nest. Perhaps it had been such a home for a young couple that she had entered on her marriage with Sir Scrope Camper, before he inherited his title and estates.

The General was at a loss to conceive what it was.

It recurred at another mention of his idea of the nature of the residence. It was almost a paroxysm. He determined not to vex her reminiscences again; and as this resolution directed his mind to his residence, thinking it pre-eminently gentlemanly, his tongue committed the error of repeating it, with 'gentleman-like' for a variation.

Elizabeth was out—he knew not where. The housemaid informed him, that Miss Elizabeth was out rowing on the water.

'Is she alone?' Lady Camper inquired of him.

'I fancy so,' the General replied.

'The poor child has no mother.'

'It has been a sad loss to us both, Lady Camper.'

'No doubt. She is too pretty to go out alone.'

'I can trust her.'

'Girls!'

'She has the spirit of a man.'

'That is well. She has a spirit; it will be tried.'

The General modestly furnished an instance or two of her spiritedness.

Lady Camper seemed to like this theme; she looked graciously interested.

'Still, you should not suffer her to go out alone,' she said.

'I place implicit confidence in her,' said the General; and Lady Camper gave it up.

She proposed to walk down the lanes to the river-side, to meet Elizabeth returning.

The General manifested alacrity checked by reluctance. Lady Camper had told him she objected to sit in a strange room by herself; after that, he could hardly leave her to dash upstairs to change his clothes; yet how, attired as he was, in a fatigue jacket, that warned him not to imagine his back view, and held him constantly a little to the rear of Lady Camper, lest she should be troubled by it;—and he knew the habit of the second rank to criticise the front—how consent to face the outer world in such style side by side with the lady he admired?

'Come,' said she; and he shot forward a step, looking as if he had missed fire.

'Are you not coming, General?'

He advanced mechanically.

Not a soul met them down the lanes, except a little one, to whom Lady Camper gave a small silver-piece, because she was a picture.

The act of charity sank into the General's heart, as any pretty performance will do upon a warm waxen bed.

Lady Camper surprised him by answering his thoughts. 'No; it's for my own pleasure.'

Presently she said, 'Here they are.'

General Ople beheld his daughter by the river-side at the end of the lane, under escort of Mr. Reginald Rolles.

It was another picture, and a pleasing one. The young lady and the young gentleman wore boating hats, and were both dressed in white, and standing by or just turning from the outrigger and light skiff they were about to leave in charge of a waterman. Elizabeth stretched a finger at arm's-length, issuing directions, which Mr. Rolles took up and worded further to the man, for the sake of emphasis; and he, rather than Elizabeth, was guilty of the half-start at sight of the persons who were approaching.

'My nephew, you should know, is intended for a working soldier,' said Lady Camper; 'I like that sort of soldier best.'

General Ople drooped his shoulders at the personal compliment.

She resumed. 'His pay is a matter of importance to him. You are aware of the smallness of a subaltern's pay.

'I,' said the General, 'I say I feel my poor half-pay, having always been a working soldier myself, very important, I was saying, very important to me!'

'Why did you retire?'

Her interest in him seemed promising. He replied conscientiously, 'Beyond the duties of General of Brigade, I could not, I say I could not, dare to aspire; I can accept and execute orders; I shrink from responsibility!'

'It is a pity,' said she, 'that you were not, like my nephew Reginald, entirely dependent on your profession.'

She laid such stress on her remark, that the General, who had just expressed a very modest estimate of his abilities, was unable to reject the flattery of her assuming him to be a man of some fortune. He coughed, and said, 'Very little.' The thought came to him that he might have to make a statement to her in time, and he emphasized, 'Very little indeed. Sufficient,' he assured her, 'for a gentlemanly appearance.'

'I have given you your warning,' was her inscrutable rejoinder, uttered within earshot of the young people, to whom, especially to Elizabeth, she was gracious. The damsel's boating uniform was praised, and her sunny flush of exercise and exposure.

Lady Camper regretted that she could not abandon her parasol: 'I freckle so easily.'

The General, puzzling over her strange words about a warning, gazed at the red rose of art on her cheek with an air of profound abstraction.

'I freckle so easily,' she repeated, dropping her parasol to defend her face from the calculating scrutiny.

'I burn brown,' said Elizabeth.

Lady Camper laid the bud of a Falcot rose against the young girl's cheek, but fetched streams of colour, that overwhelmed the momentary comparison of the sunswarthed skin with the rich dusky yellow of the rose in its deepening inward to soft brown.

Reginald stretched his hand for the privileged flower, and she let him take it; then she looked at the General; but the General was looking, with his usual air of satisfaction, nowhere.

CHAPTER III

'Lady Camper is no common enigma,' General Ople observed to his daughter.

Elizabeth inclined to be pleased with her, for at her suggestion the General had bought a couple of horses, that she might ride in the park, accompanied by her father or the little groom. Still, the great lady was hard to read. She tested the resources of his income by all sorts of instigation to expenditure, which his gallantry could not withstand; she encouraged him to talk of his deeds in arms; she was friendly, almost affectionate, and most bountiful in the presents of fruit, peaches, nectarines, grapes, and hot-house wonders, that she showered on his table; but she was an enigma in her evident dissatisfaction with him for something he seemed to have left unsaid. And what could that be?

At their last interview she had asked him, 'Are you sure, General, you have nothing more to tell me?'

And as he remarked, when relating it to Elizabeth, 'One might really be tempted to misapprehend her ladyship's... I say one might commit oneself beyond recovery. Now, my dear, what do you think she intended?'

Elizabeth was 'burning brown,' or darkly blushing, as her manner was.

She answered, 'I am certain you know of nothing that would interest her; nothing, unless...'

'Well?' the General urged her.

'How can I speak it, papa?'

'You really can't mean...'

'Papa, what could I mean?'

'If I were fool enough!' he murmured. 'No, no, I am an old man. I was saying, I am past the age of folly.'

One day Elizabeth came home from her ride in a thoughtful mood. She had not, further than has been mentioned, incited her father to think of the age of folly; but voluntarily or not, Lady Camper had, by an excess of graciousness amounting to downright invitation; as thus, 'Will you persist in withholding your confidence from me, General?' She added, 'I am not so difficult a person.' These prompting speeches occurred on the morning of the day when Elizabeth sat at his table, after a long ride into the country, profoundly meditative.

A note was handed to General Ople, with the request that he would step in to speak with Lady Camper in the course of the evening, or next morning. Elizabeth waited till his hat was on, then said, 'Papa, on my ride to-day, I met Mr. Rolles.'

'I am glad you had an agreeable escort, my dear.'

'I could not refuse his company.'

'Certainly not. And where did you ride?'

'To a beautiful valley; and there we met.... '

'Her ladyship?'

'Yes.'

'She always admires you on horseback.'

'So you know it, papa, if she should speak of it.'

'And I am bound to tell you, my child,' said the General, 'that this morning Lady Camper's manner to me was... if I were a fool... I say, this morning I beat a retreat, but apparently she... I see no way out of it, supposing she...'

'I am sure she esteems you, dear papa,' said Elizabeth. 'You take to her, my dear?' the General inquired anxiously; 'a little?—a little afraid of her?'

'A little,' Elizabeth replied, 'only a little.'

'Don't be agitated about me.'

'No, papa; you are sure to do right.'

'But you are trembling.'

'Oh! no. I wish you success.'

General Ople was overjoyed to be reinforced by his daughter's good wishes. He kissed her to thank her. He turned back to her to kiss her again. She had greatly lightened the difficulty at least of a delicate position.

It was just like the imperious nature of Lady Camper to summon him in the evening to terminate the conversation of the morning, from the visible pitfall of which he had beaten a rather precipitate retreat. But if his daughter cordially wished him success, and Lady Camper offered him the crown of it, why then he had only to pluck up spirit, like a good commander who has to pass a fordable river in the enemy's presence; a dash, a splash, a rattling volley or two, and you are over, established on the opposite bank. But you must be positive of victory, otherwise, with the river behind you, your new position is likely to be ticklish. So the General entered Lady Camper's drawing-room warily, watching the fair enemy. He knew he was captivating, his old conquests whispered in his ears, and her reception of him all but pointed to a footstool at her feet. He might have fallen there at once, had he not remembered a hint that Mr. Reginald Rolles had dropped concerning Lady Camper's amazing variability.

Lady Camper began.

'General, you ran away from me this morning. Let me speak. And, by the way, I must reproach you; you should not have left it to me. Things have now gone so far that I cannot pretend to be blind. I know your feelings as a father. Your daughter's happiness...'

'My lady,' the General interposed, 'I have her distinct assurance that it is, I say it is wrapt up in mine.'

'Let me speak. Young people will say anything. Well, they have a certain excuse for selfishness; we have not. I am in some degree bound to my nephew; he is my sister's son.'

'Assuredly, my lady. I would not stand in his light, be quite assured. If I am, I was saying if I am not mistaken, I... and he is, or has the making of an excellent soldier in him, and is likely to be a distinguished cavalry officer.'

'He has to carve his own way in the world, General.'

'All good soldiers have, my lady. And if my position is not, after a considerable term of service, I say if...'

'To continue,' said Lady Camper: 'I never have liked early marriages. I was married in my teens before I knew men. Now I do know them, and now....'

The General plunged forward: 'The honour you do us now:—a mature experience is worth:—my dear Lady Camper, I have admired you:—and your objection to early marriages cannot apply to... indeed, madam, vigour, they say... though youth, of course... yet young people, as you observe... and I have, though perhaps my reputation is against it, I was saying I have a natural timidity with your sex, and I am grey-headed, white-headed, but happily without a single malady.'

Lady Camper's brows showed a trifling bewilderment. 'I am speaking of these young people, General Ople.'

'I consent to everything beforehand, my dear lady. He should be, I say Mr. Rolles should be provided for.'

'So should she, General, so should Elizabeth.'

'She shall be, she will, dear madam. What I have, with your permission, if—good heaven! Lady Camper, I scarcely know where I am. She would .... I shall not like to lose her: you would not wish it. In time she will.... she has every quality of a good wife.'

'There, stay there, and be intelligible,' said Lady Camper. 'She has every quality. Money should be one of them. Has she money?'

'Oh! my lady,' the General exclaimed, 'we shall not come upon your purse when her time comes.'

'Has she ten thousand pounds?'

'Elizabeth? She will have, at her father's death... but as for my income, it is moderate, and only sufficient to maintain a gentlemanly appearance in proper self-respect. I make no show. I say I make no show. A wealthy marriage is the last thing on earth I should have aimed at. I prefer quiet and retirement. Personally, I mean. That is my personal taste. But if the lady... I say if it should happen that the lady ... and indeed I am not one to press a suit: but if she who distinguishes and honours me should chance to be wealthy, all I can do is to leave her wealth at her disposal, and that I do: I do that unreservedly. I feel I am very confused, alarmingly confused. Your ladyship merits a superior... I trust I have not... I am entirely at your ladyship's mercy.'

'Are you prepared, if your daughter is asked in marriage, to settle ten thousand pounds on her, General Ople?'

The General collected himself. In his heart he thoroughly appreciated the moral beauty of Lady Camper's extreme solicitude on behalf of his daughter's provision; but he would have desired a postponement of that and other material questions belonging to a distant future until his own fate was decided.

So he said: 'Your ladyship's generosity is very marked. I say it is very marked.'

'How, my good General Ople! how is it marked in any degree?' cried Lady Camper. 'I am not generous. I don't pretend to be; and certainly I don't want the young people to think me so. I want to be just. I have assumed that you intend to be the same. Then will you do me the favour to reply to me?'

The General smiled winningly and intently, to show her that he prized her, and would not let her escape his eulogies.

'Marked, in this way, dear madam, that you think of my daughter's future more than I. I say, more than her father himself does. I know I ought to speak more warmly, I feel warmly. I was never an eloquent man, and if you take me as a soldier, I am, as, I have ever been in the service, I was saying I am Wilson Ople, of the grade of General, to be relied on for executing orders; and, madam, you are Lady Camper, and you command me. I cannot be more precise. In fact, it is the feeling of the necessity for keeping close to the business that destroys what I would say. I am in fact lamentably incompetent to conduct my own case.'

Lady Camper left her chair.

'Dear me, this is very strange, unless I am singularly in error,' she said.

The General now faintly guessed that he might be in error, for his part.

But he had burned his ships, blown up his bridges; retreat could not be thought of.

He stood, his head bent and appealing to her sideface, like one pleadingly in pursuit, and very deferentially, with a courteous vehemence, he entreated first her ladyship's pardon for his presumption, and then the gift of her ladyship's hand.

As for his language, it was the tongue of General Ople. But his bearing was fine. If his clipped white silken hair spoke of age, his figure breathed manliness. He was a picture, and she loved pictures.

For his own sake, she begged him to cease. She dreaded to hear of something 'gentlemanly.'

'This is a new idea to me, my dear General,' she said. 'You must give me time. People at our age have to think of fitness. Of course, in a sense, we are both free to do as we like. Perhaps I may be of some aid to you. My preference is for absolute independence. And I wished to talk of a different affair. Come to me tomorrow. Do not be hurt if I decide that we had better remain as we are.'

The General bowed. His efforts, and the wavering of the fair enemy's flag, had inspired him with a positive re-awakening of masculine passion to gain this fortress. He said well: 'I have, then, the happiness, madam, of being allowed to hope until to-morrow?'

She replied, 'I would not deprive you of a moment of happiness. Bring good sense with you when you do come.'

The General asked eagerly, 'I have your ladyship's permission to come early?'

'Consult your happiness,' she answered; and if to his mind she seemed returning to the state of enigma, it was on the whole deliciously. She restored him his youth. He told Elizabeth that night; he really must begin to think of marrying her to some worthy young fellow. 'Though,' said he, with an air of frank intoxication, 'my opinion is, the young ones are not so lively as the old in these days, or I should have been besieged before now.'

The exact substance of the interview he forbore to relate to his inquisitive daughter, with a very honourable discretion.

CHAPTER IV

Elizabeth came riding home to breakfast from a gallop round the park, and passing Lady Camper's gates, received the salutation of her parasol. Lady Camper talked with her through the bars. There was not a sign to tell of a change or twist in her neighbourly affability. She remarked simply enough, that it was her nephew's habit to take early gallops, and possibly Elizabeth might have seen him, for his quarters were proximate; but she did not demand an answer. She had passed a rather restless night, she said. 'How is the General?'

'Papa must have slept soundly, for he usually calls to me through his door when he hears I am up,' said Elizabeth.

Lady Camper nodded kindly and walked on.

Early in the morning General Ople was ready for battle. His forces were, the anticipation of victory, a carefully arranged toilet, and an unaccustomed spirit of enterprise in the realms of speech; for he was no longer in such awe of Lady Camper.

'You have slept well?' she inquired.

'Excellently, my lady:

'Yes, your daughter tells me she heard you, as she went by your door in the morning for a ride to meet my nephew. You are, I shall assume, prepared for business.'

'Elizabeth?... to meet...?' General Ople's impression of anything extraneous to his emotion was feeble and passed instantly. 'Prepared! Oh, certainly'; and he struck in a compliment on her ladyship's fresh morning bloom.

'It can hardly be visible,' she responded; 'I have not painted yet.'

'Does your ladyship proceed to your painting in the very early morning?'

'Rouge. I rouge.'

'Dear me! I should not have supposed it.'

'You have speculated on it very openly, General. I remember your trying to see a freckle through the rouge; but the truth is, I am of a supernatural paleness if I do not rouge, so I do. You understand, therefore, I have a false complexion. Now to business.'

'If your ladyship insists on calling it business. I have little to offer—myself!'

'You have a gentlemanly residence.'

'It is, my lady, it is. It is a bijou.'

'Ah!' Lady Camper sighed dejectedly.

'It is a perfect bijou!'

'Oblige me, General, by not pronouncing the French word as if you were swearing by something in English, like a trooper.'

General Ople started, admitted that the word was French, and apologized for his pronunciation. Her variability was now visible over a corner of the battlefield like a thunder-cloud.

'The business we have to discuss concerns the young people, General.'

'Yes,' brightened by this, he assented: 'Yes, dear Lady Camper; it is a part of the business; it is a secondary part; it has to be discussed; I say I subscribe beforehand. I may say, that honouring, esteeming you as I do, and hoping ardently for your consent....

'They must have a home and an income, General.'

'I presume, dearest lady, that Elizabeth will be welcome in your home. I certainly shall never chase Reginald out of mine.'

Lady Camper threw back her head. 'Then you are not yet awake, or you practice the art of sleeping with open eyes! Now listen to me. I rouge, I have told you. I like colour, and I do not like to see wrinkles or have them seen. Therefore I rouge. I do not expect to deceive the world so flagrantly as to my age, and you I would not deceive for a moment. I am seventy.'

The effect of this noble frankness on the General, was to raise him from his chair in a sitting posture as if he had been blown up.

Her countenance was inexorably imperturbable under his alternate blinking and gazing that drew her close and shot her distant, like a mysterious toy.

'But,' said she, 'I am an artist; I dislike the look of extreme age, so I conceal it as well as I can. You are very kind to fall in with the deception: an innocent and, I think, a proper one, before the world, though not to the gentleman who does me the honour to propose to me for my hand. You desire to settle our business first. You esteem me; I suppose you mean as much as young people mean when they say they love. Do you? Let us come to an understanding.'

'I can,' the melancholy General gasped, 'I say I can—I cannot—I cannot credit your ladyship's...'

'You are at liberty to call me Angela.'

'Ange...' he tried it, and in shame relapsed. 'Madam, yes. Thanks.'

'Ah,' cried Lady Camper, 'do not use these vulgar contractions of decent speech in my presence. I abhor the word "thanks." It is fit for fribbles.'

'Dear me, I have used it all my life,' groaned the General.

'Then, for the remainder, be it understood that you renounce it. To continue, my age is...'

'Oh, impossible, impossible,' the General almost wailed; there was really a crack in his voice.

'Advancing to seventy. But, like you, I am happy to say I have not a malady. I bring no invalid frame to a union that necessitates the leaving of the front door open day and night to the doctor. My belief is, I could follow my husband still on a campaign, if he were a warrior instead of a pensioner.'

General Ople winced.

He was about to say humbly, 'As General of Brigade...'

'Yes, yes, you want a commanding officer, and that I have seen, and that has caused me to meditate on your proposal,' she interrupted him; while he, studying her countenance hard, with the painful aspect of a youth who lashes a donkey memory in an examination by word of mouth, attempted to marshal her signs of younger years against her awful confession of the extremely ancient, the witheringly ancient. But for the manifest rouge, manifest in spite of her declaration that she had not yet that morning proceeded to her paintbrush, he would have thrown down his glove to challenge her on the subject of her age. She had actually charms. Her mouth had a charm; her eyes were lively; her figure, mature if you like, was at least full and good; she stood upright, she had a queenly seat. His mental ejaculation was, 'What a wonderful constitution!'

By a lapse of politeness, he repeated it to himself half aloud; he was shockingly nervous.

'Yes, I have finer health than many a younger woman,' she said. 'An ordinary calculation would give me twenty good years to come. I am a widow, as you know. And, by the way, you have a leaning for widows. Have you not? I thought I had heard of a widow Barcop in this parish. Do not protest. I assure you I am a stranger to jealousy. My income...'

The General raised his hands.

'Well, then,' said the cool and self-contained lady, 'before I go farther, I may ask you, knowing what you have forced me to confess, are you still of the same mind as to marriage? And one moment, General. I promise you most sincerely that your withdrawing a step shall not, as far as it touches me, affect my neighbourly and friendly sentiments; not in any degree. Shall we be as we were?'

Lady Camper extended her delicate hand to him.

He took it respectfully, inspected the aristocratic and unshrunken fingers, and kissing them, said, 'I never withdraw from a position, unless I am beaten back. Lady Camper, I...'

'My name is Angela.'

The General tried again: he could not utter the name.

To call a lady of seventy Angela is difficult in itself. It is, it seems, thrice difficult in the way of courtship.

'Angela!' said she.

'Yes. I say, there is not a more beautiful female name, dear Lady Camper.'

'Spare me that word "female" as long as you live. Address me by that name, if you please.'

The General smiled. The smile was meant for propitiation and sweetness. It became a brazen smile.

'Unless you wish to step back,' said she.

'Indeed, no. I am happy, Lady Camper. My life is yours. I say, my life is devoted to you, dear madam.'

'Angela!'

General Ople was blushingly delivered of the name.

'That will do,' said she. 'And as I think it possible one may be admired too much as an artist, I must request you to keep my number of years a secret.'

'To the death, madam,' said the General.

'And now we will take a turn in the garden, Wilson Ople. And beware of one thing, for a commencement, for you are full of weeds, and I mean to pluck out a few: never call any place a gentlemanly residence in my hearing, nor let it come to my ears that you have been using the phrase elsewhere. Don't express astonishment. At present it is enough that I dislike it. But this only,' Lady Camper added, 'this only if it is not your intention to withdraw from your position.'

'Madam, my lady, I was saying—hem!—Angela, I could not wish to withdraw.'

Lady Camper leaned with some pressure on his arm, observing, 'You have a curious attachment to antiquities.'

'My dear lady, it is your mind; I say, it is your mind: I was saying, I am in love with your mind,' the General endeavoured to assure her, and himself too.

'Or is it my powers as an artist?'

'Your mind, your extraordinary powers of mind.'

'Well,' said Lady Camper, 'a veteran General of Brigade is as good a crutch as a childless old grannam can have.'

And as a crutch, General Ople, parading her grounds with the aged woman, found himself used and treated.

The accuracy of his perceptions might be questioned. He was like a man stunned by some great tropical fruit, which responds to the longing of his eyes by falling on his head; but it appeared to him, that she increased in bitterness at every step they took, as if determined to make him realize her wrinkles.

He was even so inconsequent, or so little recognized his position, as to object in his heart to hear himself called Wilson.

It is true that she uttered Wilsonople as if the names formed one word. And on a second occasion (when he inclined to feel hurt) she remarked, 'I fear me, Wilsonople, if we are to speak plainly, thou art but a fool.' He, perhaps, naturally objected to that. He was, however, giddy, and barely knew.

Yet once more the magical woman changed. All semblance of harshness, and harridan-like spike-tonguedness vanished when she said adieu.

The astronomer, looking at the crusty jag and scoria of the magnified moon through his telescope, and again with naked eyes at the soft-beaming moon, when the crater-ridges are faint as eyebrow-pencillings, has a similar sharp alternation of prospect to that which mystified General Ople.

But between watching an orb that is only variable at our caprice, and contemplating a woman who shifts and quivers ever with her own, how vast the difference!

And consider that this woman is about to be one's wife! He could have believed (if he had not known full surely that such things are not) he was in the hands of a witch.

Lady Camper's 'adieu' was perfectly beautiful—a kind, cordial, intimate, above all, to satisfy his present craving, it was a lady-like adieu—the adieu of a delicate and elegant woman, who had hardly left her anchorage by forty to sail into the fifties.

Alas! he had her word for it, that she was not less than seventy. And, worse, she had betrayed most melancholy signs of sourness and agedness as soon as he had sworn himself to her fast and fixed.

'The road is open to you to retreat,' were her last words.

'My road,' he answered gallantly, 'is forward.'

He was drawing backward as he said it, and something provoked her to smile.

CHAPTER V

It is a noble thing to say that your road is forward, and it befits a man of battles. General Ople was too loyal a gentleman to think of any other road. Still, albeit not gifted with imagination, he could not avoid the feeling that he had set his face to Winter. He found himself suddenly walking straight into the heart of Winter, and a nipping Winter. For her ladyship had proved acutely nipping. His little customary phrases, to which Lady Camper objected, he could see no harm in whatever. Conversing with her in the privacy of domestic life would never be the flowing business that it is for other men. It would demand perpetual vigilance, hop, skip, jump, flounderings, and apologies.

This was not a pleasing prospect.

On the other hand, she was the niece of an earl. She was wealthy. She might be an excellent friend to Elizabeth; and she could be, when she liked, both commandingly and bewitchingly ladylike.

Good! But he was a General Officer of not more than fifty-five, in his full vigour, and she a woman of seventy!

The prospect was bleak. It resembled an outlook on the steppes. In point of the discipline he was to expect, he might be compared to a raw recruit, and in his own home!

However, she was a woman of mind. One would be proud of her.

But did he know the worst of her? A dreadful presentiment, that he did not know the worst of her, rolled an ocean of gloom upon General Ople, striking out one solitary thought in the obscurity, namely, that he was about to receive punishment for retiring from active service to a life of ease at a comparatively early age, when still in marching trim. And the shadow of the thought was, that he deserved the punishment!

He was in his garden with the dawn. Hard exercise is the best of opiates for dismal reflections. The General discomposed his daughter by offering to accompany her on her morning ride before breakfast. She considered that it would fatigue him. 'I am not a man of eighty!' he cried. He could have wished he had been.

He led the way to the park, where they soon had sight of young Rolles, who checked his horse and spied them like a vedette, but, perceiving that he had been seen, came cantering, and hailing the General with hearty wonderment.

'And what's this the world says, General?' said he. 'But we all applaud your taste. My aunt Angela was the handsomest woman of her time.'

The General murmured in confusion, 'Dear me!' and looked at the young man, thinking that he could not have known the time.

'Is all arranged, my dear General?'

'Nothing is arranged, and I beg—I say I beg... I came out for fresh air and pace.'..

The General rode frantically.

In spite of the fresh air, he was unable to eat at breakfast. He was bound, of course, to present himself to Lady Camper, in common civility, immediately after it.

And first, what were the phrases he had to avoid uttering in her presence? He could remember only the 'gentlemanly residence.' And it was a gentlemanly residence, he thought as he took leave of it. It was one, neatly named to fit the place. Lady Camper is indeed a most eccentric person! he decided from his experience of her.

He was rather astonished that young Rolles should have spoken so coolly of his aunt's leaning to matrimony; but perhaps her exact age was unknown to the younger members of her family.

This idea refreshed him by suggesting the extremely honourable nature of Lady Camper's uncomfortable confession.

He himself had an uncomfortable confession to make. He would have to speak of his income. He was living up to the edges of it.

She is an upright woman, and I must be the same! he said, fortunately not in her hearing.

The subject was disagreeable to a man sensitive on the topic of money, and feeling that his prudence had recently been misled to keep up appearances.

Lady Camper was in her garden, reclining under her parasol. A chair was beside her, to which, acknowledging the salutation of her suitor, she waved him.

'You have met my nephew Reginald this morning, General?'

'Curiously, in the park, this morning, before breakfast, I did, yes. Hem! I, I say I did meet him. Has your ladyship seen him?'

'No. The park is very pretty in the early morning.'

'Sweetly pretty.'

Lady Camper raised her head, and with the mildness of assured dictatorship, pronounced: 'Never say that before me.'

'I submit, my lady,' said the poor scourged man.

'Why, naturally you do. Vulgar phrases have to be endured, except when our intimates are guilty, and then we are not merely offended, we are compromised by them. You are still of the mind in which you left me yesterday? You are one day older. But I warn you, so am I.'

'Yes, my lady, we cannot, I say we cannot check time. Decidedly of the same mind. Quite so.'

'Oblige me by never saying "Quite so." My lawyer says it. It reeks of the City of London. And do not look so miserable.'

'I, madam? my dear lady!' the General flashed out in a radiance that dulled instantly.

'Well,' said she cheerfully, 'and you're for the old woman?'

'For Lady Camper.'

'You are seductive in your flatteries, General. Well, then, we have to speak of business.'

'My affairs—' General Ople was beginning, with perturbed forehead; but Lady Camper held up her finger.

'We will touch on your affairs incidentally. Now listen to me, and do not exclaim until I have finished. You know that these two young ones have been whispering over the wall for some months. They have been meeting on the river and in the park habitually, apparently with your consent.'

'My lady!'

'I did not say with your connivance.'

'You mean my daughter Elizabeth?'

'And my nephew Reginald. We have named them, if that advances us. Now, the end of such meetings is marriage, and the sooner the better, if they are to continue. I would rather they should not; I do not hold it good for young soldiers to marry. But if they do, it is very certain that their pay will not support a family; and in a marriage of two healthy young people, we have to assume the existence of the family. You have allowed matters to go so far that the boy is hot in love; I suppose the girl is, too. She is a nice girl. I do not object to her personally. But I insist that a settlement be made on her before I give my nephew one penny. Hear me out, for I am not fond of business, and shall be glad to have done with these explanations. Reginald has nothing of his own. He is my sister's son, and I loved her, and rather like the boy. He has at present four hundred a year from me. I will double it, on the condition that you at once make over ten thousand—not less; and let it be yes or no!—to be settled on your daughter and go to her children, independent of the husband—cela va sans dire. Now you may speak, General.'

The General spoke, with breath fetched from the deeps:

'Ten thousand pounds! Hem! Ten! Hem, frankly—ten, my lady! One's income—I am quite taken by surprise. I say Elizabeth's conduct—though, poor child! it is natural to her to seek a mate, I mean, to accept a mate and an establishment, and Reginald is a very hopeful fellow—I was saying, they jump on me out of an ambush, and I wish them every happiness. And she is an ardent soldier, and a soldier she must marry. But ten thousand!'

'It is to secure the happiness of your daughter, General.'

'Pounds! my lady. It would rather cripple me.'

'You would have my house, General; you would have the moiety, as the lawyers say, of my purse; you would have horses, carriages, servants; I do not divine what more you would wish to have.'

'But, madam—a pensioner on the Government! I can look back on past services, I say old services, and I accept my position. But, madam, a pensioner on my wife, bringing next to nothing to the common estate! I fear my self-respect would, I say would...'

'Well, and what would it do, General Ople?'

'I was saying, my self-respect as my wife's pensioner, my lady. I could not come to her empty-handed.'

'Do you expect that I should be the person to settle money on your daughter, to save her from mischances? A rakish husband, for example; for Reginald is young, and no one can guess what will be made of him.'

'Undoubtedly your ladyship is correct. We might try absence for the poor girl. I have no female relation, but I could send her to the sea-side to a lady-friend.'

'General Ople, I forbid you, as you value my esteem, ever—and I repeat, I forbid you ever—to afflict my ears with that phrase, "lady-friend!"'

The General blinked in a state of insurgent humility.

These incessant whippings could not but sting the humblest of men; and 'lady-friend,' he was sure, was a very common term, used, he was sure, in the very best society. He had never heard Her Majesty speak at levees of a lady-friend, but he was quite sure that she had one; and if so, what could be the objection to her subjects mentioning it as a term to suit their own circumstances?

He was harassed and perplexed by old Lady Camper's treatment of him, and he resolved not to call her Angela even upon supplication—not that day, at least.

She said, 'You will not need to bring property of any kind to the common estate; I neither look for it nor desire it. The generous thing for you to do would be to give your daughter all you have, and come to me.'

'But, Lady Camper, if I denude myself or curtail my income—a man at his wife's discretion, I was saying a man at his wife's mercy...!'

General Ople was really forced, by his manly dignity, to make this protest on its behalf. He did not see how he could have escaped doing so; he was more an agent than a principal. 'My wife's mercy,' he said again, but simply as a herald proclaiming superior orders.

Lady Camper's brows were wrathful. A deep blood-crimson overcame the rouge, and gave her a terrible stormy look.

'The congress now ceases to sit, and the treaty is not concluded,' was all she said.

She rose, bowed to him, 'Good morning, General,' and turned her back.

He sighed. He was a free man. But this could not be denied—whatever the lady's age, she was a grand woman in her carriage, and when looking angry, she had a queenlike aspect that raised her out of the reckoning of time.

So now he knew there was a worse behind what he had previously known. He was precipitate in calling it the worst. 'Now,' said he to himself, 'I know the worst!'

No man should ever say it. Least of all, one who has entered into relations with an eccentric lady.

CHAPTER VI

Politeness required that General Ople should not appear to rejoice in his dismissal as a suitor, and should at least make some show of holding himself at the beck of a reconsidering mind. He was guilty of running up to London early next day, and remaining absent until nightfall; and he did the same on the two following days. When he presented himself at Lady Camper's lodge-gates, the astonishing intelligence, that her ladyship had departed for the Continent and Egypt gave him qualms of remorse, which assumed a more definite shape in something like awe of her triumphant constitution. He forbore to mention her age, for he was the most honourable of men, but a habit of tea-table talkativeness impelled him to say and repeat an idea that had visited him, to the effect, that Lady Camper was one of those wonderful women who are comparable to brilliant generals, and defend themselves from the siege of Time by various aggressive movements. Fearful of not being understood, owing to the rarity of the occasions when the squat plain squad of honest Saxon regulars at his command were called upon to explain an idea, he re-cast the sentence. But, as it happened that the regulars of his vocabulary were not numerous, and not accustomed to work upon thoughts and images, his repetitions rather succeeded in exposing the piece of knowledge he had recently acquired than in making his meaning plainer. So we need not marvel that his acquaintances should suppose him to be secretly aware of an extreme degree in which Lady Camper was a veteran.

General Ople entered into the gaieties of the neighbourhood once more, and passed through the Winter cheerfully. In justice to him, however, it should be said that to the intent dwelling of his mind upon Lady Camper, and not to the festive life he led, was due his entire ignorance of his daughter's unhappiness. She lived with him, and yet it was in other houses he learnt that she was unhappy. After his last interview with Lady Camper, he had informed Elizabeth of the ruinous and preposterous amount of money demanded of him for a settlement upon her and Elizabeth, like the girl of good sense that she was, had replied immediately, 'It could not be thought of, papa.'

He had spoken to Reginald likewise. The young man fell into a dramatic tearing-of-hair and long-stride fury, not ill becoming an enamoured dragoon. But he maintained that his aunt, though an eccentric, was a cordially kind woman. He seemed to feel, if he did not partly hint, that the General might have accepted Lady Camper's terms. The young officer could no longer be welcome at Douro Lodge, so the General paid him a morning call at his quarters, and was distressed to find him breakfasting very late, tapping eggs that he forgot to open—one of the surest signs of a young man downright and deep in love, as the General knew from experience—and surrounded by uncut sporting journals of past weeks, which dated from the day when his blow had struck him, as accurately as the watch of the drowned man marks his minute. Lady Camper had gone to Italy, and was in communication with her nephew: Reginald was not further explicit. His legs were very prominent in his despair, and his fingers frequently performed the part of blunt combs; consequently the General was impressed by his passion for Elizabeth. The girl who, if she was often meditative, always met his eyes with a smile, and quietly said 'Yes, papa,' and 'No, papa,' gave him little concern as to the state of her feelings. Yet everybody said now that she was unhappy. Mrs. Barcop, the widow, raised her voice above the rest. So attentive was she to Elizabeth that the General had it kindly suggested to him, that some one was courting him through his daughter. He gazed at the widow. Now she was not much past thirty; and it was really singular—he could have laughed—thinking of Mrs. Barcop set him persistently thinking of Lady Camper. That is to say, his mad fancy reverted from the lady of perhaps thirty-five to the lady of seventy.

Such, thought he, is genius in a woman! Of his neighbours generally, Mrs. Baerens, the wife of a German merchant, an exquisite player on the pianoforte, was the most inclined to lead him to speak of Lady Camper. She was a kind prattling woman, and was known to have been a governess before her charms withdrew the gastronomic Gottfried Baerens from his devotion to the well-served City club, where, as he exclaimed (ever turning fondly to his wife as he vocalized the compliment), he had found every necessity, every luxury, in life, 'as you cannot have dem out of London—all save de female!' Mrs. Baerens, a lady of Teutonic extraction, was distinguishable as of that sex; at least, she was not masculine. She spoke with great respect of Lady Camper and her family, and seemed to agree in the General's eulogies of Lady Camper's constitution. Still he thought she eyed him strangely.

One April morning the General received a letter with the Italian postmark. Opening it with his usual calm and happy curiosity, he perceived that it was composed of pen-and-ink drawings. And suddenly his heart sank like a scuttled ship. He saw himself the victim of a caricature.

The first sketch had merely seemed picturesque, and he supposed it a clever play of fancy by some travelling friend, or perhaps an actual scene slightly exaggerated. Even on reading, 'A distant view of the city of Wilsonople,' he was only slightly enlightened. His heart beat still with befitting regularity. But the second and the third sketches betrayed the terrible hand. The distant view of the city of Wilsonople was fair with glittering domes, which, in the succeeding near view, proved to have been soap-bubbles, for a place of extreme flatness, begirt with crazy old-fashioned fortifications, was shown; and in the third view, representing the interior, stood for sole place of habitation, a sentry-box.

Most minutely drawn, and, alas! with fearful accuracy, a military gentleman in undress occupied the box. Not a doubt could exist as to the person it was meant to be.

The General tried hard to remain incredulous. He remembered too well who had called him Wilsonople.

But here was the extraordinary thing that sent him over the neighbourhood canvassing for exclamations: on the fourth page was the outline of a lovely feminine hand, holding a pen, as in the act of shading, and under it these words: 'What I say is, I say I think it exceedingly unladylike.'

Now consider the General's feelings when, turning to this fourth page, having these very words in his mouth, as the accurate expression of his thoughts, he discovered them written!

An enemy who anticipates the actions of our mind, has a quality of the malignant divine that may well inspire terror. The senses of General Ople were struck by the aspect of a lurid Goddess, who penetrated him, read him through, and had both power and will to expose and make him ridiculous for ever.

The loveliness of the hand, too, in a perplexing manner contested his denunciation of her conduct. It was ladylike eminently, and it involved him in a confused mixture of the moral and material, as great as young people are known to feel when they make the attempt to separate them, in one of their frenzies.

With a petty bitter laugh he folded the letter, put it in his breast-pocket, and sallied forth for a walk, chiefly to talk to himself about it. But as it absorbed him entirely, he showed it to the rector, whom he met, and what the rector said is of no consequence, for General Ople listened to no remarks, calling in succession on the Pollingtons, the Goslings, the Baerens, and others, early though it was, and the lords of those houses absent amassing hoards; and to the ladies everywhere he displayed the sketches he had received, observing, that Wilsonople meant himself; and there he was, he said, pointing at the capped fellow in the sentry-box, done unmistakably. The likeness indeed was remarkable. 'She is a woman of genius,' he ejaculated, with utter melancholy. Mrs. Baerens, by the aid of a magnifying glass, assisted him to read a line under the sentry-box, that he had taken for a mere trembling dash; it ran, A gentlemanly residence.

'What eyes she has!' the General exclaimed; 'I say it is miraculous what eyes she has at her time of... I was saying, I should never have known it was writing.'

He sighed heavily. His shuddering sensitiveness to caricature was increased by a certain evident dread of the hand which struck; the knowing that he was absolutely bare to this woman, defenceless, open to exposure in his little whims, foibles, tricks, incompetencies, in what lay in his heart, and the words that would come to his tongue. He felt like a man haunted.

So deeply did he feel the blow, that people asked how it was that he could be so foolish as to dance about assisting Lady Camper in her efforts to make him ridiculous; he acted the parts of publisher and agent for the fearful caricaturist. In truth, there was a strangely double reason for his conduct; he danced about for sympathy, he had the intensest craving for sympathy, but more than this, or quite as much, he desired to have the powers of his enemy widely appreciated; in the first place, that he might be excused to himself for wincing under them, and secondly, because an awful admiration of her, that should be deepened by a corresponding sentiment around him, helped him to enjoy luxurious recollections of an hour when he was near making her his own—his own, in the holy abstract contemplation of marriage, without realizing their probable relative conditions after the ceremony.

'I say, that is the very image of her ladyship's hand,' he was especially fond of remarking, 'I say it is a beautiful hand.'

He carried the letter in his pocket-book; and beginning to fancy that she had done her worst, for he could not imagine an inventive malignity capable of pursuing the theme, he spoke of her treatment of him with compassionate regret, not badly assumed from being partly sincere.

Two letters dated in France, the one Dijon, the other Fontainebleau, arrived together; and as the General knew Lady Camper to be returning to England, he expected that she was anxious to excuse herself to him. His fingers were not so confident, for he tore one of the letters to open it.

The City of Wilsonople was recognizable immediately. So likewise was the sole inhabitant.

General Ople's petty bitter laugh recurred, like a weak-chested patient's cough in the shifting of our winds eastward.

A faceless woman's shadow kneels on the ground near the sentry-box, weeping. A faceless shadow of a young man on horseback is beheld galloping toward a gulf. The sole inhabitant contemplates his largely substantial full fleshed face and figure in a glass.

Next, we see the standard of Great Britain furled; next, unfurled and borne by a troop of shadows to the sentry-box. The officer within says, 'I say I should be very happy to carry it, but I cannot quit this gentlemanly residence.'

Next, the standard is shown assailed by popguns. Several of the shadows are prostrate. 'I was saying, I assure you that nothing but this gentlemanly residence prevents me from heading you,' says the gallant officer.

General Ople trembled with protestant indignation when he saw himself reclining in a magnified sentry-box, while detachments of shadows hurry to him to show him the standard of his country trailing in the dust; and he is maliciously made to say, 'I dislike responsibility. I say I am a fervent patriot, and very fond of my comforts, but I shun responsibility.'

The second letter contained scenes between Wilsonople and the Moon.

He addresses her as his neighbour, and tells her of his triumphs over the sex.

He requests her to inform him whether she is a 'female,' that she may be triumphed over.

He hastens past her window on foot, with his head bent, just as the General had been in the habit of walking.

He drives a mouse-pony furiously by.

He cuts down a tree, that she may peep through.

Then, from the Moon's point of view, Wilsonople, a Silenus, is discerned in an arm-chair winking at a couple too plainly pouting their lips for a doubt of their intentions to be entertained.

A fourth letter arrived, bearing date of Paris. This one illustrated Wilsonople's courtship of the Moon, and ended with his 'saying,' in his peculiar manner, 'In spite of her paint I could not have conceived her age to be so enormous.'

How break off his engagement with the Lady Moon? Consent to none of her terms!

Little used as he was to read behind a veil, acuteness of suffering sharpened the General's intelligence to a degree that sustained him in animated dialogue with each succeeding sketch, or poisoned arrow whirring at him from the moment his eyes rested on it; and here are a few samples:

'Wilsonople informs the Moon that she is "sweetly pretty."

'He thanks her with "thanks" for a handsome piece of lunar green cheese.

'He points to her, apparently telling some one, "my lady-friend."

'He sneezes "Bijou! bijou! bijou!"'

They were trifles, but they attacked his habits of speech; and he began to grow more and more alarmingly absurd in each fresh caricature of his person.

He looked at himself as the malicious woman's hand had shaped him. It was unjust; it was no resemblance—and yet it was! There was a corner of likeness left that leavened the lump; henceforth he must walk abroad with this distressing image of himself before his eyes, instead of the satisfactory reflex of the man who had, and was happy in thinking that he had, done mischief in his time. Such an end for a conquering man was too pathetic.

The General surprised himself talking to himself in something louder than a hum at neighbours' dinner-tables. He looked about and noticed that people were silently watching him.

CHAPTER VII

Lady Camper's return was the subject of speculation in the neighbourhood, for most people thought she would cease to persecute the General with her preposterous and unwarrantable pen-and-ink sketches when living so closely proximate; and how he would behave was the question. Those who made a hero of him were sure he would treat her with disdain. Others were uncertain. He had been so severely hit that it seemed possible he would not show much spirit.

He, for his part, had come to entertain such dread of the post, that Lady Camper's return relieved him of his morning apprehensions; and he would have forgiven her, though he feared to see her, if only she had promised to leave him in peace for the future. He feared to see her, because of the too probable furnishing of fresh matter for her ladyship's hand. Of course he could not avoid being seen by her, and that was a particular misery. A gentlemanly humility, or demureness of aspect, when seen, would, he hoped, disarm his enemy. It should, he thought. He had borne unheard-of things. No one of his friends and acquaintances knew, they could not know, what he had endured. It has caused him fits of stammering. It had destroyed the composure of his gait. Elizabeth had informed him that he talked to himself incessantly, and aloud. She, poor child, looked pale too. She was evidently anxious about him.

Young Rolles, whom he had met now and then, persisted in praising his aunt's good heart. So, perhaps, having satiated her revenge, she might now be inclined for peace, on the terms of distant civility.

'Yes! poor Elizabeth!' sighed the General, in pity of the poor girl's disappointment; 'poor Elizabeth! she little guesses what her father has gone through. Poor child! I say, she hasn't an idea of my sufferings.'

General Ople delivered his card at Lady Camper's lodgegates and escaped to his residence in a state of prickly heat that required the brushing of his hair with hard brushes for several minutes to comfort and re-establish him.

He had fallen to working in his garden, when Lady Camper's card was brought to him an hour after the delivery of his own; a pleasing promptitude, showing signs of repentance, and suggesting to the General instantly some sharp sarcasms upon women, which he had come upon in quotations in the papers and the pulpit, his two main sources of information.

Instead of handing back the card to the maid, he stuck it in his hat and went on digging.

The first of a series of letters containing shameless realistic caricatures was handed to him the afternoon following. They came fast and thick. Not a day's interval of grace was allowed. Niobe under the shafts of Diana was hardly less violently and mortally assailed. The deadliness of the attack lay in the ridicule of the daily habits of one of the most sensitive of men, as to his personal appearance, and the opinion of the world. He might have concealed the sketches, but he could not have concealed the bruises, and people were perpetually asking the unhappy General what he was saying, for he spoke to himself as if he were repeating something to them for the tenth time.

'I say,' said he, 'I say that for a lady, really an educated lady, to sit, as she must—I was saying, she must have sat in an attic to have the right view of me. And there you see—this is what she has done. This is the last, this is the afternoon's delivery. Her ladyship has me correctly as to costume, but I could not exhibit such a sketch to ladies.'

A back view of the General was displayed in his act of digging.

'I say I could not allow ladies to see it,' he informed the gentlemen, who were suffered to inspect it freely.

'But you see, I have no means of escape; I am at her mercy from morning to night,' the General said, with a quivering tongue, 'unless I stay at home inside the house; and that is death to me, or unless I abandon the place, and my lease; and I shall—I say, I shall find nowhere in England for anything like the money or conveniences such a gent—a residence you would call fit for a gentleman. I call it a bi... it is, in short, a gem. But I shall have to go.'

Young Rolles offered to expostulate with his aunt Angela.

The General said, 'Tha... I thank you very much. I would not have her ladyship suppose I am so susceptible. I hardly know,' he confessed pitiably, 'what it is right to say, and what not—what not. I-I-I never know when I am not looking a fool. I hurry from tree to tree to shun the light. I am seriously affected in my appetite. I say, I shall have to go.'

Reginald gave him to understand that if he flew, the shafts would follow him, for Lady Camper would never forgive his running away, and was quite equal to publishing a book of the adventures of Wilsonople.

Sunday afternoon, walking in the park with his daughter on his arm, General Ople met Mr. Rolles. He saw that the young man and Elizabeth were mortally pale, and as the very idea of wretchedness directed his attention to himself, he addressed them conjointly on the subject of his persecution, giving neither of them a chance of speaking until they were constrained to part.

A sketch was the consequence, in which a withered Cupid and a fading Psyche were seen divided by Wilsonople, who keeps them forcibly asunder with policeman's fists, while courteously and elegantly entreating them to hear him. 'Meet,' he tells them, 'as often as you like, in my company, so long as you listen to me'; and the pathos of his aspect makes hungry demand for a sympathetic audience.

Now, this, and not the series representing the martyrdom of the old couple at Douro Lodge Gates, whose rigid frames bore witness to the close packing of a gentlemanly residence, this was the sketch General Ople, in his madness from the pursuing bite of the gadfly, handed about at Mrs. Pollington's lawn-party. Some have said, that he should not have betrayed his daughter; but it is reasonable to suppose he had no idea of his daughter's being the Psyche. Or if he had, it was indistinct, owing to the violence of his personal emotion. Assuming this to have been the very sketch; he handed it to two or three ladies in turn, and was heard to deliver himself at intervals in the following snatches: 'As you like, my lady, as you like; strike, I say strike; I bear it; I say I bear it. ... If her ladyship is unforgiving, I say I am enduring.... I may go, I was saying I may go mad, but while I have my reason I walk upright, I walk upright.'

Mr. Pollington and certain City gentlemen hearing the poor General's renewed soliloquies, were seized with disgust of Lady Camper's conduct, and stoutly advised an application to the Law Courts.

He gave ear to them abstractedly, but after pulling out the whole chapter of the caricatures (which it seemed that he kept in a case of morocco leather in his breast-pocket), showing them, with comments on them, and observing, 'There will be more, there must be more, I say I am sure there are things I do that her ladyship will discover and expose,' he declined to seek redress or simple protection; and the miserable spectacle was exhibited soon after of this courtly man listening to Mrs. Barcop on the weather, and replying in acquiescence: 'It is hot.—If your ladyship will only abstain from colours. Very hot as you say, madam,—I do not complain of pen and ink, but I would rather escape colours. And I dare say you find it hot too?'

Mrs. Barcop shut her eyes and sighed over the wreck of a handsome military officer.

She asked him: 'What is your objection to colours?'

His hand was at his breast-pocket immediately, as he said: 'Have you not seen?'—though but a few minutes back he had shown her the contents of the packet, including a hurried glance of the famous digging scene.

By this time the entire district was in fervid sympathy with General Ople. The ladies did not, as their lords did, proclaim astonishment that a man should suffer a woman to goad him to a state of semi-lunacy; but one or two confessed to their husbands, that it required a great admiration of General Ople not to despise him, both for his susceptibility and his patience. As for the men, they knew him to have faced the balls in bellowing battle-strife; they knew him to have endured privation, not only cold but downright want of food and drink—an almost unimaginable horror to these brave daily feasters; so they could not quite look on him in contempt; but his want of sense was offensive, and still more so his submission to a scourging by a woman. Not one of them would have deigned to feel it. Would they have allowed her to see that she could sting them? They would have laughed at her. Or they would have dragged her before a magistrate.

It was a Sunday in early Summer when General Ople walked to morning service, unaccompanied by Elizabeth, who was unwell. The church was of the considerate old-fashioned order, with deaf square pews, permitting the mind to abstract itself from the sermon, or wrestle at leisure with the difficulties presented by the preacher, as General Ople often did, feeling not a little in love with his sincere attentiveness for grappling with the knotty point and partially allowing the struggle to be seen.

The Church was, besides, a sanctuary for him. Hither his enemy did not come. He had this one place of refuge, and he almost looked a happy man again.

He had passed into his hat and out of it, which he habitually did standing, when who should walk up to within a couple of yards of him but Lady Camper. Her pew was full of poor people, who made signs of retiring. She signified to them that they were to sit, then quietly took her seat among them, fronting the General across the aisle.

During the sermon a low voice, sharp in contradistinction to the monotone of the preacher's, was heard to repeat these words: 'I say I am not sure I shall survive it.' Considerable muttering in the same quarter was heard besides.

After the customary ceremonious game, when all were free to move, of nobody liking to move first, Lady Camper and a charity boy were the persons who took the lead. But Lady Camper could not quit her pew, owing to the sticking of the door. She smiled as with her pretty hand she twice or thrice essayed to shake it open. General Ople strode to her aid. He pulled the door, gave the shadow of a respectful bow, and no doubt he would have withdrawn, had not Lady Camper, while acknowledging the civility, placed her prayer-book in his hands to carry at her heels. There was no choice for him. He made a sort of slipping dance back for his hat, and followed her ladyship. All present being eager to witness the spectacle, the passage of Lady Camper dragging the victim General behind her was observed without a stir of the well-dressed members of the congregation, until a desire overcame them to see how Lady Camper would behave to her fish when she had him outside the sacred edifice.

None could have imagined such a scene. Lady Camper was in her carriage; General Ople was holding her prayer-book, hat in hand, at the carriage step, and he looked as if he were toasting before the bars of a furnace; for while he stood there, Lady Camper was rapidly pencilling outlines in a small pocket sketchbook. There are dogs whose shyness is put to it to endure human observation and a direct address to them, even on the part of their masters; and these dear simple dogs wag tail and turn their heads aside waveringly, as though to entreat you not to eye them and talk to them so. General Ople, in the presence of the sketchbook, was much like the nervous animal. He would fain have run away. He glanced at it, and round about, and again at it, and at the heavens. Her ladyship's cruelty, and his inexplicable submission to it, were witnessed of the multitude.

The General's friends walked very slowly. Lady Camper's carriage whirled by, and the General came up with them, accosting them and himself alternately. They asked him where Elizabeth was, and he replied, 'Poor child, yes! I am told she is pale, but I cannot, believe I am so perfectly, I say so perfectly ridiculous, when I join the responses.' He drew forth half a dozen sheets, and showed them sketches that Lady Camper had taken in church, caricaturing him in the sitting down and the standing up. She had torn them out of the book, and presented them to him when driving off. 'I was saying, worship in the ordinary sense will be interdicted to me if her ladyship...,' said the General, woefully shuffling the sketch-paper sheets in which he figured.

He made the following odd confession to Mr. and Mrs. Gosling on the road:—that he had gone to his chest, and taken out his sword-belt to measure his girth, and found himself thinner than when he left the service, which had not been the case before his attendance at the last levee of the foregoing season. So the deduction was obvious, that Lady Camper had reduced him. She had reduced him as effectually as a harassing siege.

'But why do you pay attention to her? Why...!' exclaimed Mr. Gosling, a gentleman of the City, whose roundness would have turned a rifle-shot.

'To allow her to wound you so seriously!' exclaimed Mrs. Gosling.

'Madam, if she were my wife,' the General explained, 'I should feel it. I say it is the fact of it; I feel it, if I appear so extremely ridiculous to a human eye, to any one eye.'

'To Lady Camper's eye.'

He admitted it might be that. He had not thought of ascribing the acuteness of his pain to the miserable image he presented in this particular lady's eye. No; it really was true, curiously true: another lady's eye might have transformed him to a pumpkin shape, exaggerated all his foibles fifty-fold, and he, though not liking it, of course not, would yet have preserved a certain manly equanimity. How was it Lady Camper had such power over him?—a lady concealing seventy years with a rouge-box or paint-pot! It was witchcraft in its worst character. He had for six months at her bidding been actually living the life of a beast, degraded in his own esteem; scorched by every laugh he heard; running, pursued, overtaken, and as it were scored or branded, and then let go for the process to be repeated.

CHAPTER VIII

Our young barbarians have it all their own way with us when they fall into love-liking; they lead us whither they please, and interest us in their wishings, their weepings, and that fine performance, their kissings. But when we see our veterans tottering to their fall, we scarcely consent to their having a wish; as for a kiss, we halloo at them if we discover them on a byway to the sacred grove where such things are supposed to be done by the venerable. And this piece of rank injustice, not to say impoliteness, is entirely because of an unsound opinion that Nature is not in it, as though it were our esteem for Nature which caused us to disrespect them. They, in truth, show her to us discreet, civilized, in a decent moral aspect: vistas of real life, views of the mind's eye, are opened by their touching little emotions; whereas those bully youngsters who come bellowing at us and catch us by the senses plainly prove either that we are no better than they, or that we give our attention to Nature only when she makes us afraid of her. If we cared for her, we should be up and after her reverentially in her sedater steps, deeply studying her in her slower paces. She teaches them nothing when they are whirling. Our closest instructors, the true philosophers—the story-tellers, in short-will learn in time that Nature is not of necessity always roaring, and as soon as they do, the world may be said to be enlightened. Meantime, in the contemplation of a pair of white whiskers fluttering round a pair of manifestly painted cheeks, be assured that Nature is in it: not that hectoring wanton—but let the young have their fun. Let the superior interest of the passions of the aged be conceded, and not a word shall be said against the young.

If, then, Nature is in it, how has she been made active? The reason of her launch upon this last adventure is, that she has perceived the person who can supply the virtue known to her by experience to be wanting. Thus, in the broader instance, many who have journeyed far down the road, turn back to the worship of youth, which they have lost. Some are for the graceful worldliness of wit, of which they have just share enough to admire it. Some are captivated by hands that can wield the rod, which in earlier days they escaped to their cost. In the case of General Ople, it was partly her whippings of him, partly her penetration; her ability, that sat so finely on a wealthy woman, her indifference to conventional manners, that so well beseemed a nobly-born one, and more than all, her correction of his little weaknesses and incompetencies, in spite of his dislike of it, won him. He began to feel a sort of nibbling pleasure in her grotesque sketches of his person; a tendency to recur to the old ones while dreading the arrival of new. You hear old gentlemen speak fondly of the swish; and they are not attached to pain, but the instrument revives their feeling of youth; and General Ople half enjoyed, while shrinking, Lady Camper's foregone outlines of him. For in the distance, the whip's-end may look like a clinging caress instead of a stinging flick. But this craven melting in his heart was rebuked by a very worthy pride, that flew for support to the injury she had done to his devotions, and the offence to the sacred edifice. After thinking over it, he decided that he must quit his residence; and as it appeared to him in the light of duty, he, with an unspoken anguish, commissioned the house-agent of his town to sell his lease or let the house furnished, without further parley.

From the house-agent's shop he turned into the chemist's, for a tonic—a foolish proceeding, for he had received bracing enough in the blow he had just dealt himself, but he had been cogitating on tonics recently, imagining certain valiant effects of them, with visions of a former careless happiness that they were likely to restore. So he requested to have the tonic strong, and he took one glass of it over the counter.

Fifteen minutes after the draught, he came in sight of his house, and beholding it, he could have called it a gentlemanly residence aloud under Lady Camper's windows, his insurgency was of such violence. He talked of it incessantly, but forbore to tell Elizabeth, as she was looking pale, the reason why its modest merits touched him so. He longed for the hour of his next dose, and for a caricature to follow, that he might drink and defy it. A caricature was really due to him, he thought; otherwise why had he abandoned his bijou dwelling? Lady Camper, however, sent none. He had to wait a fortnight before one came, and that was rather a likeness, and a handsome likeness, except as regarded a certain disorderliness in his dress, which he knew to be very unlike him. Still it despatched him to the looking-glass, to bring that verifier of facts in evidence against the sketch. While sitting there he heard the housemaid's knock at the door, and the strange intelligence that his daughter was with Lady Camper, and had left word that she hoped he would not forget his engagement to go to Mrs. Baerens' lawn-party.

The General jumped away from the glass, shouting at the absent Elizabeth in a fit of wrath so foreign to him, that he returned hurriedly to have another look at himself, and exclaimed at the pitch of his voice, 'I say I attribute it to an indigestion of that tonic. Do you hear?' The housemaid faintly answered outside the door that she did, alarming him, for there seemed to be confusion somewhere. His hope was that no one would mention Lady Camper's name, for the mere thought of her caused a rush to his head. 'I believe I am in for a touch of apoplexy,' he said to the rector, who greeted him, in advance of the ladies, on Mr. Baerens' lawn. He said it smilingly, but wanting some show of sympathy, instead of the whisper and meaningless hand at his clerical band, with which the rector responded, he cried, 'Apoplexy,' and his friend seemed then to understand, and disappeared among the ladies.

Several of them surrounded the General, and one inquired whether the series was being continued. He drew forth his pocket-book, handed her the latest, and remarked on the gross injustice of it; for, as he requested them to take note, her ladyship now sketched him as a person inattentive to his dress, and he begged them to observe that she had drawn him with his necktie hanging loose. 'And that, I say that has never been known of me since I first entered society.'

The ladies exchanged looks of profound concern; for the fact was, the General had come without any necktie and any collar, and he appeared to be unaware of the circumstance. The rector had told them, that in answer to a hint he had dropped on the subject of neckties, General Ople expressed a slight apprehension of apoplexy; but his careless or merely partial observance of the laws of buttonment could have nothing to do with such fears. They signified rather a disorder of the intelligence. Elizabeth was condemned for leaving him to go about alone. The situation was really most painful, for a word to so sensitive a man would drive him away in shame and for good; and still, to let him parade the ground in the state, compared with his natural self, of scarecrow, and with the dreadful habit of talking to himself quite rageing, was a horrible alternative. Mrs. Baerens at last directed her husband upon the General, trembling as though she watched for the operations of a fish torpedo; and other ladies shared her excessive anxiousness, for Mr. Baerens had the manner and the look of artillery, and on this occasion carried a surcharge of powder.

The General bent his ear to Mr. Baerens, whose German-English and repeated remark, 'I am to do it wid delicassy,' did not assist his comprehension; and when he might have been enlightened, he was petrified by seeing Lady Camper walk on the lawn with Elizabeth. The great lady stood a moment beside Mrs. Baerens; she came straight over to him, contemplating him in silence.

Then she said, 'Your arm, General Ople,' and she made one circuit of the lawn with him, barely speaking.

At her request, he conducted her to her carriage. He took a seat beside her, obediently. He felt that he was being sketched, and comported himself like a child's flat man, that jumps at the pulling of a string.

'Where have you left your girl, General?'

Before he could rally his wits to answer the question, he was asked:

'And what have you done with your necktie and collar?'

He touched his throat.

'I am rather nervous to-day, I forgot Elizabeth,' he said, sending his fingers in a dotting run of wonderment round his neck.

Lady Camper smiled with a triumphing humour on her close-drawn lips.

The verified absence of necktie and collar seemed to be choking him.

'Never mind, you have been abroad without them,' said Lady Camper, 'and that is a victory for me. And you thought of Elizabeth first when I drew your attention to it, and that is a victory for you. It is a very great victory. Pray, do not be dismayed, General. You have a handsome campaigning air. And no apologies, if you please; I like you well enough as you are. There is my hand.'

General Ople understood her last remark. He pressed the lady's hand in silence, very nervously.

'But do not shrug your head into your shoulders as if there were any possibility of concealing the thunderingly evident,' said Lady Camper, electrifying him, what with her cordial squeeze, her kind eyes, and her singular language. 'You have omitted the collar. Well? The collar is the fatal finishing touch in men's dress; it would make Apollo look bourgeois.'

Her hand was in his: and watching the play of her features, a spark entered General Ople's brain, causing him, in forgetfulness of collar and caricatures, to ejaculate, 'Seventy? Did your ladyship say seventy? Utterly impossible! You trifle with me.'

'We will talk when we are free of this accompaniment of carriage-wheels, General,' said Lady Camper.

'I will beg permission to go and fetch Elizabeth, madam.'

'Rightly thought of. Fetch her in my carriage. And, by the way, Mrs. Baerens was my old music-mistress, and is, I think, one year older than I. She can tell you on which side of seventy I am.'

'I shall not require to ask, my lady,' he said, sighing.

'Then we will send the carriage for Elizabeth, and have it out together at once. I am impatient; yes, General, impatient: for what?—forgiveness.'

'Of me, my lady?' The General breathed profoundly.

'Of whom else? Do you know what it is?-I don't think you do. You English have the smallest experience of humanity. I mean this: to strike so hard that, in the end, you soften your heart to the victim. Well, that is my weakness. And we of our blood put no restraint on the blows we strike when we think them wanted, so we are always overdoing it.'

General Ople assisted Lady Camper to alight from the carriage, which was forthwith despatched for Elizabeth.

He prepared to listen to her with a disconnected smile of acute attentiveness.

She had changed. She spoke of money. Ten thousand pounds must be settled on his daughter. 'And now,' said she, 'you will remember that you are wanting a collar.'

He acquiesced. He craved permission to retire for ten minutes.

'Simplest of men! what will cover you?' she exclaimed, and peremptorily bidding him sit down in the drawing-room, she took one of the famous pair of pistols in her hand, and said, 'If I put myself in a similar position, and make myself decodletee too, will that satisfy you? You see these murderous weapons. Well, I am a coward. I dread fire-arms. They are laid there to impose on the world, and I believe they do. They have imposed on you. Now, you would never think of pretending to a moral quality you do not possess. But, silly, simple man that you are! You can give yourself the airs of wealth, buy horses to conceal your nakedness, and when you are taken upon the standard of your apparent income, you would rather seem to be beating a miserly retreat than behave frankly and honestly. I have a little overstated it, but I am near the mark.'

'Your ladyship wanting courage!' cried the General.

'Refresh yourself by meditating on it,' said she. 'And to prove it to you, I was glad to take this house when I knew I was to have a gallant gentleman for a neighbour. No visitors will be admitted, General Ople, so you are bare-throated only to me: sit quietly. One day you speculated on the paint in my cheeks for the space of a minute and a half:—I had said that I freckled easily. Your look signified that you really could not detect a single freckle for the paint. I forgave you, or I did not. But when I found you, on closer acquaintance, as indifferent to your daughter's happiness as you had been to her reputation...'

'My daughter! her reputation! her happiness!'

General Ople raised his eyes under a wave, half uttering the outcries.

'So indifferent to her reputation, that you allowed a young man to talk with her over the wall, and meet her by appointment: so reckless of the girl's happiness, that when I tried to bring you to a treaty, on her behalf, you could not be dragged from thinking of yourself and your own affair. When I found that, perhaps I was predisposed to give you some of what my sisters used to call my spice. You would not honestly state the proportions of your income, and you affected to be faithful to the woman of seventy. Most preposterous! Could any caricature of mine exceed in grotesqueness your sketch of yourself? You are a brave and a generous man all the same: and I suspect it is more hoodwinking than egotism—or extreme egotism—that blinds you. A certain amount you must have to be a man. You did not like my paint, still less did you like my sincerity; you were annoyed by my corrections of your habits of speech; you were horrified by the age of seventy, and you were credulous—General Ople, listen to me, and remember that you have no collar on—you were credulous of my statement of my great age, or you chose to be so, or chose to seem so, because I had brushed your cat's coat against the fur. And then, full of yourself, not thinking of Elizabeth, but to withdraw in the chivalrous attitude of the man true to his word to the old woman, only stickling to bring a certain independence to the common stock, because—I quote you! and you have no collar on, mind—"you could not be at your wife's mercy," you broke from your proposal on the money question. Where was your consideration for Elizabeth then?

'Well, General, you were fond of thinking of yourself, and I thought I would assist you. I gave you plenty of subject matter. I will not say I meant to work a homoeopathic cure. But if I drive you to forget your collar, is it or is it not a triumph?'

'No,' added Lady Camper, 'it is no triumph for me, but it is one for you, if you like to make the most of it. Your fault has been to quit active service, General, and love your ease too well. It is the fault of your countrymen. You must get a militia regiment, or inspectorship of militia. You are ten times the man in exercise. Why, do you mean to tell me that you would have cared for those drawings of mine when marching?'

'I think so, I say I think so,' remarked the General seriously.

'I doubt it,' said she. 'But to the point; here comes Elizabeth. If you have not much money to spare for her, according to your prudent calculation, reflect how this money has enfeebled you and reduced you to the level of the people round about us here—who are, what? Inhabitants of gentlemanly residences, yes! But what kind of creature? They have no mental standard, no moral aim, no native chivalry. You were rapidly becoming one of them, only, fortunately for you, you were sensitive to ridicule.'

'Elizabeth shall have half my money settled on her,' said the General; 'though I fear it is not much. And if I can find occupation, my lady...'

'Something worthier than that,' said Lady Camper, pencilling outlines rapidly on the margin of a book, and he saw himself lashing a pony; 'or that,' and he was plucking at a cabbage; 'or that,' and he was bowing to three petticoated posts.

'The likeness is exact,' General Ople groaned.

'So you may suppose I have studied you,' said she. 'But there is no real likeness. Slight exaggerations do more harm to truth than reckless violations of it.

You would not have cared one bit for a caricature, if you had not nursed the absurd idea of being one of our conquerors. It is the very tragedy of modesty for a man like you to have such notions, my poor dear good friend. The modest are the most easily intoxicated when they sip at vanity. And reflect whether you have not been intoxicated, for these young people have been wretched, and you have not observed it, though one of them was living with you, and is the child you love. There, I have done. Pray show a good face to Elizabeth.'

The General obeyed as well as he could. He felt very like a sheep that has come from a shearing, and when released he wished to run away. But hardly had he escaped before he had a desire for the renewal of the operation. 'She sees me through, she sees me through,' he was heard saying to himself, and in the end he taught himself, to say it with a secret exultation, for as it was on her part an extraordinary piece of insight to see him through, it struck him that in acknowledging the truth of it, he made a discovery of new powers in human nature.

General Ople studied Lady Camper diligently for fresh proofs of her penetration of the mysteries in his bosom; by which means, as it happened that she was diligently observing the two betrothed young ones, he began to watch them likewise, and took a pleasure in the sight. Their meetings, their partings, their rides out and home furnished him themes of converse. He soon had enough to talk of, and previously, as he remembered, he had never sustained a conversation of any length with composure and the beneficent sense of fulness. Five thousand pounds, to which sum Lady Camper reduced her stipulation for Elizabeth's dowry, he signed over to his dear girl gladly, and came out with the confession to her ladyship that a well-invested twelve thousand comprised his fortune. She shrugged she had left off pulling him this way and that, so his chains were enjoyable, and he said to himself: 'If ever she should in the dead of night want a man to defend her!' He mentioned it to Reginald, who had been the repository of Elizabeth's lamentations about her father being left alone, forsaken, and the young man conceived a scheme for causing his aunt's great bell to be rung at midnight, which would certainly have led to a dramatic issue and the happy re-establishment of our masculine ascendancy at the close of this history. But he forgot it in his bridegroom's delight, until he was making his miserable official speech at the wedding-breakfast, and set Elizabeth winking over a tear. As she stood in the hall ready to depart, a great van was observed in the road at the gates of Douro Lodge; and this, the men in custody declared to contain the goods and knick-knacks of the people who had taken the house furnished for a year, and were coming in that very afternoon.

'I remember, I say now I remember, I had a notice,' the General said cheerily to his troubled daughter.

'But where are you to go, papa?' the poor girl cried, close on sobbing.

'I shall get employment of some sort,' said he. 'I was saying I want it, I need it, I require it.'

'You are saying three times what once would have sufficed for,' said Lady Camper, and she asked him a few questions, frowned with a smile, and offered him a lodgement in his neighbour's house.

'Really, dearest Aunt Angela?' said Elizabeth.

'What else can I do, child? I have, it seems, driven him out of a gentlemanly residence, and I must give him a ladylike one. True, I would rather have had him at call, but as I have always wished for a policeman in the house, I may as well be satisfied with a soldier.'

'But if you lose your character, my lady?' said Reginald.

'Then I must look to the General to restore it.'

General Ople immediately bowed his head over Lady Camper's fingers.

'An odd thing to happen to a woman of forty-one!' she said to her great people, and they submitted with the best grace in the world, while the General's ears tingled till he felt younger than Reginald. This, his reflections ran, or it would be more correct to say waltzed, this is the result of painting!—that you can believe a woman to be any age when her cheeks are tinted!

As for Lady Camper, she had been floated accidentally over the ridicule of the bruit of a marriage at a time of life as terrible to her as her fiction of seventy had been to General Ople; she resigned herself to let things go with the tide. She had not been blissful in her first marriage, she had abandoned the chase of an ideal man, and she had found one who was tunable so as not to offend her ears, likely ever to be a fund of amusement for her humour, good, impressible, and above all, very picturesque. There is the secret of her, and of how it came to pass that a simple man and a complex woman fell to union after the strangest division.

'Fair Chloe, we toasted of old,
As the Queen of our festival meeting;
Now Chloe is lifeless and cold;
You must go to the grave for her greeting.
Her beauty and talents were framed
To enkindle the proudest to win her;
Then let not the mem'ry be blamed
Of the purest that e'er was a sinner!'
Captain Chanter's Collection.

CHAPTER I

A proper tenderness for the Peerage will continue to pass current the illustrious gentleman who was inflamed by Cupid's darts to espouse the milkmaid, or dairymaid, under his ballad title of Duke of Dewlap: nor was it the smallest of the services rendered him by Beau Beamish, that he clapped the name upon her rustic Grace, the young duchess, the very first day of her arrival at the Wells. This happy inspiration of a wit never failing at a pinch has rescued one of our princeliest houses from the assaults of the vulgar, who are ever too rejoiced to bespatter and disfigure a brilliant coat-of-arms; insomuch that the ballad, to which we are indebted for the narrative of the meeting and marriage of the ducal pair, speaks of Dewlap in good faith—

O the ninth Duke of Dewlap I am, Susie dear!

without a hint of a domino title. So likewise the pictorial historian is merry over 'Dewlap alliances' in his description of the society of that period. He has read the ballad, but disregarded the memoirs of the beau. Writers of pretension would seem to have an animus against individuals of the character of Mr. Beamish. They will treat of the habits and manners of highwaymen, and quote obscure broadsheets and songs of the people to colour their story, yet decline to bestow more than a passing remark upon our domestic kings: because they are not hereditary, we may suppose. The ballad of 'The Duke and the Dairymaid,' ascribed with questionable authority to the pen of Mr. Beamish himself in a freak of his gaiety, was once popular enough to provoke the moralist to animadversions upon an order of composition that 'tempted every bouncing country lass to sidle an eye in a blowsy cheek' in expectation of a coronet for her pains—and a wet ditch as the result! We may doubt it to have been such an occasion of mischief. But that mischief may have been done by it to a nobility-loving people, even to the love of our nobility among the people, must be granted; and for the particular reason, that the hero of the ballad behaved so handsomely. We perceive a susceptibility to adulteration in their worship at the sight of one of their number, a young maid, suddenly snatched up to the gaping heights of Luxury and Fashion through sheer good looks. Remembering that they are accustomed to a totally reverse effect from that possession, it is very perceptible how a breach in their reverence may come of the change.

Otherwise the ballad is innocent; certainly it is innocent in design. A fresher national song of a beautiful incident of our country life has never been written. The sentiments are natural, the imagery is apt and redolent of the soil, the music of the verse appeals to the dullest ear. It has no smell of the lamp, nothing foreign and far-fetched about it, but is just what it pretends to be, the carol of the native bird. A sample will show, for the ballad is much too long to be given entire:

Sweet Susie she tripped on a shiny May morn,
As blithe as the lark from the green-springing corn,
When, hard by a stile, 'twas her luck to behold
A wonderful gentleman covered with gold!

There was gold on his breeches and gold on his coat,
His shirt-frill was grand as a fifty-pound note;
The diamonds glittered all up him so bright,
She thought him the Milky Way clothing a Sprite!

'Fear not, pretty maiden,' he said with a smile;
'And, pray, let me help you in crossing the stile.
She bobbed him a curtsey so lovely and smart,
It shot like an arrow and fixed in his heart.

As light as a robin she hopped to the stone,
But fast was her hand in the gentleman's own;
And guess how she stared, nor her senses could trust,
When this creamy gentleman knelt in the dust!

With a rhapsody upon her beauty, he informs her of his rank, for a flourish to the proposal of honourable and immediate marriage. He cannot wait. This is the fatal condition of his love: apparently a characteristic of amorous dukes. We read them in the signs extended to us. The minds of these august and solitary men have not yet been sounded; they are too distant. Standing upon their lofty pinnacles, they are as legible to the rabble below as a line of cuneiform writing in a page of old copybook roundhand. By their deeds we know them, as heathendom knows of its gods; and it is repeatedly on record that the moment they have taken fire they must wed, though the lady's finger be circled with nothing closer fitting than a ring of the bed-curtain. Vainly, as becomes a candid country lass, blue-eyed Susan tells him that she is but a poor dairymaid. He has been a student of women at Courts, in which furnace the sex becomes a transparency, so he recounts to her the catalogue of material advantages he has to offer. Finally, after his assurances that she is to be married by the parson, really by the parson, and a real parson—

Sweet Susie is off for her parents' consent,
And long must the old folk debate what it meant.
She left them the eve of that happy May morn,
To shine like the blossom that hangs from the thorn!

Apart from its historical value, the ballad is an example to poets of our day, who fly to mythological Greece, or a fanciful and morbid mediaevalism, or—save the mark!—abstract ideas, for themes of song, of what may be done to make our English life poetically interesting, if they would but pluck the treasures presented them by the wayside; and Nature being now as then the passport to popularity, they have themselves to thank for their little hold on the heart of the people. A living native duke is worth fifty Phoebus Apollos to Englishmen, and a buxom young lass of the fields mounting from a pair of pails to the estate of duchess, a more romantic object than troops of your visionary Yseults and Guineveres.

CHAPTER II

A certain time after the marriage, his Grace alighted at the Wells, and did himself the honour to call on Mr. Beamish. Addressing that gentleman, to whom he was no stranger, he communicated the purport of his visit.

'Sir, and my very good friend,' he said, 'first let me beg you to abate the severity of your countenance, for if I am here in breach of your prohibition, I shall presently depart in compliance with it. I could indeed deplore the loss of the passion for play of which you effectually cured me. I was then armed against a crueller, that allows of no interval for a man to make his vow to recover!'

'The disease which is all crisis, I apprehend,' Mr. Beamish remarked.

'Which, sir, when it takes hold of dry wood, burns to the last splinter. It is now'—the duke fetched a tender groan—'three years ago that I had a caprice to marry a grandchild!'

'Of Adam's,' Mr. Beamish said cheerfully. 'There was no legitimate bar to the union.'

'Unhappily none. Yet you are not to suppose I regret it. A most admirable creature, Mr. Beamish, a real divinity! And the better known, the more adored. There is the misfortune. At my season of life, when the greater and the minor organs are in a conspiracy to tell me I am mortal, the passion of love must be welcomed as a calamity, though one would not be free of it for the renewal of youth. You are to understand, that with a little awakening taste for dissipation, she is the most innocent of angels. Hitherto we have lived... To her it has been a new world. But she is beginning to find it a narrow one. No, no, she is not tired of my society. Very far from that. But in her present station an inclination for such gatherings as you have here, for example, is like a desire to take the air: and the healthy habits of my duchess have not accustomed her to be immured. And in fine, devote ourselves as we will, a term approaches when the enthusiasm for serving as your wife's playfellow all day, running round tables and flying along corridors before a knotted handkerchief, is mightily relaxed. Yet the dread of a separation from her has kept me at these pastimes for a considerable period beyond my relish of them. Not that I acknowledge fatigue. I have, it seems, a taste for reflection; I am now much disposed to read and meditate, which cannot be done without repose. I settle myself, and I receive a worsted ball in my face, and I am expected to return it. I comply; and then you would say a nursery in arms. It would else be the deplorable spectacle of a beautiful young woman yawning.'

'Earthquake and saltpetre threaten us less terribly,' said Mr. Beamish.

'In fine, she has extracted a promise that 'this summer she shall visit the Wells for a month, and I fear I cannot break my pledge of my word; I fear I cannot.'

'Very certainly I would not,' said Mr. Beamish.

The duke heaved a sigh. 'There are reasons, family reasons, why my company and protection must be denied to her here. I have no wish... indeed my name, for the present, until such time as she shall have found her feet... and there is ever a penalty to pay for that. Ah, Mr. Beamish, pictures are ours, when we have bought them and hung them up; but who insures us possession of a beautiful work of Nature? I have latterly betaken me to reflect much and seriously. I am tempted to side with the Divines in the sermons I have read; the flesh is the habitation of a rebellious devil.'

'To whom we object in proportion as we ourselves become quit of him,' Mr. Beamish acquiesced.

'But this mania of young people for pleasure, eternal pleasure, is one of the wonders. It does not pall on them; they are insatiate.'

'There is the cataract, and there is the cliff. Potentate to potentate, duke—so long as you are on my territory, be it understood. Upon my way to a place of worship once, I passed a Puritan, who was complaining of a butterfly that fluttered prettily abroad in desecration of the Day of Rest. "Friend," said I to him, "conclusively you prove to me that you are not a butterfly." Surly did no more than favour me with the anathema of his countenance.'

'Cousin Beamish, my complaint of these young people is, that they miss their pleasure in pursuing it. I have lectured my duchess—'

'Ha!'

'Foolish, I own,' said the duke. 'But suppose, now, you had caught your butterfly, and you could neither let it go nor consent to follow its vagaries. That poses you.'

'Young people,' said Mr. Beamish, 'come under my observation in this poor realm of mine—young and old. I find them prodigiously alike in their love of pleasure, differing mainly in their capacity to satisfy it. That is no uncommon observation. The young, have an edge which they are desirous of blunting; the old contrariwise. The cry of the young for pleasure is actually—I have studied their language—a cry for burdens. Curious! And the old ones cry for having too many on their shoulders: which is not astonishing. Between them they make an agreeable concert both to charm the ears and guide the steps of the philosopher, whose wisdom it is to avoid their tracks.'

'Good. But I have asked you for practical advice, and you give me an essay.'

'For the reason, duke, that you propose a case that suggests hanging. You mention two things impossible to be done. The alternative is, a garter and the bedpost. When we have come upon crossways, and we can decide neither to take the right hand nor the left, neither forward nor back, the index of the board which would direct us points to itself, and emphatically says, Gallows.'

'Beamish, I am distracted. If I refuse her the visit, I foresee dissensions, tears, games at ball, romps, not one day of rest remaining to me. I could be of a mind with your Puritan, positively. If I allow it, so innocent a creature in the atmosphere of a place like this must suffer some corruption. You should know that the station I took her from was ... it was modest. She was absolutely a buttercup of the fields. She has had various masters. She dances... she dances prettily, I could say bewitchingly. And so she is now for airing her accomplishments: such are women!'

'Have you heard of Chloe?' said Mr. Beamish. 'There you have an example of a young lady uncorrupted by this place—of which I would only remark that it is best unvisited, but better tasted than longed for.'

'Chloe? A lady who squandered her fortune to redeem some ill-requiting rascal: I remember to have heard of her. She is here still? And ruined, of course?'

'In purse.'

'That cannot be without the loss of reputation.'

'Chloe's champion will grant that she is exposed to the evils of improvidence. The more brightly shine her native purity, her goodness of heart, her trustfulness. She is a lady whose exaltation glows in her abasement.'

'She has, I see, preserved her comeliness,' observed the duke, with a smile.

'Despite the flying of the roses, which had not her heart's patience. 'Tis now the lily that reigns. So, then, Chloe shall be attached to the duchess during her stay, and unless the devil himself should interfere, I guarantee her Grace against any worse harm than experience; and that,' Mr. Beamish added, as the duke raised his arms at the fearful word, 'that shall be mild. Play she will; she is sure to play. Put it down at a thousand. We map her out a course of permissible follies, and she plays to lose the thousand by degrees, with as telling an effect upon a connubial conscience as we can produce.'

'A thousand,' said the duke, 'will be cheap indeed. I think now I have had a description of this fair Chloe, and from an enthusiast; a brune? elegantly mannered and of a good landed family; though she has thought proper to conceal her name. And that will be our difficulty, cousin Beamish.'

'She was, under my dominion, Miss Martinsward,' Mr. Beamish pursued. 'She came here very young, and at once her suitors were legion. In the way of women, she chose the worst among them; and for the fellow Caseldy she sacrificed the fortune she had inherited of a maternal uncle. To release him from prison, she paid all his debts; a mountain of bills, with the lawyers piled above—Pelion upon Ossa, to quote our poets. In fact, obeying the dictates of a soul steeped in generosity, she committed the indiscretion to strip herself, scandalizing propriety. This was immediately on her coming of age; and it was the death-blow to her relations with her family. Since then, honoured even by rakes, she has lived impoverished at the Wells. I dubbed her Chloe, and man or woman disrespectful to Chloe packs. From being the victim of her generous disposition, I could not save her; I can protect her from the shafts of malice.'

'She has no passion for play?' inquired the duke.

'She nourishes a passion for the man for whom she bled, to the exclusion of the other passions. She lives, and I believe I may say that it is the motive of her rising and dressing daily, in expectation of his advent.'

'He may be dead.'

'The dog is alive. And he has not ceased to be Handsome Caseldy, they say. Between ourselves, duke, there is matter to break her heart. He has been the Count Caseldy of Continental gaming tables, and he is recently Sir Martin Caseldy, settled on the estate she made him free to take up intact on his father's decease.'

'Pah! a villain!'

'With a blacker brand upon him every morning that he looks forth across his property, and leaves her to languish! She still—I say it to the redemption of our sex—has offers. Her incomparable attractions of mind and person exercise the natural empire of beauty. But she will none of them. I call her the Fair Suicide. She has died for love; and she is a ghost, a good ghost, and a pleasing ghost, but an apparition, a taper.

The duke fidgeted, and expressed a hope to hear that she was not of melancholy conversation; and again, that the subject of her discourse was not confined to love and lovers, happy or unhappy. He wished his duchess, he said, to be entertained upon gayer topics: love being a theme he desired to reserve to himself. 'This month!' he said, prognostically shaking and moaning. 'I would this month were over, and that we were well purged of it.'

Mr. Beamish reassured him. The wit and sprightliness of Chloe were so famous as to be considered medical, he affirmed; she was besieged for her company; she composed and sang impromptu verses, she played harp and harpsichord divinely, and touched the guitar, and danced, danced like the silvery moon on the waters of the mill pool. He concluded by saying that she was both humane and wise, humble-minded and amusing, virtuous yet not a Tartar; the best of companions for her Grace the young duchess. Moreover, he boldly engaged to carry the duchess through the term of her visit under a name that should be as good as a masquerade for concealing his Grace's, while giving her all the honours due to her rank.

'You strictly interpret my wishes,' said the duke; 'all honours, the foremost place, and my wrath upon man or woman gainsaying them!'

'Mine! if you please, duke,' said Mr. Beamish.

'A thousand pardons! I leave it to you, cousin. I could not be in safer hands. I am heartily bounders to you. Chloe, then. By the way, she has a decent respect for age?'

'She is reverentially inclined.'

'Not that. She is, I would ask, no wanton prattler of the charms and advantages of youth?'

'She has a young adorer that I have dubbed Alonzo, whom she scarce notices.'

'Nothing could be better. Alonzo: h'm! A faithful swain?'

'Life is his tree, upon which unceasingly he carves his mistress's initials.'

'She should not be too cruel. I recollect myself formerly: I was... Young men will, when long slighted, transfer their affections, and be warmer to the second flame than to the first. I put you on your guard. He follows her much? These lovers' paintings and puffings in the neighbourhood of the most innocent of women are contagious.'

'Her Grace will be running home all the sooner.'

'Or off!—may she forgive me! I am like a King John's Jew, forced to lend his treasure without security. What a world is ours! Nothing, Beamish, nothing desirable will you have which is not coveted! Catch a prize, and you will find you are at war with your species. You have to be on the defensive from that moment. There is no such thing as peaceable procession on earth. Let it be a beautiful young woman!—Ah!'

Mr. Beamish replied bracingly, 'The champion wrestler challenges all comers while he wears the belt.'

The duke dejectedly assented. 'True; or he is challenged, say. Is there any tale we could tell her of this Alonzo? You could deport him for the month, my dear Beamish.'

'I commit no injustice unless with sufficient reason. It is an estimable youth, as shown by his devotion to a peerless woman. To endow her with his name and fortune is his only thought.'

'I perceive; an excellent young fellow! I have an incipient liking for this young Alonzo. You must not permit my duchess to laugh at him. Encourage her rather to advance his suit. The silliness of a young man will be no bad spectacle. Chloe, then. You have set my mind at rest, Beamish, and it is but another obligation added to the heap; so, if I do not speak of payment, the reason is that I know you would not have me bankrupt.'

The remainder of the colloquy of the duke and Mr. Beamish referred to the date of her Grace's coming to the Wells, the lodgement she was to receive, and other minor arrangements bearing upon her state and comfort; the duke perpetually observing, 'But I leave it all to you, Beamish,' when he had laid down precise instructions in these respects, even to the specification of the shopkeepers, the confectioner and the apothecary, who were to balance or cancel one another in the opposite nature of their supplies, and the haberdasher and the jeweller, with whom she was to make her purchases. For the duke had a recollection of giddy shops, and of giddy shopmen too; and it was by serving as one for a day that a certain great nobleman came to victory with a jealously guarded dame beautiful as Venus. 'I would have challenged the goddess!' he cried, and subsided from his enthusiasm plaintively, like a weak wind instrument. 'So there you see the prudence of a choice of shops. But I leave it to you, Beamish.' Similarly the great military commander, having done whatsoever a careful prevision may suggest to insure him victory, casts himself upon Providence, with the hope of propitiating the unanticipated and darkly possible.

CHAPTER III

The splendid equipage of a coach and six, with footmen in scarlet and green, carried Beau Beamish five miles along the road on a sunny day to meet the young duchess at the boundary of his territory, and conduct her in state to the Wells. Chloe sat beside him, receiving counsel with regard to her prospective duties. He was this day the consummate beau, suave, but monarchical, and his manner of speech partook of his external grandeur. 'Spy me the horizon, and apprise me if somewhere you distinguish a chariot,' he said, as they drew up on the rise of a hill of long descent, where the dusty roadway sank between its brown hedges, and crawled mounting from dry rush-spotted hollows to corn fields on a companion height directly facing them, at a remove of about three-quarters of a mile. Chloe looked forth, while the beau passingly raised his hat for coolness, and murmured, with a glance down the sultry track: 'It sweats the eye to see!'

Presently Chloe said, 'Now a dust blows. Something approaches. Now I discern horses, now a vehicle; and it is a chariot!'

Orders were issued to the outriders for horns to be sounded.

Both Chloe and Beau Beamish wrinkled their foreheads at the disorderly notes of triple horns, whose pealing made an acid in the air instead of sweetness.

'You would say, kennel dogs that bay the moon!' said the wincing beau. 'Yet, as you know, these fellows have been exercised. I have had them out in a meadow for hours, baked and drenched, to get them rid of their native cacophony. But they love it, as they love bacon and beans. The musical taste of our people is in the stage of the primitive appetite for noise, and for that they are gluttons.'

'It will be pleasant to hear in the distance,' Chloe replied.

'Ay, the extremer the distance, the pleasanter to hear. Are they advancing?'

'They stop. There is a cavalier at the window. Now he doffs his hat.'

'Sweepingly?'

Chloe described a semicircle in the grand manner.

The beau's eyebrows rose. 'Powers divine!' he muttered. 'She is let loose from hand to hand, and midway comes a cavalier. We did not count on the hawks. So I have to deal with a cavalier! It signifies, my dear Chloe, that I must incontinently affect the passion if I am to be his match: nothing less.'

'He has flown,' said Chloe.

'Whom she encounters after meeting me, I care not,' quoth the beau, snapping a finger. 'But there has been an interval for damage with a lady innocent as Eve. Is she advancing?'

'The chariot is trotting down the hill. He has ridden back. She has no attendant horseman.'

'They were dismissed at my injunction ten miles off particularly to the benefit of the cavaliering horde, it would appear. In the case of a woman, Chloe, one blink of the eyelids is an omission of watchfulness.'

'That is an axiom fit for the harem of the Grand Signior.'

'The Grand Signior might give us profitable lessons for dealing with the sex.'

'Distrust us, and it is a declaration of war!'

'Trust you, and the stopper is out of the smelling-bottle.'

'Mr. Beamish, we are women, but we have souls.'

'The pip in the apple whose ruddy cheek allures little Tommy to rob the orchard is as good a preservative.'

'You admit that men are our enemies?'

'I maintain that they carry the banner of virtue.'

'Oh, Mr. Beamish, I shall expire.'

'I forbid it in my lifetime, Chloe, for I wish to die believing in one woman.'

'No flattery for me at the expense of my sisters!'

'Then fly to a hermitage; for all flattery is at somebody's expense, child. 'Tis an essence-extract of humanity! To live on it, in the fashion of some people, is bad—it is downright cannibal. But we may sprinkle our handkerchiefs with it, and we should, if we would caress our noses with an air. Society, my Chloe, is a recommencement upon an upper level of the savage system; we must have our sacrifices. As, for instance, what say you of myself beside our booted bumpkin squires?'

'Hundreds of them, Mr. Beamish!'

'That is a holocaust of squires reduced to make an incense for me, though you have not performed Druid rites and packed them in gigantic osier ribs. Be philosophical, but accept your personal dues. Grant us ours too. I have a serious intention to preserve this young duchess, and I expect my task to be severe. I carry the banner aforesaid; verily and penitentially I do. It is an error of the vulgar to suppose that all is dragon in the dragon's jaws.'

'Men are his fangs and claws.'

'Ay, but the passion for his fiery breath is in woman. She will take her leap and have her jump, will and will! And at the point where she will and she won't, the dragon gulps and down she goes! However, the business is to keep our buttercup duchess from that same point. Is she near?'

'I can see her,' said Chloe.

Beau Beamish requested a sketch of her, and Chloe began: 'She is ravishing.'

Upon which he commented, 'Every woman is ravishing at forty paces, and still more so in imagination.'

'Beautiful auburn hair, and a dazzling red and white complexion, set in a blue coif.'

'Her eyes?'

'Melting blue.'

''Tis an English witch!' exclaimed the beau, and he compassionately invoked her absent lord.

Chloe's optics were no longer tasked to discern the fair lady's lineaments, for the chariot windows came flush with those of the beau on the broad plateau of the hill. His coach door was opened. He sat upright, levelling his privileged stare at Duchess Susan until she blushed.

'Ay, madam,' quoth he, 'I am not the first.'

'La, sir!' said she; 'who are you?'

The beau deliberately raised his hat and bowed. 'He, madam, of whose approach the gentleman who took his leave of you on yonder elevation informed you.'

She looked artlessly over her shoulder, and at the beau alighting from his carriage. 'A gentleman?'

'On horseback.'

The duchess popped her head through the window on an impulse to measure the distance between the two hills.

'Never!' she cried.

'Why, madam, did he deliver no message to announce me?' said the beau, ruffling.

'Goodness gracious! You must be Mr. Beamish,' she replied.

He laid his hat on his bosom, and invited her to quit her carriage for a seat beside him. She stipulated, 'If you are really Mr. Beamish?' He frowned, and raised his head to convince her; but she would not be impressed, and he applied to Chloe to establish his identity. Hearing Chloe's name, the duchess called out, 'Oh! there, now, that's enough, for Chloe's my maid here, and I know she's a lady born, and we're going to be friends. Hand me to Chloe. And you are Chloe?' she said, after a frank stride from step to step of the carriages. 'And don't mind being my maid? You do look a nice, kind creature. And I see you're a lady born; I know in a minute. You're dark, I'm fair; we shall suit. And tell me—hush!—what dreadful long eyes he has! I shall ask you presently what you think of me. I was never at the Wells before. Dear me! the coach has turned. How far off shall we hear the bells to say I'm coming? I know I'm to have bells. Mr. Beamish, Mr. Beamish! I must have a chatter with a woman, and I'm in awe of you, sir, that I am, but men and men I see to talk to for a lift of my finger, by the dozen, in my duke's palace—though they're old ones, that's true—but a woman who's a lady, and kind enough to be my maid, I haven't met yet since I had the right to wear a coronet. There, I'll hold Chloe's hand, and that'll do. You would tell me at once, Chloe, if I was not dressed to your taste; now, wouldn't you? As for talkative, that's a sign with me of my liking people. I really don't know what to say to my duke sometimes. I sit and think it so funny to be having a duke instead of a husband. You're off!'

The duchess laughed at Chloe's laughter. Chloe excused herself, but was informed by her mistress that it was what she liked.

'For the first two years,' she resumed, 'I could hardly speak a syllable. I stammered, I reddened, I longed to be up in my room brushing and curling my hair, and was ready to curtsey to everybody. Now I'm quite at home, for I've plenty of courage—except about death, and I'm worse about death than I was when I was a simple body with a gawk's "lawks!" in her round eyes and mouth for an egg. I wonder why that is? But isn't death horrible? And skeletons!' The duchess shuddered.

'It depends upon the skeleton,' said Beau Beamish, who had joined the conversation. 'Yours, madam, I would rather not meet, because she would precipitate me into transports of regret for the loss of the flesh. I have, however, met mine own and had reason for satisfaction with the interview.'

'Your own skeleton, sir!' said the duchess wonderingly and appalled.

'Unmistakably mine. I will call you to witness by an account of him.'

Duchess Susan gaped, and, 'Oh, don't!' she cried out; but added, 'It 's broad day, and I've got some one to sleep anigh me after dark'; with which she smiled on Chloe, who promised her there was no matter for alarm.

'I encountered my gentleman as I was proceeding to my room at night,' said the beau, 'along a narrow corridor, where it was imperative that one of us should yield the 'pas;' and, I must confess it, we are all so amazingly alike in our bones, that I stood prepared to demand place of him. For indubitably the fellow was an obstruction, and at the first glance repulsive. I took him for anybody's skeleton, Death's ensign, with his cachinnatory skull, and the numbered ribs, and the extraordinary splay feet—in fact, the whole ungainly and shaky hobbledehoy which man is built on, and by whose image in his weaker moments he is haunted. I had, to be frank, been dancing on a supper with certain of our choicest Wits and Beauties. It is a recipe for conjuring apparitions. Now, then, thinks I, my fine fellow, I will bounce you; and without a salutation I pressed forward. Madam, I give you my word, he behaved to the full pitch as I myself should have done under similar circumstances. Retiring upon an inclination of his structure, he draws up and fetches me a bow of the exact middle nick between dignity and service. I advance, he withdraws, and again the bow, devoid of obsequiousness, majestically condescending. These, thinks I, be royal manners. I could have taken him for the Sable King in person, stripped of his mantle. On my soul, he put me to the blush.'

'And is that all?' asked the duchess, relieving herself with a sigh.

'Why, madam,' quoth the beau, 'do you not see that he could have been none other than mine own, who could comport himself with that grand air and gracefulness when wounded by his closest relative? Upon his opening my door for me, and accepting the 'pas,' which I now right heartily accorded him, I recognized at once both him and the reproof he had designedly dealt me—or the wine supper I had danced on, perhaps I should say' and I protest that by such a display of supreme good breeding he managed to convey the highest compliment ever received by man, namely the assurance, that after the withering away of this mortal garb, I shall still be noted for urbanity and elegancy. Nay, and more, immortally, without the slip I was guilty of when I carried the bag of wine.'

Duchess Susan fanned herself to assist her digestion of the anecdote.

'Well, it's not so frightful a story, and I know you are the great Mr. Beamish;' she said.

He questioned her whether the gentleman had signalled him to her on the hill.

'What can he mean about a gentleman?' she turned to Chloe. 'My duke told me you would meet me, sir. And you are to protect me. And if anything happens, it is to be your fault.'

'Entirely,' said the beau. 'I shall therefore maintain a vigilant guard.'

'Except leaving me free. Oof! I've been boxed up so long. I declare, Chloe, I feel like a best dress out for a holiday, and a bit afraid of spoiling. I'm a real child, more than I was when my duke married me. I seemed to go in and grow up again, after I was raised to fortune. And nobody to tell of it! Fancy that! For you can't talk to old gentlemen about what's going on in your heart.'

'How of young gentlemen?' she was asked by the beau.

And she replied, 'They find it out.'

'Not if you do not assist them,' said he.

Duchess Susan let her eyelids and her underlie half drop, as she looked at him with the simple shyness of one of nature's thoughts in her head at peep on the pastures of the world. The melting blue eyes and the cherry lip made an exceedingly quickening picture. 'Now, I wonder if that is true?' she transferred her slyness to speech.

'Beware the middle-aged!' he exclaimed.

She appealed to Chloe. 'And I'm sure they're the nicest.'

Chloe agreed that they were.

The duchess measured Chloe and the beau together, with a mind swift in apprehending all that it hungered for.

She would have pursued the pleasing theme had she not been directed to gaze below upon the towers and roofs of the Wells, shining sleepily in a siesta of afternoon Summer sunlight.

With a spread of her silken robe, she touched the edifice of her hair, murmuring to Chloe, 'I can't abide that powder. You shall see me walk in a hoop. I can. I've done it to slow music till my duke clapped hands. I'm nothing sitting to what I am on my feet. That's because I haven't got fine language yet. I shall. It seems to come last. So, there 's the place. And whereabouts do all the great people meet and prommy—?'

'They promenade where you see the trees, madam,' said Chloe.

'And where is it where the ladies sit and eat jam tarts with whipped cream on 'em, while the gentlemen stand and pay compliments?'

Chloe said it was at a shop near the pump room.

Duchess Susan looked out over the house-tops, beyond the dusty hedges.

'Oh, and that powder!' she cried. 'I hate to be out of the fashion and a spectacle. But I do love my own hair, and I have such a lot, and I like the colour, and so does my duke. Only, don't let me be fingered at. If once I begin to blush before people, my courage is gone; my singing inside me is choked; and I've a real lark going on in me all day long, rain or sunshine—hush, all about love and amusement.'

Chloe smiled, and Duchess Susan said, 'Just like a bird, for I don't know what it is.'

She looked for Chloe to say that she did.

At the moment a pair of mounted squires rode up, and the coach stopped, while Beau Beamish gave orders for the church bells to be set ringing, and the band to meet and precede his equipage at the head of the bath avenue: 'in honour of the arrival of her Grace the Duchess of Dewlap.'

He delivered these words loudly to his men, and turned an effulgent gaze upon the duchess, so that for a minute she was fascinated and did not consult her hearing; but presently she fell into an uneasiness; the signs increased, she bit her lip, and after breathing short once or twice, 'Was it meaning me, Mr. Beamish?' she said.

'You, madam, are the person whom we 'delight to honour,' he replied.

'Duchess of what?' she screwed uneasy features to hear.

'Duchess of Dewlap,' said he.

'It's not my title, sir.'

'It is your title on my territory, madam.'

She made her pretty nose and upper lip ugly with a sneer of 'Dew—! And enter that town before all those people as Duchess of... Oh, no, I won't; I just won't! Call back those men now, please; now, if you please. Pray, Mr. Beamish! You'll offend me, sir. I'm not going to be a mock. You'll offend my duke, sir. He'd die rather than have my feelings hurt. Here's all my pleasure spoilt. I won't and I sha'n't enter the town as duchess of that stupid name, so call 'em back, call 'em back this instant. I know who I am and what I am, and I know what's due to me, I do.'

Beau Beamish rejoined, 'I too. Chloe will tell you I am lord here.'

'Then I'll go home, I will. I won't be laughed at for a great lady ninny. I'm a real lady of high rank, and such I'll appear. What 's a Duchess of Dewlap? One might as well be Duchess of Cowstail, Duchess of Mopsend. And those people! But I won't be that. I won't be played with. I see them staring! No, I can make up my mind, and I beg you to call back your men, or I'll go back home.' She muttered, 'Be made fun of—made a fool of!'

'Your Grace's chariot is behind,' said the beau.

His despotic coolness provoked her to an outcry and weeping: she repeated, 'Dewlap! Dewlap!' in sobs; she shook her shoulders and hid her face.

'You are proud of your title, are you, madam?' said he.

'I am.' She came out of her hands to answer him proudly. 'That I am!' she meant for a stronger affirmation.

'Then mark me,' he said impressively; 'I am your duke's friend, and you are under my charge here. I am your guardian and you are my ward, and you can enter the town only on the condition of obedience to me. Now, mark me, madam; no one can rob you of your real name and title saving yourself. But you are entering a place where you will encounter a thousand temptations to tarnish, and haply forfeit it. Be warned do nothing that will.'

'Then I'm to have my own title?' said she, clearing up.

'For the month of your visit you are Duchess of Dewlap.'

'I say I sha'n't!'

'You shall.'

'Never, sir!'

'I command it.'

She flung herself forward, with a wail, upon Chloe's bosom. 'Can't you do something for me?' she whimpered.

'It is impossible to move Mr. Beamish,' Chloe said.

Out of a pause, composed of sobs and sighs, the duchess let loose in a broken voice: 'Then I 'm sure I think—I think I'd rather have met—have met his skeleton!'

Her sincerity was equal to wit.

Beau Beamish shouted. He cordially applauded her, and in the genuine kindness of an admiration that surprised him, he permitted himself the liberty of taking and saluting her fingers. She fancied there was another chance for her, but he frowned at the mention of it.

Upon these proceedings the exhilarating sound of the band was heard; simultaneously a festival peal of bells burst forth; and an admonishment of the necessity for concealing her chagrin and exhibiting both station and a countenance to the people, combined with the excitement of the new scenes and the marching music to banish the acuter sense of disappointment from Duchess Susan's mind; so she very soon held herself erect, and wore a face open to every wonder, impressionable as the blue lake-surface, crisped here and there by fitful breezes against a level sun.

CHAPTER IV

It was an axiom with Mr. Beamish, our first, if not our only philosophical beau and a gentleman of some thoughtfulness, that the social English require tyrannical government as much as the political are able to dispense with it: and this he explained by an exposition of the character of a race possessed of the eminent virtue of individual self-assertion, which causes them to insist on good elbowroom wherever they gather together. Society, however, not being tolerable where the smoothness of intercourse is disturbed by a perpetual punching of sides, the merits of the free citizen in them become their demerits when a fraternal circle is established, and they who have shown an example of civilization too notable in one sphere to call for eulogy, are often to be seen elbowing on the ragged edge of barbarism in the other. They must therefore be reduced to accept laws not of their own making, and of an extreme rigidity.

Here too is a further peril; for the gallant spirits distinguishing them in the state of independence may (he foresaw the melancholy experience of a later age) abandon them utterly in subjection, and the glorious boisterousness befitting the village green forsake them even in their haunts of liberal association, should they once be thoroughly tamed by authority. Our 'merrie England' will then be long-faced England, an England of fallen chaps, like a boar's head, bearing for speech a lemon in the mouth: good to feast on, mayhap; not with!

Mr. Beamish would actually seem to have foreseen the danger of a transition that he could watch over only in his time; and, as he said, 'I go, as I came, on a flash'; he had neither ancestry nor descendants: he was a genius, he knew himself a solitary, therefore, in spite of his efforts to create his like. Within his district he did effect something, enough to give him fame as one of the princely fathers of our domestic civilization, though we now appear to have lost by it more than formerly we gained. The chasing of the natural is ever fraught with dubious hazards. If it gallops back, according to the proverb, it will do so at the charge: commonly it gallops off, quite off; and then for any kind of animation our precarious dependence is upon brains: we have to live on our wits, which are ordinarily less productive than land, and cannot be remitted in entail.

Rightly or wrongly (there are differences of opinion about it) Mr. Beamish repressed the chthonic natural with a rod of iron beneath his rule. The hoyden and the bumpkin had no peace until they had given public imitations of the lady and the gentleman; nor were the lady and the gentleman privileged to be what he called 'free flags.' He could be charitable to the passion, but he bellowed the very word itself (hauled up smoking from the brimstone lake) against them that pretended to be shamelessly guilty of the peccadilloes of gallantry. His famous accost of a lady threatening to sink, and already performing like a vessel in that situation: 'So, madam, I hear you are preparing to enrol yourself in the very ancient order?'... (he named it) was a piece of insolence that involved him in some discord with the lady's husband and 'the rascal steward,' as he chose to term the third party in these affairs: yet it is reputed to have saved the lady.

Furthermore, he attacked the vulgarity of persons of quality, and he has told a fashionable dame who was indulging herself in a marked sneer of disdain, not improving to her features, 'that he would be pleased to have her assurance it was her face she presented to mankind': a thing—thanks perhaps to him chiefly—no longer possible of utterance. One of the sex asking him why he addressed his persecutions particularly to women: 'Because I fight your battles,' says he, 'and I find you in the ranks of the enemy.' He treated them as traitors.

He was nevertheless well supported by a sex that compensates for dislike of its friend before a certain age by a cordial recognition of him when it has touched the period. A phalanx of great dames gave him the terrors of Olympus for all except the natively audacious, the truculent and the insufferably obtuse; and from the midst of them he launched decree and bolt to good effect: not, of course, without receiving return missiles, and not without subsequent question whether the work of that man was beneficial to the country, who indeed tamed the bumpkin squire and his brood, but at the cost of their animal spirits and their gift of speech; viz. by making petrifactions of them. In the surgical operation of tracheotomy, a successful treatment of the patient hangs, we believe, on the promptness and skill of the introduction of the artificial windpipe; and it may be that our unhappy countrymen when cut off from the source of their breath were not neatly handled; or else that there is a physical opposition in them to anything artificial, and it must be nature or nothing. The dispute shall be left where it stands.

Now, to venture upon parading a beautiful young Duchess of Dewlap, with an odour of the shepherdess about her notwithstanding her acquired art of stepping conformably in a hoop, and to demand full homage of respect for a lady bearing such a title, who had the intoxicating attractions of the ruddy orchard apple on the tree next the roadside wall, when the owner is absent, was bold in Mr. Beamish, passing temerity; nor would even he have attempted it had he not been assured of the support of his phalanx of great ladies. They indeed, after being taken into the secret, had stipulated that first they must have an inspection of the transformed dairymaid; and the review was not unfavourable. Duchess Susan came out of it more scatheless than her duke. She was tongue-tied, and her tutored walking and really admirable stature helped her to appease, the critics of her sex; by whom her too readily blushful innocence was praised, with a reserve, expressed in the remark, that she was a monstrous fine toy for a duke's second childhood, and should never have been let fly from his nursery. Her milliner was approved. The duke was a notorious connoisseur of female charms, and would see, of course, to the decorous adornment of her person by the best of modistes. Her smiling was pretty, her eyes were soft; she might turn out good, if well guarded for a time; but these merits of the woman are not those of the great lady, and her title was too strong a beam on her character to give it a fair chance with her critics. They one and all recommended powder for her hair and cheeks. That odour of the shepherdess could be exorcised by no other means, they declared. Her blushing was indecent.

Truly the critics of the foeman sex behaved in a way to cause the blushes to swarm rosy as the troops of young Loves round Cytherea in her sea-birth, when, some soaring, and sinking some, they flutter like her loosened zone, and breast the air thick as flower petals on the summer's breath, weaving her net for the world. Duchess Susan might protest her inability to keep her blushes down; that the wrong was done by the insolent eyes, and not by her artless cheeks. Ay, but nature, if we are to tame these men, must be swathed and concealed, partly stifled, absolutely stifled upon occasion. The natural woman does not move a foot without striking earth to conjure up the horrid apparition of the natural man, who is not as she, but a cannibal savage. To be the light which leads, it is her business to don the misty vesture of an idea, that she may dwell as an idea in men's minds, very dim, very powerful, but abstruse, unseizable. Much wisdom was imparted to her on the subject, and she understood a little, and echoed hollow to the remainder, willing to show entire docility as far as her intelligence consented to be awake. She was in that stage of the dainty, faintly tinged innocence of the amorousness of themselves when beautiful young women who have not been caught for schooling in infancy deem it a defilement to be made to appear other than the blessed nature has made them, which has made them beautiful, and surely therefore deserves to be worshipped. The lectures of the great ladies and Chloe's counsels failed to persuade her to use the powder puff-ball. Perhaps too, as timidity quitted her, she enjoyed her distinctiveness in their midst.

But the distinctiveness of a Duchess of Dewlap with the hair and cheeks of our native fields, was fraught with troubles outrunning Mr. Beamish's calculations. He had perceived that she would be attractive; he had not reckoned on the homogeneousness of her particular English charms. A beauty in red, white, and blue is our goddess Venus with the apple of Paris in her hand; and after two visits to the Pump Room, and one promenade in the walks about the Assembly House, she had as completely divided the ordinary guests of the Wells into male and female in opinion as her mother Nature had done in it sex. And the men would not be silenced; they had gazed on their divinest, and it was for the women to succumb to that unwholesome state, so full of thunder. Knights and squires, military and rural, threw up their allegiance right and left to devote themselves to this robust new vision, and in their peculiar manner, with a general View-halloo, and Yoicks, Tally-ho, and away we go, pelt ahead! Unexampled as it is in England for Beauty to kindle the ardours of the scent of the fox, Duchess Susan did more—she turned all her followers into hounds; they were madmen: within a very few days of her entrance bets raged about her, and there were brawls, jolly flings at her character in the form of lusty encomium, givings of the lie, and upon one occasion a knock-down blow in public, as though the place had never known the polishing touch of Mr. Beamish.

He was thrown into great perplexity by that blow. Discountenancing the duel as much as he could, an affair of the sword was nevertheless more tolerable than the brutal fist: and of all men to be guilty of it, who would have anticipated the young Alonzo, Chloe's quiet, modest lover! He it was. The case came before Mr. Beamish for his decision; he had to pronounce an impartial judgement, and for some time, during the examination of evidence, he suffered, as he assures us in his Memoirs, a royal agony. To have to strike with the glaive of Justice them whom they most esteem, is the greatest affliction known to kings. He would have done it: he deserved to reign. Happily the evidence against the gentleman who was tumbled, Mr. Ralph Shepster, excused Mr. Augustus Camwell, otherwise Alonzo, for dealing with him promptly to shut his mouth.

This Shepster, a raw young squire, 'reeking,' Beau Beamish writes of him, 'one half of the soil, and t' other half of the town,' had involved Chloe in his familiar remarks upon the Duchess of Dewlap; and the personal respect entertained by Mr. Beamish for Chloe so strongly approved Alonzo's championship of her, that in giving judgement he laid stress on young Alonzo's passion for Chloe, to prove at once the disinterestedness of the assailant, and the judicial nature of the sentence: which was, that Mr. Ralph Shepster should undergo banishment, and had the right to demand reparation. The latter part of this decree assisted in effecting the execution of the former. Shepster declined cold steel, calling it murder, and was effusive of nature's logic on the subject.

'Because a man comes and knocks me down, I'm to go up to him and ask him to run me through!'

His shake of the head signified that he was not such a noodle. Voluble and prolific of illustration, as is no one so much as a son of nature inspired to speak her words of wisdom, he defied the mandate, and refused himself satisfaction, until in the strangest manner possible flights of white feathers beset him, and he became a mark for persecution too trying for the friendship of his friends. He fled, repeating his tale, that he had seen 'Beamish's Duchess,' and Chloe attending her, at an assignation in the South Grove, where a gentleman, unknown to the Wells, presented himself to the adventurous ladies, and they walked together—a tale ending with nods.

Shepster's banishment was one of those victories of justice upon which mankind might be congratulated if they left no commotion behind. But, as when a boy has been horsed before his comrades, dread may visit them, yet is there likewise devilry in the school; and everywhere over earth a summary punishment that does not sweep the place clear is likely to infect whom it leaves remaining. The great law-givers, Lycurgus, Draco, Solon, Beamish, sorrowfully acknowledge that they have had recourse to infernal agents, after they have thus purified their circle of an offender. Doctors confess to the same of their physic. The expelling agency has next to be expelled, and it is a subtle poison, affecting our spirits. Duchess Susan had now the incense of a victim to heighten her charms; like the treasure-laden Spanish galleon for whom, on her voyage home from South American waters, our enterprising light-craft privateers lay in wait, she had the double attraction of being desirable and an enemy. To watch above her conscientiously was a harassing business.

Mr. Beamish sent for Chloe, and she came to him at once. Her look was curious; he studied it while they conversed. So looks one who is watching the sure flight of an arrow, or the happy combinations of an intrigue. Saying, 'I am no inquisitor, child,' he ventured upon two or three modest inquisitions with regard to her mistress. The title he had disguised Duchess Susan in, he confessed to rueing as the principal cause of the agitation of his principality. 'She is courted,' he said, 'less like a citadel waving a flag than a hostelry where the demand is for sitting room and a tankard! These be our manners. Yet, I must own, a Duchess of Dewlap is a provocation, and my exclusive desire to protect the name of my lord stands corrected by the perils environing his lady. She is other than I supposed her; she is, we will hope, an excellent good creature, but too attractive for most and drawbridge and the customary defences to be neglected.

Chloe met his interrogatory with a ready report of the young duchess's innocence and good nature that pacified Mr. Beamish.

'And you?' said he.

She smiled for answer.

That smile was not the common smile; it was one of an eager exultingness, producing as he gazed the twitch of an inquisitive reflection of it on his lips. Such a smile bids us guess and quickens us to guess, warns us we burn and speeds our burning, and so, like an angel wafting us to some heaven-feasting promontory, lifts us out of ourselves to see in the universe of colour what the mouth has but pallid speech to tell. That is the very heart's language; the years are in a look, as mount and vale of the dark land spring up in lightning.

He checked himself: he scarce dared to say it.

She nodded.

'You have seen the man, Chloe?'

Her smiling broke up in the hard lines of an ecstasy neighbouring pain. 'He has come; he is here; he is faithful; he has not forgotten me. I was right. I knew! I knew!'

'Caseldy has come?'

'He has come. Do not ask. To have him! to see him! Mr. Beamish, he is here.'

'At last!'

'Cruel!'

'Well, Caseldy has come, then! But now, friend Chloe, you should be made aware that the man—'

She stopped her ears. As she did so, Mr. Beamish observed a thick silken skein dangling from one hand. Part of it was plaited, and at the upper end there was a knot. It resembled the commencement of her manufactory of a whip: she swayed it to and fro, allowing him to catch and lift the threads on his fingers for the purpose of examining her work. There was no special compliment to pay, so he dropped it without remark.

Their faces had expressed her wish to hear nothing from him of Caseldy and his submission to say nothing. Her happiness was too big; she appeared to beg to lie down with it on her bosom, in the manner of an outworn, young mother who has now first received her infant in her arms from the nurse.

CHAPTER V

Humouring Chloe with his usual considerateness, Mr. Beamish forbore to cast a shadow on her new-born joy, and even within himself to doubt the security of its foundation. Caseldy's return to the Wells was at least some assurance of his constancy, seeing that here they appointed to meet when he and Chloe last parted. All might be well, though it was unexplained why he had not presented himself earlier. To the lightest inquiry Chloe's reply was a shiver of happiness.

Moreover, Mr. Beamish calculated that Caseldy would be a serviceable ally in commanding a proper respect for her Grace the Duchess of Dewlap. So he betook himself cheerfully to Caseldy's lodgings to deliver a message of welcome, meeting, on his way thither, Mr. Augustus Camwell, with whom he had a short conversation, greatly to his admiration of the enamoured young gentleman's goodness and self-compression in speaking of Caseldy and Chloe's better fortune. Mr. Camwell seemed hurried.

Caseldy was not at home, and Mr. Beamish proceeded to the lodgings of the duchess. Chloe had found her absent. The two consulted. Mr. Beamish put on a serious air, until Chloe mentioned the pastrycook's shop, for Duchess Susan had a sweet tooth; she loved a visit to the pastrycook's, whose jam tarts were dearer to her than his more famous hot mutton pies. The pastry cook informed Mr. Beamish that her Grace had been in his shop, earlier than usual, as it happened, and accompanied by a foreign-looking gentleman wearing moustachois. Her Grace, the pastrycook said, had partaken of several tarts, in common with the gentleman, who complimented him upon his excelling the Continental confectioner. Mr. Beamish glanced at Chloe. He pursued his researches down at the Pump Room, while she looked round the ladies' coffee house. Encountering again, they walked back to the duchess's lodgings, where a band stood playing in the road, by order of her Grace; but the duchess was away, and had not been seen since her morning's departure.

'What sort of character would you give mistress Susan of Dewlap, from your personal acquaintance with it?' said Mr. Beamish to Chloe, as they stepped from the door.

Chloe mused and said, 'I would add "good" to the unkindest comparison you could find for her.'

'But accepting the comparison!' Mr. Beamish nodded, and revolved upon the circumstance of their being very much in nature's hands with Duchess Susan, of whom it might be said that her character was good, yet all the more alive to the temptations besetting the Spring season. He allied Chloe's adjective to a number of epithets equally applicable to nature and to women, according to current ideas, concluding: 'Count, they call your Caseldy at his lodgings. "The Count he is out for an airing." He is counted out. Ah! you will make him drop that "Count" when he takes you from here.'

'Do not speak of the time beyond the month,' said Chloe, so urgently on a rapid breath as to cause Mr. Beamish to cast an inquiring look at her.

She answered it, 'Is not one month of brightness as much as we can ask for?'

The beau clapped his elbows complacently to his sides in philosophical concord with her sentiment.

In the afternoon, on the parade, they were joined by Mr. Camwell, among groups of fashionable ladies and their escorts, pacing serenely, by medical prescription, for an appetite. As he did not comment on the absence of the duchess, Mr. Beamish alluded to it; whereupon he was informed that she was about the meadows, and had been there for some hours.

'Not unguarded,' he replied to Mr. Beamish.

'Aha!' quoth the latter; 'we have an Argus!' and as the duchess was not on the heights, and the sun's rays were mild in cloud, he agreed to his young friend's proposal that they should advance to meet her. Chloe walked with them, but her face was disdainful; at the stiles she gave her hand to Mr. Beamish; she did not address a word to Mr. Camwell, and he knew the reason. Nevertheless he maintained his air of soldierly resignation to the performance of duty, and held his head like a gentleman unable to conceive the ignominy of having played spy. Chloe shrank from him.

Duchess Susan was distinguished coming across a broad uncut meadow, tirra-lirraing beneath a lark, Caseldy in attendance on her. She stopped short and spoke to him; then came forward, crying ingenuously. 'Oh, Mr. Beamish, isn't this just what you wanted me to do?'

'No, madam,' said he, 'you had my injunctions to the contrary.'

'La!' she exclaimed, 'I thought I was to run about in the fields now and then to preserve my simplicity. I know I was told so, and who told me!'

Mr. Beamish bowed effusively to the introduction of Caseldy, whose fingers he touched in sign of the renewal of acquaintance, and with a laugh addressed the duchess:

'Madam, you remind me of a tale of my infancy. I had a juvenile comrade of the tenderest age, by name Tommy Plumston, and he enjoyed the privilege of intimacy with a component urchin yclept Jimmy Clungeon, with which adventurous roamer, in defiance of his mother's interdict against his leaving the house for a minute during her absence from home, he departed on a tour of the district, resulting, perhaps as a consequence of its completeness, in this, that at a distance computed at four miles from the maternal mansion, he perceived his beloved mama with sufficient clearness to feel sure that she likewise had seen him. Tommy consulted with Jimmy, and then he sprang forward on a run to his frowning mama, and delivered himself in these artless words, which I repeat as they were uttered, to give you the flavour of the innocent babe: he said, "I frink I frought I hear you call me, ma! and Jimmy Clungeon, he frought he frink so too!" So, you see, the pair of them were under the impression that they were doing right. There is a delicate distinction in the tenses of each frinking where the other frought, enough in itself to stamp sincerity upon the statement.'

Caseldy said, 'The veracity of a boy possessing a friend named Clungeon is beyond contest.'

Duchess Susan opened her eyes. 'Four miles from home! And what did his mother do to him?'

'Tommy's mama,' said Mr. Beamish, and with the resplendent licence of the period which continued still upon tolerable terms with nature under the compromise of decorous 'Oh-fie!' flatly declared the thing she did.

'I fancy, sir, that I caught sight of your figure on the hill yonder about an hour or so earlier,' said Caseldy to Mr. Camwell.

'If it was at the time when you were issuing from that wood, sir, your surmise is correct,' said the young gentleman.

'You are long-sighted, sir!'

'I am, sir.'

'And so am I.'

'And I,' said Chloe.

'Our Chloe will distinguish you accurately at a mile, and has done it,' observed Mr. Beamish.

'One guesses tiptoe on a suspicion, and if one is wrong it passes, and if one is right it is a miracle,' she said, and raised her voice on a song to quit the subject.

'Ay, ay, Chloe; so then you had a suspicion, you rogue, the day we had the pleasure of meeting the duchess, had you?' Mr. Beamish persisted.

Duchess Susan interposed. 'Such a pretty song! and you to stop her, sir!'

Caseldy took up the air.

'Oh, you two together!' she cried. 'I do love hearing music in the fields; it is heavenly. Bands in the town and voices in the green fields, I say! Couldn't you join Chloe, Mr.... Count, sir, before we come among the people, here where it 's all so nice and still. Music! and my heart does begin so to pit-a-pat. Do you sing, Mr. Alonzo?'

'Poorly,' the young gentleman replied.

'But the Count can sing, and Chloe's a real angel when she sings; and won't you, dear?' she implored Chloe, to whom Caseldy addressed a prelude with a bow and a flourish of the hand.

Chloe's voice flew forth. Caseldy's rich masculine matched it. The song was gay; he snapped his finger at intervals in foreign style, singing big-chested, with full notes and a fine abandonment, and the quickest susceptibility to his fair companion's cunning modulations, and an eye for Duchess Susan's rapture.

Mr. Beamish and Mr. Camwell applauded them.

'I never can tell what to say when I'm brimming'; the duchess let fall a sigh. 'And he can play the flute, Mr. Beamish. He promised me he would go into the orchestra and play a bit at one of your nice evening delicious concerts, and that will be nice—Oh!'

'He promised you, madam, did he so?' said the beau. 'Was it on your way to the Wells that he promised you?'

'On my way to the Wells!' she exclaimed softly. 'Why, how could anybody promise me a thing before ever he saw me? I call that a strange thing to ask a person. No, to-day, while we were promenading; and I should hear him sing, he said. He does admire his Chloe so. Why, no wonder, is it, now? She can do everything; knit, sew, sing, dance—and talk! She's never uneasy for a word. She makes whole scenes of things go round you, like a picture peep-show, I tell her. And always cheerful. She hasn't a minute of grumps; and I'm sometimes a dish of stale milk fit only for pigs.

With your late hours here, I'm sure I want tickling in the morning, and Chloe carols me one of her songs, and I say, "There's my bird!"'

Mr. Beamish added, 'And you will remember she has a heart.'

'I should think so!' said the duchess.

'A heart, madam!'

'Why, what else?'

Nothing other, the beau, by his aspect, was constrained to admit.

He appeared puzzled by this daughter of nature in a coronet; and more on her remarking, 'You know about her heart, Mr. Beamish.'

He acquiesced, for of course he knew of her life-long devotion to Caseldy; but there was archness in her tone. However, he did not expect a woman of her education to have the tone perfectly concordant with the circumstances. Speaking tentatively of Caseldy's handsome face and figure, he was pleased to hear the duchess say, 'So I tell Chloe.'

'Well,' said he, 'we must consider them united; they are one.'

Duchess Susan replied, 'That's what I tell him; she will do anything you wish.'

He repeated these words with an interjection, and decided in his mind that they were merely silly. She was a real shepherdess by birth and nature, requiring a strong guard over her attractions on account of her simplicity; such was his reading of the problem; he had conceived it at the first sight of her, and always recurred to it under the influence of her artless eyes, though his theories upon men and women were astute, and that cavalier perceived by long-sighted Chloe at Duchess Susan's coach window perturbed him at whiles. Habitually to be anticipating the simpleton in a particular person is the sure way of being sometimes the dupe, as he would not have been the last to warn a neophyte; but abstract wisdom is in need of an unappeased suspicion of much keenness of edge, if we would have it alive to cope with artless eyes and our prepossessed fancy of their artlessness.

'You talk of Chloe to him?' he said.

She answered. 'Yes, that I do. And he does love her! I like to hear him. He is one of the gentlemen who don't make me feel timid with them.'

She received a short lecture on the virtues of timidity in preserving the sex from danger; after which, considering that the lady who does not feel timid with a particular cavalier has had no sentiment awakened, he relinquished his place to Mr. Camwell, and proceeded to administer the probe to Caseldy.

That gentleman was communicatively candid. Chloe had left him, and he related how, summoned home to England and compelled to settle a dispute threatening a lawsuit, he had regretfully to abstain from visiting the Wells for a season, not because of any fear of the attractions of play—he had subdued the frailty of the desire to play—but because he deemed it due to his Chloe to bring her an untroubled face, and he wished first to be the better of the serious annoyances besetting him. For some similar reason he had not written; he wished to feast on her surprise. 'And I had my reward,' he said, as if he had been the person principally to suffer through that abstinence. 'I found—I may say it to you, Mr. Beamish love in her eyes. Divine by nature, she is one of the immortals, both in appearance and in steadfastness.'

They referred to Duchess Susan. Caseldy reluctantly owned that it would be an unkindness to remove Chloe from attendance on her during the short remaining term of her stay at the Wells; and so he had not proposed it, he said, for the duchess was a child, an innocent, not stupid by any means; but, of course, her transplanting from an inferior to an exalted position put her under disadvantages.

Mr. Beamish spoke of the difficulties of his post as guardian, and also of the strange cavalier seen at her carriage window by Chloe.

Caseldy smiled and said, 'If there was one—and Chloe is rather long—sighted—we can hardly expect her to confess it.'

'Why not, sir, if she be this piece of innocence?' Mr. Beamish was led to inquire.

'She fears you, sir,' Caseldy answered. 'You have inspired her with an extraordinary fear of you.'

'I have?' said the beau: it had been his endeavour to inspire it, and he swelled somewhat, rather with relief at the thought of his possessing a power to control his delicate charge, than with our vanity; yet would it be audacious to say that there was not a dose of the latter. He was a very human man; and he had, as we have seen, his ideas of the effect of the impression of fear upon the hearts of women. Something, in any case, caused him to forget the cavalier.

They were drawn to the three preceding them, by a lively dissension between Chloe and Mr. Camwell.

Duchess Susan explained it in her blunt style: 'She wants him to go away home, and he says he will, if she'll give him that double skein of silk she swings about, and she says she won't, let him ask as long as he pleases; so he says he sha'n't go, and I'm sure I don't see why he should; and she says he may stay, but he sha'n't have her necklace, she calls it. So Mr. Camwell snatches, and Chloe fires up. Gracious, can't she frown!—at him. She never frowns at anybody but him.'

Caseldy attempted persuasion on Mr. Camwell's behalf. With his mouth at Chloe's ear, he said, 'Give it; let the poor fellow have his memento; despatch him with it.'

'I can hear! and that is really kind,' exclaimed Duchess Susan.

'Rather a missy-missy schoolgirl sort of necklace,' Mr. Beamish observed; 'but he might have it, without the dismissal, for I cannot consent to lose Alonzo. No, madam,' he nodded at the duchess.

Caseldy continued his whisper: 'You can't think of wearing a thing like that about your neck?'

'Indeed,' said Chloe, 'I think of it.'

'Why, what fashion have you over here?'

'It is not yet a fashion,' she said.

'A silken circlet will not well become any precious pendant that I know of.'

'A bag of dust is not a very precious pendant,' she said.

'Oh, a memento mori!' cried he.

And she answered, 'Yes.'

He rallied her for her superstition, pursuing, 'Surely, my love, 'tis a cheap riddance of a pestilent, intrusive jaloux. Whip it into his hands for a mittimus.'

'Does his presence distress you?' she asked.

'I will own that to be always having the fellow dogging us, with his dejected leer, is not agreeable. He watches us now, because my lips are close by your cheek. He should be absent; he is one too many. Speed him on his voyage with the souvenir he asks for.'

'I keep it for a journey of my own, which I may have to take,' said Chloe.

'With me?'

'You will follow; you cannot help following me, Caseldy.'

He speculated on her front. She was tenderly smiling. 'You are happy, Chloe?'

'I have never known such happiness,' she said. The brilliancy of her eyes confirmed it.

He glanced over at Duchess Susan, who was like a sunflower in the sun. His glance lingered a moment. Her abundant and glowing young charms were the richest fascination an eye like his could dwell on. 'That is right,' said he. 'We will be perfectly happy till the month ends. And after it? But get us rid of Monsieur le Jeune; toss him that trifle; I spare him that. 'Twill be bliss to him, at the cost of a bit of silk thread to us. Besides, if we keep him to cure him of his passion here, might it not be—these boys veer suddenly, like the winds of Albion, from one fair object to t' other—at the cost of the precious and simple lady you are guarding? I merely hint. These two affect one another, as though it could be. She speaks of him. It shall be as you please, but a trifle like that, my Chloe, to be rid of a green eye!'

'You much wish him gone?' she said.

He shrugged. 'The fellow is in our way.'

'You think him a little perilous for my innocent lady?'

'Candidly, I do.'

She stretched the half-plaited silken rope in her two hands to try the strength of it, made a second knot, and consigned it to her pocket.

At once she wore her liveliest playfellow air, in which character no one was so enchanting as Chloe could be, for she became the comrade of men without forfeit of her station among sage sweet ladies, and was like a well-mannered sparkling boy, to whom his admiring seniors have given the lead in sallies, whims, and fights; but pleasanter than a boy, the soft hues of her sex toned her frolic spirit; she seemed her sex's deputy, to tell the coarser where they could meet, as on a bridge above the torrent separating them, gaily for interchange of the best of either, unfired and untempted by fire, yet with all the elements which make fire burn to animate their hearts.

'Lucky the man who wins for himself that life-long cordial!' Mr. Beamish said to Duchess Susan.

She had small comprehension of metaphorical phrases, but she was quick at reading faces; and comparing the enthusiasm on the face of the beau with Caseldy's look of troubled wonderment and regret, she pitied the lover conscious of not having the larger share of his mistress's affections. When presently he looked at her, the tender-hearted woman could have cried for very compassion, so sensible did he show himself of Chloe's preference of the other.

CHAPTER VI

That evening Duchess Susan played at the Pharaoh table and lost eight hundred pounds, through desperation at the loss of twenty. After encouraging her to proceed to this extremity, Caseldy checked her. He was conducting her out of the Play room when a couple of young squires of the Shepster order, and primed with wine, intercepted her to present their condolences, which they performed with exaggerated gestures, intended for broad mimicry of the courtliness imported from the Continent, and a very dulcet harping on the popular variations of her Christian name, not forgetting her singular title, 'my lovely, lovely Dewlap!'

She was excited and stunned by her immediate experience in the transfer of money, and she said, 'I 'm sure I don't know what you want.'

'Yes!' cried they, striking their bosoms as guitars, and attempting the posture of the thrummer on the instrument; 'she knows. She does know. Handsome Susie knows what we want.' And one ejaculated, mellifluously, 'Oh!' and the other 'Ah!' in flagrant derision of the foreign ways they produced in boorish burlesque—a self-consolatory and a common trick of the boor.

Caseldy was behind. He pushed forward and bowed to them. 'Sirs, will you mention to me what you want?'

He said it with a look that meant steel. It cooled them sufficiently to let him place the duchess under the protectorship of Mr. Beamish, then entering from another room with Chloe; whereupon the pair of rustic bucks retired to reinvigorate their valiant blood.

Mr. Beamish had seen that there was cause for gratitude to Caseldy, to whom he said, 'She has lost?' and he seemed satisfied on hearing the amount of the loss, and commissioned Caseldy to escort the ladies to their lodgings at once, observing, 'Adieu, Count!'

'You will find my foreign title of use to you here, after a bout or two,' was the reply.

'No bouts, if possibly to be avoided; though I perceive how the flavour of your countship may spread a wholesome alarm among our rurals, who will readily have at you with fists, but relish not the tricky cold weapon.'

Mr. Beamish haughtily bowed the duchess away.

Caseldy seized the opportunity while handing her into her sedan to say, 'We will try the fortune-teller for a lucky day to have our revenge.'

She answered: 'Oh, don't talk to me about playing again ever; I'm nigh on a clean pocket, and never knew such a sinful place as this. I feel I've tumbled into a ditch. And there's Mr. Beamish, all top when he bows to me. You're keeping Chloe waiting, sir.'

'Where was she while we were at the table?'

'Sure she was with Mr. Beamish.'

'Ah!' he groaned.

'The poor soul is in despair over her losses to-night,' he turned from the boxed-up duchess to remark to Chloe. 'Give her a comfortable cry and a few moral maxims.'

'I will,' she said. 'You love me, Caseldy?'

'Love you? I? Your own? What assurance would you have?'

'None, dear friend.'

Here was a woman easily deceived.

In the hearts of certain men, owing to an intellectual contempt of easy dupes, compunction in deceiving is diminished by the lightness of their task; and that soft confidence which will often, if but passingly, bid betrayers reconsider the charms of the fair soul they are abandoning, commends these armoured knights to pursue with redoubled earnest the fruitful ways of treachery. Their feelings are warm for their prey, moreover; and choosing to judge their victim by the present warmth of their feelings, they can at will be hurt, even to being scandalized, by a coldness that does not waken one suspicion of them. Jealousy would have a chance of arresting, for it is not impossible to tease them back to avowed allegiance; but sheer indifference also has a stronger hold on them than a, dull, blind trustfulness. They hate the burden it imposes; the blind aspect is only touching enough to remind them of the burden, and they hate if for that, and for the enormous presumption of the belief that they are everlastingly bound to such an imbecile. She walks about with her eyes shut, expecting not to stumble, and when she does, am I to blame? The injured man asks it in the course of his reasoning.

He recurs to his victim's merits, but only compassionately, and the compassion is chilled by the thought that she may in the end start across his path to thwart him. Thereat he is drawn to think of the prize she may rob him of; and when one woman is an obstacle, the other shines desirable as life beyond death; he must have her; he sees her in the hue of his desire for her, and the obstacle in that of his repulsion. Cruelty is no more than the man's effort to win the wished object.

She should not leave it to his imagination to conceive that in the end the blind may awaken to thwart him. Better for her to cast him hence, or let him know that she will do battle to keep him. But the pride of a love that has hardened in the faithfulness of love cannot always be wise on trial.

Caseldy walked considerably in the rear of the couple of chairs. He saw on his way what was coming. His two young squires were posted at Duchess Susan's door when she arrived, and he received a blow from one of them in clearing a way for her. She plucked at his hand. 'Have they hurt you?' she asked.

'Think of me to-night thanking them and heaven for this, my darling,' he replied, with a pressure that lit the flying moment to kindle the after hours.

Chloe had taken help of one of her bearers to jump out. She stretched a finger at the unruly intruders, crying sternly, 'There is blood on you—come not nigh me!' The loftiest harangue would not have been so cunning to touch their wits. They stared at one another in the clear moonlight. Which of them had blood on him? As they had not been for blood, but for rough fun, and something to boast of next day, they gesticulated according to the first instructions of the dancing master, by way of gallantry, and were out of Caseldy's path when he placed himself at his liege lady's service. 'Take no notice of them, dear,' she said.

'No, no,' said he; and 'What is it?' and his hoarse accent and shaking clasp of her arm sickened her to the sensation of approaching death.

Upstairs Duchess Susan made a show of embracing her. Both were trembling. The duchess ascribed her condition to those dreadful men. 'What makes them be at me so?' she said.

And Chloe said, 'Because you are beautiful.'

'Am I?'

'You are.'

'I am?'

'Very beautiful; young and beautiful; beautiful in the bud. You will learn to excuse them, madam.'

'But, Chloe—' The duchess shut her mouth. Out of a languid reverie, she sighed: 'I suppose I must be! My duke—oh, don't talk of him. Dear man! he's in bed and fast asleep long before this. I wonder how he came to let me come here.

I did bother him, I know. Am I very, very beautiful, Chloe, so that men can't help themselves?'

'Very, madam.'

'There, good-night. I want to be in bed, and I can't kiss you because you keep calling me madam, and freeze me to icicles; but I do love you, Chloe.'

'I am sure you do.'

'I'm quite certain I do. I know I never mean harm. But how are we women expected to behave, then? Oh, I'm unhappy, I am.'

'You must abstain from playing.'

'It's that! I've lost my money—I forgot. And I shall have to confess it to my duke, though he warned me. Old men hold their fingers up—so! One finger: and you never forget the sight of it, never. It's a round finger, like the handle of a jug, and won't point at you when they're lecturing, and the skin's like an old coat on gaffer's shoulders—or, Chloe! just like, when you look at the nail, a rumpled counterpane up to the face of a corpse. I declare, it's just like! I feel as if I didn't a bit mind talking of corpses tonight. And my money's gone, and I don't much mind. I'm a wild girl again, handsomer than when that—he is a dear, kind, good old nobleman, with his funny old finger: "Susan! Susan!" I'm no worse than others. Everybody plays here; everybody superior. Why, you have played, Chloe.'

'Never!'

'I've heard you say you played once, and a bigger stake it was, you said, than anybody ever did play.'

'Not money.'

'What then?'

'My life.'

'Goodness—yes! I understand. I understand everything to-night-men too. So you did!—They're not so shamefully wicked, Chloe. Because I can't see the wrong of human nature—if we're discreet, I mean. Now and then a country dance and a game, and home to bed and dreams. There's no harm in that, I vow. And that's why you stayed at this place. You like it, Chloe?'

'I am used to it.'

'But when you're married to Count Caseldy you'll go?'

'Yes, then.'

She uttered it so joylessly that Duchess Susan added, with intense affectionateness, 'You're not obliged to marry him, dear Chloe.'

'Nor he me, madam.'

The duchess caught at her impulsively to kiss her, and said she would undress herself, as she wished to be alone.

From that night she was a creature inflamed.

CHAPTER VII

The total disappearance of the pair of heroes who had been the latest in the conspiracy to vex his delicate charge, gave Mr. Beamish a high opinion of Caseldy as an assistant in such an office as he held. They had gone, and nothing more was heard of them. Caseldy confined his observations on the subject to the remark that he had employed the best means to be rid of that kind of worthies; and whether their souls had fled, or only their bodies, was unknown. But the duchess had quiet promenades with Caseldy to guard her, while Mr. Beamish counted the remaining days of her visit with the impatience of a man having cause to cast eye on a clock. For Duchess Susan was not very manageable now; she had fits of insurgency, and plainly said that her time was short, and she meant to do as she liked, go where she liked, play when she liked, and be an independent woman—if she was so soon to be taken away and boxed in a castle that was only a bigger sedan.

Caseldy protested he was as helpless as the beau. He described the annoyance of his incessant running about at her heels in all directions amusingly, and suggested that she must be beating the district to recover her 'strange cavalier,' of whom, or of one that had ridden beside her carriage half a day on her journey to the Wells, he said she had dropped a sort of hint. He complained of the impossibility of his getting an hour in privacy with his Chloe.

'And I, accustomed to consult with her, see too little of her,' said Mr. Beamish. 'I shall presently be seeing nothing, and already I am sensible of my loss.'

He represented his case to Duchess Susan:—that she was for ever driving out long distances and taking Chloe from him, when his occupation precluded his accompanying them; and as Chloe soon was to be lost to him for good, he deeply felt her absence.

The duchess flung him enigmatical rejoinders: 'You can change all that, Mr. Beamish, if you like, and you know you can. Oh, yes, you can. But you like being a butterfly, and when you've made ladies pale you're happy: and there they're to stick and wither for you. Never!—I've that pride. I may be worried, but I'll never sink to green and melancholy for a man.'

She bridled at herself in a mirror, wherein not a sign of paleness was reflected.

Mr. Beamish meditated, and he thought it prudent to speak to Caseldy manfully of her childish suspicions, lest she should perchance in like manner perturb the lover's mind.

'Oh, make your mind easy, my dear sir, as far as I am concerned,' said Caseldy. 'But, to tell you the truth, I think I can interpret her creamy ladyship's innuendos a little differently and quite as clearly. For my part, I prefer the pale to the blowsy, and I stake my right hand on Chloe's fidelity. Whatever harm I may have the senseless cruelty—misfortune, I may rather call it—to do that heavenly-minded woman in our days to come, none shall say of me that I was ever for an instant guilty of the baseness of doubting her purity and constancy. And, sir, I will add that I could perfectly rely also on your honour.'

Mr. Beamish bowed. 'You do but do me justice. But, say, what interpretation?'

'She began by fearing you,' said Caseldy, creating a stare that was followed by a frown. 'She fancies you neglect her. Perhaps she has a woman's suspicion that you do it to try her.'

Mr. Beamish frenetically cited his many occupations. 'How can I be ever dancing attendance on her?' Then he said, 'Pooh,' and tenderly fingered the ruffles of his wrist. 'Tush, tush,' said he, 'no, no: though if it came to a struggle between us, I might in the interests of my old friend, her lord, whom I have reasons for esteeming, interpose an influence that would make the exercise of my authority agreeable. Hitherto I have seen no actual need of it, and I watch keenly. Her eye has been on Colonel Poltermore once or twice his on her. The woman is a rose in June, sir, and I forgive the whole world for looking—and for longing too. But I have observed nothing serious.'

'He is of our party to the beacon-head to-morrow,' said Caseldy. 'She insisted that she would have him; and at least it will grant me furlough for an hour.'

'Do me the service to report to me,' said Mr. Beamish.

In this fashion he engaged Caseldy to supply him with inventions, and prepared himself to swallow them. It was Poltermore and Poltermore, the Colonel here, the Colonel there until the chase grew so hot that Mr. Beamish could no longer listen to young Mr. Camwell's fatiguing drone upon his one theme of the double-dealing of Chloe's betrothed. He became of her way of thinking, and treated the young gentleman almost as coldly as she. In time he was ready to guess of his own acuteness that the 'strange cavalier' could have been no other than Colonel Poltermore. When Caseldy hinted it, Mr. Beamish said, 'I have marked him.' He added, in highly self-satisfied style, 'With all your foreign training, my friend, you will learn that we English are not so far behind you in the art of unravelling an intrigue in the dark.' To which Caseldy replied, that the Continental world had little to teach Mr. Beamish.

Poor Colonel Poltermore, as he came to be called, was clearly a victim of the sudden affability of Duchess Susan. The transformation of a stiff military officer into a nimble Puck, a runner of errands and a sprightly attendant, could not pass without notice. The first effect of her discriminating condescension on this unfortunate gentleman was to make him the champion of her claims to breeding. She had it by nature, she was Nature's great lady, he would protest to the noble dames of the circle he moved in; and they admitted that she was different in every way from a bourgeoise elevated by marriage to lofty rank: she was not vulgar. But they remained doubtful of the perfect simplicity of a young woman who worked such changes in men as to render one of the famous conquerors of the day her agitated humble servant. By rapid degrees the Colonel had fallen to that. When not by her side, he was ever marching with sharp strides, hurrying through rooms and down alleys and groves until he had discovered and attached himself to her skirts. And, curiously, the object of his jealousy was the devoted Alonzo! Mr. Beamish laughed when he heard of it. The lady's excitement and giddy mien, however, accused Poltermore of a stage of success requiring to be combated immediately. There was mention of Duchess Susan's mighty wish to pay a visit to the popular fortune-teller of the hut on the heath, and Mr. Beamish put his veto on the expedition. She had obeyed him by abstaining from play of late, so he fully expected, that his interdict would be obeyed; and besides the fortune-teller was a rogue of a sham astrologer known to have foretold to certain tender ladies things they were only too desirous to imagine predestined by an extraordinary indication of the course of planets through the zodiac, thus causing them to sin by the example of celestial conjunctions—a piece of wanton impiety. The beau took high ground in his objections to the adventure. Nevertheless, Duchess Susan did go. She drove to the heath at an early hour of the morning, attended by Chloe, Colonel Poltermore, and Caseldy. They subsequently breakfasted at an inn where gipsy repasts were occasionally served to the fashion, and they were back at the wells as soon as the world was abroad. Their surprise then was prodigious when Mr. Beamish, accosting them full in assembly, inquired whether they were satisfied with the report of their fortunes, and yet more when he positively proved himself acquainted with the fortunes which had been recounted to each of them in privacy.

'You, Colonel Poltermore, are to be in luck's way up to the tenth milestone,—where your chariot will overset and you will be lamed for life.'

'Not quite so bad,' said the Colonel cheerfully, he having been informed of much better.

'And you, Count Caseldy, are to have it all your own way with good luck, after committing a deed of slaughter, with the solitary penalty of undergoing a visit every night from the corpse.'

'Ghost,' Caseldy smilingly corrected him.

'And Chloe would not have her fortune told, because she knew it!' Mr. Beamish cast a paternal glance at her. 'And you, madam,' he bent his brows on the duchess, 'received the communication that "All for Love" will sink you as it raised you, put you down as it took you up, furnish the feast to the raven gentleman which belongs of right to the golden eagle?'

'Nothing of the sort! And I don't believe in any of their stories,' cried the duchess, with a burning face.

'You deny it, madam?'

'I do. There was never a word of a raven or an eagle, that I'll swear, now.'

'You deny that there was ever a word of "All for Love"? Speak, madam.'

'Their conjuror's rigmarole!' she murmured, huffing. 'As if I listened to their nonsense!'

'Does the Duchess of Dewlap dare to give me the lie?' said Mr. Beamish.

'That's not my title, and you know it,' she retorted.

'What's this?' the angry beau sang out. 'What stuff is this you wear?' He towered and laid hand on a border of lace of her morning dress, tore it furiously and swung a length of it round him: and while the duchess panted and trembled at an outrage that won for her the sympathy of every lady present as well as the championship of the gentlemen, he tossed the lace to the floor and trampled on it, making his big voice intelligible over the uproar: 'Hear what she does! 'Tis a felony! She wears the stuff with Betty Worcester's yellow starch on it for mock antique! And let who else wears it strip it off before the town shall say we are disgraced—when I tell you that Betty Worcester was hanged at Tyburn yesterday morning for murder!'

There were shrieks.

Hardly had he finished speaking before the assembly began to melt; he stood in the centre like a pole unwinding streamers, amid a confusion of hurrying dresses, the sound and whirl and drift whereof was as that of the autumnal strewn leaves on a wind rising in November. The troops of ladies were off to bereave themselves of their fashionable imitation old lace adornment, which denounced them in some sort abettors and associates of the sanguinary loathed wretch, Mrs. Elizabeth Worcester, their benefactress of the previous day, now hanged and dangling on the gallows-tree.

Those ladies who wore not imitation lace or any lace in the morning, were scarcely displeased with the beau for his exposure of them that did. The gentlemen were confounded by his exhibition of audacious power. The two gentlemen nighest upon violently resenting his brutality to Duchess Susan, led her from the room in company with Chloe.

'The woman shall fear me to good purpose,' Mr. Beamish said to himself.

CHAPTER VIII

Mr. Camwell was in the ante-room as Chloe passed out behind the two incensed supporters of Duchess Susan.

'I shall be by the fir-trees on the Mount at eight this evening,' she said.

'I will be there,' he replied.

'Drive Mr. Beamish into the country, that these gentlemen may have time to cool.'

He promised her it should be done.

Close on the hour of her appointment, he stood under the fir-trees, admiring the sunset along the western line of hills, and when Chloe joined him he spoke of the beauty of the scene.

'Though nothing seems more eloquently to say farewell,' he added, with a sinking voice.

'We could say it now, and be friends,' she answered.

'Later than now, you think it unlikely that you could forgive me, Chloe.'

'In truth, sir, you are making it hard for me.'

'I have stayed here to keep watch; for no pleasure of my own,' said he.

'Mr. Beamish is an excellent protector of the duchess.'

'Excellent; and he is cleverly taught to suppose she fears him greatly; and when she offends him, he makes a display of his Jupiter's awfulness, with the effect on woman of natural spirit which you have seen, and others had foreseen, that she is exasperated and grows reckless. Tie another knot in your string, Chloe.'

She looked away, saying, 'Were you not the cause? You were in collusion with that charlatan of the heath, who told them their fortunes this morning. I see far, both in the dark and in the light.'

'But not through a curtain. I was present.'

'Hateful, hateful business of the spy! You have worked a great mischief Mr. Camwell. And how can you reconcile it to, your conscience that you should play so base a part?'

'I have but performed my duty, dear madam.'

'You pretend that it is your devotion to me! I might be flattered if I saw not so abject a figure in my service. Now have I but four days of my month of happiness remaining, and my request to you is, leave me to enjoy them. I beseech you to go. Very humbly, most earnestly, I beg your departure. Grant it to me, and do not stay to poison my last days here. Leave us to-morrow. I will admit your good intentions. I give you my hand in gratitude. Adieu, Mr. Camwell.'

He took her hand. 'Adieu. I foresee an early separation, and this dear hand is mine while I have it in mine. Adieu. It is a word to be repeated at a parting like ours. We do not blow out our light with one breath: we let it fade gradually, like yonder sunset.'

'Speak so,' said she.

'Ah, Chloe, to give one's life! And it is your happiness I have sought more than your favor.'

'I believe it; but I have not liked the means. You leave us to-morrow?'

'It seems to me that to-morrow is the term.'

Her face clouded. 'That tells me a very uncertain promise.'

'You looked forth to a month of happiness—meaning a month of delusion. The delusion expires to-night. You will awaken to see your end of it in the morning. You have never looked beyond the month since the day of his arrival.'

'Let him not be named, I supplicate you.'

'Then you consent that another shall be sacrificed for you to enjoy your state of deception an hour longer?'

'I am not deceived, sir. I wish for peace, and crave it, and that is all I would have.'

'And you make her your peace-offering, whom you have engaged to serve! Too surely your eyes have been open as well as mine. Knot by knot—I have watched you—where is it?—you have marked the points in that silken string where the confirmation of a just suspicion was too strong for you.'

'I did it, and still I continued merry?' She subsided from her scornfulness on an involuntary 'Ah!' that was a shudder.

'You acted Light Heart, madam, and too well to hoodwink me. Meanwhile you allowed that mischief to proceed, rather than have your crazy lullaby disturbed.'

'Indeed, Mr. Camwell, you presume.'

'The time, and my knowledge of what it is fraught with, demand it and excuse it. You and I, my dear and one only love on earth, stand outside of ordinary rules. We are between life and death.'

'We are so always.'

'Listen further to the preacher: We have them close on us, with the question, Which it shall be to-morrow. You are for sleeping on, but I say no; nor shall that iniquity of double treachery be committed because of your desire to be rocked in a cradle. Hear me out. The drug you have swallowed to cheat yourself will not bear the shock awaiting you tomorrow with the first light. Hear these birds! When next they sing, you will be broad awake, and of me, and the worship and service I would have dedicated to you, I do not... it is a spectral sunset of a day that was never to be!—awake, and looking on what? Back from a monstrous villainy to the forlorn wretch who winked at it with knots in a string. Count them then, and where will be your answer to heaven? I begged it of you, to save you from those blows of remorse; yes, terrible!'

'Oh, no!'

'Terrible, I say!'

'You are mistaken, Mr. Camwell. It is my soother. I tell my beads on it.'

'See how a persistent residence in this place has made a Pagan of the purest soul among us! Had you... but that day was not to lighten me! More adorable in your errors that you are than others by their virtues, you have sinned through excess of the qualities men prize. Oh, you have a boundless generosity, unhappily enwound with a pride as great. There is your fault, that is the cause of your misery. Too generous! too proud! You have trusted, and you will not cease to trust; you have vowed yourself to love, never to remonstrate, never to seem to doubt; it is too much your religion, rare verily. But bethink you of that inexperienced and most silly good creature who is on the rapids to her destruction. Is she not—you will cry it aloud to-morrow—your victim? You hear it within you now.'

'Friend, my dear, true friend,' Chloe said in her deeper voice of melody, 'set your mind at ease about to-morrow and her. Her safety is assured. I stake my life on it. She shall not be a victim. At the worst she will but have learnt a lesson. So, then, adieu! The West hangs like a garland of unwatered flowers, neglected by the mistress they adorned. Remember the scene, and that here we parted, and that Chloe wished you the happiness it was out of her power to bestow, because she was of another world, with her history written out to the last red streak before ever you knew her. Adieu; this time adieu for good!'

Mr. Camwell stood in her path. 'Blind eyes, if you like,' he said, 'but you shall not hear blind language. I forfeit the poor consideration for me that I have treasured; hate me; better hated by you than shun my duty! Your duchess is away at the first dawn this next morning; it has come to that. I speak with full knowledge. Question her.'

Chloe threw a faltering scorn of him into her voice, as much as her heart's sharp throbs would allow. 'I question you, sir, how you came to this full knowledge you boast of?'

'I have it; let that suffice. Nay, I will be particular; his coach is ordered for the time I name to you; her maid is already at a station on the road of the flight.'

'You have their servants in your pay?'

'For the mine—the countermine. We must grub dirt to match deceivers. You, madam, have chosen to be delicate to excess, and have thrown it upon me to be gross, and if you please, abominable, in my means of defending you. It is not too late for you to save the lady, nor too late to bring him to the sense of honour.'

'I cannot think Colonel Poltermore so dishonourable.'

'Poor Colonel Poltermore! The office he is made to fill is an old one. Are you not ashamed, Chloe?'

'I have listened too long,' she replied.

'Then, if it is your pleasure, depart.'

He made way for her. She passed him. Taking two hurried steps in the gloom of the twilight, she stopped, held at her heart, and painfully turning to him, threw her arms out, and let herself be seized and kissed.

On his asking pardon of her, which his long habit of respect forced him to do in the thick of rapture and repetitions, she said, 'You rob no one.'

'Oh,' he cried, 'there is a reward, then, for faithful love. But am I the man I was a minute back? I have you; I embrace you; and I doubt that I am I. Or is it Chloe's ghost?'

'She has died and visits you.'

'And will again?'

Chloe could not speak for languor.

The intensity of the happiness she gave by resting mutely where she was, charmed her senses. But so long had the frost been on them that their awakening to warmth was haunted by speculations on the sweet taste of this reward of faithfulness to him, and the strange taste of her own unfaithfulness to her. And reflecting on the cold act of speculation while strong arm and glowing mouth were pressing her, she thought her senses might really be dead, and she a ghost visiting the good youth for his comfort. So feel ghosts, she thought, and what we call happiness in love is a match between ecstasy and compliance. Another thought flew through her like a mortal shot: 'Not so with those two! with them it will be ecstasy meeting ecstasy; they will take and give happiness in equal portions.' A pang of jealousy traversed her frame. She made the shrewdness of it help to nerve her fervour in a last strain of him to her bosom, and gently releasing herself, she said, 'No one is robbed. And now, dear friend, promise me that you will not disturb Mr. Beamish.'

'Chloe,' said he, 'have you bribed me?'

'I do not wish him to be troubled.'

'The duchess, I have told you—'

'I know. But you have Chloe's word that she will watch over the duchess and die to save her. It is an oath. You have heard of some arrangements. I say they shall lead to nothing: it shall not take place. Indeed, my friend, I am awake; I see as much as you see. And those... after being where I have been, can you suppose I have a regret? But she is my dear and peculiar charge, and if she runs a risk, trust to me that there shall be no catastrophe; I swear it; so, now, adieu. We sup in company to-night. They will be expecting some of Chloe's verses, and she must sing to herself for a few minutes to stir the bed her songs take wing from; therefore, we will part, and for her sake avoid her; do not be present at our table, or in the room, or anywhere there. Yes, you rob no one,' she said, in a voice that curled through him deliciously by wavering; but I think I may blush at recollections, and I would rather have you absent. Adieu! I will not ask for obedience from you beyond to-night. Your word?'

He gave it in a stupor of felicity, and she fled.

CHAPTER IX

Chloe drew the silken string from her bosom, as she descended the dim pathway through the furies, and set her fingers travelling along it for the number of the knots. 'I have no right to be living,' she said. Seven was the number; seven years she had awaited her lover's return; she counted her age and completed it in sevens. Fatalism had sustained her during her lover's absence; it had fast hold of her now. Thereby had she been enabled to say, 'He will come'; and saying, 'He has come,' her touch rested on the first knot in the string. She had no power to displace her fingers, and the cause of the tying of the knot stood across her brain marked in dull red characters, legible neither to her eye nor to her understanding, but a reviving of the hour that brought it on her spirit with human distinctness, except of the light of day: she had a sense of having forfeited light, and seeing perhaps more clearly. Everything assured her that she saw more clearly than others; she saw too when it was good to cease to live.

Hers was the unhappy lot of one gifted with poet-imagination to throb with the woman supplanting her and share the fascination of the man who deceived. At their first meeting, in her presence, she had seen that they were not strangers; she pitied them for speaking falsely, and when she vowed to thwart this course of evil it to save a younger creature of her sex, not in rivalry. She treated them both with a proud generosity surpassing gentleness. All that there was of selfishness in her bosom resolved to the enjoyment of her one month of strongly willed delusion.

The kiss she had sunk to robbed no one, not even her body's purity, for when this knot was tied she consigned herself to her end, and had become a bag of dust. The other knots in the string pointed to verifications; this first one was a suspicion, and it was the more precious, she felt it to be more a certainty; it had come from the dark world beyond us, where all is known. Her belief that it had come thence was nourished by testimony, the space of blackness wherein she had lived since, exhausting her last vitality in a simulation of infantile happiness, which was nothing other than the carrying on of her emotion of the moment of sharp sour sweet—such as it may be, the doomed below attain for their knowledge of joy—when, at the first meeting with her lover, the perception of his treachery to the soul confiding in him, told her she had lived, and opened out the cherishable kingdom of insensibility to her for her heritage.

She made her tragic humility speak thankfully to the wound that slew her. 'Had it not been so, I should not have seen him,' she said:—Her lover would not have come to her but for his pursuit of another woman.

She pardoned him for being attracted by that beautiful transplant of the fields: pardoned her likewise. 'He when I saw him first was as beautiful to me. For him I might have done as much.'

Far away in a lighted hall of the West, her family raised hands of reproach. They were minute objects, keenly discerned as diminished figures cut in steel. Feeling could not be very warm for them, they were so small, and a sea that had drowned her ran between; and looking that way she had scarce any warmth of feeling save for a white rhaiadr leaping out of broken cloud through branched rocks, where she had climbed and dreamed when a child. The dream was then of the coloured days to come; now she was more infant in her mind, and she watched the scattered water broaden, and tasted the spray, sat there drinking the scene, untroubled by hopes as a lamb, different only from an infant in knowing that she had thrown off life to travel back to her home and be refreshed. She heard her people talk; they were unending babblers in the waterfall. Truth was with them, and wisdom. How, then, could she pretend to any right to live? Already she had no name; she was less living than a tombstone. For who was Chloe? Her family might pass the grave of Chloe without weeping, without moralizing. They had foreseen her ruin, they had foretold it, they noised it in the waters, and on they sped to the plains, telling the world of their prophecy, and making what was untold as yet a lighter thing to do.

The lamps in an irregularly dotted line underneath the hill beckoned her to her task of appearing as the gayest of them that draw their breath for the day and have pulses for the morrow.

At midnight the great supper party to celebrate the reconciliation of Mr. Beamish and Duchess Susan broke up, and beneath a soft fair sky the ladies, with their silvery chatter of gratitude for amusement, caught Chloe in their arms to kiss her, rendering it natural for their cavaliers to exclaim that Chloe was blest above mortals. The duchess preferred to walk. Her spirits were excited, and her language smelt of her origin, but the superb fleshly beauty of the woman was aglow, and crying, 'I declare I should burst in one of those boxes—just as if you'd stalled me!' she fanned a wind on her face, and sumptuously spread her spherical skirts, attended by the vanquished and captive Colonel Poltermore, a gentleman manifestly bent on insinuating sly slips of speech to serve for here a pinch of powder, there a match. 'Am I?' she was heard to say. She blew prodigious deep-chested sighs of a coquette that has taken to roaring.

Presently her voice tossed out: 'As if I would!' These vivid illuminations of the Colonel's proceedings were a pasture to the rearward groups, composed of two very grand ladies, Caseldy, Mr. Beamish, a lord, and Chloe.

'You man! Oh!' sprang from the duchess. 'What do I hear? I won't listen; I can't, I mustn't, I oughtn't.'

So she said, but her head careened, she gave him her coy reluctant ear, with total abandonment to the seductions of his whispers, and the lord let fly a peal of laughter. It had been a supper of copious wine, and the songs which rise from wine. Nature was excused by our midnight naturalists.

The two great dames, admonished by the violence of the nobleman's laughter, laid claim on Mr. Beamish to accompany them at their parting with Chloe and Duchess Susan.

In the momentary shuffling of couples incident to adieux among a company, the duchess murmured to Caseldy:

'Have I done it well.'

He praised her for perfection in her acting. 'I am at your door at three, remember.'

'My heart's in my mouth,' said she.

Colonel Poltermore still had the privilege of conducting her the few farther steps to her lodgings.

Caseldy walked beside Chloe, and silently, until he said, 'If I have not yet mentioned the subject—'

'If it is an allusion to money let me not hear it to-night,' she replied.

'I can only say that my lawyers have instructions. But my lawyers cannot pay you in gratitude. Do not think me in your hardest review of my misconduct ungrateful. I have ever esteemed you above all women; I do, and I shall; you are too much above me. I am afraid I am a composition of bad stuff; I did not win a very particularly good name on the Continent; I begin to know myself, and in comparison with you, dear Catherine—'

'You speak to Chloe,' she said. 'Catherine is a buried person. She died without pain. She is by this time dust.'

The man heaved his breast. 'Women have not an idea of our temptations.'

'You are excused by me for all your errors, Caseldy. Always remember that.'

He sighed profoundly. 'Ay, you have a Christian's heart.'

She answered, 'I have come to the conclusion that it is a Pagan's.'

'As for me,' he rejoined, 'I am a fatalist. Through life I have seen my destiny. What is to be, will be; we can do nothing.'

'I have heard of one who expired of a surfeit that he anticipated, nay proclaimed, when indulging in the last desired morsel,' said Chloe.

'He was driven to it.'

'From within.'

Caseldy acquiesced; his wits were clouded, and an illustration even coarser and more grotesque would have won a serious nod and a sigh from him. 'Yes, we are moved by other hands!'

'It is pleasant to think so: and think it of me tomorrow. Will you!' said Chloe.

He promised it heartily, to induce her to think the same of him.

Their separation was in no way remarkable. The pretty formalities were executed at the door, and the pair of gentlemen departed.

'It's quite dark still,' Duchess Susan said, looking up at the sky, and she ran upstairs, and sank, complaining of the weakness of her legs, in a chair of the ante-chamber of her bedroom, where Chloe slept. Then she asked the time of the night. She could not suppress her hushed 'Oh!' of heavy throbbing from minute to minute. Suddenly she started off at a quick stride to her own room, saying that it must be sleepiness which affected her so.

Her bedroom had a door to the sitting-room, and thence, as also from Chloe's room, the landing on the stairs was reached, for the room ran parallel with both bed-chambers. She walked in it and threw the window open, but closed it immediately; opened and shut the door, and returned and called for Chloe. She wanted to be read to. Chloe named certain composing books. The duchess chose a book of sermons. 'But we're all such dreadful sinners, it's better not to bother ourselves late at night.' She dismissed that suggestion. Chloe proposed books of poetry. 'Only I don't understand them except about larks, and buttercups, and hayfields, and that's no comfort to a woman burning,' was the answer.

'Are you feverish, madam?' said Chloe. And the duchess was sharp on her: 'Yes, madam, I am.'

She reproved herself in a change of tone: 'No, Chloe, not feverish, only this air of yours here is such an exciting air, as the doctor says; and they made me drink wine, and I played before supper—Oh! my money; I used to say I could get more, but now!' she sighed—'but there's better in the world than money. You know that, don't you, you dear? Tell me. And I want you to be happy; that you'll find. I do wish we could all be!' She wept, and spoke of requiring a little music to compose her.

Chloe stretched a hand for her guitar. Duchess Susan listened to some notes, and cried that it went to her heart and hurt her. 'Everything we like a lot has a fence and a board against trespassers, because of such a lot of people in the world,' she moaned. 'Don't play, put down that thing, please, dear. You're the cleverest creature anybody has ever met; they all say so. I wish I—Lovely women catch men, and clever women keep them: I've heard that said in this wretched place, and it 's a nice prospect for me, next door to a fool! I know I am.'

'The duke adores you, madam.'

'Poor duke! Do let him be—sleeping so woebegone with his mouth so, and that chin of a baby, like as if he dreamed of a penny whistle. He shouldn't have let me come here. Talk of Mr. Beamish. How he will miss you, Chloe!'

'He will,' Chloe said sadly.

'If you go, dear.'

'I am going.'

'Why should you leave him, Chloe?'

'I must.'

'And there, the thought of it makes you miserable!'

'It does.'

'You needn't, I'm sure.'

Chloe looked at her.

The duchess turned her head. 'Why can't you be gay, as you were at the supper-table, Chloe? You're out to him like a flower when the sun jumps over the hill; you're up like a lark in the dews; as I used to be when I thought of nothing. Oh, the early morning; and I'm sleepy. What a beast I feel, with my grandeur, and the time in an hour or two for the birds to sing, and me ready to drop. I must go and undress.'

She rushed on Chloe, kissed her hastily, declaring that she was quite dead of fatigue, and dismissed her. 'I don't want help, I can undress myself. As if Susan Barley couldn't do that for herself! and you may shut your door, I sha'n't have any frights to-night, I'm so tired out.'

'Another kiss,' Chloe said tenderly.

'Yes, take it'—the duchess leaned her cheek—'but I'm so tired I don't know what I'm doing.'

'It will not be on your conscience,' Chloe answered, kissing her warmly.

Will those words she withdrew, and the duchess closed the door. She ran a bolt in it immediately.

'I'm too tired to know anything I'm doing,' she said to herself, and stood with shut eyes to hug certain thoughts which set her bosom heaving.

There was the bed, there was the clock. She had the option of lying down and floating quietly into the day, all peril past. It seemed sweet for a minute. But it soon seemed an old, a worn, an end-of-autumn life, chill, without aim, like a something that was hungry and toothless. The bed proposing innocent sleep repelled her and drove her to the clock. The clock was awful: the hand at the hour, the finger following the minute, commanded her to stir actively, and drove her to gentle meditations on the bed. She lay down dressed, after setting her light beside the clock, that she might see it at will, and considering it necessary for the bed to appear to have been lain on. Considering also that she ought to be heard moving about in the process of undressing, she rose from the bed to make sure of her reading of the guilty clock. An hour and twenty minutes! she had no more time than that: and it was not enough for her various preparations, though it was true that her maid had packed and taken a box of the things chiefly needful; but the duchess had to change her shoes and her dress, and run at bo-peep with the changes of her mind, a sedative preface to any fatal step among women of her complexion, for so they invite indecision to exhaust their scruples, and they let the blood have its way. Having so short a space of time, she thought the matter decided, and with some relief she flung despairing on the bed, and lay down for good with her duke. In a little while her head was at work reviewing him sternly, estimating him not less accurately than the male moralist charitable to her sex would do. She quitted the bed, with a spring to escape her imagined lord; and as if she had felt him to be there, she lay down no more. A quiet life like that was flatter to her idea than a handsomely bound big book without any print on the pages, and without a picture. Her contemplation of it, contrasted with the life waved to her view by the timepiece, set her whole system rageing; she burned to fly. Providently, nevertheless, she thumped a pillow, and threw the bedclothes into proper disorder, to inform the world that her limbs had warmed them, and that all had been impulse with her. She then proceeded to disrobe, murmuring to herself that she could stop now, and could stop now, at each stage of the advance to a fresh dressing of her person, and moralizing on her singular fate, in the mouth of an observer. 'She was shot up suddenly over everybody's head, and suddenly down she went.' Susan whispered to herself: 'But it was for love!' Possessed by the rosiness of love, she finished her business, with an attention to everything needed that was equal to perfect serenity of mind. After which there was nothing to do, save to sit humped in a chair, cover her face and count the clock-tickings, that said, Yes—no; do—don't; fly—stay; fly—fly! It seemed to her she heard a moving. Well she might with that dreadful heart of hers!

Chloe was asleep, at peace by this time, she thought; and how she envied Chloe! She might be as happy, if she pleased. Why not? But what kind of happiness was it? She likened it to that of the corpse underground, and shrank distastefully.

Susan stood at her glass to have a look at the creature about whom there was all this disturbance, and she threw up her arms high for a languid, not unlovely yawn, that closed in blissful shuddering with the sensation of her lover's arms having wormed round her waist and taken her while she was defenceless. For surely they would. She took a jewelled ring, his gift, from her purse, and kissed it, and drew it on and off her finger, leaving it on. Now she might wear it without fear of inquiries and virtuous eyebrows. O heavenly now—if only it were an hour hence; and going behind galloping horses!

The clock was at the terrible moment. She hesitated internally and hastened; once her feet stuck fast, and firmly she said, 'No'; but the clock was her lord. The clock was her lover and her lord; and obeying it, she managed to get into the sitting-room, on the pretext that she merely wished to see through the front window whether daylight was coming.

How well she knew that half-light of the ebb of the wave of darkness.

Strange enough it was to see it showing houses regaining their solidity of the foregone day, instead of still fields, black hedges, familiar shapes of trees. The houses had no wakefulness, they were but seen to stand, and the light was a revelation of emptiness. Susan's heart was cunning to reproach her duke for the difference of the scene she beheld from that of the innocent open-breasted land. Yes, it was dawn in a wicked place that she never should have been allowed to visit. But where was he whom she looked for? There! The cloaked figure of a man was at the corner of the street. It was he. Her heart froze; but her limbs were strung to throw off the house, and reach air, breathe, and (as her thoughts ran) swoon, well-protected. To her senses the house was a house on fire, and crying to her to escape.

Yet she stepped deliberately, to be sure-footed in a dusky room; she touched along the wall and came to the door, where a foot-stool nearly tripped her. Here her touch was at fault, for though she knew she must be close by the door, she was met by an obstruction unlike wood, and the door seemed neither shut nor open. She could not find the handle; something hung over it. Thinking coolly, she fancied the thing must be a gown or dressing-gown; it hung heavily. Her fingers were sensible of the touch of silk; she distinguished a depending bulk, and she felt at it very carefully and mechanically, saying within herself, in her anxiety to pass it without noise, 'If I should awake poor Chloe, of all people!' Her alarm was that the door might creak. Before any other alarm had struck her brain, the hand she felt with was in a palsy, her mouth gaped, her throat thickened, the dust-ball rose in her throat, and the effort to swallow it down and get breath kept her from acute speculation while she felt again, pinched, plucked at the thing, ready to laugh, ready to shriek. Above her head, all on one side, the thing had a round white top. Could it be a hand that her touch had slid across? An arm too! this was an arm! She clutched it, imagining that it clung to her. She pulled it to release herself from it, desperately she pulled, and a lump descended, and a flash of all the torn nerves of her body told her that a dead human body was upon her.

At a quarter to four o'clock of a midsummer morning, as Mr. Beamish relates of his last share in the Tale of Chloe, a woman's voice, in piercing notes of anguish, rang out three shrieks consecutively, which were heard by him at the instant of his quitting his front doorstep, in obedience to the summons of young Mr. Camwell, delivered ten minutes previously, with great urgency, by that gentleman's lacquey. On his reaching the street of the house inhabited by Duchess Susan, he perceived many night-capped heads at windows, and one window of the house in question lifted but vacant. His first impression accused the pair of gentlemen, whom he saw bearing drawn swords in no friendly attitude of an ugly brawl that had probably affrighted her Grace, or her personal attendant, a woman capable of screaming, for he was well assured that it could not have been Chloe, the least likely of her sex to abandon herself to the use of their weapons either in terror or in jeopardy. The antagonists were Mr. Camwell and Count Caseldy. On his approaching them, Mr. Camwell sheathed his sword, saying that his work was done. Caseldy was convulsed with wrath, to such a degree as to make the part of an intermediary perilous. There had been passes between them, and Caseldy cried aloud that he would have his enemy's blood.

The night-watch was nowhere. Soon, however, certain shopmen and their apprentices assisted Mr. Beamish to preserve the peace, despite the fury of Caseldy and the provocations—'not easy to withstand,' says the chronicler—offered by him to young Camwell. The latter said to Mr. Beamish: 'I knew I should be no match, so I sent for you,' causing his friend astonishment, inasmuch as he was assured of the youth's natural valour.

Mr. Beamish was about to deliver an allocution of reproof to them in equal shares, being entirely unsuspicious of any other reason for the alarum than this palpable outbreak of a rivalry that he would have inclined to attribute to the charms of Chloe, when the house-door swung wide for them to enter, and the landlady of the house, holding clasped hands at full stretch, implored them to run up to the poor lady: 'Oh, she's dead; she's dead, dead!'

Caseldy rushed past her.

'How, dead! good woman?' Mr. Beamish questioned her most incredulously, half-smiling.

She answered among her moans: 'Dead by the neck; off the door—Oh!'

Young Camwell pressed his forehead, with a call on his Maker's name. As they reached the landing upstairs, Caseldy came out of the sitting-room.

'Which?' said Camwell to the speaking of his face.

'She!' said the other.

'The duchess?' Mr. Beamish exclaimed.

But Camwell walked into the room. He had nothing to ask after that reply.

The figure stretched along the floor was covered with a sheet. The young man fell at his length beside it, and his face was downward.

Mr. Beamish relates: 'To this day, when I write at an interval of fifteen years, I have the tragic ague of that hour in my blood, and I behold the shrouded form of the most admirable of women, whose heart was broken by a faithless man ere she devoted her wreck of life to arrest one weaker than herself on the descent to perdition. Therein it was beneficently granted her to be of the service she prayed to be through her death. She died to save. In a last letter, found upon her pincushion, addressed to me under seal of secrecy toward the parties principally concerned, she anticipates the whole confession of the unhappy duchess. Nay, she prophesies: "The duchess will tell you truly she has had enough of love!" Those actual words were reiterated to me by the poor lady daily until her lord arrived to head the funeral procession, and assist in nursing back the shattered health of his wife to a state that should fit her for travelling. To me, at least, she was constant in repeating, "No more of love!" By her behaviour to her duke, I can judge her to have been sincere. She spoke of feeling Chloe's eyes go through her with every word of hers that she recollected. Nor was the end of Chloe less effective upon the traitor. He was in the procession to her grave. He spoke to none. There is a line of the verse bearing the superscription, "My Reasons for Dying," that shows her to have been apprehensive to secure the safety of Mr. Camwell:

I die because my heart is dead

To warn a soul from sin I die:
I die that blood may not be shed, etc.

She feared he would be somewhere on the road to mar the fugitives, and she knew him, as indeed he knew himself, no match for one trained in the foreign tricks of steel, ready though he was to dispute the traitor's way. She remembers Mr. Camwell's petition for the knotted silken string in her request that it shall be cut from her throat and given to him.'

Mr. Beamish indulges in verses above the grave of Chloe. They are of a character to cool emotion. But when we find a man, who is commonly of the quickest susceptibility to ridicule as well as to what is befitting, careless of exposure, we may reflect on the truthfulness of feeling by which he is drawn to pass his own guard and come forth in his nakedness; something of the poet's tongue may breathe to us through his mortal stammering, even if we have to acknowledge that a quotation would scatter pathos.

THE HOUSE ON THE BEACH

A REALISTIC TALE

CHAPTER I

The experience of great officials who have laid down their dignities before death, or have had the philosophic mind to review themselves while still wielding the deputy sceptre, teaches them that in the exercise of authority over men an eccentric behaviour in trifles has most exposed them to hostile criticism and gone farthest to jeopardize their popularity. It is their Achilles' heel; the place where their mother Nature holds them as she dips them in our waters. The eccentricity of common persons is the entertainment of the multitude, and the maternal hand is perceived for a cherishing and endearing sign upon them; but rarely can this be found suitable for the august in station; only, indeed, when their sceptre is no more fearful than a grandmother's birch; and these must learn from it sooner or later that they are uncomfortably mortal.

When herrings are at auction on a beach, for example, the man of chief distinction in the town should not step in among a poor fraternity to take advantage of an occasion of cheapness, though it be done, as he may protest, to relieve the fishermen of a burden; nor should such a dignitary as the bailiff of a Cinque Port carry home the spoil of victorious bargaining on his arm in a basket. It is not that his conduct is in itself objectionable, so much as that it causes him to be popularly weighed; and during life, until the best of all advocates can plead before our fellow Englishmen that we are out of their way, it is prudent to avoid the process.

Mr. Tinman, however, this high-stepping person in question, happened to have come of a marketing mother. She had started him from a small shop to a big one. He, by the practice of her virtues, had been enabled to start himself as a gentleman. He was a man of this ambition, and prouder behind it. But having started himself precipitately, he took rank among independent incomes, as they are called, only to take fright at the perils of starvation besetting one who has been tempted to abandon the source of fifty per cent. So, if noble imagery were allowable in our time in prose, might alarms and partial regrets be assumed to animate the splendid pumpkin cut loose from the suckers. Deprived of that prodigious nourishment of the shop in the fashionable seaport of Helmstone, he retired upon his native town, the

Cinque Port of Crikswich, where he rented the cheapest residence he could discover for his habitation, the House on the Beach, and lived imposingly, though not in total disaccord with his old mother's principles. His income, as he observed to his widowed sister and solitary companion almost daily in their privacy, was respectable. The descent from an altitude of fifty to five per cent. cannot but be felt. Nevertheless it was a comforting midnight bolster reflection for a man, turning over to the other side between a dream and a wink, that he was making no bad debts, and one must pay to be addressed as esquire. Once an esquire, you are off the ground in England and on the ladder. An esquire can offer his hand in marriage to a lady in her own right; plain esquires have married duchesses; they marry baronets' daughters every day of the week.

Thoughts of this kind were as the rise and fall of waves in the bosom of the new esquire. How often in his Helmstone shop had he not heard titled ladies disdaining to talk a whit more prettily than ordinary women; and he had been a match for the subtlety of their pride—he understood it. He knew well that at the hint of a proposal from him they would have spoken out in a manner very different to that of ordinary women. The lightning, only to be warded by an esquire, was in them. He quitted business at the age of forty, that he might pretend to espousals with a born lady; or at least it was one of the ideas in his mind.

And here, I think, is the moment for the epitaph of anticipation over him, and the exclamation, alas! I would not be premature, but it is necessary to create some interest in him, and no one but a foreigner could feel it at present for the Englishman who is bursting merely to do like the rest of his countrymen, and rise above them to shake them class by class as the dust from his heels. Alas! then an—undertaker's pathos is better than none at all—he was not a single-minded aspirant to our social honours. The old marketing mother; to whom he owed his fortunes, was in his blood to confound his ambition; and so contradictory was the man's nature, that in revenge for disappointments, there were times when he turned against the saving spirit of parsimony. Readers deep in Greek dramatic writings will see the fatal Sisters behind the chair of a man who gives frequent and bigger dinners, that he may become important in his neighbourhood, while decreasing the price he pays for his wine, that he may miserably indemnify himself for the outlay. A sip of his wine fetched the breath, as when men are in the presence of the tremendous elements of nature. It sounded the constitution more darkly-awful, and with a profounder testimony to stubborn health, than the physician's instruments. Most of the guests at Mr. Tinman's table were so constructed that they admired him for its powerful quality the more at his announcement of the price of it; the combined strength and cheapness probably flattering them, as by another mystic instance of the national energy. It must have been so, since his townsmen rejoiced to hail him as head of their town. Here and there a solitary esquire, fished out of the bathing season to dine at the house on the beach, was guilty of raising one of those clamours concerning subsequent headaches, which spread an evil reputation as a pall. A resident esquire or two, in whom a reminiscence of Tinman's table may be likened to the hook which some old trout has borne away from the angler as the most vivid of warnings to him to beware for the future, caught up the black report and propagated it.

The Lieutenant of the Coastguard, hearing the latest conscious victim, or hearing of him, would nod his head and say he had never dined at Tinman's table without a headache ensuing and a visit to the chemist's shop; which, he was assured, was good for trade, and he acquiesced, as it was right to do in a man devoted to his country. He dined with Tinman again. We try our best to be social. For eight months in our year he had little choice but to dine with Tinman or be a hermit attached to a telescope.

"Where are you going, Lieutenant?" His frank reply to the question was, "I am going to be killed;" and it grew notorious that this meant Tinman's table. We get on together as well as we can. Perhaps if we were an acutely calculating people we should find it preferable both for trade and our physical prosperity to turn and kill Tinman, in contempt of consequences. But we are not, and so he does the business gradually for us. A generous people we must be, for Tinman was not detested. The recollection of "next morning" caused him to be dimly feared.

Tinman, meanwhile, was awake only to the Circumstance that he made no progress as an esquire, except on the envelopes of letters, and in his own esteem. That broad region he began to occupy to the exclusion of other inhabitants; and the result of such a state of princely isolation was a plunge of his whole being into deep thoughts. From the hour of his investiture as the town's chief man, thoughts which were long shots took possession of him. He had his wits about him; he was alive to ridicule; he knew he was not popular below, or on easy terms with people above him, and he meditated a surpassing stroke as one of the Band of Esq., that had nothing original about it to perplex and annoy the native mind, yet was dazzling. Few members of the privileged Band dare even imagine the thing.

It will hardly be believed, but it is historical fact, that in the act of carrying fresh herrings home on his arm, he entertained the idea of a visit to the First Person and Head of the realm, and was indulging in pleasing visions of the charms of a personal acquaintance. Nay, he had already consulted with brother jurats. For you must know that one of the princesses had recently suffered betrothal in the newspapers, and supposing her to deign to ratify the engagement, what so reasonable on the part of a Cinque Port chieftain as to congratulate his liege mistress, her illustrious mother? These are thoughts and these are deeds >which give emotional warmth and colour to the ejecter members of a population wretchedly befogged. They are our sunlight, and our brighter theme of conversation. They are necessary to the climate and the Saxon mind; and it would be foolish to put them away, as it is foolish not to do our utmost to be intimate with terrestrial splendours while we have them—as it may be said of wardens, mayors, and bailiffs-at command. Tinman was quite of this opinion. They are there to relieve our dulness. We have them in the place of heavenly; and he would have argued that we have a right to bother them too. He had a notion, up in the clouds, of a Sailors' Convalescent Hospital at Crikswich to seduce a prince with, hand him the trowel, make him "lay the stone," and then poor prince! refresh him at table. But that was a matter for by and by.

His purchase of herrings completed, Mr. Tinman walked across the mound of shingle to the house on the beach. He was rather a fresh-faced man, of the Saxon colouring, and at a distance looking good-humoured. That he should have been able to make such an appearance while doing daily battle with his wine, was a proof of great physical vigour. His pace was leisurely, as it must needs be over pebbles, where half a step is subtracted from each whole one in passing; and, besides, he was aware of a general breath at his departure that betokened a censorious assembly. Why should he not market for himself? He threw dignity into his retreating figure in response to the internal interrogation. The moment >was one when conscious rectitude =pliers man should have a tail for its just display. Philosophers have drawn attention to the power of the human face to express pure virtue, but no sooner has it passed on than the spirit erect within would seem helpless. The breadth of our shoulders is apparently presented for our critics to write on. Poor duty is done by the simple sense of moral worth, to supplant that absence of feature in the plain flat back. We are below the animals in this. How charged with language behind him is a dog! Everybody has noticed it. Let a dog turn away from a hostile circle, and his crisp and wary tail not merely defends him, it menaces; it is a weapon. Man has no choice but to surge and boil, or stiffen preposterously. Knowing the popular sentiment about his marketing—for men can see behind their backs, though they may have nothing to speak with—Tinman resembled those persons of principle who decline to pay for a "Bless your honour!" from a voluble beggar-woman, and obtain the reverse of it after they have gone by. He was sufficiently sensitive to feel that his back was chalked as on a slate. The only remark following him was, "There he goes!"

He went to the seaward gate of the house on the beach, made practicable in a low flint wall, where he was met by his sister Martha, to whom he handed the basket. Apparently he named the cost of his purchase per dozen. She touched the fish and pressed the bellies of the topmost, it might be to question them tenderly concerning their roes. Then the couple passed out of sight. Herrings were soon after this despatching their odours through the chimneys of all Crikswich, and there was that much of concord and festive union among the inhabitants.

The house on the beach had been posted where it stood, one supposes, for the sake of the sea-view, from which it turned right about to face the town across a patch of grass and salt scurf, looking like a square and scornful corporal engaged in the perpetual review of an awkward squad of recruits. Sea delighted it not, nor land either. Marine Parade fronting it to the left, shaded sickly eyes, under a worn green verandah, from a sun that rarely appeared, as the traducers of spinsters pretend those virgins are ever keenly on their guard against him that cometh not. Belle Vue Terrace stared out of lank glass panes without reserve, unashamed of its yellow complexion. A gaping public-house, calling itself newly Hotel, fell backward a step. Villas with the titles of royalty and bloody battles claimed five feet of garden, and swelled in bowwindows beside other villas which drew up firmly, commending to the attention a decent straightness and unintrusive decorum in preference. On an elevated meadow to the right was the Crouch. The Hall of Elba nestled among weather-beaten dwarf woods further toward the cliff. Shavenness, featurelessness, emptiness, clamminess scurfiness, formed the outward expression of a town to which people were reasonably glad to come from London in summer-time, for there was nothing in Crikswich to distract the naked pursuit of health. The sea tossed its renovating brine to the determinedly sniffing animal, who went to his meals with an appetite that rendered him cordially eulogistic of the place, in spite of certain frank whiffs of sewerage coming off an open deposit on the common to mingle with the brine. Tradition told of a French lady and gentleman entering the town to take lodgings for a month, and that on the morrow they took a boat from the shore, saying in their faint English to a sailor veteran of the coastguard, whom they had consulted about the weather, "It is better zis zan zat," as they shrugged between rough sea and corpselike land. And they were not seen again. Their meaning none knew. Having paid their bill at the lodging-house, their conduct was ascribed to systematic madness. English people came to Crikswich for the pure salt sea air, and they did not expect it to be cooked and dressed and decorated for them. If these things are done to nature, it is nature no longer that you have, but something Frenchified. Those French are for trimming Neptune's beard! Only wait, and you are sure to find variety in nature, more than you may like. You will find it in Neptune. What say you to a breach of the sea-wall, and an inundation of the aromatic grass-flat extending from the house on the beach to the tottering terraces, villas, cottages: and public-house transformed by its ensign to Hotel, along the frontage of the town? Such an event had occurred of old, and had given the house on the beach the serious shaking great Neptune in his wrath alone can give. But many years had intervened. Groynes had been run down to intercept him and divert him. He generally did his winter mischief on a mill and salt marshes lower westward. Mr. Tinman had always been extremely zealous in promoting the expenditure of what moneys the town had to spare upon the protection of the shore, as it were for the propitiation or defiance of the sea-god. There was a kindly joke against him an that subject among brother jurats. He retorted with the joke, that the first thing for Englishmen to look to were England's defences.

But it will not do to be dwelling too fondly on our eras of peace, for which we make such splendid sacrifices. Peace, saving for the advent of a German band, which troubled the repose of the town at intervals, had imparted to the inhabitants of Crikswich, within and without, the likeness to its most perfect image, together, it must be confessed, with a degree of nervousness that invested common events with some of the terrors of the Last Trump, when one night, just upon the passing of the vernal equinox, something happened.

CHAPTER II

A carriage Stopped short in the ray of candlelight that was fitfully and feebly capering on the windy blackness outside the open workshop of Crickledon, the carpenter, fronting the sea-beach. Mr. Tinnnan's house was inquired for. Crickledon left off planing; at half-sprawl over the board, he bawled out, "Turn to the right; right ahead; can't mistake it." He nodded to one of the cronies intent on watching his labours: "Not unless they mean to be bait for whiting-pout. Who's that for Tinman, I wonder?" The speculations of Crickledon's friends were lost in the scream of the plane.

One cast an eye through the door and observed that the carriage was there still. "Gentleman's got out and walked," said Crickledon. He was informed that somebody was visible inside. "Gentleman's wife, mayhap," he said. His friends indulged in their privilege of thinking what they liked, and there was the usual silence of tongues in the shop. He furnished them sound and motion for their amusement, and now and then a scrap of conversation; and the sedater spirits dwelling in his immediate neighbourhood were accustomed to step in and see him work up to supper-time, instead of resorting to the more turbid and costly excitement of the public-house.

Crickledon looked up from the measurement of a thumb-line. In the doorway stood a bearded gentleman, who announced himself with the startling exclamation, "Here's a pretty pickle!" and bustled to make way for a man well known to them as Ned Crummins, the upholsterer's man, on whose back hung an article of furniture, the condition of which, with a condensed brevity of humour worthy of literary admiration, he displayed by mutely turning himself about as he entered.

"Smashed!" was the general outcry.

"I ran slap into him," said the gentleman. "Who the deuce!—no bones broken, that's one thing. The fellow—there, look at him: he's like a glass tortoise."

"It's a chiwal glass," Crickledon remarked, and laid finger on the star in the centre.

"Gentleman ran slap into me," said Crummins, depositing the frame on the floor of the shop.

"Never had such a shock in my life," continued the gentleman. "Upon my soul, I took him for a door: I did indeed. A kind of light flashed from one of your houses here, and in the pitch dark I thought I was at the door of old Mart Tinman's house, and dash me if I did n't go in—crash! But what the deuce do you do, carrying that great big looking-glass at night, man? And, look here tell me; how was it you happened to be going glass foremost when you'd got the glass on your back?"

"Well, 't ain't my fault, I knows that," rejoined Crummins. "I came along as careful as a man could. I was just going to bawl out to Master Tinman, 'I knows the way, never fear me'; for I thinks I hears him call from his house, 'Do ye see the way?' and into me this gentleman runs all his might, and smash goes the glass. I was just ten steps from Master Tinman's gate, and that careful, I reckoned every foot I put down, that I was; I knows I did, though."

"Why, it was me calling, 'I'm sure I can't see the way.'

"You heard me, you donkey!" retorted the bearded gentleman. "What was the good of your turning that glass against me in the very nick when I dashed on you?"

"Well, 't ain't my fault, I swear," said Crummins. "The wind catches voices so on a pitch dark night, you never can tell whether they be on one shoulder or the other. And if I'm to go and lose my place through no fault of mine—"

"Have n't I told you, sir, I'm going to pay the damage? Here," said the gentleman, fumbling at his waistcoat, "here, take this card. Read it."

For the first time during the scene in the carpenter's shop, a certain pomposity swelled the gentleman's tone. His delivery of the card appeared to act on him like the flourish of a trumpet before great men.

"Van Diemen Smith," he proclaimed himself for the assistance of Ned Crummins in his task; the latter's look of sad concern on receiving the card seeming to declare an unscholarly conscience.

An anxious feminine voice was heard close beside Mr. Van Diemen Smith.

"Oh, papa, has there been an accident? Are you hurt?"

"Not a bit, Netty; not a bit. Walked into a big looking-glass in the dark, that's all. A matter of eight or ten pound, and that won't stúmp us. But these are what I call queer doings in Old England, when you can't take a step in the dark, on the seashore without plunging bang into a glass. And it looks like bad luck to my visit to old Mart Tinman."

"Can you," he addressed the company, "tell me of a clean, wholesome lodging-house? I was thinking of flinging myself, body and baggage, on your mayor, or whatever he is—my old schoolmate; but I don't so much like this beginning. A couple of bed-rooms and sitting-room; clean sheets, well aired; good food, well cooked; payment per week in advance."

The pebble dropped into deep water speaks of its depth by the tardy arrival of bubbles on the surface, and, in like manner, the very simple question put by Mr. Van Diemen Smith pursued its course of penetration in the assembled mind in the carpenter's shop for a considerable period, with no sign to show that it had reached the bottom.

"Surely, papa, we can go to an inn? There must be some hotel," said his daughter.

"There's good accommodation at the Cliff Hotel hard by," said Crickledon.

"But," said one of his friends, "if you don't want to go so far, sir, there's Master Crickledon's own house next door, and his wife lets lodgings, and there's not a better cook along this coast."

"Then why did n't the man mention it? Is he afraid of having me?" asked Mr. Smith, a little thunderingly. "I may n't be known much yet in England; but I'll tell you, you inquire the route to Mr. Van Diemen Smith over there in Australia."

"Yes, papa," interrupted his daughter, "only you must consider that it may not be convenient to take us in at this hour—so late."

"It's not that, miss, begging your pardon," said Crickledon. "I make a point of never recommending my own house. That's where it is. Otherwise you're welcome to try us."

"I was thinking of falling bounce on my old schoolmate, and putting Old English hospitality to the proof," Mr. Smith meditated. "But it's late. Yes, and that confounded glass! No, we'll bide with you, Mr. Carpenter. I'll send my card across to Mart Tinman to-morrow, and set him agog at his breakfast."

Mr. Van Diemen Smith waved his hand for Crickledon to lead the way.

Hereupon Ned Crummins looked up from the card he had been turning over and over, more and more like one arriving at a condemnatory judgment of a fish.

"I can't go and give my master a card instead of his glass," he remarked.

"Yes, that reminds me; and I should like to know what you meant by bringing that glass away from Mr. Tinman's house at night," said Mr. Smith. "If I'm to pay for it, I've a right to know. What's the meaning of moving it at night? Eh, let's hear. Night's not the time for moving big glasses like that. I'm not so sure I haven't got a case."

"If you'll step round to my master along o' me, sir," said Crummins, "perhaps he'll explain."

Crummins was requested to state who his master was, and he replied, "Phippun and Company;" but Mr. Smith positively refused to go with him.

"But here," said he, "is a crown for you, for you're a civil fellow. You'll know where to find me in the morning; and mind, I shall expect Phippun and Company to give me a very good account of their reason for moving a big looking-glass on a night like this. There, be off."

The crown-piece in his hand effected a genial change in Crummins' disposition to communicate. Crickledon spoke to him about the glass; two or three of the others present jogged him. "What did Mr. Tinman want by having the glass moved so late in the day, Ned? Your master wasn't nervous about his property, was he?"

"Not he," said Crummins, and began to suck down his upper lip and agitate his eyelids and stand uneasily, glimmering signs of the setting in of the tide of narration.

He caught the eye of Mr. Smith, then looked abashed at Miss.

Crickledon saw his dilemma. "Say what's uppermost, Ned; never mind how you says it. English is English. Mr. Tinman sent for you to take the glass away, now, did n't he?"

"He did," said Crummins.

"And you went to him."

"Ay, that I did."

"And he fastened the chiwal glass upon your back"

"He did that."

"That's all plain sailing. Had he bought the glass?"

"No, he had n't bought it. He'd hired it."

As when upon an enforced visit to the dentist, people have had one tooth out, the remaining offenders are more willingly submitted to the operation, insomuch that a poetical licence might hazard the statement that they shed them like leaves of the tree, so Crummins, who had shrunk from speech, now volunteered whole sentences in succession, and how important they were deemed by his fellow-townsman, Mr. Smith, and especially Miss Annette Smith, could perceive in their ejaculations, before they themselves were drawn into the strong current of interest.

And this was the matter: Tinman had hired the glass for three days. Latish, on the very first day of the hiring, close upon dark, he had despatched imperative orders to Phippun and Company to take the glass out of his house on the spot. And why? Because, as he maintained, there was a fault in the glass causing an incongruous and absurd reflection; and he was at that moment awaiting the arrival of another chiwal-glass.

"Cut along, Ned," said Crickledon.

"What the deuce does he want with a chiwal-glass at all?" cried Mr. Smith, endangering the flow of the story by suggesting to the narrator that he must "hark back," which to him was equivalent to the jumping of a chasm hindward. Happily his brain had seized a picture:

"Mr. Tinman, he's a-standin' in his best Court suit."

Mr. Tinmau's old schoolmate gave a jump; and no wonder.

"Standing?" he cried; and as the act of standing was really not extraordinary, he fixed upon the suit: "Court?"

"So Mrs. Cavely told me, it was what he was standin' in, and as I found 'm I left 'm," said Crummins.

"He's standing in it now?" said Mr. Van Diemen Smith, with a great gape.

Crummins doggedly repeated the statement. Many would have ornamented it in the repetition, but he was for bare flat truth.

"He must be precious proud of having a Court suit," said Mr. Smith, and gazed at his daughter so glassily that she smiled, though she was impatient to proceed to Mrs. Crickledon's lodgings.

"Oh! there's where it is?" interjected the carpenter, with a funny frown at a low word from Ned Crummins. "Practicing, is he? Mr. Tinman's practicing before the glass preparatory to his going to the palace in London."

"He gave me a shillin'," said Crummins.

Crickledon comprehended him immediately. "We sha'n't speak about it, Ned."

What did you see? was thus cautiously suggested.

The shilling was on Crummins' tongue to check his betrayal of the secret scene. But remembering that he had only witnessed it by accident, and that Mr. Tinman had not completely taken him into his confidence, he thrust his hand down his pocket to finger the crown-piece lying in fellowship with the coin it multiplied five times, and was inspired to think himself at liberty to say: "All I saw was when the door opened. Not the house-door. It was the parlour-door. I saw him walk up to the glass, and walk back from the glass. And when he'd got up to the glass he bowed, he did, and he went back'ards just so."

Doubtless the presence of a lady was the active agent that prevented Crummins from doubling his body entirely, and giving more than a rapid indication of the posture of Mr. Tinman in his retreat before the glass. But it was a glimpse of broad burlesque, and though it was received with becoming sobriety by the men in the carpenter's shop, Annette plucked at her father's arm.

She could not get him to depart. That picture of his old schoolmate Martin Tinman practicing before a chiwal glass to present himself at the palace in his Court suit, seemed to stupefy his Australian intelligence.

"What right has he got to go to Court?" Mr. Van Diemen Smith inquired, like the foreigner he had become through exile.

"Mr. Tinman's bailiff of the town," said Crickledon.

"And what was his objection to that glass I smashed?"

"He's rather an irritable gentleman," Crickledon murmured, and turned to Crummins.

Crummins growled: "He said it was misty, and gave him a twist."

"What a big fool he must be! eh?" Mr. Smith glanced at Crickledon and the other faces for the verdict of Tinman's townsmen upon his character.

They had grounds for thinking differently of Tinman.

"He's no fool," said Crickledon.

Another shook his head. "Sharp at a bargain."

"That he be," said the chorus.

Mr. Smith was informed that Mr. Tinman would probably end by buying up half the town.

"Then," said Mr. Smith, "he can afford to pay half the money for that glass, and pay he shall."

A serious view of the recent catastrophe was presented by his declaration.

In the midst of a colloquy regarding the cost of the glass, during which it began to be seen by Mr. Tinman's townsmen that there was laughing-stuff for a year or so in the scene witnessed by Crummins, if they postponed a bit their right to the laugh and took it in doses, Annette induced her father to signal to Crickledon his readiness to go and see the lodgings. No sooner had he done it than he said, "What on earth made us wait all this time here? I'm hungry, my dear; I want supper."

"That is because you have had a disappointment. I know you, papa," said Annette.

"Yes, it's rather a damper about old Mart Tinman," her father assented. "Or else I have n't recovered the shock of smashing that glass, and visit it on him. But, upon my honour, he's my only friend in England, I have n't a single relative that I know of, and to come and find your only friend making a donkey of himself, is enough to make a man think of eating and drinking."

Annette murmured reproachfully: "We can hardly say he is our only friend in England, papa, can we?"

"Do you mean that young fellow? You'll take my appetite away if you talk of him. He's a stranger. I don't believe he's worth a penny. He owns he's what he calls a journalist."

These latter remarks were hurriedly exchanged at the threshold of Crickledon's house.

"It don't look promising," said Mr. Smith.

"I didn't recommend it," said Crickledon.

"Why the deuce do you let your lodgings, then?"

"People who have come once come again."

"Oh! I am in England," Annette sighed joyfully, feeling at home in some trait she had detected in Crickledon.

CHAPTER III

The story of the shattered chiwal-glass and the visit of Tinman's old schoolmate fresh from Australia, was at many a breakfast-table before. Tinman heard a word of it, and when he did he had no time to spare for such incidents, for he was reading to his widowed sister Martha, in an impressive tone, at a tolerably high pitch of the voice, and with a suppressed excitement that shook away all things external from his mind as violently as it agitated his body. Not the waves without but the engine within it is which gives the shock and tremor to the crazy steamer, forcing it to cut through the waves and scatter them to spray; and so did Martin Tinman make light of the external attack of the card of VAN DIEMEN SMITH, and its pencilled line: "An old chum of yours, eh, matey?" Even the communication of Phippun & Co. concerning the chiwal-glass, failed to divert him from his particular task. It was indeed a public duty; and the chiwal-glass, though pertaining to it, was a private business. He that has broken the glass, let that man pay for it, he pronounced—no doubt in simpler fashion, being at his ease in his home, but with the serenity of one uplifted. As to the name VAN DIEMEN SMITH, he knew it not, and so he said to himself while accurately recollecting the identity of the old chum who alone of men would have thought of writing eh, matey?

Mr. Van Diemen Smith did not present the card in person. "At Crickledon's," he wrote, apparently expecting the bailiff of the town to rush over to him before knowing who he was.

Tinman was far too busy. Anybody can read plain penmanship or print, but ask anybody not a Cabinet Minister or a Lord-in-Waiting to read out loud and clear in a Palace, before a Throne. Oh! the nature of reading is distorted in a trice, and as Tinman said to his worthy sister: "I can do it, but I must lose no time in preparing myself." Again, at a reperusal, he informed her: "I must habituate myself." For this purpose he had put on the suit overnight.

The articulation of faultless English was his object. His sister Martha sat vice-regally to receive his loyal congratulations on the illustrious marriage, and she was pensive, less nervous than her brother from not having to speak continuously, yet somewhat perturbed. She also had her task, and it was to avoid thinking herself the Person addressed by her suppliant brother, while at the same time she took possession of the scholarly training and perfect knowledge of diction and rules of pronunciation which would infallibly be brought to bear on him in the terrible hour of the delivery of the Address. It was no small task moreover to be compelled to listen right through to the end of the Address, before the very gentlest word of criticism was allowed. She did not exactly complain of the renewal of the rehearsal: a fatigue can be endured when it is a joy. What vexed her was her failing memory for the points of objection, as in her imagined High Seat she conceived them; for, in painful truth, the instant her brother had finished she entirely lost her acuteness of ear, and with that her recollection: so there was nothing to do but to say: "Excellent! Quite unobjectionable, dear Martin, quite:" so she said, and emphatically; but the addition of the word "only" was printed on her contracted brow, and every faculty of Tinman's mind and nature being at strain just then, he asked her testily: "What now? what's the fault now?" She assured him with languor that there was not a fault. "It's not your way of talking," said he, and what he said was true. His discernment was extraordinary; generally he noticed nothing.

Not only were his perceptions quickened by the preparations for the day of great splendour: day of a great furnace to be passed through likewise!—he, was learning English at an astonishing rate into the bargain. A pronouncing Dictionary lay open on his table. To this he flew at a hint of a contrary method, and disputes, verifications and triumphs on one side and the other ensued between brother and sister. In his heart the agitated man believed his sister to be a misleading guide. He dared not say it, he thought it, and previous to his African travel through the Dictionary he had thought his sister infallible on these points. He dared not say it, because he knew no one else before whom he could practice, and as it was confidence that he chiefly wanted—above all things, confidence and confidence comes of practice, he preferred the going on with his practice to an absolute certainty as to correctness.

At midday came another card from Mr. Van Diemen Smith bearing the superscription: alias Phil R.

"Can it be possible," Tinman asked his sister, "that Philip Ribstone has had the audacity to return to this country? I think," he added, "I am right in treating whoever sends me this card as a counterfeit."

Martha's advice was, that he should take no notice of the card.

"I am seriously engaged," said Tinman. With a "Now then, dear," he resumed his labours.

Messages had passed between Tinman and Phippun; and in the afternoon Phippun appeared to broach the question of payment for the chiwal-glass. He had seen Mr. Van Diemen Smith, had found him very strange, rather impracticable. He was obliged to tell Tinman that he must hold him responsible for the glass; nor could he send a second until payment was made for the first. It really seemed as if Tinman would be compelled, by the force of circumstances, to go and shake his old friend by the hand. Otherwise one could clearly see the man might be off: he might be off at any minute, leaving a legal contention behind him. On the other hand, supposing he had come to Crikswich for assistance in money? Friendship is a good thing, and so is hospitality, which is an essentially English thing, and consequently one that it behoves an Englishman to think it his duty to perform, but we do not extend it to paupers. But should a pauper get so close to us as to lay hold of us, vowing he was once our friend, how shake him loose? Tinman foresaw that it might be a matter of five pounds thrown to the dogs, perhaps ten, counting the glass. He put on his hat, full of melancholy presentiments; and it was exactly half-past five o'clock of the spring afternoon when he knocked at Crickledon's door.

Had he looked into Crickledon's shop as he went by, he would have perceived Van Diemen Smith astride a piece of timber, smoking a pipe. Van Diemen saw Tinman. His eyes cocked and watered. It is a disgraceful fact to record of him without periphrasis. In truth, the bearded fellow was almost a woman at heart, and had come from the Antipodes throbbing to slap Martin Tinman on the back, squeeze his hand, run over England with him, treat him, and talk of old times in the presence of a trotting regiment of champagne. That affair of the chiwal-glass had temporarily damped his enthusiasm. The absence of a reply to his double transmission of cards had wounded him; and something in the look of Tinman disgusted his rough taste. But the well-known features recalled the days of youth. Tinman was his one living link to the country he admired as the conqueror of the world, and imaginatively delighted in as the seat of pleasures, and he could not discard the feeling of some love for Tinman without losing his grasp of the reason why, he had longed so fervently and travelled so breathlessly to return hither. In the days of their youth, Van Diemen had been Tinman's cordial spirit, at whom he sipped for cheerful visions of life, and a good honest glow of emotion now and then. Whether it was odd or not that the sipper should be oblivious, and the cordial spirit heartily reminiscent of those times, we will not stay to inquire.

Their meeting took place in Crickledon's shop. Tinman was led in by Mrs. Crickledon. His voice made a sound of metal in his throat, and his air was that of a man buttoned up to the palate, as he read from the card, glancing over his eyelids, "Mr. Van Diemen Smith, I believe."

"Phil Ribstone, if you like," said the other, without rising.

"Oh, ah, indeed!" Tinman temperately coughed.

"Yes, dear me. So it is. It strikes you as odd?"

"The change of name," said Tinman.

"Not nature, though!"

"Ah! Have you been long in England?"

"Time to run to Helmstone, and on here. You've been lucky in business, I hear."

"Thank you; as things go. Do you think of remaining in England?"

"I've got to settle about a glass I broke last night."

"Ah! I have heard of it. Yes, I fear there will have to be a settlement."

"I shall pay half of the damage. You'll have to stump up your part."

Van Diemen smiled roguishly.

"We must discuss that," said Tinman, smiling too, as a patient in bed may smile at a doctor's joke; for he was, as Crickledon had said of him, no fool on practical points, and Van Diemen's mention of the half-payment reassured him as to his old friend's position in the world, and softly thawed him. "Will you dine with me to-day?"

"I don't mind if I do. I've a girl. You remember little Netty? She's walking out on the beach with a young fellow named Fellingham, whose acquaintance we made on the voyage, and has n't left us long to ourselves. Will you have her as well? And I suppose you must ask him. He's a newspaper man; been round the world; seen a lot."

Tinman hesitated. An electrical idea of putting sherry at fifteen shillings per dozen on his table instead of the ceremonial wine at twenty-five shillings, assisted him to say hospitably, "Oh! ah! yes; any friend of yours."

"And now perhaps you'll shake my fist," said Van Diemen.

"With pleasure," said Tinman. "It was your change of name, you know, Philip."

"Look here, Martin. Van Diemen Smith was a convict, and my benefactor. Why the deuce he was so fond of that name, I can't tell you; but his dying wish was for me to take it and carry it on. He left me his fortune, for Van Diemen Smith to enjoy life, as he never did, poor fellow, when he was alive. The money was got honestly, by hard labour at a store. He did evil once, and repented after. But, by Heaven!"—Van Diemen jumped up and thundered out of a broad chest—"the man was one of the finest hearts that ever beat. He was! and I'm proud of him. When he died, I turned my thoughts home to Old England and you, Martin."

"Oh!" said Tinman; and reminded by Van Diemen's way of speaking, that cordiality was expected of him, he shook his limbs to some briskness, and continued, "Well, yes, we must all die in our native land if we can. I hope you're comfortable in your lodgings?"

"I'll give you one of Mrs. Crickledon's dinners to try. You're as good as mayor of this town, I hear?"

"I am the bailiff of the town," said Mr. Tinman.

"You're going to Court, I'm told."

"The appointment," replied Mr. Tinman, "will soon be made. I have not yet an appointed day."

On the great highroad of life there is Expectation, and there is Attainment, and also there is Envy. Mr. Tinman's posture stood for Attainment shadowing Expectation, and sunning itself in the glass of Envy, as he spoke of the appointed day. It was involuntary, and naturally evanescent, a momentary view of the spirit.

He unbent, and begged to be excused for the present, that he might go and apprise his sister of guests coming.

"All right. I daresay we shall see, enough of one another," said Van Diemen. And almost before the creak of Tinman's heels was deadened on the road outside the shop, he put the funny question to Crickledon, "Do you box?"

"I make 'em," Crickledon replied.

"Because I should like to have a go in at something, my friend."

Van Diemen stretched and yawned.

Crickledon recommended the taking of a walk.

"I think I will," said the other, and turned back abruptly. "How long do you work in the day?"

"Generally, all the hours of light," Crickledon replied; "and always up to supper-time."

"You're healthy and happy?"

"Nothing to complain of."

"Good appetite?"

"Pretty regular."

"You never take a holiday?"

"Except Sundays."

"You'd like to be working then?"

"I won't say that."

"But you're glad to be up Monday morning?"

"It feels cheerfuller in the shop."

"And carpentering's your joy?"

"I think I may say so."

Van Diemen slapped his thigh. "There's life in Old England yet!"

Crickledon eyed him as he walked away to the beach to look for his daughter, and conceived that there was a touch of the soldier in him.

CHAPTER IV

Annette Smith's delight in her native England made her see beauty and kindness everywhere around her; it put a halo about the house on the beach, and thrilled her at Tinman's table when she heard the thunder of the waves hard by. She fancied it had been a most agreeable dinner to her father and Mr. Herbert Fellingham—especially to the latter, who had laughed very much; and she was astonished to hear them at breakfast both complaining of their evening. In answer to which, she exclaimed, "Oh, I think the situation of the house is so romantic!"

"The situation of the host is exceedingly so," said Mr. Fellingham; "but I think his wine the most unromantic liquid I have ever tasted."

"It must be that!" cried Van Diemen, puzzled by novel pains in the head. "Old Martin woke up a little like his old self after dinner."

"He drank sparingly," said Mr. Fellingham.

"I am sure you were satirical last night," Annette said reproachfully.

"On the contrary, I told him I thought he was in a romantic situation."

"But I have had a French mademoiselle for my governess and an Oxford gentleman for my tutor; and I know you accepted French and English from Mr. Tinman and his sister that I should not have approved."

"Netty," said Van Diemen, "has had the best instruction money could procure; and if she says you were satirical, you may depend on it you were."

"Oh, in that case, of course!" Mr. Fellingham rejoined. "Who could help it?"

He thought himself warranted in giving the rein to his wicked satirical spirit, and talked lightly of the accidental character of the letter H in Tinman's pronunciation; of how, like somebody else's hat in a high wind, it descended on somebody else's head, and of how his words walked about asking one another who they were and what they were doing, danced together madly, snapping their fingers at signification; and so forth. He was flippant.

Annette glanced at her father, and dropped her eyelids.

Mr. Fellingham perceived that he was enjoined to be on his guard.

He went one step farther in his fun; upon which Van Diemen said, with a frown, "If you please!"

Nothing could withstand that.

"Hang old Mart Tinman's wine!" Van Diemen burst out in the dead pause. "My head's a bullet. I'm in a shocking bad temper. I can hardly see. I'm bilious."

Mr. Fellingham counselled his lying down for an hour, and he went grumbling, complaining of Mart Tinman's incredulity about the towering beauty of a place in Australia called Gippsland.

Annette confided to Mr. Fellingham, as soon as they were alone, the chivalrous nature of her father in his friendships, and his indisposition to hear a satirical remark upon his old schoolmate, the moment he understood it to be satire.

Fellingham pleaded: "The man's a perfect burlesque. He's as distinctly made to be laughed at as a mask in a pantomime."

"Papa will not think so," said Annette; "and papa has been told that he is not to be laughed at as a man of business."

"Do you prize him for that?"

"I am no judge. I am too happy to be in England to be a judge of anything."

"You did not touch his wine!"

"You men attach so much importance to wine!"

"They do say that powders is a good thing after Mr. Tinman's wine," observed Mrs. Crickledon, who had come into the sitting-room to take away the breakfast things.

Mr. Fellingham gave a peal of laughter; but Mrs Crickledon bade him be hushed, for Mr. Van Diemen Smith had gone to lay down his poor aching head on his pillow. Annette ran upstairs to speak to her father about a doctor.

During her absence, Mr. Fellingham received the popular portrait of Mr. Tinman from the lips of Mrs. Crickledon. He subsequently strolled to the carpenter's shop, and endeavoured to get a confirmation of it.

"My wife talks too much," said Crickledon.

When questioned by a gentleman, however, he was naturally bound to answer to the extent of his knowledge.

"What a funny old country it is!" Mr. Fellingham said to Annette, on their walk to the beach.

She implored him not to laugh at anything English.

"I don't, I assure you," said he. "I love the country, too. But when one comes back from abroad, and plunges into their daily life, it's difficult to retain the real figure of the old country seen from outside, and one has to remember half a dozen great names to right oneself. And Englishmen are so funny! Your father comes here to see his old friend, and begins boasting of the Gippsland he has left behind. Tinman immediately brags of Helvellyn, and they fling mountains at one another till, on their first evening together, there's earthquake and rupture—they were nearly at fisticuffs at one time."

"Oh! surely no," said Annette. "I did not hear them. They were good friends when you came to the drawingroom. Perhaps the wine did affect poor papa, if it was bad wine. I wish men would never drink any. How much happier they would be."

"But then there would cease to be social meetings in England. What should we do?"

"I know that is a sneer; and you were nearly as enthusiastic as I was on board the vessel," Annette said, sadly.

"Quite true. I was. But see what quaint creatures we have about us! Tinman practicing in his Court suit before the chiwal-glass! And that good fellow, the carpenter, Crickledon, who has lived with the sea fronting him all his life, and has never been in a boat, and he confesses he has only once gone inland, and has never seen an acorn!"

"I wish I could see one—of a real English oak," said Annette.

"And after being in England a few months you will be sighing for the Continent."

"Never!"

"You think you will be quite contented here?"

"I am sure I shall be. May papa and I never be exiles again! I did not feel it when I was three years old, going out to Australia; but it would be like death to me now. Oh!" Annette shivered, as with the exile's chill.

"On my honour," said Mr. Fellingham, as softly as he could with the wind in his teeth, "I love the old country ten times more from your love of it."

"That is not how I want England to be loved," returned Annette.

"The love is in your hands."

She seemed indifferent on hearing it.

He should have seen that the way to woo her was to humour her prepossession by another passion. He could feel that it ennobled her in the abstract, but a latent spite at Tinman on account of his wine, to which he continued angrily to attribute as unwonted dizziness of the head and slight irascibility, made him urgent in his desire that she should separate herself from Tinman and his sister by the sharp division of derision.

Annette declined to laugh at the most risible caricatures of Tinman. In her antagonism she forced her simplicity so far as to say that she did not think him absurd. And supposing Mr. Tinman to have proposed to the titled widow, Lady Ray, as she had heard, and to other ladies young and middle-aged in the neighbourhood, why should he not, if he wished to marry? If he was economical, surely he had a right to manage his own affairs. Her dread was lest Mr. Tinman and her father should quarrel over the payment for the broken chiwal-glass: that she honestly admitted, and Fellingham was so indiscreet as to roar aloud, not so very cordially.

Annette thought him unkindly satirical; and his thoughts of her reduced her to the condition of a commonplace girl with expressive eyes.

She had to return to her father. Mr. Fellingham took a walk on the springy turf along the cliffs; and "certainly she is a commonplace girl," he began by reflecting; with a side eye at the fact that his meditations were excited by Tinman's poisoning of his bile. "A girl who can't see the absurdity of Tinman must be destitute of common intelligence." After a while he sniffed the fine sharp air of mingled earth and sea delightedly, and he strode back to the town late in the afternoon, laughing at himself in scorn of his wretched susceptibility to bilious impressions, and really all but hating Tinman as the cause of his weakness—in the manner of the criminal hating the detective, perhaps. He cast it altogether on Tinman that Annette's complexion of character had become discoloured to his mind; for, in spite of the physical freshness with which he returned to her society, he was incapable of throwing off the idea of her being commonplace; and it was with regret that he acknowledged he had gained from his walk only a higher opinion of himself.

Her father was the victim of a sick headache, [Migraine—D.W.]and lay, a groaning man, on his bed, ministered to by Mrs. Crickledon chiefly. Annette had to conduct the business with Mr. Phippun and Mr. Tinman as to payment for the chiwal-glass. She was commissioned to offer half the price for the glass on her father's part; more he would not pay. Tinman and Phippun sat with her in Crickledon's cottage, and Mrs. Crickledon brought down two messages from her invalid, each positive, to the effect that he would fight with all the arms of English law rather than yield his point.

Tinman declared it to be quite out of the question that he should pay a penny. Phippun vowed that from one or the other of them he would have the money.

Annette naturally was in deep distress, and Fellingham postponed the discussion to the morrow.

Even after such a taste of Tinman as that, Annette could not be induced to join in deriding him privately. She looked pained by Mr. Fellingham's cruel jests. It was monstrous, Fellingham considered, that he should draw on himself a second reprimand from Van Diemen Smith, while they were consulting in entire agreement upon the case of the chiwal-glass.

"I must tell you this, mister sir," said Van Diemen, "I like you, but I'll be straightforward and truthful, or I'm not worthy the name of Englishman; and I do like you, or I should n't have given you leave to come down here after us two. You must respect my friend if you care for my respect. That's it. There it is. Now you know my conditions."

"I 'm afraid I can't sign the treaty," said Fellingham.

"Here's more," said Van Diemen. "I'm a chilly man myself if I hear a laugh and think I know the aim of it. I'll meet what you like except scorn. I can't stand contempt. So I feel for another. And now you know."

"It puts a stopper on the play of fancy, and checks the throwing off of steam," Fellingham remonstrated. "I promise to do my best, but of all the men I've ever met in my life—Tinman!—the ridiculous! Pray pardon me; but the donkey and his looking-glass! The glass was misty! He—as particular about his reflection in the glass as a poet with his verses! Advance, retire, bow; and such murder of the Queen's English in the very presence! If I thought he was going to take his wine with him, I'd have him arrested for high treason."

"You've chosen, and you know what you best like," said Van Diemen, pointing his accents—by which is produced the awkward pause, the pitfall of conversation, and sometimes of amity.

Thus it happened that Mr. Herbert Fellingham journeyed back to London a day earlier than he had intended, and without saying what he meant to say.

CHAPTER V

A month later, after a night of sharp frost on the verge of the warmer days of spring, Mr. Fellingham entered Crikswich under a sky of perfect blue that was in brilliant harmony with the green downs, the white cliffs and sparkling sea, and no doubt it was the beauty before his eyes which persuaded him of his delusion in having taken Annette for a commonplace girl. He had come in a merely curious mood to discover whether she was one or not. Who but a commonplace girl would care to reside in Crikswich, he had asked himself; and now he was full sure that no commonplace girl would ever have had the idea. Exquisitely simple, she certainly was; but that may well be a distinction in a young lady whose eyes are expressive.

The sound of sawing attracted him to Crickledon's shop, and the industrious carpenter soon put him on the tide of affairs.

Crickledon pointed to the house on the beach as the place where Mr. Van Diemen Smith and his daughter were staying.

"Dear me! and how does he look?" said Fellingham.

"Our town seems to agree with him, sir."

"Well, I must not say any more, I suppose." Fellingham checked his tongue. "How have they settled that dispute about the chiwal-glass?"

"Mr. Tinman had to give way."

"Really."

"But," Crickledon stopped work, "Mr. Tinman sold him a meadow."

"I see."

"Mr. Smith has been buying a goodish bit of ground here. They tell me he's about purchasing Elba. He has bought the Crouch. He and Mr. Tinman are always out together. They're over at Helmstone now. They've been to London."

"Are they likely to be back to-day?"

"Certain, I should think. Mr. Tinman has to be in London to-morrow."

Crickledon looked. He was not the man to look artful, but there was a lighted corner in his look that revived Fellingham's recollections, and the latter burst out:

"The Address? I 'd half forgotten it. That's not over yet? Has he been practicing much?"

"No more glasses ha' been broken."

"And how is your wife, Crickledon?"

"She's at home, sir, ready for a talk, if you've a mind to try her."

Mrs. Crickledon proved to be very ready. "That Tinman," was her theme. He had taken away her lodgers, and she knew his objects. Mr. Smith repented of leaving her, she knew, though he dared not say it in plain words. She knew Miss Smith was tired to death of constant companionship with Mrs. Cavely, Tinman's sister. She generally came once in the day just to escape from Mrs. Cavely, who would not, bless you! step into a cottager's house where she was not allowed to patronize. Fortunately Miss Smith had induced her father to get his own wine from the merchants.

"A happy resolution," said Fellingham; "and a saving one."

He heard further that Mr. Smith would take possession of the Crouch next month, and that Mrs. Cavely hung over Miss Smith like a kite.

"And that old Tinman, old enough to be her father!" said Mrs. Crickledon.

She dealt in the flashes which connect ideas. Fellingham, though a man, and an Englishman, was nervously wakeful enough to see the connection.

"They'll have to consult the young lady first, ma'am."

"If it's her father's nod she'll bow to it; now mark me," Mrs. Crickledon said, with emphasis. "She's a young lady who thinks for herself, but she takes her start from her father where it's feeling. And he's gone stone-blind over that Tinman."

While they were speaking, Annette appeared.

"I saw you," she said to Fellingham; gladly and openly, in the most commonplace manner.

"Are you going to give me a walk along the beach?" said he.

She proposed the country behind the town, and that was quite as much to his taste. But it was not a happy walk. He had decided that he admired her, and the notion of having Tinman for a rival annoyed him. He overflowed with ridicule of Tinman, and this was distressing to Annette, because not only did she see that he would not control himself before her father, but he kindled her own satirical spirit in opposition to her father's friendly sentiments toward his old schoolmate.

"Mr. Tinman has been extremely hospitable to us," she said, a little coldly.

"May I ask you, has he consented to receive instruction in deportment and pronunciation?"

Annette did not answer.

"If practice makes perfect, he must be near the mark by this time."

She continued silent.

"I dare say, in domestic life, he's as amiable as he is hospitable, and it must be a daily gratification to see him in his Court suit."

"I have not seen him in his Court suit."

"That is his coyness."

"People talk of those things."

"The common people scandalize the great, about whom they know nothing, you mean! I am sure that is true, and living in Courts one must be keenly aware of it. But what a splendid sky and-sea!"

"Is it not?"

Annette echoed his false rapture with a candour that melted him.

He was preparing to make up for lost time, when the wild waving of a parasol down a road to the right, coming from the town, caused Annette to stop and say, "I think that must be Mrs. Cavely. We ought to meet her."

Fellingham asked why.

"She is so fond of walks," Anisette replied, with a tooth on her lip

Fellingham thought she seemed fond of runs.

Mrs. Cavely joined them, breathless. "My dear! the pace you go at!" she shouted. "I saw you starting. I followed, I ran, I tore along. I feared I never should catch you. And to lose such a morning of English scenery!

"Is it not heavenly?"

"One can't say more," Fellingham observed, bowing.

"I am sure I am very glad to see you again, sir. You enjoy Crikswich?"

"Once visited, always desired, like Venice, ma'am. May I venture to inquire whether Mr. Tinman has presented his Address?"

"The day after to-morrow. The appointment is made with him," said Mrs. Cavely, more officially in manner, "for the day after to-morrow. He is excited, as you may well believe. But Mr. Smith is an immense relief to him—the very distraction he wanted. We have become one family, you know."

"Indeed, ma'am, I did not know it," said Fellingham.

The communication imparted such satiric venom to his further remarks, that Annette resolved to break her walk and dismiss him for the day.

He called at the house on the beach after the dinner-hour, to see Mr. Van Diemen Smith, when there was literally a duel between him and Tinman; for Van Diemen's contribution to the table was champagne, and that had been drunk, but Tinman's sherry remained. Tinman would insist on Fellingham's taking a glass. Fellingham parried him with a sedate gravity of irony that was painfully perceptible to Anisette. Van Diemen at last backed Tinman's hospitable intent, and, to Fellingham's astonishment, he found that he had been supposed by these two men to be bashfully retreating from a seductive offer all the time that his tricks of fence and transpiercings of one of them had been marvels of skill.

Tinman pushed the glass into his hand.

"You have spilt some," said Fellingham.

"It won't hurt the carpet," said Tinman.

"Won't it?" Fellingham gazed at the carpet, as if expecting a flame to arise.

He then related the tale of the magnanimous Alexander drinking off the potion, in scorn of the slanderer, to show faith in his friend.

"Alexander—Who was that?" said Tinman, foiled in his historical recollections by the absence of the surname.

"General Alexander," said Fellingham. "Alexander Philipson, or he declared it was Joveson; and very fond of wine. But his sherry did for him at last."

"Ah! he drank too much, then," said Tinman.

"Of his own!"

Anisette admonished the vindictive young gentleman by saying, "How long do you stay in Crikswich, Mr. Fellingham?"

He had grossly misconducted himself. But an adversary at once offensive and helpless provokes brutality. Anisette prudently avoided letting her father understand that satire was in the air; and neither he nor Tinman was conscious of it exactly: yet both shrank within themselves under the sensation of a devilish blast blowing. Fellingham accompanied them and certain jurats to London next day.

Yes, if you like: when a mayor visits Majesty, it is an important circumstance, and you are at liberty to argue at length that it means more than a desire on his part to show his writing power and his reading power: it is full of comfort the people, as an exhibition of their majesty likewise; and it is an encouragement to men to strive to become mayors, bailiffs, or prime men of any sort; but a stress in the reporting of it—the making it appear too important a circumstance—will surely breathe the intimation to a politically-minded people that satire is in the air, and however dearly they cherish the privilege of knocking at the first door of the kingdom, and walking ceremoniously in to read their writings, they will, if they are not in one of their moods for prostration, laugh. They will laugh at the report.

All the greater reason is it that we should not indulge them at such periods; and I say woe's me for any brother of the pen, and one in some esteem, who dressed the report of that presentation of the Address of congratulation by Mr. Bailiff Tinman, of Crikswich! Herbert Fellingham wreaked his personal spite on Tinman. He should have bethought him that it involved another than Tinman that is to say, an office— which the fitful beast rejoices to paw and play with contemptuously now and then, one may think, as a solace to his pride, and an indemnification for those caprices of abject worship so strongly recalling the days we see through Mr. Darwin's glasses.

He should not have written the report. It sent a titter over England. He was so unwise as to despatch a copy of the newspaper containing it to Van Diemen Smith. Van Diemen perused it with satisfaction. So did Tinman. Both of these praised the able young writer. But they handed the paper to the Coastguard Lieutenant, who asked Tinman how he liked it; and visitors were beginning to drop in to Crikswich, who made a point of asking for a sight of the chief man; and then came a comic publication, all in the Republican tone of the time, with Man's Dignity for the standpoint, and the wheezy laughter residing in old puns to back it, in eulogy of the satiric report of the famous Address of congratulation of the Bailiff of Crikswich.

"Annette," Van Diemen said to his daughter, "you'll not encourage that newspaper fellow to come down here any more. He had his warning."

CHAPTER VI

One of the most difficult lessons for spirited young men to learn is, that good jokes are not always good policy. They have to be paid for, like good dinners, though dinner and joke shall seem to have been at somebody else's expense. Young Fellingham was treated rudely by Van Diemen Smith, and with some cold reserve by Annette: in consequence of which he thought her more than ever commonplace. He wrote her a letter of playful remonstrance, followed by one that appealed to her sentiments.

But she replied to neither of them. So his visits to Crikswich came to an end.

Shall a girl who has no appreciation of fun affect us? Her expressive eyes, and her quaint simplicity, and her enthusiasm for England, haunted Mr. Fellingham; being conjured up by contrast with what he met about him. But shall a girl who would impose upon us the task of holding in our laughter at Tinman be much regretted? There could be no companionship between us, Fellingham thought.

On an excursion to the English Lakes he saw the name of Van Diemen Smith in a visitors' book, and changed his ideas on the subject of companionship. Among mountains, or on the sea, or reading history, Annette was one in a thousand. He happened to be at a public ball at Helmstone in the Winter season, and who but Annette herself came whirling before him on the arm of an officer! Fellingham did not miss his chance of talking to her. She greeted him gaily, and speaking with the excitement of the dance upon her, appeared a stranger to the serious emotions he was willing to cherish. She had been to the Lakes and to Scotland. Next summer she was going to Wales. All her experiences were delicious. She was insatiable, but satisfied.

"I wish I had been with you," said Fellingham.

"I wish you had," said she.

Mrs. Cavely was her chaperon at the ball, and he was not permitted to enjoy a lengthened conversation sitting with Annette. What was he to think of a girl who could be submissive to Mrs. Cavely, and danced with any number of officers, and had no idea save of running incessantly over England in the pursuit of pleasure? Her tone of saying, "I wish you had," was that of the most ordinary of wishes, distinctly, if not designedly different from his own melodious depth.

She granted him one waltz, and he talked of her father and his whimsical vagrancies and feeling he had a positive liking for Van Diemen, and he sagaciously said so.

Annette's eyes brightened. "Then why do you never go to see him? He has bought Elba. We move into the Hall after Christmas. We are at the Crouch at present. Papa will be sure to make you welcome. Do you not know that he never forgets a friend or breaks a friendship?"

"I do, and I love him for it," said Fellingham.

If he was not greatly mistaken a gentle pressure on the fingers of his left hand rewarded him.

This determined him. It should here be observed that he was by birth the superior of Annette's parentage, and such is the sentiment of a better blood that the flattery of her warm touch was needed for him to overlook the distinction.

Two of his visits to Crikswich resulted simply in interviews and conversations with Mrs. Crickledon. Van Diemen and his daughter were in London with Tinman and Mrs. Cavely, purchasing furniture for Elba Hall. Mrs. Crickledon had no scruple in saying, that Mrs. Cavely meant her brother to inhabit the Hall, though Mr. Smith had outbid him in the purchase. According to her, Tinman and Mr. Smith had their differences; for Mr. Smith was a very outspoken gentleman, and had been known to call Tinman names that no man of spirit would bear if he was not scheming.

Fellingham returned to London, where he roamed the streets famous for furniture warehouses, in the vain hope of encountering the new owner of Elba.

Failing in this endeavour, he wrote a love-letter to Annette.

It was her first. She had liked him. Her manner of thinking she might love him was through the reflection that no one stood in the way. The letter opened a world to her, broader than Great Britain.

Fellingham begged her, if she thought favourably of him, to prepare her father for the purport of his visit. If otherwise, she was to interdict the visit with as little delay as possible and cut him adrift.

A decided line of conduct was imperative. Yet you have seen that she was not in love. She was only not unwilling to be in love. And Fellingham was just a trifle warmed. Now mark what events will do to light the fires.

Van Diemen and Tinman, old chums re-united, and both successful in life, had nevertheless, as Mrs. Crickledon said, their differences. They commenced with an opposition to Tinman's views regarding the expenditure of town moneys. Tinman was ever for devoting them to the patriotic defence of "our shores;" whereas Van Diemen, pointing in detestation of the town sewerage reeking across the common under the beach, loudly called on him to preserve our lives, by way of commencement. Then Van Diemen precipitately purchased Elba at a high valuation, and Tinman had expected by waiting to buy it at his own valuation, and sell it out of friendly consideration to his friend afterwards, for a friendly consideration. Van Diemen had joined the hunt. Tinman could not mount a horse. They had not quarrelled, but they had snapped about these and other affairs. Van Diemen fancied Tinman was jealous of his wealth. Tinman shrewdly suspected Van Diemen to be contemptuous of his dignity. He suffered a loss in a loan of money; and instead of pitying him, Van Diemen had laughed him to scorn for expecting security for investments at ten per cent. The bitterness of the pinch to Tinman made him frightfully sensitive to strictures on his discretion. In his anguish he told his sister he was ruined, and she advised him to marry before the crash. She was aware that he exaggerated, but she repeated her advice. She went so far as to name the person. This is known, because she was overheard by her housemaid, a gossip of Mrs. Crickledon's, the subsequently famous "Little Jane."

Now, Annette had shyly intimated to her father the nature of Herbert Fellingham's letter, at the same time professing a perfect readiness to submit to his directions; and her father's perplexity was very great, for Annette had rather fervently dramatized the young man's words at the ball at Helmstone, which had pleasantly tickled him, and, besides, he liked the young man. On the other hand, he did not at all like the prospect of losing his daughter; and he would have desired her to be a lady of title. He hinted at her right to claim a high position. Annette shrank from the prospect, saying, "Never let me marry one who might be ashamed of my father!"

"I shouldn't stomach that," said Van Diemen, more disposed in favour of the present suitor.

Annette was now in a tremor. She had a lover; he was coming. And if he did not come, did it matter? Not so very much, except to her pride. And if he did, what was she to say to him? She felt like an actress who may in a few minutes be called on the stage, without knowing her part. This was painfully unlike love, and the poor girl feared it would be her conscientious duty to dismiss him—most gently, of course; and perhaps, should he be impetuous and picturesque, relent enough to let him hope, and so bring about a happy postponement of the question. Her father had been to a neighbouring town on business with Mr. Tinman. He knocked at her door at midnight; and she, in dread of she knew not what—chiefly that the Hour of the Scene had somehow struck—stepped out to him trembling. He was alone. She thought herself the most childish of mortals in supposing that she could have been summoned at midnight to declare her sentiments, and hardly noticed his gloomy depression. He asked her to give him five minutes; then asked her for a kiss, and told her to go to bed and sleep. But Annette had seen that a great present affliction was on him, and she would not be sent to sleep. She promised to listen patiently, to bear anything, to be brave. "Is it bad news from home?" she said, speaking of the old home where she had not left her heart, and where his money was invested.

"It's this, my dear Netty," said Van Diemen, suffering her to lead him into her sitting-room; "we shall have to leave the shores of England."

"Then we are ruined."

"We're not; the rascal can't do that. We might be off to the Continent, or we might go to America; we've money. But we can't stay here. I'll not live at any man's mercy."

"The Continent! America!" exclaimed the enthusiast for England. "Oh, papa, you love living in England so!"

"Not so much as all that, my dear. You do, that I know. But I don't see how it's to be managed. Mart Tinman and I have been at tooth and claw to-day and half the night; and he has thrown off the mask, or he's dashed something from my sight, I don't know which. I knocked him down."

"Papa!"

"I picked him up."

"Oh," cried Annette, "has Mr. Tinman been hurt?"

"He called me a Deserter!"

Anisette shuddered.

She did not know what this thing was, but the name of it opened a cabinet of horrors, and she touched her father timidly, to assure him of her constant love, and a little to reassure herself of his substantial identity.

"And I am one," Van Diemen made the confession at the pitch of his voice. "I am a Deserter; I'm liable to be branded on the back. And it's in Mart Tinman's power to have me marched away to-morrow morning in the sight of Crikswich, and all I can say for myself, as a man and a Briton, is, I did not desert before the enemy. That I swear I never would have done. Death, if death's in front; but your poor mother was a handsome woman, my child, and there—I could not go on living in barracks and leaving her unprotected. I can't tell a young woman the tale. A hundred pounds came on me for a legacy, as plump in my hands out of open heaven, and your poor mother and I saw our chance; we consulted, and we determined to risk it, and I got on board with her and you, and over the seas we went, first to shipwreck, ultimately to fortune."

Van Diemen laughed miserably. "They noticed in the hunting-field here I had a soldier-like seat. A soldier-like seat it'll be, with a brand on it. I sha'n't be asked to take a soldier-like seat at any of their tables again. I may at Mart Tinman's, out of pity, after I've undergone my punishment. There's a year still to run out of the twenty of my term of service due. He knows it; he's been reckoning; he has me. But the worst cat-o'-nine-tails for me is the disgrace. To have myself pointed at, 'There goes the Deserter' He was a private in the Carbineers, and he deserted.' No one'll say, 'Ay, but he clung to the idea of his old schoolmate when abroad, and came back loving him, and trusted him, and was deceived."

Van Diemen produced a spasmodic cough with a blow on his chest. Anisette was weeping.

"There, now go to bed," said he. "I wish you might have known no more than you did of our flight when I got you on board the ship with your poor mother; but you're a young woman now, and you must help me to think of another cut and run, and what baggage we can scrape together in a jiffy, for I won't live here at Mart Tinman's mercy."

Drying her eyes to weep again, Annette said, when she could speak: "Will nothing quiet him? I was going to bother you with all sorts of silly questions, poor dear papa; but I see I can understand if I try. Will nothing—Is he so very angry? Can we not do something to pacify him? He is fond of money. He—oh, the thought of leaving England! Papa, it will kill you; you set your whole heart on England. We could—I could—could I not, do you not think?—step between you as a peacemaker. Mr. Tinman is always very courteous to me."

At these words of Annette's, Van Diemen burst into a short snap of savage laughter. "But that's far away in the background, Mr. Mart Tinman!" he said. "You stick to your game, I know that; but you'll find me flown, though I leave a name to stink like your common behind me. And," he added, as a chill reminder, "that name the name of my benefactor. Poor old Van Diemen! He thought it a safe bequest to make."

"It was; it is! We will stay; we will not be exiled," said Annette. "I will do anything. What was the quarrel about, papa?"

"The fact is, my dear, I just wanted to show him—and take down his pride—I'm by my Australian education a shrewder hand than his old country. I bought the house on the beach while he was chaffering, and then I sold it him at a rise when the town was looking up—only to make him see. Then he burst up about something I said of Australia. I will have the common clean. Let him live at the Crouch as my tenant if he finds the house on the beach in danger."

"Papa, I am sure," Annette repeated—"sure I have influence with Mr. Tinman."

"There are those lips of yours shutting tight," said her father. "Just listen, and they make a big O. The donkey! He owns you've got influence, and he offers he'll be silent if you'll pledge your word to marry him. I'm not sure he didn't say, within the year. I told him to look sharp not to be knocked down again. Mart Tinman for my son-in-law! That's an upside down of my expectations, as good as being at the antipodes without a second voyage back! I let him know you were engaged."

Annette gazed at her father open-mouthed, as he had predicted; now with a little chilly dimple at one corner of the mouth, now at another—as a breeze curves the leaden winter lake here and there. She could not get his meaning into her sight, and she sought, by looking hard, to understand it better; much as when some solitary maiden lady, passing into her bedchamber in the hours of darkness, beholds—tradition telling us she has absolutely beheld foot of burglar under bed; and lo! she stares, and, cunningly to moderate her horror, doubts, yet cannot but believe that there is a leg, and a trunk, and a head, and two terrible arms, bearing pistols, to follow. Sick, she palpitates; she compresses her trepidation; she coughs, perchance she sings a bar or two of an aria. Glancing down again, thrice horrible to her is it to discover that there is no foot! For had it remained, it might have been imagined a harmless, empty boot. But the withdrawal has a deadly significance of animal life....

In like manner our stricken Annette perceived the object; so did she gradually apprehend the fact of her being asked for Tinman's bride, and she could not think it credible. She half scented, she devised her plan of escape from another single mention of it. But on her father's remarking, with a shuffle, frightened by her countenance, "Don't listen to what I said, Netty. I won't paint him blacker than he is"—then Annette was sure she had been proposed for by Mr. Tinman, and she fancied her father might have revolved it in his mind that there was this means of keeping Tinman silent, silent for ever, in his own interests.

"It was not true, when you told Mr. Tinman I was engaged, papa," she said.

"No, I know that. Mart Tinman only half-kind of hinted. Come, I say! Where's the unmarried man wouldn't like to have a girl like you, Netty! They say he's been rejected all round a circuit of fifteen miles; and he's not bad-looking, neither—he looks fresh and fair. But I thought it as well to let him know he might get me at a disadvantage, but he couldn't you. Now, don't think about it, my love."

"Not if it is not necessary, papa," said Annette; and employed her familiar sweetness in persuading him to go to bed, as though he were the afflicted one requiring to be petted.

CHAPTER VII

Round under the cliffs by the sea, facing South, are warm seats in winter. The sun that shines there on a day of frost wraps you as in a mantle. Here it was that Mr. Herbert Fellingham found Annette, a chalk-block for her chair, and a mound of chalk-rubble defending her from the keen-tipped breath of the east, now and then shadowing the smooth blue water, faintly, like reflections of a flight of gulls.

Infants are said to have their ideas, and why not young ladies? Those who write of their perplexities in descriptions comical in their length are unkind to them, by making them appear the simplest of the creatures of fiction; and most of us, I am sure, would incline to believe in them if they were only some bit more lightly touched. Those troubled sentiments of our young lady of the comfortable classes are quite worthy of mention. Her poor little eye poring as little fishlike as possible upon the intricate, which she takes for the infinite, has its place in our history, nor should we any of us miss the pathos of it were it not that so large a space is claimed for the exposure. As it is, one has almost to fight a battle to persuade the world that she has downright thoughts and feelings, and really a superhuman delicacy is required in presenting her that she may be credible. Even then—so much being accomplished the thousands accustomed to chapters of her when she is in the situation of Annette will be disappointed by short sentences, just as of old the Continental eater of oysters would have been offended at the offer of an exchange of two live for two dozen dead ones. Annette was in the grand crucial position of English imaginative prose. I recognize it, and that to this the streamlets flow, thence pours the flood. But what was the plain truth? She had brought herself to think she ought to sacrifice herself to Tinman, and her evasions with Herbert, manifested in tricks of coldness alternating with tones of regret, ended, as they had commenced, in a mysterious half-sullenness. She had hardly a word to say. Let me step in again to observe that she had at the moment no pointed intention of marrying Tinman. To her mind the circumstances compelled her to embark on the idea of doing so, and she saw the extremity in an extreme distance, as those who are taking voyages may see death by drowning. Still she had embarked.

"At all events, I have your word for it that you don't dislike me?" said Herbert.

"Oh! no," she sighed. She liked him as emigrants the land they are leaving.

"And you have not promised your hand?"

"No," she said, but sighed in thinking that if she could be induced to promise it, there would not be a word of leaving England.

"Then, as you are not engaged, and don't hate me, I have a chance?" he said, in the semi-wailful interrogative of an organ making a mere windy conclusion.

Ocean sent up a tiny wave at their feet.

"A day like this in winter is rarer than a summer day," Herbert resumed encouragingly.

Annette was replying, "People abuse our climate—"

But the thought of having to go out away from this climate in the darkness of exile, with her father to suffer under it worse than herself, overwhelmed her, and fetched the reality of her sorrow in the form of Tinman swimming before her soul with the velocity of a telegraph-pole to the window of the flying train. It was past as soon as seen, but it gave her a desperate sensation of speed.

She began to feel that this was life in earnest.

And Herbert should have been more resolute, fierier. She needed a strong will.

But he was not on the rapids of the masterful passion. For though going at a certain pace, it was by his own impulsion; and I am afraid I must, with many apologies, compare him to the skater—to the skater on easy, slippery ice, be it understood; but he could perform gyrations as he went, and he rather sailed along than dashed; he was careful of his figuring. Some lovers, right honest lovers, never get beyond this quaint skating-stage; and some ladies, a right goodly number in a foggy climate, deceived by their occasional runs ahead, take them for vessels on the very torrent of love. Let them take them, and let the race continue. Only we perceive that they are skating; they are careering over a smooth icy floor, and they can stop at a signal, with just half-a-yard of grating on the heel at the outside. Ice, and not fire nor falling water, has been their medium of progression.

Whether a man should unveil his own sex is quite another question. If we are detected, not solely are we done for, but our love-tales too. However, there is not much ground for anxiety on that head. Each member of the other party is blind on her own account.

To Annette the figuring of Herbert was graceful, but it did not catch her up and carry her; it hardly touched her: He spoke well enough to make her sorry for him, and not warmly enough to make her forget her sorrow for herself.

Herbert could obtain no explanation of the singularity of her conduct from Annette, and he went straight to her father, who was nearly as inexplicable for a time. At last he said:

"If you are ready to quit the country with us, you may have my consent."

"Why quit the country?" Herbert asked, in natural amazement.

Van Diemen declined to tell him.

But seeing the young man look stupefied and wretched he took a turn about the room, and said: "I have n't robbed," and after more turns, "I have n't murdered." He growled in his menagerie trot within the four walls. "But I'm, in a man's power. Will that satisfy you? You'll tell me, because I'm rich, to snap my fingers. I can't. I've got feelings. I'm in his power to hurt me and disgrace me. It's the disgrace—to my disgrace I say it—I dread most. You'd be up to my reason if you had ever served in a regiment. I mean, discipline—if ever you'd known discipline—in the police if you like—anything—anywhere where there's what we used to call spiny de cor. I mean, at school. And I'm," said Van Diemen, "a rank idiot double D. dolt, and flat as a pancake, and transparent as a pane of glass. You see through me. Anybody could. I can't talk of my botheration without betraying myself. What good am I among you sharp fellows in England?"

Language of this kind, by virtue of its unintelligibility, set Mr. Herbert Fellingham's acute speculations at work. He was obliged to lean on Van Diemen's assertion, that he had not robbed and had not murdered, to be comforted by the belief that he was not once a notorious bushranger, or a defaulting manager of mines, or any other thing that is naughtily Australian and kangarooly.

He sat at the dinner-table at Elba, eating like the rest of mankind, and looking like a starved beggarman all the while.

Annette, in pity of his bewilderment, would have had her father take him into their confidence. She suggested it covertly, and next she spoke of it to him as a prudent measure, seeing that Mr. Fellingham might find out his exact degree of liability. Van Diemen shouted; he betrayed himself in his weakness as she could not have imagined him. He was ready to go, he said—go on the spot, give up Elba, fly from Old England: what he could not do was to let his countrymen know what he was, and live among them afterwards. He declared that the fact had eternally been present to his mind, devouring him; and Annette remembered his kindness to the artillerymen posted along the shore westward of Crikswich, though she could recall no sign of remorse. Van Diemen said: "We have to do with Martin Tinman; that's one who has a hold on me, and one's enough. Leak out my secret to a second fellow, you double my risks." He would not be taught to see how the second might counteract the first. The singularity of the action of his character on her position was, that though she knew not a soul to whom she could unburden her wretchedness, and stood far more isolated than in her Australian home, fever and chill struck her blood in contemplation of the necessity of quitting England.

Deep, then, was her gratitude to dear good Mrs. Cavely for stepping in to mediate between her father and Mr. Tinman. And well might she be amazed to hear the origin of their recent dispute.

"It was," Mrs. Cavely said, "that Gippsland."

Annette cried: "What?"

"That Gippsland of yours, my dear. Your father will praise Gippsland whenever my Martin asks him to admire the beauties of our neighbourhood. Many a time has Martin come home to me complaining of it. We have no doubt on earth that Gippsland is a very fine place; but my brother has his idea's of dignity, you must know, and I only wish he had been more used to contradiction, you may believe me. He is a lamb by nature. And, as he says, 'Why underrate one's own country?' He cannot bear to hear boasting. Well! I put it to you, dear Annette, is he so unimportant a person? He asks to be respected, and especially by his dearest friend. From that to blows! It's the way with men. They begin about trifles, they drink, they quarrel, and one does what he is sorry for, and one says more than he means. All my Martin desires is to shake your dear father's hand, forgive and forget. To win your esteem, darling Annette, he would humble himself in the dust. Will you not help me to bring these two dear old friends together once more? It is unreasonable of your dear papa to go on boasting of Gippsland if he is so fond of England, now is it not? My brother is the offended party in the eye of the law. That is quite certain. Do you suppose he dreams of taking advantage of it? He is waiting at home to be told he may call on your father. Rank, dignity, wounded feelings, is nothing to him in comparison with friendship."

Annette thought of the blow which had felled him, and spoke the truth of her heart in saying, "He is very generous."

"You understand him." Mrs. Cavely pressed her hand. "We will both go to your dear father. He may," she added, not without a gleam of feminine archness, "praise Gippsland above the Himalayas to me. What my Martin so much objected to was, the speaking of Gippsland at all when there was mention of our Lake scenery. As for me, I know how men love to boast of things nobody else has seen."

The two ladies went in company to Van Diemen, who allowed himself to be melted. He was reserved nevertheless. His reception of Mr. Tinman displeased his daughter. Annette attached the blackest importance to a blow of the fist. In her mind it blazed fiendlike, and the man who forgave it rose a step or two on the sublime. Especially did he do so considering that he had it in his power to dismiss her father and herself from bright beaming England before she had looked on all the cathedrals and churches, the sea-shores and spots named in printed poetry, to say nothing of the nobility.

"Papa, you were not so kind to Mr. Tinman as I could have hoped," said Annette.

"Mart Tinman has me at his mercy, and he'll make me know it," her father returned gloomily. "He may let me off with the Commander-in-chief. He'll blast my reputation some day, though. I shall be hanging my head in society, through him."

Van Diemen imitated the disconsolate appearance of a gallows body, in one of those rapid flashes of spontaneous veri-similitude which spring of an inborn horror painting itself on the outside.

"A Deserter!" he moaned.

He succeeded in impressing the terrible nature of the stigma upon Annette's imagination.

The guest at Elba was busy in adding up the sum of his own impressions, and dividing it by this and that new circumstance; for he was totally in the dark. He was attracted by the mysterious interview of Mrs. Cavely and Annette. Tinman's calling and departing set him upon new calculations. Annette grew cold and visibly distressed by her consciousness of it.

She endeavoured to account for this variation of mood. "We have been invited to dine at the house on the beach to-morrow. I would not have accepted, but papa... we seemed to think it a duty. Of course the invitation extends to you. We fancy you do not greatly enjoy dining there. The table will be laid for you here, if you prefer."

Herbert preferred to try the skill of Mrs. Crickledon.

Now, for positive penetration the head prepossessed by a suspicion is unmatched; for where there is no daylight; this one at least goes about with a lantern. Herbert begged Mrs. Crickledon to cook a dinner for him, and then to give the right colour to his absence from the table of Mr. Tinman, he started for a winter day's walk over the downs as sharpening a business as any young fellow, blunt or keen, may undertake; excellent for men of the pen, whether they be creative, and produce, or slaughtering, and review; good, then, for the silly sheep of letters and the butchers. He sat down to Mrs. Crickledon's table at half-past six. She was, as she had previously informed him, a forty-pound-a-year cook at the period of her courting by Crickledon. That zealous and devoted husband had made his first excursion inland to drop over the downs to the great house, and fetch her away as his bride, on the death of her master, Sir Alfred Pooney, who never would have parted with her in life; and every day of that man's life he dirtied thirteen plates at dinner, nor more, nor less, but exactly that number, as if he believed there was luck in it. And as Crickledon said, it was odd. But it was always a pleasure to cook for him. Mrs. Crickledon could not abide cooking for a mean eater. And when Crickledon said he had never seen an acorn, he might have seen one had he looked about him in the great park, under the oaks, on the day when he came to be married.

"Then it's a standing compliment to you, Mrs. Crickledon, that he did not," said Herbert.

He remarked with the sententiousness of enforced philosophy, that no wine was better than bad wine.

Mrs. Crickledon spoke of a bottle left by her summer lodgers, who had indeed left two, calling the wine invalid's wine; and she and her husband had opened one on the anniversary of their marriage day in October. It had the taste of doctor's shop, they both agreed; and as no friend of theirs could be tempted beyond a sip, they were advised, because it was called a tonic, to mix it with the pig-wash, so that it should not be entirely lost, but benefit the constitution of the pig. Herbert sipped at the remaining bottle, and finding himself in the superior society of an old Manzanilla, refilled his glass.

"Nothing I knows of proves the difference between gentlefolks and poor persons as tastes in wine," said Mrs. Crickledon, admiring him as she brought in a dish of cutlets,—with Sir Alfred Pooney's favourite sauce Soubise, wherein rightly onion should be delicate as the idea of love in maidens' thoughts, albeit constituting the element of flavour. Something of such a dictum Sir Alfred Pooney had imparted to his cook, and she repeated it with the fresh elegance of, such sweet sayings when transfused through the native mind:

"He said, I like as it was what you would call a young gal's blush at a kiss round a corner."

The epicurean baronet had the habit of talking in that way.

Herbert drank to his memory. He was well-filled; he had no work to do, and he was exuberant in spirits, as Mrs. Crickledon knew her countrymen should and would be under those conditions. And suddenly he drew his hand across a forehead so wrinkled and dark, that Mrs. Crickledon exclaimed, "Heart or stomach?"

"Oh, no," said he. "I'm sound enough in both, I hope."

"That old Tinman's up to one of his games," she observed.

"Do you think so?"

"He's circumventing Miss Annette Smith."

"Pooh! Crickledon. A man of his age can't be seriously thinking of proposing for a young lady."

"He's a well-kept man. He's never racketed. He had n't the rackets in him. And she may n't care for him. But we hear things drop."

"What things have you heard drop, Crickledon? In a profound silence you may hear pins; in a hubbub you may hear cannon-balls. But I never believe in eavesdropping gossip."

"He was heard to say to Mr. Smith," Crickledon pursued, and she lowered her voice, "he was heard to say, it was when they were quarreling over that chiwal, and they went at one another pretty hard before Mr. Smith beat him and he sold Mr. Smith that meadow; he was heard to say, there was worse than transportation for Mr. Smith if he but lifted his finger. They Tinmans have awful tempers. His old mother died malignant, though she was a saving woman, and never owed a penny to a Christian a hour longer than it took to pay the money. And old Tinman's just such another."

"Transportation!" Herbert ejaculated, "that's sheer nonsense, Crickledon. I'm sure your husband would tell you so."

"It was my husband brought me the words," Mrs. Crickledon rejoined with some triumph. "He did tell me, I own, to keep it shut: but my speaking to you, a friend of Mr. Smith's, won't do no harm. He heard them under the battery, over that chiwal glass: 'And you shall pay,' says Mr. Smith, and 'I sha'n't,' says old Tinman. Mr. Smith said he would have it if he had to squeeze a deathbed confession from a sinner. Then old Tinman fires out, 'You!' he says, 'you' and he stammered. 'Mr. Smith,' my husband said and you never saw a man so shocked as my husband at being obliged to hear them at one another Mr. Smith used the word damn. 'You may laugh, sir.'"

"You say it so capitally, Crickledon."

"And then old Tinman said, 'And a D. to you; and if I lift my finger, it's Big D. on your back."

"And what did Mr. Smith say, then?"

"He said, like a man shot, my husband says he said, 'My God!'"

Herbert Fellingham jumped away from the table.

"You tell me, Crickledon, your husband actually heard that—just those words?—the tones?"

"My husband says he heard him say, 'My God!' just like a poor man shot or stabbed. You may speak to Crickledon, if you speaks to him alone, sir. I say you ought to know. For I've noticed Mr. Smith since that day has never looked to me the same easy-minded happy gentleman he was when we first knew him. He would have had me go to cook for him at Elba, but Crickledon thought I'd better be independent, and Mr. Smith said to me, 'Perhaps you're right, Crickledon, for who knows how long I may be among you?'"

Herbert took the solace of tobacco in Crickledon's shop. Thence, with the story confirmed to him, he sauntered toward the house on the beach.

CHAPTER VIII

The moon was over sea. Coasting vessels that had run into the bay for shelter from the North wind lay with their shadows thrown shoreward on the cold smooth water, almost to the verge of the beach, where there was neither breath nor sound of wind, only the lisp at the pebbles.

Mrs. Crickledon's dinner and the state of his heart made young Fellingham indifferent to a wintry atmosphere. It sufficed him that the night was fair. He stretched himself on the shingle, thinking of the Manzanilla, and Annette, and the fine flavour given to tobacco by a dry still air in moonlight—thinking of his work, too, in the background, as far as mental lassitude would allow of it. The idea of taking Annette to see his first play at the theatre when it should be performed—was very soothing. The beach rather looked like a stage, and the sea like a ghostly audience, with, if you will, the broadside bulks of black sailing craft at anchor for representatives of the newspaper piers. Annette was a nice girl; if a little commonplace and low-born, yet sweet. What a subject he could make of her father! "The Deserter" offered a new complication. Fellingham rapidly sketched it in fancy—Van Diemen, as a Member of the Parliament of Great Britain, led away from the House of Commons to be branded on the bank! What a magnificent fall! We have so few intensely dramatic positions in English real life that the meditative author grew enamoured of this one, and laughed out a royal "Ha!" like a monarch reviewing his well-appointed soldiery.

"There you are," said Van Diemen's voice; "I smelt your pipe. You're a rum fellow, to belying out on the beach on a cold night. Lord! I don't like you the worse for it. Twas for the romance of the moon in my young days."

"Where is Annette?" said Fellingham, jumping to his feet.

"My daughter? She 's taking leave of her intended."

"What's that?" Fellingham gasped. "Good heavens, Mr. Smith, what do you mean?"

"Pick up your pipe, my lad. Girls choose as they please, I suppose"

"Her intended, did you say, sir? What can that mean?"

"My dear good young fellow, don't make a fuss. We're all going to stay here, and very glad to see you from time to time. The fact is, I oughtn't to have quarrelled with Mart Tinman as I've done; I'm too peppery by nature. The fact is, I struck him, and he forgave it. I could n't have done that myself. And I believe I'm in for a headache to-morrow; upon my soul, I do. Mart Tinman would champagne us; but, poor old boy, I struck him, and I couldn't make amends—didn't see my way; and we joined hands over the glass—to the deuce with the glass!—and the end of it is, Netty—she did n't propose it, but as I'm in his—I say, as I had struck him, she—it was rather solemn, if you had seen us—she burst into tears, and there was Mrs. Cavely, and old Mart, and me as big a fool—if I'm not a villain!"

Fellingham perceived a more than common effect of Tin man's wine. He touched Van Diemen on the shoulder. "May I beg to hear exactly what has happened?"

"Upon my soul, we're all going to live comfortably in Old England, and no more quarreling and decamping," was the stupid rejoinder. "Except that I did n't exactly—I think you said I exactly'?—I did n't bargain for old Mart as my—but he's a sound man; Mart's my junior; he's rich. He's eco ... he's eco... you know—my Lord! where's my brains?—but he's upright—'nomical!"

"An economical man," said Fellingham, with sedate impatience.

"My dear sir, I'm heartily obliged to you for your assistance," returned Van Diemen. "Here she is."

Annette had come out of the gate in the flint wall. She started slightly on seeing Herbert, whom she had taken for a coastguard, she said. He bowed. He kept his head bent, peering at her intrusively.

"It's the air on champagne," Van Diemen said, calling on his lungs to clear themselves and right him. "I was n't a bit queer in the house."

"The air on Tinman's champagne!" said Fellingham.

"It must be like the contact of two hostile chemical elements."

Annette walked faster.

They descended from the shingle to the scant-bladed grass-sweep running round the salted town-refuse on toward Elba. Van Diemen sniffed, ejaculating, "I'll be best man with Mart Tinman about this business! You'll stop with us, Mr.—what's your Christian name? Stop with us as long as you like. Old friends for me! The joke of it is that Nelson was my man, and yet I went and enlisted in the cavalry. If you talk of chemical substances, old Mart Tinman was a sneak who never cared a dump for his country; and I'm not to speak a single sybbarel about that..... over there... Australia... Gippsland! So down he went, clean over. Very sorry for what we have done. Contrite. Penitent."

"Now we feel the wind a little," said Annette.

Fellingham murmured, "Allow me; your shawl is flying loose."

He laid his hands on her arms, and, pressing her in a tremble, said, "One sign! It's not true? A word! Do you hate me?"

"Thank you very much, but I am not cold," she replied and linked herself to her father.

Van Diemen immediately shouted, "For we are jolly boys! for we are jolly boys! It's the air on the champagne. And hang me," said he, as they entered the grounds of Elba, "if I don't walk over my property."

Annette interposed; she stood like a reed in his way.

"No! my Lord! I'll see what I sold you for!" he cried. "I'm an owner of the soil of Old England, and care no more for the title of squire than Napoleon Bonaparty. But I'll tell you what, Mr. Hubbard: your mother was never so astonished at her dog as old Van Diemen would be to hear himself called squire in Old England. And a convict he was, for he did wrong once, but he worked his redemption. And the smell of my own property makes me feel my legs again. And I'll tell you what, Mr. Hubbard, as Netty calls you when she speaks of you in private: Mart Tinman's ideas of wine are pretty much like his ideas of healthy smells, and when I'm bailiff of Crikswich, mind, he'll find two to one against him in our town council. I love my country, but hang me if I don't purify it—"

Saying this, with the excitement of a high resolve a upon him, Van Diemen bored through a shrubbery-brake, and Fellingham said to Annette:

"Have I lost you?"

"I belong to my father," said she, contracting and disengaging her feminine garments to step after him in the cold silver-spotted dusk of the winter woods.

Van Diemen came out on a fish-pond.

"Here you are, young ones!" he said to the pair. "This way, Fellowman. I'm clearer now, and it's my belief I've been talking nonsense. I'm puffed up with money, and have n't the heart I once had. I say, Fellowman, Fellowbird, Hubbard—what's your right name?—fancy an old carp fished out of that pond and flung into the sea. That's exile! And if the girl don't mind, what does it matter?"

"Mr. Herbert Fellingham, I think, would like to go to bed, papa," said Annette.

"Miss Smith must be getting cold," Fellingham hinted.

"Bounce away indoors," replied Van Diemen, and he led them like a bull.

Annette was disinclined to leave them together in the smoking-room, and under the pretext of wishing to see her father to bed she remained with them, though there was a novel directness and heat of tone in Herbert that alarmed her, and with reason. He divined in hideous outlines what had happened. He was no longer figuring on easy ice, but desperate at the prospect of a loss to himself, and a fate for Annette, that tossed him from repulsion to incredulity, and so back.

Van Diemen begged him to light his pipe.

"I'm off to London to-morrow," said Fellingham. "I don't want to go, for very particular reasons; I may be of more use there. I have a cousin who's a General officer in the army, and if I have your permission—you see, anything's better, as it seems to me, than that you should depend for peace and comfort on one man's tongue not wagging, especially when he is not the best of tempers if I have your permission—without mentioning names, of course—I'll consult him."

There was a dead silence.

"You know you may trust me, sir. I love your daughter with all my heart. Your honour and your interests are mine."

Van Diemen struggled for composure.

"Netty, what have you been at?" he said.

"It is untrue, papa!" she answered the unworded accusation.

"Annette has told me nothing, sir. I have heard it. You must brace your mind to the fact that it is known. What is known to Mr. Tinman is pretty sure to be known generally at the next disagreement."

"That scoundrel Mart!" Van Diemen muttered.

"I am positive Mr. Tinman did not speak of you, papa," said Annette, and turned her eyes from the half-paralyzed figure of her father on Herbert to put him to proof.

"No, but he made himself heard when it was being discussed. At any rate, it's known; and the thing to do is to meet it."

"I'm off. I'll not stop a day. I'd rather live on the Continent," said Van Diemen, shaking himself, as to prepare for the step into that desert.

"Mr. Tinman has been most generous!" Annette protested tearfully.

"I won't say no: I think you are deceived and lend him your own generosity," said Herbert. "Can you suppose it generous, that even in the extremest case, he should speak of the matter to your father, and talk of denouncing him? He did it."

"He was provoked."

"A gentleman is distinguished by his not allowing himself to be provoked."

"I am engaged to him, and I cannot hear it said that he is not a gentleman."

The first part of her sentence Annette uttered bravely; at the conclusion she broke down. She wished Herbert to be aware of the truth, that he might stay his attacks on Mr. Tinman; and she believed he had only been guessing the circumstances in which her father was placed; but the comparison between her two suitors forced itself on her now, when the younger one spoke in a manner so self-contained, brief, and full of feeling.

She had to leave the room weeping.

"Has your daughter engaged herself, sir?" said Herbert.

"Talk to me to-morrow; don't give us up if she has we were trapped, it's my opinion," said Van Diemen. "There's the devil in that wine of—Mart Tinman's. I feel it still, and in the morning it'll be worse. What can she see in him? I must quit the country; carry her off. How he did it, I don't know. It was that woman, the widow, the fellow's sister. She talked till she piped her eye—talked about our lasting union. On my soul, I believe I egged Netty on! I was in a mollified way with that wine; all of a sudden the woman joins their hands! And I—a man of spirit will despise me!—what I thought of was, 'now my secret's safe!' You've sobered me, young sir. I see myself, if that's being sober. I don't ask your opinion of me; I am a deserter, false to my colours, a breaker of his oath. Only mark this: I was married, and a common trooper, married to a handsome young woman, true as steel; but she was handsome, and we were starvation poor, and she had to endure persecution from an officer day by day. Bear that situation in your mind.... Providence dropped me a hundred pounds out of the sky. Properly speaking, it popped up out of the earth, for I reaped it, you may say, from a relative's grave. Rich and poor 's all right, if I'm rich and you're poor; and you may be happy though you're poor; but where there are many poor young women, lots of rich men are a terrible temptation to them. That's my dear good wife speaking, and had she been spared to me I never should have come back to Old England, and heart's delight and heartache I should not have known. She was my backbone, she was my breast-comforter too. Why did she stick to me? Because I had faith in her when appearances were against her. But she never forgave this country the hurt to her woman's pride. You'll have noticed a squarish jaw in Netty. That's her mother. And I shall have to encounter it, supposing I find Mart Tinman has been playing me false. I'm blown on somehow. I'll think of what course I'll take 'twixt now and morning. Good night, young gentleman."

"Good night; sir," said Herbert, adding, "I will get information from the Horse Guards; as for the people knowing it about here, you're not living much in society—"

"It's not other people's feelings, it's my own," Van Diemen silenced him. "I feel it, if it's in the wind; ever since Mart Tinman spoke the thing out, I've felt on my skin cold and hot."

He flourished his lighted candle and went to bed, manifestly solaced by the idea that he was the victim of his own feelings.

Herbert could not sleep. Annette's monstrous choice of Tinman in preference to himself constantly assailed and shook his understanding. There was the "squarish jaw" mentioned by her father to think of. It filled him with a vague apprehension, but he was unable to imagine that a young girl, and an English girl, and an enthusiastic young English girl, could be devoid of sentiment; and presuming her to have it, as one must, there was no fear, that she would persist in her loathsome choice when she knew her father was against it.

Annette did not shun him next morning. She did not shun the subject, either. But she had been exact in arranging that she should not be more than a few minutes downstairs before her father. Herbert found, that compared with her, girls of sentiment are commonplace indeed. She had conceived an insane idea of nobility in Tinman that blinded her to his face, figure, and character—his manners, likewise. He had forgiven a blow!

Silly as the delusion might be, it clothed her in whimsical attractiveness.

It was a beauty in her to dwell so firmly upon moral quality. Overthrown and stunned as he was, and reduced to helplessness by her brief and positive replies, Herbert was obliged to admire the singular young lady, who spoke, without much shyness, of her incongruous, destined mate though his admiration had an edge cutting like irony. While in the turn for candour, she ought to have told him, that previous to her decision she had weighed the case of the diverse claims of himself and Tinman, and resolved them according to her predilection for the peaceful residence of her father and herself in England. This she had done a little regretfully, because of the natural sympathy of the young girl for the younger man. But the younger man had seemed to her seriously-straightforward mind too light and airy in his wooing, like one of her waltzing officers—very well so long as she stepped the measure with him, and not forcible enough to take her off her feet. He had changed, and now that he had become persuasive, she feared he would disturb the serenity with which she desired and strove to contemplate her decision. Tinman's magnanimity was present in her imagination to sustain her, though she was aware that Mrs. Cavely had surprised her will, and caused it to surrender unconsulted by her wiser intelligence.

"I cannot listen to you," she said to Herbert, after listening longer than was prudent. "If what you say of papa is true, I do not think he will remain in Crikswich, or even in England. But I am sure the old friend we used, to speak of so much in Australia has not wilfully betrayed him."

Herbert would have had to say, "Look on us two!" to proceed in his baffled wooing; and the very ludicrousness of the contrast led him to see the folly and shame of proposing it.

Van Diemen came down to breakfast looking haggard and restless. "I have 'nt had my morning's walk—I can't go out to be hooted," he said, calling to his daughter for tea, and strong tea; and explaining to Herbert that he knew it to be bad for the nerves, but it was an antidote to bad champagne.

Mr. Herbert Fellingham had previously received an invitation on behalf of a sister of his to Crikswich. A dull sense of genuine sagacity inspired him to remind Annette of it. She wrote prettily to Miss Mary Fellingham, and Herbert had some faint joy in carrying away the letter of her handwriting.

"Fetch her soon, for we sha'n't be here long," Van Diemen said to him at parting. He expressed a certain dread of his next meeting with Mart Tinman.

Herbert speedily brought Mary Fellingham to Elba, and left her there. The situation was apparently unaltered. Van Diemen looked worn, like a man who has been feeding mainly on his reflections, which was manifest in his few melancholy bits of speech. He said to Herbert: "How you feel a thing when you are found out!" and, "It doesn't do for a man with a heart to do wrong!" He designated the two principal roads by which poor sinners come to a conscience. His own would have slumbered but for discovery; and, as he remarked, if it had not been for his heart leading him to Tinman, he would not have fallen into that man's power.

The arrival of a young lady of fashionable appearance at Elba was matter of cogitation to Mrs. Cavely. She was disposed to suspect that it meant something, and Van Diemen's behaviour to her brother would of itself have fortified any suspicion. He did not call at the house on the beach, he did not invite Martin to dinner, he was rarely seen, and when he appeared at the Town Council he once or twice violently opposed his friend Martin, who came home ruffled, deeply offended in his interests and his dignity.

"Have you noticed any difference in Annette's treatment of you, dear?" Mrs. Cavely inquired.

"No," said Tinman; "none. She shakes hands. She asks after my health. She offers me my cup of tea."

"I have seen all that. But does she avoid privacy with you?"

"Dear me, no! Why should she? I hope, Martha, I am a man who may be confided in by any young lady in England."

"I am sure you may, dear Martin."

"She has an objection to name the... the day," said Martin. "I have informed her that I have an objection to long engagements. I don't like her new companion: She says she has been presented at Court. I greatly doubt it."

"It's to give herself a style, you may depend. I don't believe her!" exclaimed Mrs. Cavely, with sharp personal asperity.

Brother and sister examined together the Court Guide they had purchased on the occasion at once of their largest outlay and most thrilling gratification; in it they certainly found the name of General Fellingham. "But he can't be related to a newspaper-writer," said Mrs. Cavely.

To which her brother rejoined, "Unless the young man turned scamp. I hate unproductive professions."

"I hate him, Martin." Mrs. Cavely laughed in scorn, "I should say, I pity him. It's as clear to me as the sun at noonday, he wanted Annette. That's why I was in a hurry. How I dreaded he would come that evening to our dinner! When I saw him absent, I could have cried out it was Providence! And so be careful—we have had everything done for us from on High as yet—but be careful of your temper, dear Martin. I will hasten on the union; for it's a shame of a girl to drag a man behind her till he's old at the altar. Temper, dear, if you will only think of it, is the weak point."

"Now he has begun boasting to me of his Australian wines!" Tinman ejaculated.

"Bear it. Bear it as you do Gippsland. My dear, you have the retort in your heart:—Yes! but have you a Court in Australia?"

"Ha! and his Australian wines cost twice the amount I pay for mine!"

"Quite true. We are not obliged to buy them, I should hope. I would, though—a dozen—if I thought it necessary, to keep him quiet."

Tinman continued muttering angrily over the Australian wines, with a word of irritation at Gippsland, while promising to be watchful of his temper.

"What good is Australia to us," he asked, "if it does n't bring us money?"

"It's going to, my dear," said Mrs. Cavely. "Think of that when he begins boasting his Australia. And though it's convict's money, as he confesses—"

"With his convict's money!" Tinman interjected tremblingly. "How long am I expected to wait?"

"Rely on me to hurry on the day," said Mrs. Cavely. "There is no other annoyance?"

"Wherever I am going to buy, that man outbids me and then says it's the old country's want of pluck and dash, and doing things large-handed! A man who'd go on his knees to stop in England!" Tinman vociferated in a breath; and fairly reddened by the effort: "He may have to do it yet. I can't stand insult."

"You are less able to stand insult after Honours," his sister said, in obedience to what she had observed of him since his famous visit to London. "It must be so, in nature. But temper is everything just now. Remember, it was by command of temper, and letting her father put himself in the wrong, you got hold of Annette. And I would abstain even from wine. For sometimes after it, you have owned it disagreed. And I have noticed these eruptions between you and Mr. Smith—as he calls himself—generally after wine."

"Always the poor! the poor! money for the poor!" Tinman harped on further grievances against Van Diemen. "I say doctors have said the drain on the common is healthy; it's a healthy smell, nourishing. We've always had it and been a healthy town. But the sea encroaches, and I say my house and my property is in danger. He buys my house over my head, and offers me the Crouch to live in at an advanced rent. And then he sells me my house at an advanced price, and I buy, and then he votes against a penny for the protection of the shore! And we're in Winter again! As if he was not in my power!"

"My dear Martin, to Elba we go, and soon, if you will govern your temper," said Mrs. Cavely. "You're an angel to let me speak of it so, and it's only that man that irritates you. I call him sinfully ostentatious."

"I could blow him from a gun if I spoke out, and he knows it! He's wanting in common gratitude, let alone respect," Tinman snorted.

"But he has a daughter, my dear."

Tinman slowly and crackingly subsided.

His main grievance against Van Diemen was the non-recognition of his importance by that uncultured Australian, who did not seem to be conscious of the dignities and distinctions we come to in our country. The moneyed daughter, the prospective marriage, for an economical man rejected by every lady surrounding him, advised him to lock up his temper in submission to Martha.

"Bring Annette to dine with us," he said, on Martha's proposing a visit to the dear young creature.

Martha drank a glass of her brother's wine at lunch, and departed on the mission.

Annette declined to be brought. Her excuse was her guest, Miss Fellingham.

"Bring her too, by all means—if you'll condescend, I am sure," Mrs. Cavely said to Mary.

"I am much obliged to you; I do not dine out at present," said the London lady.

"Dear me! are you ill?"

"No."

"Nothing in the family, I hope?"

"My family?"

"I am sure, I beg pardon," said Mrs. Cavely, bridling with a spite pardonable by the severest moralist.

"Can I speak to you alone?" she addressed Annette.

Miss Fellingham rose.

Mrs. Cavely confronted her. "I can't allow it; I can't think of it. I'm only taking a little liberty with one I may call my future sister-in-law."

"Shall I come out with you?" said Annette, in sheer lassitude assisting Mary Fellingham in her scheme to show the distastefulness of this lady and her brother.

"Not if you don't wish to."

"I have no objection."

"Another time will do."

"Will you write?"

"By post indeed!"

Mrs. Cavely delivered a laugh supposed to, be peculiar to the English stage.

"It would be a penny thrown away," said Annette. "I thought you could send a messenger."

Intercommunication with Miss Fellingham had done mischief to her high moral conception of the pair inhabiting the house on the beach. Mrs. Cavely saw it, and could not conceal that she smarted.

Her counsel to her brother, after recounting the offensive scene to him in animated dialogue, was, to give Van Diemen a fright.

"I wish I had not drunk that glass of sherry before starting," she exclaimed, both savagely and sagely. "It's best after business. And these gentlemen's habits of yours of taking to dining late upset me. I'm afraid I showed temper; but you, Martin, would not have borne one-tenth of what I did."

"How dare you say so!" her brother rebuked her indignantly; and the house on the beach enclosed with difficulty a storm between brother and sister, happily not heard outside, because of loud winds raging.

Nevertheless Tinman pondered on Martha's idea of the wisdom of giving Van Diemen a fright.

CHAPTER X

The English have been called a bad-tempered people, but this is to judge of them by their manifestations; whereas an examination into causes might prove them to be no worse tempered than that man is a bad sleeper who lies in a biting bed. If a sagacious instinct directs them to discountenance realistic tales, the realistic tale should justify its appearance by the discovery of an apology for the tormented souls. Once they sang madrigals, once they danced on the green, they revelled in their lusty humours, without having recourse to the pun for fun, an exhibition of hundreds of bare legs for jollity, a sentimental wailing all in the throat for music. Evidence is procurable that they have been an artificially-reared people, feeding on the genius of inventors, transposers, adulterators, instead of the products of nature, for the last half century; and it is unfair to affirm of them that they are positively this or that. They are experiments. They are the sons and victims of a desperate Energy, alluring by cheapness, satiating with quantity, that it may mount in the social scale, at the expense of their tissues. The land is in a state of fermentation to mount, and the shop, which has shot half their stars to their social zenith, is what verily they would scald themselves to wash themselves free of. Nor is it in any degree a reprehensible sign that they should fly as from hue and cry the title of tradesman. It is on the contrary the spot of sanity, which bids us right cordially hope. Energy, transferred to the moral sense, may clear them yet.

Meanwhile this beer, this wine, both are of a character to have killed more than the tempers of a less gifted people. Martin Tinman invited Van Diemen Smith to try the flavour of a wine that, as he said, he thought of "laying down."

It has been hinted before of a strange effect upon the minds of men who knew what they were going to, when they received an invitation to dine with Tinman. For the sake of a little social meeting at any cost, they accepted it; accepted it with a sigh, midway as by engineering measurement between prospective and retrospective; as nearly mechanical as things human may be, like the Mussulman's accustomed cry of Kismet. Has it not been related of the little Jew babe sucking at its mother's breast in Jerusalem, that this innocent, long after the Captivity, would start convulsively, relinquishing its feast, and indulging in the purest. Hebrew lamentation of the most tenacious of races, at the passing sound of a Babylonian or a Ninevite voice? In some such manner did men, unable to refuse, deep in what remained to them of nature, listen to Tinman; and so did Van Diemen, sighing heavily under the operation of simple animal instinct.

"You seem miserable," said Tinman, not oblivious of his design to give his friend a fright.

"Do I? No, I'm all right," Van Diemen replied. "I'm thinking of alterations at the Hall before Summer, to accommodate guests—if I stay here."

"I suppose you would not like to be separated from Annette."

"Separated? No, I should think I shouldn't. Who'd do it?"

"Because I should not like to leave my good sister Martha all to herself in a house so near the sea—"

"Why not go to the Crouch, man?"

"Thank you."

"No thanks needed if you don't take advantage of the offer."

They were at the entrance to Elba, whither Mr. Tinman was betaking himself to see his intended. He asked if Annette was at home, and to his great stupefaction heard that she had gone to London for a week.

Dissembling the spite aroused within him, he postponed his very strongly fortified design, and said, "You must be lonely."

Van Diemen informed him that it would be for a night only, as young Fellingham was coming down to keep him company.

"At six o'clock this evening, then," said Tinman. "We're not fashionable in Winter."

"Hang me, if I know when ever we were!" Van Diemen rejoined.

"Come, though, you'd like to be. You've got your ambition, Philip, like other men."

"Respectable and respected—that 's my ambition, Mr. Mart."

Tinman simpered: "With your wealth!"

"Ay, I 'm rich—for a contented mind."

"I 'm pretty sure you 'll approve my new vintage," said Tinman. "It's direct from Oporto, my wine-merchant tells me, on his word."

"What's the price?"

"No, no, no. Try it first. It's rather a stiff price."

Van Diemen was partially reassured by the announcement. "What do you call a stiff price?"

"Well!—over thirty."

"Double that, and you may have a chance."

"Now," cried Tinman, exasperated, "how can a man from Australia know anything about prices for port? You can't divest your ideas of diggers' prices. You're like an intoxicating drink yourself on the tradesmen of our town. You think it fine—ha! ha! I daresay, Philip, I should be doing the same if I were up to your mark at my banker's. We can't all of us be lords, nor baronets."

Catching up his temper thus cleverly, he curbed that habitual runaway, and retired from his old friend's presence to explode in the society of the solitary Martha.

Annette's behaviour was as bitterly criticized by the sister as by the brother.

"She has gone to those Fellingham people; and she may be thinking of jilting us," Mrs. Cavely said.

"In that case, I have no mercy," cried her brother. "I have borne"—he bowed with a professional spiritual humility—"as I should, but it may get past endurance. I say I have borne enough; and if the worst comes to the worst, and I hand him over to the authorities—I say I mean him no harm, but he has struck me. He beat me as a boy and he has struck me as a man, and I say I have no thought of revenge, but I cannot have him here; and I say if I drive him out of the country back to his Gippsland!"

Martin Tinman quivered for speech, probably for that which feedeth speech, as is the way with angry men.

"And what?—what then?" said Martha, with the tender mellifluousness of sisterly reproach. "What good can you expect of letting temper get the better of you, dear?"

Tinman did not enjoy her recent turn for usurping the lead in their consultations, and he said, tartly, "This good, Martha. We shall get the Hall at my price, and be Head People here. Which," he raised his note, "which he, a Deserter, has no right to pretend to give himself out to be. What your feelings may be as an old inhabitant, I don't know, but I have always looked up to the people at Elba Hall, and I say I don't like to have a Deserter squandering convict's money there—with his forty-pound-a-year cook, and his champagne at seventy a dozen. It's the luxury of Sodom and Gomorrah."

"That does not prevent its being very nice to dine there," said Mrs. Cavely; "and it shall be our table for good if I have any management."

"You mean me, ma'am," bellowed Tinman.

"Not at all," she breathed, in dulcet contrast. "You are good-looking, Martin, but you have not half such pretty eyes as the person I mean. I never ventured to dream of managing you, Martin. I am thinking of the people at Elba."

"But why this extraordinary treatment of me, Martha?"

"She's a child, having her head turned by those Fellinghams. But she's honourable; she has sworn to me she would be honourable."

"You do think I may as well give him a fright?" Tinman inquired hungrily.

"A sort of hint; but very gentle, Martin. Do be gentle—casual like—as if you did n't want to say it. Get him on his Gippsland. Then if he brings you to words, you can always laugh back, and say you will go to Kew and see the Fernery, and fancy all that, so high, on Helvellyn or the Downs. Why"—Mrs. Cavely, at the end of her astute advices and cautionings, as usual, gave loose to her natural character—"Why that man came back to England at all, with his boastings of Gippsland, I can't for the life of me find out. It 's a perfect mystery."

"It is," Tinman sounded his voice at a great depth, reflectively. Glad of taking the part she was perpetually assuming of late, he put out his hand and said: "But it may have been ordained for our good, Martha."

"True, dear," said she, with an earnest sentiment of thankfulness to the Power which had led him round to her way of thinking and feeling.

CHAPTER XI

Annette had gone to the big metropolis, which burns in colonial imaginations as the sun of cities, and was about to see something of London, under the excellent auspices of her new friend, Mary Fellingham, and a dense fog. She was alarmed by the darkness, a little in fear, too, of Herbert; and these feelings caused her to chide herself for leaving her father.

Hearing her speak of her father sadly, Herbert kindly proposed to go down to Crikswich on the very day of her coming. She thanked him, and gave him a taste of bitterness by smiling favourably on his offer; but as he wished her to discern and take to heart the difference between one man and another, in the light of a suitor, he let her perceive that it cost him heavy pangs to depart immediately, and left her to brood on his example. Mary Fellingham liked Annette. She thought her a sensible girl of uncultivated sensibilities, the reverse of thousands; not commonplace, therefore; and that the sensibilities were expanding was to be seen in her gradual unreadiness to talk of her engagement to Mr. Tinman, though her intimacy with Mary warmed daily. She considered she was bound to marry the man at some distant date, and did not feel unhappiness yet. She had only felt uneasy when she had to greet and converse with her intended; especially when the London young lady had been present. Herbert's departure relieved her of the pressing sense of contrast. She praised him to Mary for his extreme kindness to her father, and down in her unsounded heart desired that her father might appreciate it even more than she did.

Herbert drove into Crikswich at night, and stopped at Crickledon's, where he heard that Van Diemen was dining with Tinman.

Crickledon the carpenter permitted certain dry curves to play round his lips like miniature shavings at the name of Tinman; but Herbert asked, "What is it now?" in vain, and he went to Crickledon the cook.

This union of the two Crickledons, male and female; was an ideal one, such as poor women dream of; and men would do the same, if they knew how poor they are. Each had a profession, each was independent of the other, each supported the fabric. Consequently there was mutual respect, as between two pillars of a house. Each saw the other's faults with a sly wink to the world, and an occasional interchange of sarcasm that was tonic, very strengthening to the wits without endangering the habit of affection. Crickledon the cook stood for her own opinions, and directed the public conduct of Crickledon the carpenter; and if he went astray from the line she marked out, she put it down to human nature, to which she was tolerant. He, when she had not followed his advice, ascribed it to the nature of women. She never said she was the equal of her husband; but the carpenter proudly acknowledged that she was as good as a man, and he bore with foibles derogatory to such high stature, by teaching himself to observe a neatness of domestic and general management that told him he certainly was not as good as a woman. Herbert delighted in them. The cook regaled the carpenter with skilful, tasty, and economic dishes; and the carpenter, obedient to her supplications, had promised, in the event of his outliving her, that no hands but his should have the making of her coffin. "It is so nice," she said, "to think one's own husband will put together the box you are to lie in, of his own make!" Had they been even a doubtfully united pair, the cook's anticipation of a comfortable coffin, the work of the best carpenter in England, would have kept them together; and that which fine cookery does for the cementing of couples needs not to be recounted to those who have read a chapter or two of the natural history of the male sex.

"Crickledon, my dear soul, your husband is labouring with a bit of fun," Herbert said to her.

"He would n't laugh loud at Punch, for fear of an action," she replied. "He never laughs out till he gets to bed, and has locked the door; and when he does he says 'Hush!' to me. Tinman is n't bailiff again just yet, and where he has his bailiff's best Court suit from, you may ask. He exercises in it off and on all the week, at night, and sometimes in the middle of the day."

Herbert rallied her for her gossip's credulity.

"It's truth," she declared. "I have it from the maid of the house, little Jane, whom he pays four pound a year for all the work of the house: a clever little thing with her hands and her head she is; and can read and write beautiful; and she's a mind to leave 'em if they don't advance her. She knocked and went in while he was full blaze, and bowing his poll to his glass. And now he turns the key, and a child might know he was at it."

"He can't be such a donkey!"

"And he's been seen at the window on the seaside. 'Who's your Admiral staying at the house on the beach?' men have inquired as they come ashore. My husband has heard it. Tinman's got it on his brain. He might be cured by marriage to a sound-headed woman, but he 'll soon be wanting to walk about in silk legs if he stops a bachelor. They tell me his old mother here had a dress value twenty pound; and pomp's inherited. Save as he may, there's his leak."

Herbert's contempt for Tinman was intense; it was that of the young and ignorant who live in their imaginations like spendthrifts, unaware of the importance of them as the food of life, and of how necessary it is to seize upon the solider one among them for perpetual sustenance when the unsubstantial are vanishing. The great event of his bailiff's term of office had become the sun of

Tinman's system. He basked in its rays. He meant to be again the proud official, royally distinguished; meantime, though he knew not that his days were dull, he groaned under the dulness; and, as cart or cab horses, uncomplaining as a rule, show their view of the nature of harness when they have release to frisk in a field, it is possible that existence was made tolerable to the jogging man by some minutes of excitement in his bailiff's Court suit. Really to pasture on our recollections we ought to dramatize them. There is, however, only the testimony of a maid and a mariner to show that Tinman did it, and those are witnesses coming of particularly long-bow classes, given to magnify small items of fact.

On reaching the hall Herbert found the fire alight in the smoking-room, and soon after settling himself there he heard Van Diemen's voice at the hall-door saying good night to Tinman.

"Thank the Lord! there you are," said Van Diemen, entering the room. "I couldn't have hoped so much. That rascal!" he turned round to the door. "He has been threatening me, and then smoothing me. Hang his oil! It's combustible. And hang the port he's for laying down, as he calls it. 'Leave it to posterity,' says I. 'Why?' says he. 'Because the young ones 'll be better able to take care of themselves,' says I, and he insists on an explanation. I gave it to him. Out he bursts like a wasp's nest. He may have said what he did say in temper. He seemed sorry afterwards—poor old Mart! The scoundrel talked of Horse Guards and telegraph wires."

"Scoundrel, but more ninny," said Herbert, full of his contempt. "Dare him to do his worst. The General tells me they 'd be glad to overlook it at the Guards, even if they had all the facts. Branding 's out of the question."

"I swear it was done in my time," cried Van Diemen, all on fire.

"It's out of the question. You might be advised to leave England for a few months. As for the society here—"

"If I leave, I leave for good. My heart's broken. I'm disappointed. I'm deceived in my friend. He and I in the old days! What's come to him? What on earth is it changes men who stop in England so? It can't be the climate. And did you mention my name to General Fellingham?"

"Certainly not," said Herbert. "But listen to me, sir, a moment. Why not get together half-a-dozen friends of the neighbourhood, and make a clean breast of it. Englishmen like that kind of manliness, and they are sure to ring sound to it."

"I couldn't!" Van Diemen sighed. "It's not a natural feeling I have about it—I 've brooded on the word. If I have a nightmare, I see Deserter written in sulphur on the black wall."

"You can't remain at his mercy, and be bullied as you are. He makes you ill, sir. He won't do anything, but he'll go on worrying you. I'd stop him at once. I'd take the train to-morrow and get an introduction to the Commander-in-Chief. He's the very man to be kind to you in a situation like this. The General would get you the introduction."

"That's more to my taste; but no, I couldn't," Van Diemen moaned in his weakness. "Money has unmanned me. I was n't this kind of man formerly; nor more was Mart Tinman, the traitor! All the world seems changeing for the worse, and England is n't what she used to be."

"You let that man spoil it for you, sir." Herbert related Mrs. Crickledon's tale of Mr. Tinman, adding, "He's an utter donkey. I should defy him. What I should do would be to let him know to-morrow morning that you don't intend to see him again. Blow for, blow, is the thing he requires. He'll be cringing to you in a week."

"And you'd like to marry Annette," said Van Diemen, relishing, nevertheless, the advice, whose origin and object he perceived so plainly.

"Of course I should," said Herbert, franker still in his colour than his speech.

"I don't see him my girl's husband." Van Diemen eyed the red hollow in the falling coals. "When I came first, and found him a healthy man, good-looking enough for a trifle over forty, I 'd have given her gladly, she nodding Yes. Now all my fear is she's in earnest. Upon my soul, I had the notion old Mart was a sort of a boy still; playing man, you know. But how can you understand? I fancied his airs and stiffness were put on; thought I saw him burning true behind it. Who can tell? He seems to be jealous of my buying property in his native town. Something frets him. I ought never to have struck him! There's my error, and I repent it. Strike a friend! I wonder he didn't go off to the Horse Guards at once. I might have done it in his place, if I found I couldn't lick him. I should have tried kicking first."

"Yes, shinning before peaching," said Herbert, astonished almost as much as he was disgusted by the inveterate sentimental attachment of Van Diemen to his old friend.

Martin Tinman anticipated good things of the fright he had given the man after dinner. He had, undoubtedly, yielded to temper, forgetting pure policy, which it is so exceeding difficult to practice. But he had soothed the startled beast; they had shaken hands at parting, and Tinman hoped that the week of Annette's absence would enable him to mould her father. Young Fellingham's appointment to come to Elba had slipped Mr. Tinman's memory. It was annoying to see this intruder. "At all events, he's not with Annette," said Mrs. Cavely. "How long has her father to run on?"

"Five months," Tinman replied. "He would have completed his term of service in five months."

"And to think of his being a rich man because he deserted," Mrs. Cavely interjected. "Oh! I do call it immoral. He ought to be apprehended and punished, to be an example for the good of society. If you lose time, my dear Martin, your chance is gone. He's wriggling now. And if I could believe he talked us over to that young impudent, who has n't a penny that he does n't get from his pen, I'd say, denounce him to-morrow. I long for Elba. I hate this house. It will be swallowed up some day; I know it; I have dreamt it. Elba at any cost. Depend upon it, Martin, you have been foiled in your suits on account of the mean house you inhabit. Enter Elba as that girl's husband, or go there to own it, and girls will crawl to you."

"You are a ridiculous woman, Martha," said Tinman, not dissenting.

The mixture of an idea of public duty with a feeling of personal rancour is a strong incentive to the pursuit of a stern line of conduct; and the glimmer of self-interest superadded does not check the steps of the moralist. Nevertheless, Tinman held himself in. He loved peace. He preached it, he disseminated it. At a meeting in the town he strove to win Van Diemen's voice in favour of a vote for further moneys to protect "our shores." Van Diemen laughed at him, telling him he wanted a battery. "No," said Tinman, "I've had enough to do with soldiers."

"How's that?"

"They might be more cautious. I say, they might learn to know their friends from their enemies."

"That's it, that's it," said Van Diemen. "If you say much more, my hearty, you'll find me bidding against you next week for Marine Parade and Belle Vue Terrace. I've a cute eye for property, and this town's looking up."

"You look about you before you speculate in land and house property here," retorted Tinman.

Van Diemen bore so much from him that he asked himself whether he could be an Englishman. The title of Deserter was his raw wound. He attempted to form the habit of stigmatizing himself with it in the privacy of his chamber, and he succeeded in establishing the habit of talking to himself, so that he was heard by the household, and Annette, on her return, was obliged to warn him of his indiscretion. This development of a new weakness exasperated him. Rather to prove his courage by defiance than to baffle Tinman's ambition to become the principal owner of houses in Crikswich, by outbidding him at the auction for the sale of Marine Parade and Belle Vue Terrace, Van Diemen ran the houses up at the auction, and ultimately had Belle Vue knocked down to him. So fierce was the quarrel that Annette, in conjunction with Mrs. Cavely; was called on to interpose with her sweetest grace. "My native place," Tinman said to her; "it is my native place. I have a pride in it; I desire to own property in it, and your father opposes me. He opposes me. Then says I may have it back at auction price, after he has gone far to double the price! I have borne—I repeat I have borne too much."

"Are n't your properties to be equal to one?" said Mrs. Cavely, smiling mother—like from Tinman to Annette.

He sought to produce a fondling eye in a wry face, and said, "Yes, I will remember that."

"Annette will bless you with her dear hand in a month or two at the outside," Mrs. Cavely murmured, cherishingly.

"She will?" Tinman cracked his body to bend to her.

"Oh, I cannot say; do not distress me. Be friendly with papa," the girl resumed, moving to escape.

"That is the essential," said Mrs. Cavely; and continued, when Annette had gone, "The essential is to get over the next few months, miss, and then to snap your fingers at us. Martin, I would force that man to sell you Belle Vue under the price he paid for it, just to try your power."

Tinman was not quite so forcible. He obtained Belle Vue at auction price, and his passion for revenge was tipped with fire by having it accorded as a friend's favour.

The poisoned state of his mind was increased by a December high wind that rattled his casements, and warned him of his accession of property exposed to the elements. Both he and his sister attributed their nervousness to the sinister behaviour of Van Diemen. For the house on the beach had only, in most distant times, been threatened by the sea, and no house on earth was better protected from man,— Neptune, in the shape of a coastguard, being paid by Government to patrol about it during the hours of darkness. They had never had any fears before Van Diemen arrived, and caused them to give thrice their ordinary number of dinners to guests per annum. In fact, before Van Diemen came, the house on the beach looked on Crikswich without a rival to challenge its anticipated lordship over the place, and for some inexplicable reason it seemed to its inhabitants to have been a safer as well as a happier residence.

They were consoled by Tinman's performance of a clever stroke in privately purchasing the cottages west of the town, and including Crickledon's shop, abutting on Marine Parade. Then from the house on the beach they looked at an entire frontage of their property.

They entered the month of February. No further time was to be lost, "or we shall wake up to find that man has fooled us," Mrs. Cavely said. Tinman appeared at Elba to demand a private interview with Annette. His hat was blown into the hall as the door opened to him, and he himself was glad to be sheltered by the door, so violent was the gale. Annette and her father were sitting together. They kept the betrothed gentleman waiting a very long time. At last Van Diemen went to him, and said, "Netty 'll see you, if you must. I suppose you have no business with me?"

"Not to-day," Tinman replied.

Van Diemen strode round the drawing-room with his hands in his pockets. "There's a disparity of ages," he said, abruptly, as if desirous to pour out his lesson while he remembered it. "A man upwards of forty marries a girl under twenty, he's over sixty before she's forty; he's decaying when she's only mellow. I ought never to have struck you, I know. And you're such an infernal bad temper at times, and age does n't improve that, they say; and she's been educated tip-top. She's sharp on grammar, and a man may n't like that much when he's a husband. See her, if you must. But she does n't take to the idea; there's the truth. Disparity of ages and unsuitableness of dispositions—what was it Fellingham said?—like two barrel-organs grinding different tunes all day in a house."

"I don't want to hear Mr. Fellingham's comparisons," Tinman snapped.

"Oh! he's nothing to the girl," said Van Diemen. "She doesn't stomach leaving me."

"My dear Philip! why should she leave you? When we have interests in common as one household—"

"She says you're such a damned bad temper."

Tinman was pursuing amicably, "When we are united—" But the frightful charge brought against his temper drew him up. "Fiery I may be. Annette has seen I am forgiving. I am a Christian. You have provoked me; you have struck me."

"I 'll give you a couple of thousand pounds in hard money to be off the bargain, and not bother the girl," said Van Diemen.

"Now," rejoined Tinman, "I am offended. I like money, like most men who have made it. You do, Philip. But I don't come courting like a pauper. Not for ten thousand; not for twenty. Money cannot be a compensation to me for the loss of Annette. I say I love Annette."

"Because," Van Diemen continued his speech, "you trapped us into that engagement, Mart. You dosed me with the stuff you buy for wine, while your sister sat sugaring and mollifying my girl; and she did the trick in a minute, taking Netty by surprise when I was all heart and no head; and since that you may have seen the girl turn her head from marriage like my woods from the wind."

"Mr. Van Diemen Smith!" Tinman panted; he mastered himself. "You shall not provoke me. My introductions of you in this neighbourhood, my patronage, prove my friendship."

"You'll be a good old fellow, Mart, when you get over your hopes of being knighted."

"Mr. Fellingham may set you against my wine, Philip. Let me tell you—I know you—you would not object to have your daughter called Lady."

"With a spindle-shanked husband capering in a Court suit before he goes to bed every night, that he may n't forget what a fine fellow he was one day bygone! You're growing lean on it, Mart, like a recollection fifty years old."

"You have never forgiven me that day, Philip!"

"Jealous, am I? Take the money, give up the girl, and see what friends we'll be. I'll back your buyings, I'll advertise your sellings. I'll pay a painter to paint you in your Court suit, and hang up a copy of you in my diningroom."

"Annette is here," said Tinman, who had been showing Etna's tokens of insurgency.

He admired Annette. Not till latterly had Herbert Fellingham been so true an admirer of Annette as Tinman was. She looked sincere and she dressed inexpensively. For these reasons she was the best example of womankind that he knew, and her enthusiasm for England had the sympathetic effect on him of obscuring the rest of the world, and thrilling him with the reassuring belief that he was blest in his blood and his birthplace—points which her father, with his boastings of Gippsland, and other people talking of scenes on the Continent, sometimes disturbed in his mind.

"Annette," said he, "I come requesting to converse with you in private."

"If you wish it—I would rather not," she answered.

Tinman raised his head, as often at Helmstone when some offending shopwoman was to hear her doom.

He bent to her. "I see. Before your father, then!"

"It isn't an agreeable bit of business, to me," Van Diemen grumbled, frowning and shrugging.

"I have come, Annette, to ask you, to beg you, entreat—before a third person—laughing, Philip?"

"The wrong side of my mouth, my friend. And I'll tell you what: we're in for heavy seas, and I 'm not sorry you've taken the house on the beach off my hands."

"Pray, Mr. Tinman, speak at once, if you please, and I will do my best. Papa vexes you."

"No, no," replied Tinman.

He renewed his commencement. Van Diemen interrupted him again.

"Hang your power over me, as you call it. Eh, old Mart? I'm a Deserter. I'll pay a thousand pounds to the British army, whether they punish me or not. March me off tomorrow!"

"Papa, you are unjust, unkind." Annette turned to him in tears.

"No, no," said Tinman, "I do not feel it. Your father has misunderstood me, Annette."

"I am sure he has," she said fervently. "And, Mr. Tinman, I will faithfully promise that so long as you are good to my dear father, I will not be untrue to my engagement, only do not wish me to name any day. We shall be such very good dear friends if you consent to this. Will you?"

Pausing for a space, the enamoured man unrolled his voice in lamentation: "Oh! Annette, how long will you keep me?"

"There; you'll set her crying!" said Van Diemen. "Now you can run upstairs, Netty. By jingo! Mart Tinman, you've got a bass voice for love affairs."

"Annette," Tinman called to her, and made her turn round as she was retiring. "I must know the day before the end of winter. Please. In kind consideration. My arrangements demand it."

"Do let the girl go," said Van Diemen. "Dine with me tonight and I'll give you a wine to brisk your spirits, old boy."

"Thank you. When I have ordered dinner at home, I—and my wine agrees with ME," Tinman replied.

"I doubt it."

"You shall not provoke me, Philip."

They parted stiffly.

Mrs. Cavely had unpleasant domestic news to communicate to her brother, in return for his tale of affliction and wrath. It concerned the ungrateful conduct of their little housemaid Jane, who, as Mrs. Cavely said, "egged on by that woman Crickledon," had been hinting at an advance of wages.

"She didn't dare speak, but I saw what was in her when she broke a plate, and wouldn't say she was sorry. I know she goes to Crickledon and talks us over. She's a willing worker, but she has no heart."

Tinman had been accustomed in his shop at Helmstone—where heaven had blessed him with the patronage of the rich, as visibly as rays of supernal light are seen selecting from above the heads of prophets in the illustrations to cheap holy books—to deal with willing workers that have no hearts. Before the application for an advance of wages—and he knew the signs of it coming—his method was to calculate how much he might be asked for, and divide the estimated sum by the figure 4; which, as it seemed to come from a generous impulse, and had been unsolicited, was often humbly accepted, and the willing worker pursued her lean and hungry course in his service. The treatment did not always agree with his males. Women it suited; because they do not like to lift up their voices unless they are in a passion; and if you take from them the grounds of temper, you take their words away—you make chickens of them. And as Tinman said, "Gratitude I never expect!" Why not? For the reason that he knew human nature. He could record shocking instances of the ingratitude of human nature, as revealed to him in the term of his tenure of the shop at Helmstone. Blest from above, human nature's wickedness had from below too frequently besulphured and suffumigated him for his memory to be dim; and though he was ever ready to own himself an example that heaven prevaileth, he could cite instances of scandal-mongering shop-women dismissed and working him mischief in the town, which pointed to him in person for a proof that the Powers of Good and Evil were still engaged in unhappy contention. Witness Strikes! witness Revolutions!

"Tell her, when she lays the cloth, that I advance her, on account of general good conduct, five shillings per annum. Add," said Tinman, "that I wish no thanks. It is for her merits—to reward her; you understand me, Martha?"

"Quite; if you think it prudent, Martin."

"I do. She is not to breathe a syllable to cook."

"She will."

"Then keep your eye on cook."

Mrs. Cavely promised she would do so. She felt sure she was paying five shillings for ingratitude; and, therefore, it was with humility that she owned her error when, while her brother sipped his sugared acrid liquor after dinner (in devotion to the doctor's decree, that he should take a couple of glasses, rigorously as body-lashing friar), she imparted to him the singular effect of the advance of wages upon little Jane—"Oh, ma'am! and me never asked you for it!" She informed her brother how little Jane had confided to her that they were called "close," and how little Jane had vowed she would—the willing little thing!—go about letting everybody know their kindness.

"Yes! Ah!" Tinman inhaled the praise. "No, no; I don't want to be puffed," he said. "Remember cook. I have," he continued, meditatively, "rarely found my plan fail. But mind, I give the Crickledons notice to quit to-morrow. They are a pest. Besides, I shall probably think of erecting villas."

"How dreadful the wind is!" Mrs. Cavely exclaimed. "I would give that girl Annette one chance more. Try her by letter."

Tinman despatched a business letter to Annette, which brought back a vague, unbusiness-like reply. Two days afterward Mrs. Cavely reported to her brother the presence of Mr. Fellingham and Miss Mary Fellingham in Crikswich. At her dictation he wrote a second letter. This time the reply came from Van Diemen:

"My DEAR MARTIN,—Please do not go on bothering my girl. She does not like the idea of leaving me, and my experience tells me I could not live in the house with you. So there it is. Take it friendly. I have always wanted to be, and am,

"Your friend,

"PHIL."

Tinman proceeded straight to Elba; that is, as nearly straight as the wind would allow his legs to walk. Van Diemen was announced to be out; Miss Annette begged to be excused, under the pretext that she was unwell; and Tinman heard of a dinner-party at Elba that night.

He met Mr. Fellingham on the carriage drive. The young Londoner presumed to touch upon Tinman's private affairs by pleading on behalf of the Crikledons, who were, he said, much dejected by the notice they had received to quit house and shop.

"Another time," bawled Tinman. "I can't hear you in this wind."

"Come in," said Fellingham.

"The master of the house is absent," was the smart retort roared at him; and Tinman staggered away, enjoying it as he did his wine.

His house rocked. He was backed by his sister in the assurance that he had been duped.

The process he supposed to be thinking, which was the castigation of his brains with every sting wherewith a native touchiness could ply immediate recollection, led him to conclude that he must bring Van Diemen to his senses, and Annette running to him for mercy.

He sat down that night amid the howling of the storm, wind whistling, water crashing, casements rattling, beach desperately dragging, as by the wide-stretched star-fish fingers of the half-engulphed.

He hardly knew what he wrote. The man was in a state of personal terror, burning with indignation at Van Diemen as the main cause of his jeopardy. For, in order to prosecute his pursuit of Annette, he had abstained from going to Helmstone to pay moneys into his bank there, and what was precious to life as well as life itself, was imperilled by those two—Annette and her father—who, had they been true, had they been honest, to say nothing of honourable, would by this time have opened Elba to him as a fast and safe abode.

His letter was addressed, on a large envelope,

"To the Adjutant-General,

"HORSE GUARDS."

But if ever consigned to the Post, that post-office must be in London; and Tinman left the letter on his desk till the morning should bring counsel to him as to the London friend to whom he might despatch it under cover for posting, if he pushed it so far.

Sleep was impossible. Black night favoured the tearing fiends of shipwreck, and looking through a back window over sea, Tinman saw with dismay huge towering ghostwhite wreaths, that travelled up swiftly on his level, and lit the dark as they flung themselves in ruin, with a gasp, across the mound of shingle at his feet.

He undressed: His sister called to him to know if they were in danger. Clothed in his dressing-gown, he slipped along to her door, to vociferate to her hoarsely that she must not frighten the servants; and one fine quality in the training of the couple, which had helped them to prosper, a form of self-command, kept her quiet in her shivering fears.

For a distraction Tinman pulled open the drawers of his wardrobe. His glittering suit lay in one. And he thought, "What wonderful changes there are in the world!" meaning, between a man exposed to the wrath of the elements, and the same individual reading from vellum, in that suit, in a palace, to the Head of all of us!

The presumption is; that he must have often done it before. The fact is established, that he did it that night. The conclusion drawn from it is, that it must have given him a sense of stability and safety.

At any rate that he put on the suit is quite certain.

Probably it was a work of ingratiation and degrees; a feeling of the silk, a trying on to one leg, then a matching of the fellow with it. O you Revolutionists! who would have no state, no ceremonial, and but one order of galligaskins! This man must have been wooed away in spirit to forgetfulness of the tempest scourging his mighty neighbour to a bigger and a farther leap; he must have obtained from the contemplation of himself in his suit that which would be the saving of all men, in especial of his countrymen—imagination, namely.

Certain it is, as I have said, that he attired himself in the suit. He covered it with his dressing-gown, and he lay down on his bed so garbed, to await the morrow's light, being probably surprised by sleep acting upon fatigue and nerves appeased and soothed.

CHAPTER XII

Elba lay more sheltered from South-east winds under the slopes of down than any other house in Crikswich. The South-caster struck off the cliff to a martello tower and the house on the beach, leaving Elba to repose, so that the worst wind for that coast was one of the most comfortable for the owner of the hall, and he looked from his upper window on a sea of crumbling grey chalk, lashed unremittingly by the featureless piping gale, without fear that his elevated grounds and walls would be open at high tide to the ravage of water. Van Diemen had no idea of calamity being at work on land when he sat down to breakfast. He told Herbert that he had prayed for poor fellows at sea last night. Mary Fellingham and Annette were anxious to finish breakfast and mount the down to gaze on the sea, and receiving a caution from Van Diemen not to go too near the cliff, they were inclined to think he was needlessly timorous on their account.

Before they were half way through the meal, word was brought in of great breaches in the shingle, and water covering the common. Van Diemen sent for his head gardener, whose report of the state of things outside took the comprehensive form of prophecy; he predicted the fall of the town.

"Nonsense; what do you mean, John Scott?" said Van Diemen, eyeing his orderly breakfast table and the man in turns. "It does n't seem like that, yet, does it?"

"The house on the beach won't stand an hour longer, sir."

"Who says so?"

"It's cut off from land now, and waves mast-high all about it."

"Mart Tinman?" cried Van Diemen.

All started; all jumped up; and there was a scampering for hats and cloaks. Maids and men of the house ran in and out confirming the news of inundation. Some in terror for the fate of relatives, others pleasantly excited, glad of catastrophe if it but killed monotony, for at any rate it was a change of demons.

The view from the outer bank of Elba was of water covering the space of the common up to the stones of Marine Parade and Belle Vue. But at a distance it had not the appearance of angry water; the ladies thought it picturesque, and the house on the beach was seen standing firm. A second look showed the house completely isolated; and as the party led by Van Diemen circled hurriedly toward the town, they discerned heavy cataracts of foam pouring down the wrecked mound of shingle on either side of the house.

"Why, the outer wall's washed away," said Van Diemen. "Are they in real danger?" asked Annette, her teeth chattering, and the cold and other matters at her heart precluding for the moment such warmth of sympathy as she hoped soon to feel for them. She was glad to hear her father say:

"Oh! they're high and dry by this time. We shall find them in the town And we'll take them in and comfort them. Ten to one they have n't breakfasted. They sha'n't go to an inn while I'm handy."

He dashed ahead, followed closely by Herbert. The ladies beheld them talking to townsfolk as they passed along the upper streets, and did not augur well of their increase of speed. At the head of the town water was visible, part of the way up the main street, and crossing it, the ladies went swiftly under the old church, on the tower of which were spectators, through the churchyard to a high meadow that dropped to a stone wall fixed between the meadow and a grass bank above the level of the road, where now salt water beat and cast some spray. Not less than a hundred people were in this field, among them Crickledon and his wife. All were in silent watch of the house on the beach, which was to east of the field, at a distance of perhaps three stonethrows. The scene was wild. Continuously the torrents poured through the shingleclefts, and momently a thunder sounded, and high leapt a billow that topped the house and folded it weltering.

"They tell me Mart Tinman's in the house," Van Diemen roared to Herbert. He listened to further information, and bellowed: "There's no boat!"

Herbert answered: "It must be a mistake, I think; here's Crickledon says he had a warning before dawn and managed to move most of his things, and the people over there must have been awakened by the row in time to get off."

"I can't hear a word you say;" Van Diemen tried to pitch his voice higher than the wind. "Did you say a boat? But where?"

Crickledon the carpenter made signal to Herbert. They stepped rapidly up the field.

"Women feels their weakness in times like these, my dear," Mrs. Crickledon said to Annette. "What with our clothes and our cowardice it do seem we're not the equals of men when winds is high."

Annette expressed the hope to her that she had not lost much property. Mrs. Crickledon said she was glad to let her know she was insured in an Accident Company. "But," said she, "I do grieve for that poor man Tinman, if alive he be, and comes ashore to find his property wrecked by water. Bless ye! he wouldn't insure against anything less common than fire; and my house and Crickledon's shop are floating timbers by this time; and Marine Parade and Belle Vue are safe to go. And it'll be a pretty welcome for him, poor man, from his investments."

A cry at a tremendous blow of a wave on the doomed house rose from the field. Back and front door were broken down, and the force of water drove a round volume through the channel, shaking the walls.

"I can't stand this," Van Diemen cried.

Annette was too late to hold him back. He ran up the field. She was preparing to run after when Mrs. Crickledon touched her arm and implored her: "Interfere not with men, but let them follow their judgements when it's seasons of mighty peril, my dear. If any one's guilty it's me, for minding my husband of a boat that was launched for a life-boat here, and wouldn't answer, and is at the shed by the Crouch—left lying there, I've often said, as if it was a-sulking. My goodness!"

A linen sheet bad been flung out from one of the windows of the house on the beach, and flew loose and flapping in sign of distress.

"It looks as if they had gone mad in that house, to have waited so long for to declare theirselves, poor souls," Mrs. Crickledon said, sighing.

She was assured right and left that signals had been seen before, and some one stated that the cook of Mr. Tinman, and also Mrs. Cavely, were on shore.

"It's his furniture, poor man, he sticks to: and nothing gets round the heart so!" resumed Mrs. Crickledon. "There goes his bed-linen!"

The sheet was whirled and snapped away by the wind; distended doubled, like a flock of winter geese changeing alphabetical letters on the clouds, darted this way and that, and finally outspread on the waters breaking against Marine Parade.

"They cannot have thought there was positive danger in remaining," said Annette.

"Mr. Tinman was waiting for the cheapest Insurance office," a man remarked to Mrs. Crickledon.

"The least to pay is to the undertaker," she replied, standing on tiptoe. "And it's to be hoped he 'll pay more to-day. If only those walls don't fall and stop the chance of the boat to save him for more outlay, poor man! What boats was on the beach last night, high up and over the ridge as they was, are planks by this time and only good for carpenters."

"Half our town's done for," one old man said; and another followed him in a pious tone: "From water we came and to water we go."

They talked of ancient inroads of the sea, none so serious as this threatened to be for them. The gallant solidity, of the house on the beach had withstood heavy gales: it was a brave house. Heaven be thanked, no fishing boats were out. Chiefly well-to-do people would be the sufferers—an exceptional case. For it is the mysterious and unexplained dispensation that: "Mostly heaven chastises we."

A knot of excited gazers drew the rest of the field to them. Mrs. Crickledon, on the edge of the crowd, reported what was doing to Annette and Miss Fellingham. A boat had been launched from the town. "Praise the Lord, there's none but coastguard in it!" she exclaimed, and excused herself for having her heart on her husband.

Annette was as deeply thankful that her father was not in the boat.

They looked round and saw Herbert beside them. Van Diemen was in the rear, panting, and straining his neck to catch sight of the boat now pulling fast across a tumbled sea to where Tinman himself was perceived, beckoning them wildly, half out of one of the windows.

"A pound apiece to those fellows, and two if they land Mart Tinman dry; I've promised it, and they'll earn it. Look at that! Quick, you rascals!"

To the east a portion of the house had fallen, melted away. Where it stood, just below the line of shingle, it was now like a structure wasting on a tormented submerged reef. The whole line was given over to the waves.

"Where is his sister?" Annette shrieked to her father.

"Safe ashore; and one of the women with her. But Mart Tinman would stop, the fool! to-poor old boy! save his papers and things; and has n't a head to do it, Martha Cavely tells me. They're at him now! They've got him in! There's another? Oh! it's a girl, who would n't go and leave him. They'll pull to the field here. Brave lads!—By jingo, why ain't Englishmen always in danger!—eh? if you want to see them shine!"

"It's little Jane," said Mrs. Crickledon, who had been joined by her husband, and now that she knew him to be no longer in peril, kept her hand on him to restrain him, just for comfort's sake.

The boat held under the lee of the house-wreck a minute; then, as if shooting a small rapid, came down on a wave crowned with foam, to hurrahs from the townsmen.

"They're all right," said Van Diemen, puffing as at a mist before his eyes. "They'll pull westward, with the wind, and land him among us. I remember when old Mart and I were bathing once, he was younger than me, and could n't swim much, and I saw him going down. It'd have been hard to see him washed off before one's eyes thirty years afterwards. Here they come. He's all right. He's in his dressing-gown!"

The crowd made way for Mr. Van Diemen Smith to welcome his friend. Two of the coastguard jumped out, and handed him to the dry bank, while Herbert, Van Diemen, and Crickledon took him by hand and arm, and hoisted him on to the flint wall, preparatory to his descent into the field. In this exposed situation the wind, whose pranks are endless when it is once up, seized and blew Martin Tinman's dressing-gown wide as two violently flapping wings on each side of him, and finally over his head.

Van Diemen turned a pair of stupefied flat eyes on Herbert, who cast a sly look at the ladies. Tinman had sprung down. But not before the world, in one tempestuous glimpse, had caught sight of the Court suit.

Perfect gravity greeted him from the crowd.

"Safe, old Mart! and glad to be able to say it," said Van Diemen.

"We are so happy," said Annette.

"House, furniture, property, everything I possess!" ejaculated Tinman, shivering.

"Fiddle, man; you want some hot breakfast in you. Your sister has gone on—to Elba. Come you too, old Man; and where's that plucky little girl who stood by—"

"Was there a girl?" said Tinman.

"Yes, and there was a boy wanted to help." Van Diemen pointed at Herbert.

Tinman looked, and piteously asked, "Have you examined Marine Parade and Belle Vue? It depends on the tide!"

"Here is little Jane, sir," said Mrs. Crickledon.

"Fall in," Van Diemen said to little Jane.

The girl was bobbing curtseys to Annette, on her introduction by Mrs. Crickledon.

"Martin, you stay at my house; you stay at Elba till you get things comfortable about you, and then you shall have the Crouch for a year, rent free. Eh, Netty?"

Annette chimed in: "Anything we can do, anything. Nothing can be too much."

Van Diemen was praising little Jane for her devotion to her master.

"Master have been so kind to me," said little Jane.

"Now, march; it is cold," Van Diemen gave the word, and Herbert stood by Mary rather dejectedly, foreseeing that his prospects at Elba were darkened.

"Now then, Mart, left leg forward," Van Diemen linked his arm in his friend's.

"I must have a look," Tinman broke from him, and cast a forlorn look of farewell on the last of the house on the beach.

"You've got me left to you, old Mart; don't forget that," said Van Diemen.

Tinman's chest fell. "Yes, yes," he responded. He was touched.

"And I told those fellows if they landed you dry they should have—I'd give them double pay; and I do believe they've earned their money."

"I don't think I'm very wet, I'm cold," said Tinman.

"You can't help being cold, so come along."

"But, Philip!" Tinman lifted his voice; "I've lost everything. I tried to save a little. I worked hard, I exposed my life, and all in vain."

The voice of little Jane was heard.

"What's the matter with the child?" said Van Diemen.

Annette went up to her quietly.

But little Jane was addressing her master.

"Oh! if you please, I did manage to save something the last thing when the boat was at the window, and if you please, sir, all the bundles is lost, but I saved you a papercutter, and a letter Horse Guards, and here they are, sir."

The grateful little creature drew the square letter and paper-cutter from her bosom, and held them out to Mr. Tinman.

It was a letter of the imposing size, with THE HORSE GUARDS very distinctly inscribed on it in Tinman's best round hand, to strike his vindictive spirit as positively intended for transmission, and give him sight of his power to wound if it pleased him; as it might.

"What!" cried he, not clearly comprehending how much her devotion had accomplished for him.

"A letter to the Horse Guards!" cried Van Diemen.

"Here, give it me," said little Jane's master, and grasped it nervously.

"What's in that letter?" Van Diemen asked. "Let me look at that letter. Don't tell me it's private correspondence."

"My dear Philip, dear friend, kind thanks; it's not a letter," said Tinman.

"Not a letter! why, I read the address, 'Horse Guards.' I read it as it passed into your hands. Now, my man, one look at that letter, or take the consequences."

"Kind thanks for your assistance, dear Philip, indeed! Oh! this? Oh! it's nothing." He tore it in halves.

His face was of the winter sea-colour, with the chalk wash on it.

"Tear again, and I shall know what to think of the contents," Van Diemen frowned. "Let me see what you've said. You've sworn you would do it, and there it is at last, by miracle; but let me see it and I'll overlook it, and you shall be my house-mate still. If not!—"

Tinman tore away.

"You mistake, you mistake, you're entirely wrong," he said, as he pursued with desperation his task of rendering every word unreadable.

Van Diemen stood fronting him; the accumulation of stores of petty injuries and meannesses which he had endured from this man, swelled under the whip of the conclusive exhibition of treachery. He looked so black that Annette called, "Papa!"

"Philip," said Tinman. "Philip! my best friend!"

"Pooh, you're a poor creature. Come along and breakfast at Elba, and you can sleep at the Crouch, and goodnight to you. Crickledon," he called to the houseless couple, "you stop at Elba till I build you a shop."

With these words, Van Diemen led the way, walking alone. Herbert was compelled to walk with Tinman.

Mary and Annette came behind, and Mary pinched Annette's arm so sharply that she must have cried out aloud had it been possible for her to feel pain at that moment, instead of a personal exultation, flying wildly over the clash of astonishment and horror, like a sea-bird over the foam.

In the first silent place they came to, Mary murmured the words: "Little Jane."

Annette looked round at Mrs. Crickledon, who wound up the procession, taking little Jane by the hand. Little Jane was walking demurely, with a placid face. Annette glanced at Tinman. Her excited feelings nearly rose to a scream of laughter. For hours after, Mary had only to say to her: "Little Jane," to produce the same convulsion. It rolled her heart and senses in a headlong surge, shook her to burning tears, and seemed to her ideas the most wonderful running together of opposite things ever known on this earth. The young lady was ashamed of her laughter; but she was deeply indebted to it, for never was mind made so clear by that beneficent exercise.

(An early uncompleted and hitherto unpublished fragment.)

CHAPTER I

HE

Passing over Ickleworth Bridge and rounding up the heavily-shadowed river of our narrow valley, I perceived a commotion as of bathers in a certain bright space immediately underneath the vicar's terrace-garden steps. My astonishment was considerable when it became evident to me that the vicar himself was disporting in the water, which, reaching no higher than his waist, disclosed him in the ordinary habiliments of his cloth. I knew my friend to be one of the most absent-minded of men, and my first effort to explain the phenomenon of his appearance there, suggested that he might have walked in, the victim of a fit of abstraction, and that he had not yet fully comprehended his plight; but this idea was dispersed when I beheld the very portly lady, his partner in joy and adversity, standing immersed, and perfectly attired, some short distance nearer to the bank. As I advanced along the bank opposed to them, I was further amazed to hear them discoursing quite equably together, so that it was impossible to say on the face of it whether a catastrophe had occurred, or the great heat of a cloudless summer day had tempted an eccentric couple to seek for coolness in the directest fashion, without absolute disregard to propriety. I made a point of listening for the accentuation of the 'my dear' which was being interchanged, but the key-note to the harmony existing between husband and wife was neither excessively unctuous, nor shrewd, and the connubial shuttlecock was so well kept up on both sides that I chose to await the issue rather than speculate on the origin of this strange exhibition. I therefore, as I could not be accused of an outrage to modesty, permitted myself to maintain what might be invidiously termed a satyr-like watch from behind a forward flinging willow, whose business in life was to look at its image in a brown depth, branches, trunk, and roots. The sole indication of discomfort displayed by the pair was that the lady's hand worked somewhat fretfully to keep her dress from ballooning and puffing out of all proportion round about her person, while the vicar, who stood without his hat, employed a spongy handkerchief from time to time in tempering the ardours of a vertical sun. If you will consent to imagine a bald blackbird, his neck being shrunk in apprehensively, as you may see him in the first rolling of the thunder, you will gather an image of my friend's appearance.

He performed his capital ablutions with many loud 'poofs,' and a casting up of dazzled eyes, an action that gave point to his recital of the invocation of Chryses to Smintheus which brought upon the Greeks disaster and much woe. Between the lines he replied to his wife, whose remarks increased in quantity, and also, as I thought, in emphasis, under the river of verse which he poured forth unbaffled, broadening his chest to the sonorous Greek music in a singular rapture of obliviousness.

A wise man will not squander his laughter if he can help it, but will keep the agitation of it down as long as he may. The simmering of humour sends a lively spirit into the mind, whereas the boiling over is but a prodigal expenditure and the disturbance of a clear current: for the comic element is visible to you in all things, if you do but keep your mind charged with the perception of it, as I have heard a great expounder deliver himself on another subject; and he spoke very truly. So, I continued to look on with the gravity of Nature herself, and I could not but fancy, and with less than our usual wilfulness when we fancy things about Nature's moods, that the Mother of men beheld this scene with half a smile, differently from the simple observation of those cows whisking the flies from their flanks at the edge of the shorn meadow and its aspens, seen beneath the curved roof of a broad oak-branch. Save for this happy upward curve of the branch, we are encompassed by breathless foliage; even the gloom was hot; the little insects that are food for fish tried a flight and fell on the water's surface, as if panting. Here and there, a sullen fish consented to take them, and a circle spread, telling of past excitement.

I had listened to the vicar's Homeric lowing for the space of a minute or so—what some one has called, the great beast-like, bellow-like, roar and roll of the Iliad hexameter: it stopped like a cut cord. One of the numerous daughters of his house appeared in the arch of white cluster-roses on the lower garden-terrace, and with an exclamation, stood petrified at the extraordinary spectacle, and then she laughed outright. I had hitherto resisted, but the young lady's frank and boisterous laughter carried me along, and I too let loose a peal, and discovered myself. The vicar, seeing me, acknowledged a consciousness of his absurd position with a laugh as loud. As for the scapegrace girl, she went off into a run of high-pitched shriekings like twenty woodpeckers, crying: I Mama, mama, you look as if you were in Jordan!'

The vicar cleared his throat admonishingly, for it was apparent that Miss Alice was giving offence to her mother, and I presume he thought it was enough for one of the family to have done so.

'Wilt thou come out of Jordan?' I cried.

'I am sufficiently baptized with the water,' said the helpless man...

'Indeed, Mr. Amble,' observed his spouse, 'you can lecture a woman for not making the best of circumstances; I hope you'll bear in mind that it's you who are irreverent. I can endure this no longer. You deserve Mr. Pollingray's ridicule.'

Upon this, I interposed: 'Pray, ma'am, don't imagine that you have anything but sympathy from me.'— but as I was protesting, having my mouth open, the terrible Miss Alice dragged the laughter remorselessly out of me.

They have been trying Frank's new boat, Mr. Pollingray, and they've upset it. Oh! oh' and again there was the woodpeckers' chorus.

'Alice, I desire you instantly to go and fetch John the gardener,' said the angry mother.

'Mama, I can't move; wait a minute, only a minute. John's gone about the geraniums. Oh! don't look so resigned, papa; you'll kill me! Mama, come and take my hand. Oh! oh!'

The young lady put her hands in against her waist and rolled her body like a possessed one.

'Why don't you come in through the boat-house?' she asked when she had mastered her fit.

'Ah!' said the vicar. I beheld him struck by this new thought.

'How utterly absurd you are, Mr. Amble!' exclaimed his wife, 'when you know that the boat-house is locked, and that the boat was lying under the camshot when you persuaded me to step into it.'

Hearing this explanation of the accident, Alice gave way to an ungovernable emotion.

'You see, my dear,' the vicar addressed his wife, she can do nothing; it's useless. If ever patience is counselled to us, it is when accidents befall us, for then, as we are not responsible, we know we are in other hands, and it is our duty to be comparatively passive. Perhaps I may say that in every difficulty, patience is a life-belt. I beg of you to be patient still.'

'Mr. Amble, I shall think you foolish,' said the spouse, with a nod of more than emphasis.

My dear, you have only to decide,' was the meek reply.

By this time, Miss Alice had so far conquered the fiend of laughter that she could venture to summon her mother close up to the bank and extend a rescuing hand. Mrs. Amble waded to within reach, her husband following. Arrangements were made for Alice to pull, and the vicar to push; both in accordance with Mrs. Amble's stipulations, for even in her extremity of helplessness she affected rule and sovereignty. Unhappily, at the decisive moment, I chanced (and I admit it was more than an inadvertence on my part, it was a most ill-considered thing to do) I chanced, I say, to call out—and that I refrained from quoting Voltaire is something in my favour:

'How on earth did you manage to tumble in?'

There can be no contest of opinion that I might have kept my curiosity waiting, and possibly it may be said with some justification that I was the direct cause of my friend's unparalleled behaviour; but could a mortal man guess that in the very act of assisting his wife's return to dry land, and while she was—if I may put it so—modestly in his hands, he would turn about with a quotation that compared him to old Palinurus, all the while allowing his worthy and admirable burden to sink lower and dispread in excess upon the surface of the water, until the vantage of her daughter's help was lost to her; I beheld the consequences of my indiscretion, dismayed. I would have checked the preposterous Virgilian, but in contempt of my uplifted hand and averted head, and regardless of the fact that his wife was then literally dependent upon him, the vicar declaimed (and the drenching effect produced by Latin upon a lady at such a season, may be thought on):

Vix primos inopina quies laxaverat artus,
Et super incumbens, cum puppis parte revulsa
Cumque gubernaclo liquidas projecit in undas.'

It is not easy when you are unacquainted with the language, to retort upon Latin, even when the attempt to do so is made in English. Very few even of the uneducated ears can tolerate such anti-climax vituperative as English after sounding Latin. Mrs. Amble kept down those sentiments which her vernacular might have expressed. I heard but one groan that came from her as she lay huddled indistinguishably in the arms of her husband.

'Not—praecipitem! I am happy to say,' my senseless friend remarked further, and laughed cheerfully as he fortified his statement with a run of negatives. 'No, no'; in a way peculiar to him. 'No, no. If I plant my grey hairs anywhere, it will be on dry land: no. But, now, my dear; he returned to his duty; why, you're down again. Come: one, two, and up.'

He was raising a dead weight. The passion for sarcastic speech was manifestly at war with common prudence in the bosom of Mrs. Amble; prudence, however, overcame it. She cast on him a look of a kind that makes matrimony terrific in the dreams of bachelors, and then wedding her energy to the assistance given she made one of those senseless springs of the upper half of the body, which strike the philosophic eye with the futility of an effort that does not arise from a solid basis. Owing to the want of concert between them, the vicar's impulsive strength was expended when his wife's came into play. Alice clutched her mother bravely. The vicar had force enough to stay his wife's descent; but Alice (she boasts of her muscle) had not the force in the other direction—and no wonder. There are few young ladies who could pull fourteen stone sheer up a camshot.

Mrs. Amble remained in suspense between the two.

Oh, Mr. Pollingray, if you were only on this side to help us,' Miss Alice exclaimed very piteously, though I could see that she was half mad with the internal struggle of laughter at the parents and concern for them.

'Now, pull, Alice,' shouted the vicar.

'No, not yet,' screamed Mrs. Amble; I'm sinking.'

'Pull, Alice.'

'Now, Mama.'

'Oh!'

'Push, Papa.'

'I'm down.'

'Up, Ma'am; Jane; woman, up.'

'Gently, Papa: Abraham, I will not.'

'My dear, but you must.'

'And that man opposite.'

'What, Pollingray? He's fifty.'

I found myself walking indignantly down the path. Even now I protest my friend was guilty of bad manners, though I make every allowance for him; I excuse, I pass the order; but why—what justifies one man's bawling out another man's age? What purpose does it serve? I suppose the vicar wished to reassure his wife, on the principle (I have heard him enunciate it) that the sexes are merged at fifty—by which he means, I must presume, that something which may be good or bad, and is generally silly—of course, I admire and respect modesty and pudeur as much as any man—something has gone: a recognition of the bounds of division. There is, if that is a lamentable matter, a loss of certain of our young tricks at fifty. We have ceased to blush readily: and let me ask you to define a blush. Is it an involuntary truth or an ingenuous lie? I know that this will sound like the language of a man not a little jealous of his youthful compeers. I can but leave it to rightly judging persons to consider whether a healthy man in his prime, who has enough, and is not cursed by ambition, need be jealous of any living soul.

A shriek from Miss Alice checked my retreating steps. The vicar was staggering to support the breathing half of his partner while she regained her footing in the bed of the river. Their effort to scale the camshot had failed. Happily at this moment I caught sight of Master Frank's boat, which had floated, bottom upwards, against a projecting mud-bank of forget-me-nots. I contrived to reach it and right it, and having secured one of the sculls, I pulled up to the rescue; though not before I had plucked a flower, actuated by a motive that I cannot account for. The vicar held the boat firmly against the camshot, while I, at the imminent risk of joining them (I shall not forget the combined expression of Miss Alice's retreating eyes and the malicious corners of her mouth) hoisted the lady in, and the river with her. From the seat of the boat she stood sufficiently high to project the step towards land without peril. When she had set her foot there, we all assumed an attitude of respectful attention, and the vicar, who could soar over calamity like a fairweather swallow, acknowledged the return of his wife to the element with a series of apologetic yesses and short coughings.

'That would furnish a good concert for the poets,' he remarked. 'A parting, a separation of lovers; "even as a body from the watertorn," or "from the water plucked"; eh? do you think—"so I weep round her, tearful in her track," an excellent—'

But the outraged woman, dripping in grievous discomfort above him, made a peremptory gesture.

'Mr. Amble, will you come on shore instantly, I have borne with your stupidity long enough. I insist upon your remembering, sir, that you have a family dependent upon you. Other men may commit these follies.'

This was a blow at myself, a bachelor whom the lady had never persuaded to dream of relinquishing his freedom.

'My dear, I am coming,' said the vicar.

'Then, come at once, or I shall think you idiotic,' the wife retorted.

'I have been endeavouring,' the vicar now addressed me, 'to prove by a practical demonstration that women are capable of as much philosophy as men, under any sudden and afflicting revolution of circumstances.'

'And if you get a sunstroke, you will be rightly punished, and I shall not be sorry, Mr. Amble.'

'I am coming, my dear Jane. Pray run into the house and change your things.'

'Not till I see you out of the water, sir.'

'You are losing your temper, my love.'

'You would make a saint lose his temper, Mr. Amble.'

'There were female saints, my dear,' the vicar mildly responded; and addressed me further: 'Up to this point, I assure you, Pollingray, no conduct could have been more exemplary than Mrs. Amble's. I had got her into the boat—a good boat, a capital boat—but getting in myself, we overturned. The first impulse of an ordinary woman would have been to reproach and scold; but Mrs. Amble succumbed only to the first impulse. Discovering that all effort unaided to climb the bank was fruitless, she agreed to wait patiently and make the best of circumstances; and she did; and she learnt to enjoy it. There is marrow in every bone. My dear. Jane, I have never admired you so much. I tried her, Pollingray, in metaphysics. I talked to her of the opera we last heard, I think fifty years ago. And as it is less endurable for a woman to be patient in tribulation—the honour is greater, when she overcomes the fleshy trial. Insomuch,' the vicar put on a bland air of abnegation of honour, 'that I am disposed to consider any male philosopher our superior; when you've found one, ha, ha—when you've found one. O sol pulcher! I am ready to sing that the day has been glorious, so far. Pulcher ille dies.'

Mrs. Amble appealed to me. 'Would anybody not swear that he is mad to see him standing waist-deep in the water and the sun on his bald head, I am reduced to entreat you not to—though you have no family of your own—not to encourage him. It is amusing to you. Pray, reflect that such folly is too often fatal. Compel him to come on shore.'

The logic of the appeal was no doubt distinctly visible in the lady's mind, though it was not accurately worded. I saw that I stood marked to be the scape goat of the day, and humbly continued to deserve well, notwithstanding. By dint of simple signs and nods of affirmative, and a constant propulsion of my friend's arm, I drew him into the boat, and thence projected him up to the level with his wife, who had perhaps deigned to understand that it was best to avoid the arresting of his divergent mind by any remark during the passage, and remained silent. No sooner was he established on his feet, than she plucked him away.

'Your papa's hat,' she called, flashing to her daughter, and streamed up the lawn into the rose-trellised pathways leading on aloft to the vicarage house. Behind roses the weeping couple disappeared. The last I saw of my friend was a smiting of his hand upon his head in a vain effort to catch at one of the fleeting ideas sowed in him by the quick passage of objects before his vision, and shaken out of him by abnormal hurry. The Rev. Abraham Amble had been lord of his wife in the water, but his innings was over. He had evidently enjoyed it vastly, and I now understood why he had chosen to prolong it as much as possible. Your eccentric characters are not uncommonly amateurs of petty artifice. There are hours of vengeance even for henpecked men.

I found myself sighing over the enslaved condition of every Benedict of my acquaintance, when the thought came like a surprise that I was alone with Alice. The fair and pleasant damsel made a clever descent into the boat, and having seated herself, she began to twirl the scull in the rowlock, and said: 'Do you feel disposed to join me in looking after the other scull and papa's hat, Mr. Pollingray?' I suggested 'Will you not get your feet wet? I couldn't manage to empty all the water in the boat.'

'Oh' cried she, with a toss of her head; I wet feet never hurt young people.'

There was matter for an admonitory lecture in this. Let me confess I was about to give it, when she added: But Mr. Pollingray, I am really afraid that your feet are wet! You had to step into the water when you righted the boat:

My reply was to jump down by her side with as much agility as I could combine with a proper discretion. The amateur craft rocked threateningly, and I found myself grasped by and grasping the pretty damsel, until by great good luck we were steadied and preserved from the same misfortune which had befallen her parents. She laughed and blushed, and we tottered asunder.

'Would you have talked metaphysics to me in the water, Mr. Pollingray?'

Alice was here guilty of one of those naughty sort of innocent speeches smacking of Eve most strongly; though, of course, of Eve in her best days.

I took the rudder lines to steer against the sculling of her single scull, and was Adam enough to respond to temptation: 'I should perhaps have been grateful to your charitable construction of it as being metaphysics.'

She laughed colloquially, to fill a pause. It had not been coquetry: merely the woman unconsciously at play. A man is bound to remember the seniority of his years when this occurs, for a veteran of ninety and a worn out young debauchee will equally be subject to it if they do not shun the society of the sex. My long robust health and perfect self-reliance apparently tend to give me unguarded moments, or lay me open to fitful impressions. Indeed there are times when I fear I have the heart of a boy, and certainly nothing more calamitous can be conceived, supposing that it should ever for one instant get complete mastery of my head. This is the peril of a man who has lived soberly. Do we never know when we are safe? I am, in reflecting thereupon, positively prepared to say that if there is no fool like what they call an old fool (and a man in his prime, who can be laughed at, is the world's old fool) there is wisdom in the wild oats theory, and I shall come round to my nephew's way of thinking: that is, as far as Master Charles by his acting represents his thinking. I shall at all events be more lenient in my judgement of him, and less stern in my allocutions, for I shall have no text to preach from.

We picked up the hat and the scull in one of the little muddy bays of our brown river, forming an amphitheatre for water-rats and draped with great dockleaves, nettle-flowers, ragged robins, and other weeds for which the learned young lady gave the botanical names. It was pleasant to hear her speak with the full authority of absolute knowledge of her subject. She has intelligence. She is decidedly too good for Charles, unless he changes his method of living.

'Shall we row on?' she asked, settling her arms to work the pair of sculls.

'You have me in your power,' said I, and she struck out. Her shape is exceedingly graceful; I was charmed by the occasional tightening in of her lips as she exerted her muscle, while at intervals telling me of her race with one of her boastful younger brothers, whom she had beaten. I believe it is only when they are using physical exertion that the eyes of young girls have entire simplicity—the simplicity of nature as opposed to that other artificial simplicity which they learn from their governesses, their mothers, and the admiration of witlings. Attractive purity, or the nice glaze of no comprehension of anything which is considered to be improper in a wicked world, and is no doubt very useful, is not to my taste. French girls, as a rule, cannot compete with our English in the purer graces. They are only incomparable when as women they have resort to art.

Alice could look at me as she rowed, without thinking it necessary to force a smile, or to speak, or to snigger and be foolish. I felt towards the girl like a comrade.

We went no further than Hatchard's mile, where the water plumps the poor sleepy river from a sidestream, and, as it turned the boat's head quite round, I let the boat go. These studies of young women are very well as a pastime; but they soon cease to be a recreation. She forms an agreeable picture when she is rowing, and possesses a musical laugh. Now and then she gives way to the bad trick of laughing without caring or daring to explain the cause for it. She is moderately well-bred. I hope that she has principle. Certain things a man of my time of life learns by associating with very young people which are serviceable to him. What a different matter this earth must be to that girl from what it is to me! I knew it before. And—mark the difference—I feel it now.

CHAPTER II

SHE

Papa never will cease to meet with accidents and adventures. If he only walks out to sit for half an hour with one of his old dames, as he calls them, something is sure to happen to him, and it is almost as sure that Mr. Pollingray will be passing at the time and mixed up in it.

Since Mr. Pollingray's return from his last residence on the Continent, I have learnt to know him and like him. Charles is unjust to his uncle. He is not at all the grave kind of man I expected from Charles's description. He is extremely entertaining, and then he understands the world, and I like to hear him talk, he is so unpretentious and uses just the right words. No one would imagine his age, from his appearance, and he has more fun than any young man I have listened to.

But, I am convinced I have discovered his weakness. It is my fatal. peculiarity that I cannot be with people ten minutes without seeing some point about them where they are tenderest. Mr. Pollingray wants to be thought quite youthful. He can bear any amount of fatigue; he is always fresh and a delightful companion; but you cannot get him to show even a shadow of exhaustion or to admit that he ever knew what it was to lie down beaten. This is really to pretend that he is superhuman. I like him so much that I could wish him superior to such—it is nothing other than—vanity. Which is worse? A young man giving himself the air of a sage, or—but no one can call Mr. Pollingray an old man. He is a confirmed bachelor. That puts the case. Charles, when he says of him that he is a 'gentleman in a good state of preservation,' means to be ironical. I doubt whether Charles at fifty would object to have the same said of Mr. Charles Everett. Mr. Pollingray has always looked to his health. He has not been disappointed. I am sure he was always very good. But, whatever he was, he is now very pleasant, and he does not talk to women as if he thought them singular, and feel timid, I mean, confused, as some men show that they feel—the good ones. Perhaps he felt so once, and that is why he is still free. Charles's dread that his uncle will marry is most unworthy. He never will, but why should he not? Mama declares that he is waiting for a woman of intellect, I can hear her: 'Depend upon it, a woman of intellect will marry Dayton Manor.' Should that mighty event not come to pass, poor Charles will have to sink the name of Everett in that of Pollingray. Mr. Pollingray's name is the worst thing about him. When I think of his name I see him ten times older than he is. My feelings are in harmony with his pedigree concerning the age of the name. One would have to be a woman of profound intellect to see the advantage of sharing it.

'Mrs. Pollingray!' She must be a lady with a wig.

It was when we were rowing up by Hatchard's mill that I first perceived his weakness, he was looking at me so kindly, and speaking of his friendship for papa, and how glad he was to be fixed at last, near to us at Dayton. I wished to use some term of endearment in reply, and said, I remember, 'Yes, and we are also glad, Godpapa.' I was astonished that he should look so disconcerted, and went on: 'Have you forgotten that you are my godpapa?'

He answered: 'Am I? Oh! yes—the name of Alice.'

Still he looked uncertain, uncomfortable, and I said, 'Do you want to cancel the past, and cast me off?'

'No, certainly not'; he, I suppose, thought he was assuring me.

I saw his lips move at the words I cancel the past,' though he did not speak them out. He positively blushed. I know the sort of young man he must have been. Exactly the sort of young man mama would like for a son-in-law, and her daughters would accept in pure obedience when reduced to be capable of the virtue by rigorous diet, or consumption.

He let the boat go round instantly. This was enough for me. It struck me then that when papa had said to mama (as he did in that absurd situation) 'He is fifty,' Mr. Pollingray must have heard it across the river, for he walked away hurriedly. He came back, it is true, with the boat, but I have my own ideas. He is always ready to do a service, but on this occasion I think it was an afterthought. I shall not venture to call him 'Godpapa' again.

Indeed, if I have a desire, it is that I may be blind to people's weakness. My insight is inveterate. Papa says he has heard Mr. Pollingray boast of his age. If so, there has come a change over him. I cannot be deceived. I see it constantly. After my unfortunate speech, Mr. Pollingray shunned our house for two whole weeks, and scarcely bowed to us when coming out of church. Miss Pollingray idolises him—spoils him. She says that he is worth twenty of Charles. Nous savons ce que nous savons, nous autres. Charles is wild, but Charles would be above these littlenesses. How could Miss Pollingray comprehend the romance of Charles's nature?

My sister Evelina is now Mr. Pollingray's favourite. She could not say Godpapa to him, if she would. Persons who are very much petted at home, are always establishing favourites abroad. For my part, let them praise me or not, I know that I can do any thing I set my mind upon. At present I choose to be frivolous. I know I am frivolous. What then? If there is fun in the world am I not to laugh at it? I shall astonish them by and by. But, I will laugh while I can. I am sure, there is so much misery in the world, it is a mercy to be able to laugh. Mr. Pollingray may think what he likes of me. When Charles tells me that I must do my utmost to propitiate his uncle, he cannot mean that I am to refrain from laughing, because that is being a hypocrite, which I may become when I have gone through all the potential moods and not before.

It is preposterous to suppose that I am to be tied down to the views of life of elderly people.

I dare say I did laugh a little too much the other night, but could I help it? We had a dinner party. Present were Mr. Pollingray, Mrs. Kershaw, the Wilbury people (three), Charles, my brother Duncan, Evelina, mama, papa, myself, and Mr. and Mrs. (put them last for emphasis) Romer Pattlecombe, Mrs. Pattlecombe (the same number of syllables as Pollingray, and a 'P' to begin with) is thirty-one years her husband's junior, and she is twenty-six; full of fun, and always making fun of him, the mildest, kindest, goody old thing, who has never distressed himself for anything and never will. Mrs. Romer not only makes fun, but is fun. When you have done laughing with her, you can laugh at her. She is the salt of society in these parts. Some one, as we were sitting on the lawn after dinner, alluded to the mishap to papa and mama, and mama, who has never forgiven Mr. Pollingray for having seen her in her ridiculous plight, said that men were in her opinion greater gossips than women. 'That is indisputable, ma'am,' said Mr. Pollingray, he loves to bewilder her; 'only, we never mention it.'

'There is an excuse for us,' said Mrs. Romer; 'our trials are so great, we require a diversion, and so we talk of others.'

'Now really,' said Charles, 'I don't think your trials are equal to ours.'

For which remark papa bantered him, and his uncle was sharp on him; and Charles, I know, spoke half seriously, though he was seeking to draw Mrs. Romer out: he has troubles.

From this, we fell upon a comparison of sufferings, and Mrs. Romer took up the word. She is a fair, smallish, nervous woman, with delicate hands and outlines, exceedingly sympathetic; so much so that while you are telling her anything, she makes half a face in anticipation, and is ready to shriek with laughter or shake her head with uttermost grief; and sometimes, if you let her go too far in one direction, she does both. All her narrations are with ups and downs of her hands, her eyes, her chin, and her voice. Taking poor, good old Mr. Romer by the roll of his coat, she made as if posing him, and said: 'There! Now, it's all very well for you to say that there is anything equal to a woman's sufferings in this world. I do declare you know nothing of what we unhappy women have to endure. It's dreadful! No male creature can possibly know what tortures I have to undergo.'

Mama neatly contrived, after interrupting her, to divert the subject. I think that all the ladies imagined they were in jeopardy, but I knew Mrs. Romer was perfectly to be trusted. She has wit which pleases, jusqu'aux ongles, and her sense of humour never overrides her discretion with more than a glance— never with preparation.

'Now,' she pursued, 'let me tell you what excruciating trials I have to go through. This man,' she rocked the patient old gentleman to and fro, 'this man will be the death of me. He is utterly devoid of a sense of propriety. Again and again I say to him—cannot the tailor cut down these trowsers of yours? Yes, Mr. Amble, you preach patience to women, but this is too much for any woman's endurance. Now, do attempt to picture to yourself what an agony it must be to me:—he will shave, and he will wear those enormously high trowsers that, when they are braced, reach up behind to the nape of his neck! Only yesterday morning, as I was lying in bed, I could see him in his dressing-room. I tell you: he will shave, and he will choose the time for shaving early after he has braced these immensely high trowsers that make such a placard of him. Oh, my goodness! My dear Romer, I have said to him fifty times if I have said it once, my goodness me! why can you not get decent trowsers such as other men wear? He has but one answer—he has been accustomed to wear those trowsers, and he would not feel at home in another pair. And what does he say if I continue to complain? and I cannot but continue to complain, for it is not only moral, it is physical torment to see the sight he makes of himself; he says: "My dear, you should not have married an old man." What! I say to him, must an old man wear antiquated trowsers? No! nothing will turn him; those are his habits. But, you have not heard the worst. The sight of those hideous trowsers totally destroying all shape in the man, is horrible enough; but it is absolutely more than a woman can bear to see him—for he will shave—first cover his face with white soap with that ridiculous centre-piece to his trowsers reaching quite up to his poll, and then, you can fancy a woman's rage and anguish! the figure lifts its nose by the extremist tip. Oh! it's degradation! What respect can a woman have for her husband after that sight? Imagine it! And I have implored him to spare me. It's useless. You sneer at our hbops and say that you are inconvenienced by them but you gentlemen are not degraded,—Oh! unutterably!—as I am every morning of my life by that cruel spectacle of a husband.'

I have but faintly sketched Mrs. Romer's style. Evelina, who is prudish and thinks her vulgar, refused to laugh, but it came upon me, as the picture of 'your own old husband,' with so irresistibly comic an effect that I was overcome by convulsions of laughter. I do not defend myself. It was as much a fit as any other attack. I did all I could to arrest it. At last, I ran indoors and upstairs to my bedroom and tried hard to become dispossessed. I am sure I was an example of the sufferings of my sex. It could hardly have been worse for Mrs. Romer than it was for me. I was drowned in internal laughter long after I had got a grave face. Early in the evening Mr. Pollingray left us.

CHAPTER III

HE

I am carried by the fascination of a musical laugh. Apparently I am doomed to hear it at my own expense. We are secure from nothing in this life.

I have determined to stand for the county. An unoccupied man is a prey to every hook of folly. Be dilettante all your days, and you might as fairly hope to reap a moral harvest as if you had chased butterflies. The activities created by a profession or determined pursuit are necessary to the growth of the mind.

Heavens! I find myself writing like an illegitimate son of La Rochefoucauld, or of Vauvenargues. But, it is true that I am fifty years old, and I am not mature. I am undeveloped somewhere.

The question for me to consider is, whether this development is to be accomplished by my being guilty of an act of egregious folly.

Dans la cinquantaine! The reflection should produce a gravity in men. Such a number of years will not ring like bridal bells in a man's ears. I have my books about me, my horses, my dogs, a contented household. I move in the centre of a perfect machine, and I am dissatisfied. I rise early. I do not digest badly. What is wrong?

The calamity of my case is that I am in danger of betraying what is wrong with me to others, without knowing it myself. Some woman will be suspecting and tattling, because she has nothing else to do. Girls have wonderfully shrewd eyes for a weakness in the sex which they are instructed to look upon as superior. But I am on my guard.

The fact is manifest: I feel I have been living more or less uselessly. It is a fat time. There are a certain set of men in every prosperous country who, having wherewithal, and not being compelled to toil, become subjected to the moral ideal. Most of them in the end sit down with our sixth Henry or second Richard and philosophise on shepherds. To be no better than a simple hind! Am I better? Prime bacon and an occasional draft of shrewd beer content him, and they do not me. Yet I am sound, and can sit through the night and be ready, and on the morrow I shall stand for the county.

I made the announcement that I had thoughts of entering Parliament, before I had half formed the determination, at my sister's lawn party yesterday.

'Gilbert!' she cried, and raised her hands. A woman is hurt if you do not confide to her your plans as soon as you can conceive them. She must be present to assist at the birth, or your plans are unblessed plans.

I had been speaking aside in a casual manner to my friend Amble, whose idea is that the Church is not represented with sufficient strength in the Commons, and who at once, as I perceived, grasped the notion of getting me to promote sundry measures connected with schools and clerical stipends, for his eyes dilated; he said: 'Well, if you do, I can put you up to several things,' and imparting the usual chorus of yesses to his own mind, he continued absently: 'Pollingray might be made strong on church rates. There is much to do. He has lived abroad and requires schooling in these things. We want a man. Yes, yes, yes. It's a good idea; a notion.'

My sister, however, was of another opinion. She did me the honour to take me aside.

'Gilbert, were you serious just now?'

'Quite serious. Is it not my characteristic?'

'Not on these occasions. I saw the idea come suddenly upon you. You were looking at Charles.'

'Continue: and at what was he looking?'

'He was looking at Alice Amble.'

'And the young lady?'

'She looked at you.'

I was here attacked by a singularly pertinacious fly, and came out of the contest with a laugh.

'Did she have that condescension towards me? And from the glance, my resolution to enter Parliament was born? It is the French vaudevilliste's doctrine of great events from little causes. The slipper of a soubrette trips the heart of a king and changes the destiny of a nation-the history of mankind. It may be true. If I were but shot into the House from a little girl's eye!'

With this I took her arm gaily, walked with her, and had nearly overreached myself with excess of cunning. I suppose we are reduced to see more plainly that which we systematically endeavour to veil from others. It is best to flutter a handkerchief, instead of nailing up a curtain. The principal advantage is that you may thereby go on deceiving yourself, for this reason: few sentiments are wholly matter of fact; but when they are half so, you make them concrete by deliberately seeking either to crush or conceal them, and you are doubly betrayed—betrayed to the besieging eye and to yourself. When a sentiment has grown to be a passion (mercifully may I be spared!) different tactics are required. By that time, you will have already betrayed yourself too deeply to dare to be flippant: the investigating eye is aware that it has been purposely diverted: knowing some things, it makes sure of the rest from which you turn it away. If you want to hide a very grave case, you must speak gravely about it.—At which season, be but sure of your voice, and simulate a certain depth of sentimental philosophy, and you may once more, and for a long period, bewilder the investigator of the secrets of your bosom. To sum up: in the preliminary stages of a weakness, be careful that you do not show your own alarm, or all will be suspected. Should the weakness turn to fever, let a little of it be seen, like a careless man, and nothing will really be thought.

I can say this, I can do this; and is it still possible that a pin's point has got through the joints of the armour of a man like me?

Elizabeth quitted my side with the conviction that I am as considerate an uncle as I am an affectionate brother.

I said to her, apropos, 'I have been observing those two. It seems to me they are deciding things for themselves.'

'I have been going to speak to you about them Gilbert,' said she.

And I: 'The girl must be studied. The family is good. While Charles is in Wales, you must have her at Dayton. She laughs rather vacantly, don't you think? but the sound of it has the proper wholesome ring. I will give her what attention I can while she is here, but in the meantime I must have a bride of my own and commence courting.'

'Parliament, you mean,' said Elizabeth with a frank and tender smile. The hostess was summoned to welcome a new guest, and she left me, pleased with her successful effort to reach my meaning, and absorbed by it.

I would not have challenged Machiavelli; but I should not have encountered the Florentine ruefully. I feel the same keen delight in intellectual dexterity. On some points my sister is not a bad match for me. She can beat me seven games out of twelve at chess; but the five I win sequently, for then I am awake. There is natural art and artificial art, and the last beats the first. Fortunately for us, women are strangers to the last. They have had to throw off a mask before they have, got the schooling; so, when they are thus armed we know what we meet, and what are the weapons to be used.

Alice, if she is a fine fencer at all, will expect to meet the ordinary English squire in me. I have seen her at the baptismal font! It is inconceivable. She will fancy that at least she is ten times more subtle than I. When I get the mastery—it is unlikely to make me the master. What may happen is, that the nature of the girl will declare itself, under the hard light of intimacy, vulgar. Charles I cause to be absent for six weeks; so there will be time enough for the probation. I do not see him till he returns. If by chance I had come earlier to see him and he to allude to her, he would have had my conscience on his side, and that is what a scrupulous man takes care to prevent.

I wonder whether my friends imagine me to be the same man whom they knew as Gilbert Pollingray a month back? I see the change, I feel the change; but I have no retrospection, no remorse, no looking forward, no feeling: none for others, very little, for myself. I am told that I am losing fluency as a dinner-table talker. There is now more savour to me in a silvery laugh than in a spiced wit. And this is the man who knows women, and is far too modest to give a decided opinion upon any of their merits. Search myself through as I may, I cannot tell when the change began, or what the change consists of, or what is the matter with me, or what charm there is in the person who does the mischief. She is the counterpart of dozens of girls; lively, brown-eyed, brown-haired, underbred—it is not too harsh to say so—underbred slightly; half-educated, whether quickwitted I dare not opine. She is undoubtedly the last whom I or another person would have fixed upon as one to work me this unmitigated evil. I do not know her, and I believe I do not care to know her, and I am thirsting for the hour to come when I shall study her. Is not this to have the poison of a bite in one's blood? The wrath of Venus is not a fable. I was a hard reader and I despised the sex in my youth, before the family estates fell to me; since when I have playfully admired the sex; I have dallied with a passion, and not read at all, save for diversion: her anger is not a fable. You may interpret many a mythic tale by the facts which lie in your own blood. My emotions have lain altogether dormant in sentimental attachment. I have, I suppose, boasted of, Python slain, and Cupid has touched me up with an arrow. I trust to my own skill rather than to his mercy for avoiding a second from his quiver. I will understand this girl if I have to submit to a close intimacy with her for six months. There is no doubt of the elegance of her movements. Charles might as well take his tour, and let us see him again next year. Yes, her movements are (or will be) gracious. In a year's time she will have acquired the fuller tones and poetry of womanliness. Perhaps then, too, her smile will linger instead of flashing. I have known infinitely lovelier women than she. One I have known! but let her be. Louise and I have long since said adieu.

CHAPTER IV

SHE

Behold me installed in Dayton Manor House, and brought here for the express purpose (so Charles has written me word) of my being studied, that it may be seen whether I am worthy to be, on some august future occasion—possibly—a member (Oh, so much to mumble!) of this great family. Had I known it when I was leaving home, I should have countermanded the cording of my boxes. If you please, I do the packing, and not the cording. I must practise being polite, or I shall be horrifying these good people.

I am mortally offended. I am very very angry. I shall show temper. Indeed, I have shown it. Mr. Pollingray must and does think me a goose. Dear sir, and I think you are justified. If any one pretends to guess how, I have names to suit that person. I am a ninny, an ape, and mind I call myself these bad things because I deserve worse. I am flighty, I believe I am heartless. Charles is away, and I suffer no pangs. The truth is, I fancied myself so exceedingly penetrating, and it was my vanity looking in a glass. I saw something that answered to my nods and howd'ye-do's and—but I am ashamed, and so penitent I might begin making a collection of beetles. I cannot lift up my head.

Mr. Pollingray is such a different man from the one I had imagined! What that one was, I have now quite forgotten. I remember too clearly what the wretched guesser was. I have been three weeks at Dayton, and if my sisters know me when I return to the vicarage, they are not foolish virgins. For my part, I know that I shall always hate Mrs. Romer Pattlecombe, and that I am unjust to the good woman, but I do hate her, and I think the stories shocking, and wonder intensely what it was that I could have found in them to laugh at. I shall never laugh again for many years. Perhaps, when I am an old woman, I may. I wish the time had come. All young people seem to me so helplessly silly. I am one of them for the present, and have no hope that I can appear to be anything else. The young are a crowd—a shoal of small fry. Their elders are the select of the world.

On the morning of the day when I was to leave home for Dayton, a distance of eight miles, I looked out of my window while dressing—as early as halfpast seven—and I saw Mr. Pollingray's groom on horseback, leading up and down the walk a darling little, round, plump, black cob that made my heart leap with an immense bound of longing to be on it and away across the downs. And then the maid came to my door with a letter:

'Mr. Pollingray, in return for her considerate good behaviour and saving of trouble to him officially, begs his goddaughter to accept the accompanying little animal: height 14 h., age 31 years; hunts, is sure-footed, and likely to be the best jumper in the county.'

I flew downstairs. I rushed out of the house and up to my treasure, and kissed his nose and stroked his mane. I could not get my fingers away from him. Horses are so like the very best and beautifullest of women when you caress them. They show their pleasure so at being petted. They curve their necks, and paw, and look proud. They take your flattery like sunshine and are lovely in it. I kissed my beauty, peering at his black-mottled skin, which is like Allingborough Heath in the twilight. The smell of his new saddle and bridle-leather was sweeter than a garden to me. The man handed me a large riding-whip mounted with silver. I longed to jump up and ride till midnight.

Then mama and papa came out and read the note and looked, at my darling little cob, and my sisters saw him and kissed me, for they are not envious girls. The most distressing thing was that we had not a riding-habit in the family. I was ready to wear any sort. I would have ridden as a guy rather than not ride at all. But mama gave me a promise that in two days a riding-habit should be sent on to Dayton, and I had to let my pet be led back from where he came. I had no life till I was following him. I could have believed him to be a fairy prince who had charmed me. I called him Prince Leboo, because he was black and good. I forgive anybody who talks about first love after what my experience has been with Prince Leboo.

What papa thought of the present I do not know, but I know very well what mama thought: and for my part I thought everything, not distinctly including that, for I could not suppose such selfishness in one so generous as Mr. Pollingray. But I came to Dayton in a state of arrogant pride, that gave assurance if not ease to my manners. I thanked Mr. Pollingray warmly, but in a way to let him see it was the matter of a horse between us. 'You give, I register thanks, and there's an end.'

'He thinks me a fool! a fool!

'My habit,' I said, 'comes after me. I hope we shall have some rides together.'

'Many,' replied Mr. Pollingray, and his bow inflated me with ideas of my condescension.

And because Miss Pollingray (Queen Elizabeth he calls her) looked half sad, I read it—! I do not write what I read it to be.

Behold the uttermost fool of all female creation led over the house by Mr. Pollingray. He showed me the family pictures.

'I am no judge of pictures, Mr. Pollingray.'

'You will learn to see the merits of these.'

'I'm afraid not, though I were to study them for years.'

'You may have that opportunity.'

'Oh! that is more than I can expect.'

'You will develop intelligence on such subjects by and by.'

A dull sort of distant blow struck me in this remark; but I paid no heed to it.

He led me over the gardens and the grounds. The Great John Methlyn Pollingray planted those trees, and designed the house, and the flower-garden still speaks of his task; but he is not my master, and consequently I could not share his three great-grandsons' veneration for him. There are high fir-woods and beech woods, and a long ascending narrow meadow between them, through which a brook falls in continual cascades. It is the sort of scene I love, for it has a woodland grandeur and seclusion that leads, me to think, and makes a better girl of me. But what I said was: 'Yes, it is the place of all others to come and settle in for the evening of one's days.'

'You could not take to it now?' said Mr. Pollingray.

'Now?' my expression of face must have been a picture.

'You feel called upon to decline such a residence in the morning of your days?'

He persisted in looking at me as he spoke, and I felt like something withering scarlet.

I am convinced he saw through me, while his face was polished brass. My self-possession returned, for my pride was not to be dispersed immediately.

'Please, take me to the stables,' I entreated; and there I was at home. There I saw my Prince Leboo, and gave him a thousand caresses.'

'He knows me already,' I said.

Then he is some degrees in advance of me,' said Mr. Pollingray.

Is not cold dissection of one's character a cruel proceeding? And I think, too, that a form of hospitality like this by which I am invited to be analysed at leisure, is both mean and base. I have been kindly treated and I am grateful, but I do still say (even though I may have improved under it) it is unfair.

To proceed: the dinner hour arrived. The atmosphere of his own house seems to favour Mr. Pollingray as certain soils and sites favour others. He walked into the dining-room between us with his hands behind him, talking to us both so easily and smoothly cheerfully—naturally and pleasantly—inimitable by any young man! You hardly feel the change of room. We were but three at table, but there was no lack of entertainment. Mr. Pollingray is an admirable host; he talks just enough himself and helps you to talk. What does comfort me is that it gives him real pleasure to see a hearty appetite. Young men, I know it for a certainty, never quite like us to be so human. Ah! which is right? I would not miss the faith in our nobler essence which Charles has. But, if it nobler? One who has lived longer in the world ought to know better, and Mr. Pollingray approves of naturalness in everything. I have now seen through Charles's eyes for several months; so implicitly that I am timid when I dream of trusting to another's judgement. It is, however, a fact that I am not quite natural with Charles.

Every day Mr. Pollingray puts on evening dress out of deference to his sister. If young men had these good habits they would gain our respect, and lose their own self-esteem less early.

After dinner I sang. Then Mr. Pollingray read an amusing essay to us, and retired to his library. Miss Pollingray sat and talked to me of her brother, and of her nephew—for whom it is that Mr. Pollingray is beginning to receive company, and is going into society. Charles's subsequently received letter explained the 'receive company.' I could not comprehend it at the time.

'The house has been shut up for years, or rarely inhabited by us for more than a month in the year. Mr. Pollingray prefers France. All his associations, I may say his sympathies, are in France. Latterly he seems to have changed a little; but from Normandy to Touraine and Dauphiny—we had a triangular home over there. Indeed, we have it still. I am never certain of my brother.'

While Miss Pollingray was speaking, my eyes were fixed on a Vidal crayon drawing, faintly coloured with chalks, of a foreign lady—I could have sworn to her being French—young, quite girlish, I doubt if her age was more than mine.

She is pretty, is she not?' said Miss Pollingray.

She is almost beautiful,' I exclaimed, and Miss Pollingray, seeing my curiosity, was kind enough not to keep me in suspense.

'That is the Marquise de Mazardouin—nee Louise de Riverolles. You will see other portraits of her in the house. This is the most youthful of them, if I except one representing a baby, and bearing her initials.'

I remembered having noticed a similarity of feature in some of the portraits in the different rooms. My longing to look at them again was like a sudden jet of flame within me. There was no chance of seeing them till morning; so, promising myself to dream of the face before me, I dozed through a conversation with my hostess, until I had got the French lady's eyes and hair and general outline stamped accurately, as I hoped, on my mind. I was no sooner on my way to bed than all had faded. The torment of trying to conjure up that face was inconceivable. I lay, and tossed, and turned to right and to left, and scattered my sleep; but by and by my thoughts reverted to Mr. Pollingray, and then like sympathetic ink held to the heat, I beheld her again; but vividly, as she must have been when she was sitting to the artist. The hair was naturally crisped, waving thrice over the forehead and brushed clean from the temples, showing the small ears, and tied in a knot loosely behind. Her eyebrows were thick and dark, but soft; flowing eyebrows; far lovelier, to my thinking, than any pencilled arch. Dark eyes, and full, not prominent. I find little expression of inward sentiment in very prominent eyes. On the contrary they seem to have a fish-like dependency of gaze on what is without, and show fishy depths, if any. For instance, my eyes are rather prominent, and I am just the little fool—but the French lady is my theme. Madame la Marquise, your eyes are sweeter to me than celestial. I never saw such candour and unaffected innocence in eyes before. Accept the compliment of the pauvre Anglaise. Did you do mischief with them? Did Vidal's delicate sketch do justice to you? Your lips and chin and your throat all repose in such girlish grace, that if ever it is my good fortune to see you, you will not be aged to me!

I slept and dreamed of her.

In the morning, I felt certain that she had often said: 'Mon cher Gilbert,' to Mr. Pollingray. Had he ever said: 'Ma chere Louise?' He might have said: 'Ma bien aimee!' for it was a face to be loved.

My change of feeling towards him dates from that morning. He had previously seemed to me a man so much older. I perceived in him now a youthfulness beyond mere vigour of frame. I could not detach him from my dreams of the night. He insists upon addressing me by the terms of our 'official' relationship, as if he made it a principle of our intercourse.

'Well, and is your godpapa to congratulate you on your having had a quiet rest?' was his greeting.

I answered stupidly: 'Oh, yes, thank you,' and would have given worlds for the courage to reply in French, but I distrusted my accent. At breakfast, the opportunity or rather the excuse for an attempt, was offered. His French valet, Francois, waits on him at breakfast. Mr. Pollingray and his sister asked for things in the French tongue, and, as if fearing some breach of civility, Mr. Pollingray asked me if I knew French.

Yes, I know it; that is, I understand it,' I stuttered. Allons, nous parlerons francais,' said he. But I shook my head, and remained like a silly mute.

I was induced towards the close of the meal to come out with a few French words. I was utterly shamefaced. Mr. Pollingray has got the French manner of protesting that one is all but perfect in one's speaking. I know how absurd it must have sounded. But I felt his kindness, and in my heart I thanked him humbly. I believe now that a residence in France does not deteriorate an Englishman. Mr. Pollingray, when in his own house, has the best qualities of the two countries. He is gay, and, yes, while he makes a study of me, I am making a study of him. Which of us two will know the other first? He was papa's college friend—papa's junior, of course, and infinitely more papa's junior now. I observe that weakness in him, I mean, his clinging to youthfulness, less and less; but I do see it, I cannot be quite in error. The truth is, I begin to feel that I cannot venture to mistrust my infallible judgement, or I shall have no confidence in myself at all.

After breakfast, I was handed over to Miss Pollingray, with the intimation that I should not see him till dinner.

'Gilbert is anxious to cultivate the society of his English neighbours, now that he has, as he supposes, really settled among them,' she remarked to me. 'At his time of life, the desire to be useful is almost a malady. But, he cherishes the poor, and that is more than an occupation, it is a virtue.'

Her speech has become occasionally French in the construction of the sentences.

'Mais oui,' I said shyly, and being alone with her, I was not rebuffed by her smile, especially as she encouraged me on.

I am, she told me, to see a monde of French people here in September. So, the story of me is to be completer, or continued in September. I could not get Miss Pollingray to tell me distinctly whether Madame la Marquise will be one of the guests. But I know that she is not a widow. In that case, she has a husband. In that case, what is the story of her relations towards Mr. Pollingray? There must be some story. He would not surely have so many portraits of her about the house (and they travel with him wherever he goes) if she were but a lovely face to him. I cannot understand it. They were frequent, constant visitors to one another's estates in France; always together. Perhaps a man of Mr. Pollingray's age, or perhaps M. le Marquis—and here I lose myself. French habits are so different from ours. One thing I am certain of: no charge can be brought against my Englishman. I read perfect rectitude in his face. I would cast anchor by him. He must have had a dreadful unhappiness.

Mama kept her promise by sending my riding habit and hat punctually, but I had run far ahead of all the wishes I had formed when I left home, and I half feared my ride out with Mr. Pollingray. That was before I had received Charles's letter, letting me know the object of my invitation here. I require at times a morbid pride to keep me up to the work. I suppose I rode befittingly, for Mr. Pollingray praised my seat on horseback. I know I can ride, or feel the 'blast of a horse like my own'—as he calls it. Yet he never could have had a duller companion. My conversation was all yes and no, as if it went on a pair of crutches like a miserable cripple. I was humiliated and vexed. All the while I was trying to lead up to the French lady, and I could not commence with a single question. He appears to, have really cancelled the past in every respect save his calling me his goddaughter. His talk was of the English poor, and vegetation, and papa's goodness to his old dames in Ickleworth parish, and defects in my education acknowledged by me, but not likely to restore me in my depressed state. The ride was beautiful. We went the length of a twelve-mile ridge between Ickleworth and Hillford, over high commons, with immense views on both sides, and through beech-woods, oakwoods, and furzy dells and downs spotted with juniper and yewtrees—old picnic haunts of mine, but Mr. Pollingray's fresh delight in the landscape made them seem new and strange. Home through the valley.

The next day Miss Pollingray joined us, wearing a feutre gris and green plume, which looked exceedingly odd until you became accustomed to it. Her hair has decided gray streaks, and that, and the Queen Elizabeth nose, and the feutre gris!—but she is so kind, I could not even smile in my heart. It is singular that Mr. Pollingray, who's but three years her junior, should look at least twenty years younger—at the very least. His moustache and beard are of the colour of a corn sheaf, and his blue eyes shining over them remind me of summer. That describes him. He is summer, and has not fallen into his autumn yet. Miss Pollingray helped me to talk a little. She tried to check her brother's enthusiasm for our scenery, and extolled the French paysage. He laughed at her, for when they were in France it was she who used to say, 'There is nothing here like England!' Miss Fool rode between them attentive to the jingling of the bells in her cap: 'Yes' and 'No' at anybody's command, in and out of season.

Thank you, Charles, for your letter! I was beginning to think my invitation to Dayton inexplicable, when that letter arrived. I cannot but deem it an unworthy baseness to entrap a girl to study her without a warning to her. I went up to my room after I had read it, and wrote in reply till the breakfast-bell rang. I resumed my occupation an hour later, and wrote till one o'clock. In all, fifteen pages of writing, which I carefully folded and addressed to Charles; sealed the envelope, stamped it, and destroyed it. I went to bed. 'No, I won't ride out to-day, I have a headache!' I repeated this about half-a-dozen times to nobody's knocking on the door, and when at last somebody knocked I tried to repeat it once, but having the message that Mr. Pollingray particularly wished to have my company in a ride, I rose submissively and cried. This humiliation made my temper ferocious. Mr. Pollingray observed my face, and put it down in his notebook. 'A savage disposition,' or, no, 'An untamed little rebel'; for he has hopes of me. He had the cruelty to say so.

'What I am, I shall remain,' said I.

He informed me that it was perfectly natural for me to think it; and on my replying that persons ought to know themselves best: 'At my age, perhaps,' he said, and added, 'I cannot speak very confidently of my knowledge of myself.'

'Then you make us out to be nothing better than puppets, Mr. Pollingray.'

'If we have missed an early apprenticeship to the habit of self-command, ma filleule.'

'Merci, mon parrain.'

He laughed. My French, I suppose.

I determined that, if he wanted to study me, I would help him.

'I can command myself when I choose, but it is only when I choose.'

This seemed to me quite a reasonable speech, until I found him looking for something to follow, in explanation, and on coming to sift my meaning, I saw that it was temper, and getting more angry, continued:

'The sort of young people who have such wonderful command of themselves are not the pleasantest.'

'No,' he said; 'they disappoint us. We expect folly from the young.'

I shut my lips. Prince Leboo knew that he must go, and a good gallop reconciled me to circumstances. Then I was put to jumping little furzes and ditches, which one cannot pretend to do without a fair appearance of gaiety; for, while you are running the risk of a tumble, you are compelled to look cheerful and gay, at least, I am. To fall frowning will never do. I had no fall. My gallant Leboo made my heart leap with love of him, though mill-stones were tied to it. I may be vexed when I begin, but I soon ride out a bad temper. And he is mine! I am certainly inconstant to Charles, for I think of Leboo fifty times more. Besides, there is no engagement as yet between Charles and me. I have first to be approved worthy by Mr. and Miss Pollingray: two pairs of eyes and ears, over which I see a solemnly downy owl sitting, conning their reports of me. It is a very unkind ordeal to subject any inexperienced young woman to. It was harshly conceived and it is being remorselessly executed. I would complain more loudly—in shrieks—if I could say I was unhappy; but every night I look out of my window before going to bed and see the long falls of the infant river through the meadow, and the dark woods seeming to enclose the house from harm: I dream of the old inhabitant, his ancestors, and the numbers and numbers of springs when the wildflowers have flourished in those woods and the nightingales have sung there. And I feel there will never be a home to me like Dayton.

CHAPTER V

For twenty years of my life I have embraced the phantom of the fairest woman that ever drew breath. I have submitted to her whims, I have worshipped her feet, I have, I believe, strengthened her principle. I have done all in my devotion but adopt her religious faith. And I have, as I trusted some time since, awakened to perceive that those twenty years were a period of mere sentimental pastime, perfectly useless, fruitless, unless, as is possible, it has saved me from other follies. But it was a folly in itself. Can one's nature be too stedfast? The question whether a spice of frivolousness may not be a safeguard has often risen before me. The truth, I must learn to think, is, that my mental power is not the match for my ideal or sentimental apprehension and native tenacity of attachment. I have fallen into one of the pits of a well-meaning but idle man. The world discredits the existence of pure platonism in love. I myself can barely look back on those twenty years of amatory servility with a full comprehension of the part I have been playing in them. And yet I would not willingly forfeit the exalted admiration of Louise for my constancy: as little willingly as I would have imperilled her purity. I cling to the past as to something in which I have deserved well, though I am scarcely satisfied with it. According to our English notions I know my name. English notions, however, are not to be accepted in all matters, any more than the flat declaration of a fact will develop it in alt its bearings. When our English society shall have advanced to a high civilization, it will be less expansive in denouncing the higher stupidities. Among us, much of the social judgement of Bodge upon the relations of men to women is the stereotyped opinion of the land. There is the dictum here for a man who adores a woman who is possessed by a husband. If he has long adored her, and known himself to be preferred by her in innocency of heart; if he has solved the problem of being her bosom's lord, without basely seeking to degrade her to being his mistress; the epithets to characterise him in our vernacular will probably be all the less flattering. Politically we are the most self-conscious people upon earth, and socially the frankest animals. The terrorism of our social laws is eminently serviceable, for without it such frank animals as we are might run into bad excesses. I judge rather by the abstract evidence than by the examples our fair matrons give to astounded foreigners when abroad.

Louise writes that her husband is paralysed. The Marquis de Mazardouin is at last tasting of his mortality. I bear in mind the day when he married her. She says that he has taken to priestly counsel, and, like a woman, she praises him for that. It is the one thing which I have not done to please her. She anticipates his decease. Should she be free—what then? My heart does not beat the faster for the thought. There are twenty years upon it, and they make a great load. But I have a desire that she should come over to us. The old folly might rescue me from the new one. Not that I am any further persecuted by the dread that I am in imminent danger here. I have established a proper mastery over my young lady. 'Nous avons change de role'. Alice is subdued; she laughs feebly, is becoming conscious—a fact to be regretted, if I desired to check the creature's growth. There is vast capacity in the girl. She has plainly not centred her affections upon Charles, so that a man's conscience might be at ease if—if he chose to disregard what is due to decency. But, why, when I contest it, do I bow to the world's opinion concerning disparity of years between husband and wife? I know innumerable cases of an old husband making a young wife happy. My friend, Dr. Galliot, married his ward, and he had the best wife of any man of my acquaintance. She has been publishing his learned manuscripts ever since his death. That is an extreme case, for he was forty-five years her senior, and stood bald at the altar. Old General Althorpe married Julia Dahoop, and, but for his preposterous jealousy of her, might be cited in proof that the ordinary reckonings are not to be a yoke on the neck of one who earnestly seeks to spouse a fitting mate, though late in life. But, what are fifty years? They mark the prime of a healthy man's existence. He has by that time seen the world, can decide, and settle, and is virtually more eligible—to use the cant phrase of gossips—than a young man, even for a young girl. And may not some fair and fresh reward be justly claimed as the crown of a virtuous career?

I say all this, yet my real feeling is as if I were bald as Dr. Galliot and jealous as General Althorpe. For, with my thorough knowledge of myself, I, were I like either one of them, should not have offered myself to the mercy of a young woman, or of the world. Nor, as I am and know myself to be, would I offer myself to the mercy of Alice Amble. When my filleule first drove into Dayton she had some singularly audacious ideas of her own. Those vivid young feminine perceptions and untamed imaginations are desperate things to encounter. There is nothing beyond their reach. Our safety from them lies in the fact that they are always seeing too much, and imagining too wildly; so that, with a little help from us, they may be taught to distrust themselves; and when they have once distrusted themselves, we need not afterwards fear them: their supernatural vitality has vanished. I fancy my pretty Alice to be in this state now. She leaves us to-morrow. In the autumn we shall have her with us again, and Louise will scan her compassionately. I desire that they should meet. It will be hardly fair to the English girl, but, if I stand in the gap between them, I shall summon up no small quantity of dormant compatriotic feeling. The contemplation of the contrast, too, may save me from both: like the logic ass with the two trusses of hay on either side of him.

CHAPTER VI

SHE

I am at home. There was never anybody who felt so strange in her home. It is not a month since I left my sisters, and I hardly remember that I know them. They all, and even papa, appear to be thinking about such petty things. They complain that I tell them nothing. What have I to tell? My Prince! my own Leboo, if I might lie in the stall with you, then I should feel thoroughly happy! That is, if I could fall asleep. Evelina declares we are not eight miles from Dayton. It seems to me I am eight millions of miles distant, and shall be all my life travelling along a weary road to get there again just for one long sunny day. And it might rain when I got there after all! My trouble nobody knows. Nobody knows a thing!

The night before my departure, Miss Pollingray did me the honour to accompany me up to my bedroom. She spoke to me searchingly about Charles; but she did not demand compromising answers. She is not in favour of early marriages, so she merely wishes to know the footing upon which we stand: that of friends. I assured her we were simply friends. 'It is the firmest basis of an attachment,' she said; and I did not look hurried.

But I gained my end. I led her to talk of the beautiful Marquise. This is the tale. Mr. Pollingray, when a very young man, and comparatively poor, went over to France with good introductions, and there saw and fell in love with Louise de Riverolles. She reciprocated his passion. If he would have consented to abjure his religion and worship with her, Madame de Riverolles, her mother, would have listened to her entreaties. But Gilbert was firm. Mr. Pollingray, I mean, refused to abandon his faith. Her mother, consequently, did not interfere, and Monsieur de Riverolles, her father, gave her to the Marquis de Marzardouin, a roue young nobleman, immensely rich, and shockingly dissipated. And she married him. No, I cannot understand French girls. Do as I will, it is quite incomprehensible to me how Louise, loving another, could suffer herself to be decked out in bridal finery and go to the altar and take the marriage oaths. Not if perdition had threatened would I have submitted. I have a feeling that Mr. Pollingray should have shown at least one year's resentment at such conduct; and yet I admire him for his immediate generous forgiveness of her. It was fatherly. She was married at sixteen. His forgiveness was the fruit of his few years' seniority, said Miss Pollingray, whose opinion of the Marquise I cannot arrive at. At any rate, they have been true and warm friends ever since, constantly together interchangeing visits. That is why Mr. Pollingray has been more French than English for those long years.

Miss Pollingray concluded by asking me what I thought of the story. I said: 'It is very strange French habits are so different from ours. I dare say... I hope..., perhaps... indeed, Mr. Pollingray seems happy now.' Her idea of my wits must be that they are of the schoolgirl order—a perfect receptacle for indefinite impressions.

'Ah!' said she. 'Gilbert has burnt his heart to ashes by this time.'

I slept with that sentence in my brain. In the morning, I rose and dressed, dreaming. As I was turning the handle of my door to go down to breakfast, suddenly I swung round in a fit of tears. It was so piteous to think that he should have waited by her twenty years in a slow anguish, his heart burning out, without a reproach or a complaint. I saw him, I still see him, like a martyr.

'Some people,' Miss Pollingray said, I permitted themselves to think evil of my brother's assiduous devotion to a married woman. There is not a spot on his character, or on that of the person whom Gilbert loved.'

I would believe it in the teeth of calumny. I would cling to my belief in him if I were drowning.

I consider that those twenty years are just nothing, if he chooses to have them so. He has lived embalmed in a saintly affection. No wonder he considers himself still youthful. He is entitled to feel that his future is before him.

No amount of sponging would get the stains away from my horrid red eyelids. I slunk into my seat at the breakfast-table, not knowing that one of the maids had dropped a letter from Charles into my hand, and that I had opened it and was holding it open. The letter, as I found afterwards, told me that Charles has received an order from his uncle to go over to Mr. Pollingray's estate in Dauphiny on business. I am not sorry that they should have supposed I was silly enough to cry at the thought of Charles's crossing the Channel. They did imagine it, I know; for by and by Miss Pollingray whispered: 'Les absents n'auront pas tort, cette fois, n'est-ce-pas? 'And Mr. Pollingray was cruelly gentle: an air of 'I would not intrude on such emotions'; and I heightened their delusions as much as I could: there was no other way of accounting for my pantomime face. Why should he fancy I suffered so terribly? He talked with an excited cheerfulness meant to relieve me, of course, but there was no justification for his deeming me a love-sick kind of woe-begone ballad girl. It caused him likewise to adopt a manner—what to call it, I cannot think: tender respect, frigid regard, anything that accompanies and belongs to the pressure of your hand with the finger-tips. He said goodbye so tenderly that I would have kissed his sleeve. The effort to restrain myself made me like an icicle. Oh! adieu, mon parrain!

THE SENTIMENTALISTS

AN UNFINISHED COMEDY

HOMEWARE
PROFESSOR SPIRAL
ARDEN, In love with Astraea.
SWITHIN, Sympathetics.
OSIER,
DAME DRESDEN, Sister to Homeware.
ASTRAEA, Niece to Dame Dresden and Homeware.
LYRA, A Wife.
LADY OLDLACE.
VIRGINIA.
WINIFRED.

THE SENTIMENTALISTS. AN UNFINISHED COMEDY

The scene is a Surrey garden in early summer. The paths are shaded by tall box-wood hedges. The—time is some sixty years ago.

SCENE I

PROFESSOR SPIRAL, DAME DRESDEN, LADY OLDLACE, VIRGINIA, WINIFRED, SWITHIN, and **OSIER**

(As they slowly promenade the garden, the **PROFESSOR** is delivering one of his exquisite orations on Woman.)

SPIRAL
One husband! The woman consenting to marriage takes but one. For her there is no widowhood. That punctuation of the sentence called death is not the end of the chapter for her. It is the brilliant proof of her having a soul. So she exalts her sex. Above the wrangle and clamour of the passions she is a fixed star. After once recording her obedience to the laws of our common nature—that is to say, by descending once to wedlock—she passes on in sovereign disengagement—a dedicated widow.

(By this time they have disappeared from view. **HOMEWARE** appears; he craftily avoids joining their party, like one who is unworthy of such noble oratory. He desires privacy and a book, but is disturbed by the arrival of **ARDEN**, who is painfully anxious to be polite to 'her uncle Homeware.')

SCENE II

HOMEWARE, ARDEN

ARDEN: A glorious morning, sir.

HOMEWARE: The sun is out, sir.

ARDEN: I am happy in meeting you, Mr. Homeware.

HOMEWARE: I can direct you to the ladies, Mr. Arden. You will find them up yonder avenue.

ARDEN: They are listening, I believe, to an oration from the mouth of Professor Spiral.

HOMEWARE: On an Alpine flower which has descended to flourish on English soil. Professor Spiral calls it Nature's 'dedicated widow.'

ARDEN: 'Dedicated widow'?

HOMEWARE: The reference you will observe is to my niece Astraea.

ARDEN: She is dedicated to whom?

HOMEWARE: To her dead husband! You see the reverse of Astraea, says the professor, in those world-infamous widows who marry again.

ARDEN: Bah!

HOMEWARE: Astraea, it is decided, must remain solitary, virgin cold, like the little Alpine flower. Professor Spiral has his theme.

ARDEN: He will make much of it. May I venture to say that I prefer my present company?

HOMEWARE: It is a singular choice. I can supply you with no weapons for the sort of stride in which young men are usually engaged. You belong to the camp you are avoiding.

ARDEN: Achilles was not the worse warrior, sir, for his probation in petticoats.

HOMEWARE: His deeds proclaim it. But Alexander was the better chieftain until he drank with Lais.

ARDEN: No, I do not plead guilty to Bacchus.

HOMEWARE: You are confessing to the madder form of drunkenness.

ARDEN: How, sir, I beg?

HOMEWARE: How, when a young man sees the index to himself in everything spoken!

ARDEN: That might have the look. I did rightly in coming to you, sir.

HOMEWARE: 'Her uncle Homeware'?

ARDEN: You read through us all, sir.

HOMEWARE: It may interest you to learn that you are the third of the gentlemen commissioned to consult the lady's uncle Homeware.

ARDEN: The third.

HOMEWARE: Yes, she is pursued. It could hardly be otherwise. Her attractions are acknowledged, and the house is not a convent. Yet, Mr. Arden, I must remind you that all of you are upon an enterprise held to be profane by the laws of this region. Can you again forget that Astraea is a widow?

ARDEN: She was a wife two months; she has been a widow two years.

HOMEWARE: The widow of the great and venerable Professor Towers is not to measure her widowhood by years. His, from the altar to the tomb. As it might be read, a one day's walk!

ARDEN: Is she, in the pride of her youth, to be sacrificed to a whimsical feminine delicacy?

HOMEWARE: You have argued it with her?

ARDEN: I have presumed.

HOMEWARE: And still she refused her hand!

ARDEN: She commended me to you, sir. She has a sound judgement of persons.

HOMEWARE: I should put it that she passes the Commissioners of Lunacy, on the ground of her being a humorous damsel. Your predecessors had also argued it with her; and they, too, discovered their enemy in a whimsical feminine delicacy. Where is the difference between you? Evidently she cannot perceive it, and I have to seek: You will have had many conversations with Astraea?

ARDEN: I can say, that I am thrice the man I was before I had them.

HOMEWARE: You have gained in manhood from conversations with a widow in her twenty-second year; and you want more of her.

ARDEN: As much as I want more wisdom.

HOMEWARE: You would call her your Muse?

ARDEN: So prosaic a creature as I would not dare to call her that.

HOMEWARE: You have the timely mantle of modesty, Mr. Arden. She has prepared you for some of the tests with her uncle Homeware.

ARDEN: She warned me to be myself, without a spice of affectation.

HOMEWARE: No harder task could be set a young man in modern days. Oh, the humorous damsel. You sketch me the dimple at her mouth.

ARDEN: Frankly, sir, I wish you to know me better; and I think I can bear inspection. Astraea sent me to hear the reasons why she refuses me a hearing.

HOMEWARE: Her reason, I repeat, is this; to her idea, a second wedlock is unholy. Further, it passes me to explain. The young lady lands us where we were at the beginning; such must have been her humorous intention.

ARDEN: What can I do?

HOMEWARE: Love and war have been compared. Both require strategy and tactics, according to my recollection of the campaign.

ARDEN: I will take to heart what you say, sir.

HOMEWARE: Take it to head. There must be occasional descent of lovers' heads from the clouds. And Professor Spiral,—But here we have a belated breeze of skirts.

(The reference is to the arrival of **LYRA**, breathless.)

SCENE III

HOMEWARE, ARDEN, LYRA

LYRA: My own dear uncle Homeware!

HOMEWARE: But where is Pluriel?

LYRA: Where is a woman's husband when she is away from him?

HOMEWARE: In Purgatory, by the proper reckoning. But hurry up the avenue, or you will be late for Professor Spiral's address.

LYRA: I know it all without hearing. Their Spiral! Ah, Mr. Arden! You have not chosen badly. The greater my experience, the more do I value my uncle Homeware's company.

(She is affectionate to excess but has a roguish eye withal, as of one who knows that uncle Homeware suspects all young men and most young women.)

HOMEWARE: Agree with the lady promptly, my friend.

ARDEN: I would gladly boast of so lengthened an experience, Lady Pluriel.

LYRA: I must have a talk with Astraea, my dear uncle. Her letters breed suspicions. She writes feverishly. The last one hints at service on the West Coast of Africa.

HOMEWARE: For the draining of a pestiferous land, or an enlightenment of the benighted black, we could not despatch a missionary more effective than the handsomest widow in Great Britain.

LYRA: Have you not seen signs of disturbance?

HOMEWARE: A great oration may be a sedative.

LYRA: I have my suspicions.

HOMEWARE: Mr. Arden, I could counsel you to throw yourself at Lady Pluriel's feet, and institute her as your confessional priest.

ARDEN: Madam, I am at your feet. I am devoted to the lady.

LYRA: Devoted. There cannot be an objection. It signifies that a man asks for nothing in return!

HOMEWARE: Have a thought upon your words with this lady, Mr. Arden!

ARDEN: Devoted, I said. I am. I would give my life for her.

LYRA: Expecting it to be taken to-morrow or next day? Accept my encomiums. A male devotee is within an inch of a miracle. Women had been looking for this model for ages, uncle.

HOMEWARE: You are the model, Mr Arden!

LYRA: Can you have intended to say that it is in view of marriage you are devoted to the widow of Professor Towers?

ARDEN: My one view.

LYRA: It is a star you are beseeching to descend.

ARDEN: It is.

LYRA: You disappoint me hugely. You are of the ordinary tribe after all; and your devotion craves an enormous exchange, infinitely surpassing the amount you bestow.

ARDEN: It does. She is rich in gifts; I am poor. But I give all I have.

LYRA: These lovers, uncle Homeware!

HOMEWARE: A honey-bag is hung up and we have them about us. They would persuade us that the chief business of the world is a march to the altar.

ARDEN: With the right partner, if the business of the world is to be better done.

LYRA: Which right partner has been chosen on her part, by a veiled woman, who marches back from the altar to discover that she has chained herself to the skeleton of an idea, or is in charge of that devouring tyrant, an uxorious husband. Is Mr. Arden in favour with the Dame, uncle?

HOMEWARE: My sister is an unsuspicious potentate, as you know. Pretenders to the hand of an inviolate widow bite like waves at a rock.

LYRA: Professor Spiral advances rapidly.

HOMEWARE: Not, it would appear, when he has his audience of ladies and their satellites.

LYRA: I am sure I hear a spring-tide of enthusiasm coming.

ARDEN: I will see.

(He goes up the path.)

LYRA: Now! my own dear uncle, save me from Pluriel. I have given him the slip in sheer desperation; but the man is at his shrewdest when he is left to guess at my heels. Tell him I am anywhere but here. Tell him I ran away to get a sense of freshness in seeing him again. Let me have one day of liberty, or, upon my word, I shall do deeds; I shall console young Arden: I shall fly to Paris and set my cap at presidents and foreign princes. Anything rather than be eaten up every minute, as I am. May no woman of my acquaintance marry a man of twenty years her senior! She marries a gigantic limpet. At that period of his life a man becomes too voraciously constant.

HOMEWARE: Cupid clipped of wing is a destructive parasite.

LYRA: I am in dead earnest, uncle, and I will have a respite, or else let decorum beware!

(Arden returns.)

ARDEN: The ladies are on their way.

LYRA: I must get Astraea to myself.

HOMEWARE: My library is a virgin fortress, Mr. Arden. Its gates are open to you on other topics than the coupling of inebriates.

(He enters the house—**LYRA** disappears in the garden—Spiral's audience reappear without him.)

SCENE IV

DAME DRESDEN, LADY OLDLACE, VIRGINIA, WINIFRED, ARDEN, SWITHIN, OSIER

LADY OLDLACE: Such perfect rhythm!

WINIFRED: Such oratory!

LADY OLDLACE: A master hand. I was in a trance from the first sentence to the impressive close.

OSIER: Such oratory is a whole orchestral symphony.

VIRGINIA: Such command of intonation and subject!

SWITHIN: That resonant voice!

LADY OLDLACE: Swithin, his flow of eloquence! He launched forth!

SWITHIN: Like an eagle from a cliff.

OSIER: The measure of the words was like a beat of wings.

SWITHIN: He makes poets of us.

DAME DRESDEN: Spiral achieved his pinnacle to-day!

VIRGINIA: How treacherous is our memory when we have most the longing to recall great sayings!

OSIER: True, I conceive that my notes will be precious.

WINIFRED: You could take notes!

LADY OLDLACE: It seems a device for missing the quintessential.

SWITHIN: Scraps of the body to the loss of the soul of it. We can allow that our friend performed good menial service.

WINIFRED: I could not have done the thing.

SWITHIN: In truth; it does remind one of the mess of pottage.

LADY OLDLACE: One hardly felt one breathed.

VIRGINIA: I confess it moved me to tears.

SWITHIN: There is a pathos for us in the display of perfection. Such subtle contrast with our individual poverty affects us.

WINIFRED: Surely there were passages of a distinct and most exquisite pathos.

LADY OLDLACE: As in all great oratory! The key of it is the pathos.

VIRGINIA: In great oratory, great poetry, great fiction; you try it by the pathos. All our critics agree in stipulating for the pathos. My tears were no feminine weakness, I could not be a discordant instrument.

SWITHIN: I must make confession. He played on me too.

OSIER: We shall be sensible for long of that vibration from the touch of a master hand.

ARDEN: An accomplished player can make a toy-shop fiddle sound you a Stradivarius.

DAME DRESDEN: Have you a right to a remark, Mr. Arden? What could have detained you?

ARDEN: Ah, Dame. It may have been a warning that I am a discordant instrument. I do not readily vibrate.

DAME DRESDEN: A discordant instrument is out of place in any civil society. You have lost what cannot be recovered.

ARDEN: There are the notes.

OSIER: Yes, the notes.

SWITHIN: You can be satisfied with the dog's feast at the table, Mr. Arden!

OSIER: Ha!

VIRGINIA: Never have I seen Astraea look sublimer in her beauty than with her eyes uplifted to the impassioned speaker, reflecting every variation of his tones.

ARDEN: Astraea!

LADY OLDLACE: She was entranced when he spoke of woman descending from her ideal to the gross reality of man.

OSIER: Yes, yes. I have the words [reads]: 'Woman is to the front of man, holding the vestal flower of a purer civilization. I see,' he says, 'the little taper in her hands transparent round the light, against rough winds.'

DAME DRESDEN: And of Astraea herself, what were the words? 'Nature's dedicated widow.'

SWITHIN: Vestal widow, was it not?

VIRGINIA: Maiden widow, I think.

DAME DRESDEN: We decide for 'dedicated.'

WINIFRED: Spiral paid his most happy tribute to the memory of her late husband, the renowned Professor Towers.

VIRGINIA: But his look was at dear Astraea.

ARDEN: At Astraea? Why?

VIRGINIA: For her sanction doubtless.

ARDEN: Ha!

WINIFRED: He said his pride would ever be in his being received as the successor of Professor Towers.

ARDEN: Successor!

SWITHIN: Guardian was it not?

OSIER: Tutor. I think he said.

(The three **GENTLEMEN** consult Osier's notes uneasily.)

DAME DRESDEN: Our professor must by this time have received in full Astraea's congratulations, and Lyra is hearing from her what it is to be too late. You will join us at the luncheon table, if you do not feel yourself a discordant instrument there, Mr. Arden?

ARDEN (going to her): The allusion to knife and fork tunes my strings instantly, Dame.

DAME DRESDEN: You must help me to-day, for the professor will be tired, though we dare not hint at it in his presence. No reference, ladies, to the great speech we have been privileged to hear; we have expressed our appreciation and he could hardly bear it.

ARDEN: Nothing is more distasteful to the orator!

VIRGINIA: As with every true genius, he is driven to feel humbly human by the exultation of him.

SWITHIN: He breathes in a rarified air.

OSIER: I was thrilled, I caught at passing beauties. I see that here and there I have jotted down incoherencies, lines have seduced me, so that I missed the sequence—the precious part. Ladies, permit me to rank him with Plato as to the equality of women and men.

WINIFRED: It is nobly said.

OSIER: And with the Stoics, in regard to celibacy.

(By this time all the ladies have gone into the house.)

ARDEN: Successor! Was the word successor?

(**ARDEN**, **SWITHIN**, and **OSIER** are excitedly searching the notes when **SPIRAL** passes and strolls into the house. His air of self-satisfaction increases their uneasiness they follow him. **ASTRAEA** and **LYRA** come down the path.)

SCENE V

ASTRAEA, LYRA

LYRA: Oh! Pluriel, ask me of him! I wish I were less sure he would not be at the next corner I turn.

ASTRAEA: You speak of your husband strangely, Lyra.

LYRA: My head is out of a sack. I managed my escape from him this morning by renouncing bath and breakfast; and what a relief, to be in the railway carriage alone! that is, when the engine snorted. And if I set eyes on him within a week, he will hear some truths. His idea of marriage is, the taking of the woman into custody. My hat is on, and on goes Pluriel's. My foot on the stairs; I hear his boot behind me. In my boudoir I am alone one minute, and then the door opens to the inevitable. I pay a visit, he is passing the house as I leave it. He will not even affect surprise. I belong to him, I am cat's mouse. And he will look doating on me in public. And when I speak to anybody, he is that fearful picture of all smirks. Fling off a kid glove after a round of calls; feel your hand—there you have me now that I am out of him for my half a day, if for as long.

ASTRAEA: This is one of the world's happy marriages!

LYRA: This is one of the world's choice dishes! And I have it planted under my nostrils eternally. Spare me the mention of Pluriel until he appears; that's too certain this very day. Oh! good husband! good kind of man! whatever you please; only some peace, I do pray, for the husband-haunted wife. I like him, I like him, of course, but I want to breathe. Why, an English boy perpetually bowled by a Christmas pudding would come to loathe the mess.

ASTRAEA: His is surely the excess of a merit.

LYRA: Excess is a poison. Excess of a merit is a capital offence in morality. It disgusts, us with virtue. And you are the cunningest of fencers, tongue, or foils. You lead me to talk of myself, and I hate the subject. By the way, you have practised with Mr. Arden.

ASTRAEA: A tiresome instructor, who lets you pass his guard to compliment you on a hit.

LYRA: He rather wins me.

ASTRAEA: He does at first.

LYRA: Begins Plurielizing, without the law to back him, does he?

ASTRAEA: The fencing lessons are at an end.

LYRA: The duetts with Mr. Swithin's violoncello continue?

ASTRAEA: He broke through the melody.

LYRA: There were readings in poetry with Mr. Osier, I recollect.

ASTRAEA: His own compositions became obtrusive.

LYRA: No fencing, no music, no poetry! no West Coast of Africa either, I suppose.

ASTRAEA: Very well! I am on my defence. You at least shall not misunderstand me, Lyra. One intense regret I have; that I did not live in the time of the Amazons. They were free from this question of marriage; this babble of love. Why am I so persecuted? He will not take a refusal. There are sacred reasons. I am supported by every woman having the sense of her dignity. I am perverted, burlesqued by the fury of wrath I feel at their incessant pursuit. And I despise Mr. Osier and Mr. Swithin because they have an air of pious agreement with the Dame, and are conspirators behind their mask.

LYRA: False, false men!

ASTRAEA: They come to me. I am complimented on being the vulnerable spot.

LYRA: The object desired is usually addressed by suitors, my poor Astraea!

ASTRAEA: With the assumption, that as I am feminine I must necessarily be in the folds of the horrible constrictor they call Love, and that I leap to the thoughts of their debasing marriage.

LYRA: One of them goes to Mr. Homeware.

ASTRAEA: All are sent to him in turn. He can dispose of them.

LYRA: Now that is really masterly fun, my dear; most creditable to you! Love, marriage, a troop of suitors, and uncle Homeware. No, it would not have occurred to me, and—I am considered to have some humour. Of course, he disposes of them. He seemed to have a fairly favourable opinion of Mr. Arden.

ASTRAEA: I do not share it. He is the least respectful of the sentiments entertained by me. Pray, spare me the mention of him, as you say of your husband. He has that pitiful conceit in men, which sets them thinking that a woman must needs be susceptible to the declaration of the mere existence of their passion. He is past argument. Impossible for him to conceive a woman's having a mind above the conditions of her sex. A woman, according to him, can have no ideal of life, except as a ball to toss in the air and catch in a cup. Put him aside.... We creatures are doomed to marriage, and if we shun it, we are a kind of cripple. He is grossly earthy in his view of us. We are unable to move a step in thought or act unless we submit to have a husband. That is his reasoning. Nature! Nature! I have to hear of Nature! We must be above Nature, I tell him, or, we shall be very much below. He is ranked among our clever young men; and he can be amusing. So far he passes muster; and he has a pleasant voice. I dare say he is an uncle Homeware's good sort of boy. Girls like him. Why does he not fix his attention upon one of them; Why upon me? We waste our time in talking of him.... The secret of it is, that he has no reverence. The marriage he vaunts is a mere convenient arrangement for two to live together under command of nature. Reverence for the state of marriage is unknown to him. How explain my feeling? I am driven into silence. Cease to speak of him.... He is the dupe of his eloquence—his passion, he calls it. I have only to trust myself to him, and—I shall be one of the world's married women! Words are useless. How am I to make him see that it is I who respect the state of marriage by refusing; not he by perpetually soliciting. Once married, married for ever. Widow is but a term. When women hold their own against him, as I have done, they will be more esteemed. I have resisted and conquered. I am sorry I do not share in the opinion of your favourite.

LYRA: Mine?

ASTRAEA: You spoke warmly of him.

LYRA: Warmly, was it?

ASTRAEA: You are not blamed, my dear: he has a winning manner.

LYRA: I take him to be a manly young fellow, smart enough; handsome too.

ASTRAEA: Oh, he has good looks.

LYRA: And a head, by repute.

ASTRAEA: For the world's work, yes.

LYRA: Not romantic.

ASTRAEA: Romantic ideas are for dreamy simperers.

LYRA: Amazons repudiate them.

ASTRAEA: Laugh at me. Half my time I am laughing at myself. I should regain my pride if I could be resolved on a step. I am strong to resist; I have not strength to move.

LYRA: I see the sphinx of Egypt!

ASTRAEA: And all the while I am a manufactory of gunpowder in this quiet old-world Sabbath circle of dear good souls, with their stereotyped interjections, and orchestra of enthusiasms; their tapering delicacies: the rejoicing they have in their common agreement on all created things. To them it is restful. It spurs me to fly from rooms and chairs and beds and houses. I sleep hardly a couple of hours. Then into the early morning air, out with the birds; I know no other pleasure.

LYRA: Hospital work for a variation: civil or military. The former involves the house-surgeon: the latter the grateful lieutenant.

ASTRAEA: Not if a woman can resist... I go to it proof-armoured.

LYRA: What does the Dame say?

ASTRAEA: Sighs over me! Just a little maddening to hear.

LYRA: When we feel we have the strength of giants, and are bidden to sit and smile! You should rap out some of our old sweet-innocent garden oaths with her—'Carnation! Dame!' That used to make her dance on her seat.—'But, dearest Dame, it is as natural an impulse for women to have that relief as for men; and natural will out, begonia! it will!' We ran through the book of Botany for devilish objurgations. I do believe our misconduct caused us to be handed to the good man at the altar as the right corrective. And you were the worst offender.

ASTRAEA: Was I? I could be now, though I am so changed a creature.

LYRA: You enjoy the studies with your Spiral, come!

ASTRAEA: Professor Spiral is the one honest gentleman here. He does homage to my principles. I have never been troubled by him: no silly hints or side-looks—you know, the dog at the forbidden bone.

LYRA: A grand orator.

ASTRAEA: He is. You fix on the smallest of his gifts. He is intellectually and morally superior.

LYRA: Praise of that kind makes me rather incline to prefer his inferiors. He fed gobble-gobble on your puffs of incense. I coughed and scraped the gravel; quite in vain; he tapped for more and more.

ASTRAEA: Professor Spiral is a thinker; he is a sage. He gives women their due.

LYRA: And he is a bachelor too—or consequently.

ASTRAEA: If you like you may be as playful with me as the Lyra of our maiden days used to be. My dear, my dear, how glad I am to have you here! You remind me that I once had a heart. It will beat again with you beside me, and I shall look to you for protection. A novel request from me. From annoyance, I mean. It has entirely altered my character. Sometimes I am afraid to think of what I was, lest I should suddenly romp, and perform pirouettes and cry 'Carnation!' There is the bell. We must not be late when the professor condescends to sit for meals.

LYRA: That rings healthily in the professor.

ASTRAEA: Arm in arm, my Lyra.

LYRA: No Pluriel yet!

(They enter the house, and the time changes to evening of the same day. The scene is still the garden.)

SCENE VI

ASTRAEA, ARDEN

ASTRAEA: Pardon me if I do not hear you well.

ARDEN: I will not even think you barbarous.

ASTRAEA: I am. I am the object of the chase.

ARDEN: The huntsman draws the wood, then, and not you.

ASTRAEA: At any instant I am forced to run,
Or turn in my defence: how can I be
Other than barbarous? You are the cause.

ARDEN: No: heaven that made you beautiful's the cause.

ASTRAEA: Say, earth, that gave you instincts. Bring me down
To instincts! When by chance I speak awhile
With our professor, you appear in haste,
Full cry to sight again the missing hare.
Away ideas! All that's divinest flies!
I have to bear in mind how young you are.

ARDEN: You have only to look up to me four years,
Instead of forty!

ASTRAEA: Sir?

ARDEN: There's my misfortune!
And worse that, young, I love as a young man.
Could I but quench the fire, I might conceal
The youthfulness offending you so much.

ASTRAEA: I wish you would. I wish it earnestly.

ARDEN: Impossible. I burn.

ASTRAEA: You should not burn.

ARDEN: 'Tis more than I. 'Tis fire. It masters will.
You would not say I should not' if you knew fire.
It seizes. It devours.

ASTRAEA: Dry wood.

ARDEN: Cold wit!
How cold you can be! But be cold, for sweet
You must be. And your eyes are mine: with them
I see myself: unworthy to usurp
The place I hold a moment. While I look
I have my happiness.

ASTRAEA: You should look higher.

ARDEN: Through you to the highest. Only through you!
Through you
The mark I may attain is visible,
And I have strength to dream of winning it.
You are the bow that speeds the arrow: you
The glass that brings the distance nigh. My world
Is luminous through you, pure heavenly,
But hangs upon the rose's outer leaf,
Not next her heart. Astraea! my own beloved!

ASTRAEA: We may be excellent friends. And I have faults.

ARDEN: Name them: I am hungering for more to love.

ASTRAEA: I waver very constantly: I have
No fixity of feeling or of sight.
I have no courage: I can often dream
Of daring: when I wake I am in dread.
I am inconstant as a butterfly,
And shallow as a brook with little fish!
Strange little fish, that tempt the small boy's net,
But at a touch straight dive! I am any one's,
And no one's! I am vain.
Praise of my beauty lodges in my ears.
The lark reels up with it; the nightingale
Sobs bleeding; the flowers nod; I could believe
A poet, though he praised me to my face.

ARDEN: Never had poet so divine a fount
To drink of!

ASTRAEA: Have I given you more to love

ARDEN: More! You have given me your inner mind,
Where conscience in the robes of Justice shoots
Light so serenely keen that in such light
Fair infants, I newly criminal of earth,'
As your friend Osier says, might show some blot.
Seraphs might! More to love? Oh! these dear faults
Lead you to me like troops of laughing girls
With garlands. All the fear is, that you trifle,
Feigning them.

ASTRAEA: For what purpose?

ARDEN: Can I guess?

ASTRAEA: I think 'tis you who have the trifler's note.
My hearing is acute, and when you speak,
Two voices ring, though you speak fervidly.
Your Osier quotation jars. Beware!
Why were you absent from our meeting-place
This morning?

ARDEN: I was on the way, and met
Your uncle Homeware

ASTRAEA: Ah!

ARDEN: He loves you.

ASTRAEA: He loves me: he has never understood.
He loves me as a creature of the flock;
A little whiter than some others.
Yes; He loves me, as men love; not to uplift;
Not to have faith in; not to spiritualize.
For him I am a woman and a widow
One of the flock, unmarked save by a brand.
He said it!—You confess it! You have learnt
To share his error, erring fatally.

ARDEN: By whose advice went I to him?

ASTRAEA: By whose?
Pursuit that seemed incessant: persecution.
Besides, I have changed since then: I change; I change;
It is too true I change. I could esteem
You better did you change. And had you heard
The noble words this morning from the mouth
Of our professor, changed were you, or raised
Above love-thoughts, love-talk, and flame and flutter,
High as eternal snows. What said he else,
My uncle Homeware?

ARDEN: That you were not free:
And that he counselled us to use our wits.

ASTRAEA: But I am free I free to be ever free!
My freedom keeps me free! He counselled us?
I am not one in a conspiracy.
I scheme no discord with my present life.
Who does, I cannot look on as my friend.
Not free? You know me little. Were I chained,
For liberty I would sell liberty
To him who helped me to an hour's release.
But having perfect freedom...

ARDEN: No.

ASTRAEA: Good sir,
You check me?

ARDEN: Perfect freedom?

ASTRAEA: Perfect!

ARDEN: No!

ASTRAEA: Am I awake? What blinds me?

ARDEN: Filaments
The slenderest ever woven about a brain
From the brain's mists, by the little sprite called
Fancy.
A breath would scatter them; but that one breath
Must come of animation. When the heart
Is as, a frozen sea the brain spins webs.

ASTRAEA: 'Tis very singular!
I understand.
You translate cleverly. I hear in verse
My uncle Homeware's prose. He has these notions.
Old men presume to read us.

ARDEN: Young men may.
You gaze on an ideal reflecting you
Need I say beautiful? Yet it reflects
Less beauty than the lady whom I love
Breathes, radiates. Look on yourself in me.
What harm in gazing? You are this flower
You are that spirit. But the spirit fed
With substance of the flower takes all its bloom!
And where in spirits is the bloom of the flower?

ASTRAEA: 'Tis very singular. You have a tone
Quite changed.

ARDEN: You wished a change. To show you, how
I read you...

ASTRAEA: Oh! no, no. It means dissection.
I never heard of reading character
That did not mean dissection. Spare me that.
I am wilful, violent, capricious, weak,
Wound in a web of my own spinning-wheel,
A star-gazer, a riband in the wind...

ARDEN: A banner in the wind! and me you lead,
And shall! At least, I follow till I win.

ASTRAEA: Forbear, I do beseech you.

ARDEN: I have had
Your hand in mine.

ASTRAEA: Once.

ARDEN: Once!
Once! 'twas; once, was the heart alive,
Leaping to break the ice. Oh! once, was aye
That laughed at frosty May like spring's return.
Say you are terrorized: you dare not melt.
You like me; you might love me; but to dare,
Tasks more than courage. Veneration, friends,
Self-worship, which is often self-distrust,
Bar the good way to you, and make a dream
A fortress and a prison.

ASTRAEA: Changed! you have changed
Indeed. When you so boldly seized my hand
It seemed a boyish freak, done boyishly.
I wondered at Professor Spiral's choice
Of you for an example, and our hope.
Now you grow dangerous. You must have thought,
And some things true you speak-save 'terrorized.'
It may be flattering to sweet self-love
To deem me terrorized.—'Tis my own soul,
My heart, my mind, all that I hold most sacred,
Not fear of others, bids me walk aloof.
Who terrorizes me? Who could? Friends? Never!
The world? as little. Terrorized!

ARDEN: Forgive me.

ASTRAEA: I might reply, Respect me. If I loved,
If I could be so faithless as to love,
Think you I would not rather noise abroad
My shame for penitence than let friends dwell
Deluded by an image of one vowed
To superhuman, who the common mock
Of things too human has at heart become.

ARDEN: You would declare your love?

ASTRAEA: I said, my shame.
The woman that's the widow is ensnared,
Caught in the toils! away with widows!—Oh!
I hear men shouting it.

ARDEN: But shame there's none
For me in loving: therefore I may take
Your friends to witness? tell them that my pride

Is in the love of you?

ASTRAEA: 'Twill soon bring
The silence that should be between us two,
And sooner give me peace.

ARDEN: And you consent?

ASTRAEA: For the sake of peace and silence I consent,
You should be warned that you will cruelly
Disturb them. But 'tis best. You should be warned
Your pleading will be hopeless. But 'tis best.
You have my full consent. Weigh well your acts,
You cannot rest where you have cast this bolt
Lay that to heart, and you are cherished, prized,
Among them: they are estimable ladies,
Warmest of friends; though you may think they soar
Too loftily for your measure of strict sense
(And as my uncle Homeware's pupil, sir,
In worldliness, you do), just minds they have:
Once know them, and your banishment will fret.
I would not run such risks. You will offend,
Go near to outrage them; and perturbate
As they have not deserved of you. But I,
Considering I am nothing in the scales
You balance, quite and of necessity
Consent. When you have weighed it, let me hear.
My uncle Homeware steps this way in haste.
We have been talking long, and in full view!

SCENE VII

ASTRAEA, ARDEN, HOMEWARE

HOMEWARE: Astraea, child! You, Arden, stand aside.
Ay, if she were a maid you might speak first,
But being a widow she must find her tongue.
Astraea, they await you. State the fact
As soon as you are questioned, fearlessly.
Open the battle with artillery.

ASTRAEA: What is the matter, uncle Homeware?

HOMEWARE (playing fox): What?
Why, we have watched your nice preliminaries
From the windows half the evening. Now run in.
Their patience has run out, and, as I said,

Unlimber and deliver fire at once.
Your aunts Virginia and Winifred,
With Lady Oldlace, are the senators,
The Dame for Dogs. They wear terrific brows,
But be not you affrighted, my sweet chick,
And tell them uncle Homeware backs your choice,
By lawyer and by priests! by altar, fount,
And testament!

ASTRAEA: My choice! what have I chosen?

HOMEWARE: She asks? You hear her, Arden?—what and whom!

ARDEN: Surely, sir!... heavens! have you...

HOMEWARE: Surely the old fox,
 In all I have read, is wiser than the young:
And if there is a game for fox to play,
Old fox plays cunningest.

ASTRAEA: Why fox? Oh! uncle,
You make my heart beat with your mystery;
I never did love riddles. Why sit they
Awaiting me, and looking terrible?

HOMEWARE: It is reported of an ancient folk
Which worshipped idols, that upon a day
Their idol pitched before them on the floor

ASTRAEA: Was ever so ridiculous a tale!

HOMEWARE: To call the attendant fires to account
Their elders forthwith sat...

ASTRAEA: Is there no prayer
Will move you, uncle Homeware?

HOMEWARE: God-daughter,
This gentleman for you I have proposed
As husband.

ASTRAEA: Arden! we are lost.

ARDEN: Astraea!
Support him! Though I knew not his design,
It plants me in mid-heaven. Would it were
Not you, but I to bear the shock. My love!
We lost, you cry; you join me with you lost!

The truth leaps from your heart: and let it shine
To light us on our brilliant battle day
And victory

ASTRAEA: Who betrayed me!

HOMEWARE: Who betrayed?
Your voice, your eyes, your veil, your knife and fork;
Your tenfold worship of your widowhood;
As he who sees he must yield up the flag,
Hugs it oath-swearingly! straw-drowningly.
To be reasonable: you sent this gentleman
Referring him to me....

ASTRAEA: And that is false.
All's false. You have conspired. I am disgraced.
But you will learn you have judged erroneously.
I am not the frail creature you conceive.
Between your vision of life's aim, and theirs
Who presently will question me, I cling
To theirs as light: and yours I deem a den
Where souls can have no growth.

HOMEWARE: But when we touched
The point of hand-pressings, 'twas rightly time
To think of wedding ties?

ASTRAEA: Arden, adieu!

(She rushes into house.)

SCENE VIII

ARDEN, HOMEWARE

ARDEN: Adieu! she said. With her that word is final.

HOMEWARE: Strange! how young people blowing words like clouds
On winds, now fair, now foul, and as they please
Should still attach the Fates to them.

ARDEN: She's wounded
Wounded to the quick!

HOMEWARE: The quicker our success: for short
Of that, these dames, who feel for everything,
Feel nothing.

ARDEN: Your intention has been kind,
Dear sir, but you have ruined me.

HOMEWARE: Good-night.

(Going.)

ARDEN: Yet she said, we are lost, in her surprise.

HOMEWARE: Good morning.

(Returning.)

ARDEN: I suppose that I am bound
(If I could see for what I should be glad!)
To thank you, sir.

HOMEWARE: Look hard but give no thanks.
I found my girl descending on the road
Of breakneck coquetry, and barred her way.
Either she leaps the bar, or she must back.
That means she marries you, or says good-bye.

(Going again.)

ARDEN: Now she's among them.

(Looking at window.)

HOMEWARE: Now she sees her mind.

ARDEN: It is my destiny she now decides!

HOMEWARE: There's now suspense on earth and round the spheres.

ARDEN: She's mine now: mine! or I am doomed to go.

HOMEWARE: The marriage ring, or the portmanteau now!

ARDEN: Laugh as you like, air! I am not ashamed
To love and own it.

HOMEWARE: So the symptoms show.
Rightly, young man, and proving a good breed.
To further it's a duty to mankind
And I have lent my push, But recollect:
Old Ilion was not conquered in a day.

(He enters house.)

ARDEN: Ten years! If I may win her at the end!

CURTAIN

George Meredith – A Concise Bibliography

Novels

The Shaving of Shagpat (1856)
Farina (1857)
The Ordeal of Richard Feverel (1859)
Evan Harrington (1861)
Emilia in England (1864), republished as Sandra Belloni in 1887
Rhoda Fleming (1865)
Vittoria (1867)
The Adventures of Harry Richmond (1871)
Beauchamp's Career (1875)
The House on the Beach (1877)
The Case of General Ople and Lady Camper (1877)
The Tale of Chloe (1879)
The Egoist (1879)
The Tragic Comedians (1880)
Diana of the Crossways (1885)
One of our Conquerors (1891)
Lord Ormont and his Aminta (1894)
The Amazing Marriage (1895)
Celt and Saxon (1910)

Poetry

Poems (1851)
Modern Love (1862)
The Lark Ascending (1881)
Poems and Lyrics of the Joy of Earth (1883)
The Woods of Westermain (1883)
A Faith on Trial (1885)
Ballads and Poems of Tragic Life (1887)
A Reading of Earth (1888)
The Empty Purse (1892)
Odes in Contribution to the Song of French History (1898)
A Reading of Life (1901)
Selected Poems of George Meredith (1903, author's supervision)
Last Poems (1909)

Essays

Essay on Comedy (1877)